Praise for *Uprooted*

'The magic in *Uprooted*, with its realistic moral dimension, is so vividly believable that it almost seems you could work the spells. But the book will do that for you'   Ursula K. Le Guin

'*Uprooted* is enchanting, in every sense of that fine old word. A charming and inviting story that looks unflinchingly at the strangling roots of hurt and revenge'   Robin Hobb

'I didn't know how much I wanted to read a book like this until it was already in my hands. *Uprooted* has everything I love about Novik's writing style, with the added bonus of some old-world magic and the flavour of a dark faerie story'   Patrick Rothfuss

'Naomi Novik's *Uprooted* is just right. Novik combines familiar elements in a beautifully original way to give us a story that is by turns surprising, heart-pounding, tender and always engrossing'   Charlaine Harris

'*Uprooted* has everything I love: a great heroine, new takes on old myths and legends, and surprising twists and turns. A delight'   Cassandra Clare

'Magical and practical, otherworldly and planted in the real, I could NOT stop reading this book and neither will you!'   Tamora Pierce

'Wild, thrilling and deeply, darkly magical. An instant classic'

Lev Grossman

'This is a beautiful book. The magic is true magic, and the human relationships – especially those between women – complex and believable'

Ellen Kushner

'Every so often you come upon a story that seems like a lost tale of Grimm newly come to light. *Uprooted* is such a novel. Its narrative spell is confidently wrought and sympathetically cast. I might even call it bewitching'

Gregory Maguire

'Moving, heartbreaking and thoroughly satisfying, *Uprooted* is the fantasy novel I feel I've been waiting a lifetime for'

Amal El-Mohtar

UPROOTED

Naomi Novik is the acclaimed author of the Temeraire series. She has been nominated for the Hugo Award and has won the John W. Campbell Award for Best New Writer, as well as the Locus Award for Best New Writer and the Compton Crook Award for Best First Novel. She is also the author of the graphic novel *Will Supervillains Be on the Final?*

Fascinated with both history and legends, Novik is a first-generation American raised on Polish fairy tales and stories of Baba Yaga. Her own adventures include pillaging degrees in English literature and computer science from various ivory towers, designing computer games, and helping to build the Archive of Our Own for fanfiction and other fanworks. Novik is a co-founder of the Organization for Transformative Works.

She lives in New York City with husband and Hard Case Crime founder Charles Ardai and their daughter, Evidence, surrounded by an excessive number of purring computers.

@naominovik
www.facebook.com/naominovik
www.naominovik.com

BY NAOMI NOVIK

Uprooted

THE TEMERAIRE SERIES
His Majesty's Dragon
Throne of Jade
Black Powder War
Empire of Ivory
Victory of Eagles
Tongues of Serpents
Crucible of Gold
Blood of Tyrants

UPROOTED

Naomi Novik

PAN BOOKS

First published 2015 by Del Rey, an imprint of Random House,
a division of Random House LLC, a Penguin Random House Company, New York

First published in the UK 2015 by Macmillan

First published in the UK in paperback 2016 by Pan Books
an imprint of Pan Macmillan
20 New Wharf Road, London N1 9RR
Associated companies throughout the world
www.panmacmillan.com

ISBN 978-1-4472-9414-6

1 3 5 7 9 8 6 4 2

A CIP catalogue record for this book is available from the British Library.

Printed and bound by CPI Group (UK) Ltd, Croydon, CR0 4YY

UPROOTED

ONE

Our Dragon doesn't eat the girls he takes, no matter what stories they tell outside our valley. We hear them sometimes, from travelers passing through. They talk as though we were doing human sacrifice, and he were a real dragon. Of course that's not true: he may be a wizard and immortal, but he's still a man, and our fathers would band together and kill him if he wanted to eat one of us every ten years. He protects us against the Wood, and we're grateful, but not that grateful.

He doesn't devour them really; it only feels that way. He takes a girl to his tower, and ten years later he lets her go, but by then she's someone different. Her clothes are too fine and she talks like a courtier and she's been living alone with a man for ten years, so of course she's ruined, even though the girls all say he never puts a hand on them. What else could they say? And that's not the worst of it—after all, the Dragon gives them a purse full of silver for their dowry when he lets them go, so anyone would be happy to marry them, ruined or not.

But they don't want to marry anyone. They don't want to stay at all.

"They forget how to live here," my father said to me once, unexpectedly. I was riding next to him on the seat of the big empty wagon, on our way home after delivering the week's firewood. We lived in Dvernik, which wasn't the biggest village in the valley or the smallest, or the one nearest the Wood: we were seven miles away. The road took us up over a big hill, though, and at the top on a clear day you could see along the river all the way to the pale grey strip of burned earth at the leading edge, and the solid dark wall of trees beyond. The Dragon's tower was a long way in the other direction, a piece of white chalk stuck in the base of the western mountains.

I was still very small—not more than five, I think. But I already knew that we didn't talk about the Dragon, or the girls he took, so it stuck in my head when my father broke the rule.

"They remember to be afraid," my father said. That was all. Then he clucked to the horses and they pulled on, down the hill and back into the trees.

It didn't make much sense to me. We were all afraid of the Wood. But our valley was home. How could you leave your home? And yet the girls never came back to stay. The Dragon let them out of the tower, and they came back to their families for a little while—for a week, or sometimes a month, never much more. Then they took their dowry-silver and left. Mostly they would go to Kralia and go to the University. Often as not they married some city man, and otherwise they became scholars or shopkeepers, although some people did whisper about Jadwiga Bach, who'd been taken sixty years ago, that she became a courtesan and the mistress of a baron and a duke. But by the time I was born, she was just a rich old woman who sent splendid presents to all her grandnieces and nephews, and never came for a visit.

So that's hardly like handing your daughter over to be eaten, but it's not a happy thing, either. There aren't so many villages in the valley that the chances are very low—he takes only a girl of seventeen, born between one October and the next. There were eleven girls to choose from in my year, and that's worse odds than dice. Everyone says you love a Dragon-born girl differently as she gets older; you can't help it, knowing you so easily might lose her. But it wasn't like that for me, for my parents. By the time I was old enough to understand that I might be taken, we all knew he would take Kasia.

Only travelers passing through, who didn't know, ever complimented Kasia's parents or told them how beautiful their daughter was, or how clever, or how nice. The Dragon didn't always take the prettiest girl, but he always took the most special one, somehow: if there was one girl who was far and away the prettiest, or the most bright, or the best dancer, or especially kind, somehow he always picked her out, even though he scarcely exchanged a word with the girls before he made his choice.

And Kasia was all those things. She had thick wheat-golden hair that she kept in a braid to her waist, and her eyes were warm brown, and her laugh was like a song that made you want to sing it. She thought of all the best games, and could make up stories and new dances out of her head; she could cook fit for a feast, and when she spun the wool from her father's sheep, the thread came off the wheel smooth and even without a single knot or snarl.

I know I'm making her sound like something out of a story. But it was the other way around. When my mother told me stories about the spinning princess or the brave goose-girl or the river-maiden, in my head I imagined them all a little like Kasia; that was how I thought of her. And I wasn't old enough to be wise, so I loved her more, not less, because I knew she would be taken from me soon.

She didn't mind it, she said. She was fearless, too: her mother Wensa saw to that. "She'll have to be brave," I remember hearing her say to my mother once, while she prodded Kasia to climb a tree she'd hung back from, and my mother hugging her, with tears.

We lived only three houses from one another, and I didn't have a sister of my own, only three brothers much older than me. Kasia was my dearest. We played together from our cradles, first in our mothers' kitchens keeping out from underfoot and then in the streets before our houses, until we were old enough to go running wild in the woods. I never wanted to be anywhere inside when we could be running hand-in-hand beneath the branches. I imagined the trees bending their arms down to shelter us. I didn't know how I would bear it, when the Dragon took her.

My parents wouldn't have feared for me, very much, even if there hadn't been Kasia. At seventeen I was still a too-skinny colt of a girl with big feet and tangled dirt-brown hair, and my only gift, if you could call it that, was I would tear or stain or lose anything put on me between the hours of one day. My mother despaired of me by the time I was twelve and let me run around in castoffs from my older brothers, except for feast days, when I was obliged to change only twenty minutes before we left the house, and then sit on the bench before our door until we walked to church. It was still even odds whether I'd make it to the village green without catching on some branch, or spattering myself with mud.

"You'll have to marry a tailor, my little Agnieszka," my father would say, laughing, when he came home from the forest at night and I went running to meet him, grubby-faced, with at least one hole about me, and no kerchief. He swung me up anyway and kissed me; my mother only sighed a little: what parent could really be sorry, to have a few faults in a Dragon-born girl?

Our last summer before the taking was long and warm and full of tears. Kasia didn't weep, but I did. We'd linger out late in the woods, stretching each golden day as long as it would go, and then I would come home hungry and tired and go straight to lie down in the dark. My mother would come in and stroke my head, singing softly while I cried myself to sleep, and leave a plate of food by my bed for when I woke up in the middle of the night with hunger. She didn't try to comfort me otherwise: how could she? We both knew that no matter how much she loved Kasia, and Kasia's mother Wensa, she couldn't help but have a small glad knot in her belly—not *my* daughter, not *my* only one. And of course, I wouldn't really have wanted her to feel any other way.

It was just me and Kasia together, nearly all that summer. It had been that way for a long time. We'd run with the crowd of village children when we were young, but as we got older, and Kasia more beautiful, her mother had said to her, "It's best if you don't see much of the boys, for you and them." But I clung to her, and my mother did love Kasia and Wensa enough not to try and pry me loose, even though she knew that it would hurt me more in the end.

On the last day, I found us a clearing in the woods where the trees still had their leaves, golden and flame-red rustling all above us, with ripe chestnuts all over the ground. We made a little fire out of twigs and dry leaves to roast a handful. Tomorrow was the first of October, and the great feast would be held to show honor to our patron and lord. Tomorrow, the Dragon would come.

"It would be nice to be a troubadour," Kasia said, lying on her back with her eyes closed. She hummed a little: a traveling singer had come for the festival, and he'd been practicing his songs on the green that morning. The tribute wagons had been arriving all week. "To go all over Polnya, and sing for the king."

She said it thoughtfully, not like a child spinning clouds; she said it like someone really thinking about leaving the valley, going away forever. I put my hand out and gripped hers. "And you'd come home every Midwinter," I said, "and sing us all the songs you'd learned." We held on tight, and I didn't let myself remember that the girls the Dragon took never wanted to come back.

Of course at that moment I only hated him ferociously. But he wasn't a bad lord. On the other side of the northern mountains, the Baron of the Yellow Marshes kept an army of five thousand men to take to Polnya's wars, and a castle with four towers, and a wife who wore jewels the color of blood and a white fox-fur cloak, all on a domain no richer than our valley. The men had to give one day a week of work to the baron's fields, which were the best land, and he'd take likely sons for his army, and with all the soldiers wandering around, girls had to stay indoors and in company once they got to be women. And even he wasn't a *bad* lord.

The Dragon only had his one tower, and not a single man-at-arms, or even a servant, besides the one girl he took. He didn't have to keep an army: the service he owed the king was his own labor, his magic. He had to go to court sometimes, to renew his oath of loyalty, and I suppose the king could have called him to war, but for the most part his duty was to stay here and watch the Wood, and protect the kingdom from its malice.

His only extravagance was books. We were well read by the standards of villagers, because he would pay gold for a single great tome, and so the book-peddlers came all this way, even though our valley was at the very edge of Polnya. And as long as they were coming, they filled up the saddlebags of their mules with whatever worn-out or cheaper stock of books they had and sold them to us for our pennies. It was a poor house in the valley that didn't have at least two or three books proudly displayed upon the walls.

These might all seem like small and petty things, little enough cause to give up a daughter, to anyone who didn't live near enough the Wood to understand. But I had lived through the Green Summer, when a hot wind carried pollen from the Wood west a long way into the valley, into our fields and gardens. The crops grew furiously lush, but also strange and misshapen. Anyone who ate of them grew sick with anger, struck at their families, and in the end ran into the Wood and vanished, if they weren't tied down.

I was six years old at the time. My parents tried to shelter me as much as they could, but even so I remembered vividly the cold clammy sense of dread everywhere, everyone afraid, and the never-ending bite of hunger in my belly. We had eaten through all our last year's stores by then, counting on the spring. One of our neighbors ate a few green beans, driven foolish by hunger. I remember the screams from his house that night, and peering out the window to see my father running to help, taking the pitchfork from where it leaned against our barn.

One day that summer, too young to understand the danger properly, I escaped my tired, thin mother's watch and ran into the forest. I found a half-dead bramble, in a nook sheltered from the wind. I pushed through the hard dead branches to the protected heart and dug out a miraculous handful of blackberries, not misshapen at all, whole and juicy and perfect. Every one was a burst of joy in my mouth. I ate two handfuls and filled my skirt; I hurried home with them soaking purple stains through my dress and my mother wept with horror when she saw my smeared face. I didn't sicken: the bramble had somehow escaped the Wood's curse, and the blackberries were good. But her tears frightened me badly; I shied from blackberries for years after.

The Dragon had been called to court that year. He came back early and rode straight to the fields and called down magic fire to burn all that tainted harvest, every poisoned crop. That much was his duty, but afterwards he went to every house where anyone had sickened, and he gave them a taste of a magic cordial that cleared their minds. He gave orders that the villages farther west, which had escaped the blight, should share their harvest with us, and he even gave up his own tribute that year entirely so none of us would starve. The next spring, just before the planting season, he went through the fields again to burn out the few corrupted remnants before they could take fresh root.

But for all he'd saved us, we didn't love him. He never came out of his tower to stand a drink for the men at harvest-time the way the Baron of the Yellow Marshes would, or to buy some small trinket at the fair as the baron's lady and her daughters so often did. There were plays sometimes put on by traveling shows, or singers would come through over the mountain pass from Rosya. He didn't come to hear them. When the carters brought him his tribute, the doors of the tower opened by themselves, and they left all the goods in the cellar without even seeing him. He never exchanged more than a handful of words with the headwoman of our village, or even the mayor of Olshanka, the largest town of the valley, very near his tower. He didn't try to win our love at all; none of us knew him.

And of course he was also a master of dark sorcery. Lightning would flash around his tower on a clear night, even in the winter. Pale wisps that he set loose from his windows drifted along the roads and down the river at night, going to the Wood to keep watch for him. And sometimes when the Wood caught someone—a shepherd girl who had drifted too close to its edge, following her flock; a hunter who had drunk from the wrong spring; an unlucky traveler who came over the mountain pass humming a snatch of music that sank claws into your head—well, the Dragon would come down from his tower for them, too; and the ones he took away never came back at all.

He wasn't evil, but he was distant and terrible. And he was going to take Kasia away, so I hated him, and had hated him for years and years.

My feelings didn't change on that last night. Kasia and I ate our chestnuts. The sun went down and our fire went out, but we lingered in the clearing as long as the embers lasted. We didn't have a long way to go in the morning. The harvest feast was usually held in Olshanka, but in a choosing year, it was always held in a village where at least one of the girls lived, to make the travel a little easier for their families. And our village had Kasia.

I hated the Dragon even more the next day, putting on my new green overdress. My mother's hands were shaking as she braided up my hair. We knew it would be Kasia, but that didn't mean we weren't still afraid. But I held my skirts up high off the ground and climbed into the wagon as carefully as I could, looking twice for splinters and letting my father help me. I was determined to make a special effort. I knew it was no use, but I wanted Kasia to know that I loved her enough to give her a fair chance. I wasn't going to make myself look a mess or squint-eyed or slouching, the way girls sometimes did.

We gathered on the village green, all eleven of us girls in a line.

The feasting-tables were set out in a square, loaded too heavily because they weren't really big enough to hold the tribute of the entire valley. Everyone had gathered behind them. Sacks of wheat and oats were piled up on the grass at the corners in pyramids. We were the only ones standing on the grass, with our families and our headwoman Danka, who paced nervously back and forth in front of us, her mouth moving silently while she practiced her greeting.

I didn't know the other girls much. They weren't from Dvernik. All of us were silent and stiff in our nice clothes and braided hair, watching the road. There was no sign of the Dragon yet. Wild fantasies ran in my head. I imagined flinging myself in front of Kasia when the Dragon came, and telling him to take me instead, or declaring to him that Kasia didn't want to go with him. But I knew I wasn't brave enough to do any of that.

And then he came, horribly. He didn't come from the road at all, he just stepped straight out of the air. I was looking that way when he came out: fingers in midair and then an arm and a leg and then half a man, so impossible and wrong that I couldn't look away even though my stomach was folding itself over in half. The others were luckier. They didn't even notice him until he took his first step towards us, and everyone around me tried not to flinch in surprise.

The Dragon wasn't like any man of our village. He should have been old and stooped and grey; he had been living in his tower a hundred years, but he was tall, straight, beardless, his skin taut. At a quick glance in the street I might have thought him a young man, only a little older than me: someone I might have smiled at across the feast-tables, and who might have asked me to dance. But there was something unnatural in his face: a crow's-nest of lines by his eyes, as though years couldn't touch him, but use did. It wasn't an ugly face, even so, but coldness made it unpleasant: everything about him said, *I am not one of you, and don't want to be, either.*

His clothes were rich, of course; the brocade of his zupan would have fed a family for a year, even without the golden buttons. But he was as lean as a man whose harvest had gone wrong three years out of four. He held himself stiff, with all the nervous energy of a hunting dog, as though he wanted nothing more than to be off quickly. It was the worst day of all our lives, but he had no patience for us; when our headwoman Danka bowed and said to him, "My lord, let me present to you these—" he interrupted her and said, "Yes, let's get on with it."

My father's hand was warm on my shoulder as he stood beside me and bowed; my mother's hand was clenched tight on mine on the other side. They reluctantly stepped back with the other parents. Instinctively the eleven of us all edged closer to one another. Kasia and I stood near the end of the line. I didn't dare take her hand, but I stood close enough that our arms brushed, and I watched the Dragon and hated him and hated him as he stepped down the line and tipped up each girl's face, under the chin, to look at her.

He didn't speak to all of us. He didn't say a word to the girl next to me, the one from Olshanka, even though her father, Borys, was the best horse-breeder in the valley, and she wore a wool dress dyed brilliant red, her black hair in two long beautiful plaits woven with red ribbons. When it was my turn, he glanced at me with a frown— cold black eyes, pale mouth pursed—and said, "Your name, girl?"

"Agnieszka," I said, or tried to say; I discovered my mouth was dry. I swallowed. "Agnieszka," I said again, whispering. "My lord." My face was hot. I dropped my eyes. I saw that for all the care I'd taken, my skirt had three big mud stains creeping up from the hem.

The Dragon moved on. And then he paused, looking at Kasia, the way he hadn't paused for any of the rest of us. He stayed there with his hand under her chin, a thin pleased smile curving his thin hard mouth, and Kasia looked at him bravely and didn't flinch. She didn't try to make her voice rough or squeaky or anything but steady and musical as she answered, "Kasia, my lord."

He smiled at her again, not pleasantly, but with a satisfied-cat look. He went on to the end of the line only perfunctorily, barely glancing at the two girls after her. I heard Wensa drag in a breath that was nearly a sob, behind us, as he turned and came back to look at Kasia, still with that pleased look on his face. And then he frowned again, and turned his head, and looked straight at me.

I'd forgotten myself and taken Kasia's hand after all. I was squeezing the life out of it, and she was squeezing back. She quickly let go and I tucked my hands together in front of me instead, hot color in my cheeks, afraid. He only narrowed his eyes at me some more. And then he raised his hand, and in his fingers a tiny ball of blue-white flame took shape.

"She didn't mean anything," Kasia said, brave brave brave, the way I hadn't been for her. Her voice was trembling but audible, while I shook rabbit-terrified, staring at the ball. "Please, my lord—"

"Silence, girl," the Dragon said, and held his hand out towards me. "Take it."

"I—what?" I said, more bewildered than if he'd flung it into my face.

"Don't stand there like a cretin," he said. *"Take it."*

My hand was shaking so when I raised it that I couldn't help but brush against his fingers as I tried to pluck the ball from them, though I hated to; his skin felt feverish-hot. But the ball of flame was cool as a marble, and it didn't hurt me at all to touch. Startled with relief, I held it between my fingers, staring at it. He looked at me with an expression of annoyance.

"Well," he said ungraciously, "you then, I suppose." He took the ball out of my hand and closed his fist on it a moment; it vanished as quickly as it had come. He turned and said to Danka, "Send the tribute up when you can."

I still hadn't understood. I don't think anyone had, even my parents; it was all too quick, and I was shocked by having drawn his attention at all. I didn't even have a chance to turn around and say a last good-bye before he turned back and took my arm by the wrist. Only Kasia moved; I looked back at her and saw her about to reach for me in protest, and then the Dragon jerked me impatiently and ungently stumbling after him, and dragged me with him back into thin air.

I had my other hand pressed to my mouth, retching, when we stepped back out of the air. When he let go my arm, I sank to my knees and vomited without even seeing where I was. He made a muttered exclamation of disgust—I had spattered the long elegant toe of his leather boot—and said, "Useless. Stop heaving, girl, and clean that filth up." He walked away from me, his heels echoing upon the flagstones, and was gone.

I stayed there shakily until I was sure nothing more would come up, and then I wiped my mouth with the back of my hand and lifted my head to stare. I was on a floor of stone, and not just any stone, but a pure white marble laced through with veins of brilliant green. It was a small round room with narrow slitted windows, too high to look out of, but above my head the ceiling bent inward sharply. I was at the very top of the tower.

There was no furniture in the room at all, and nothing I could use to wipe up the floor. Finally I used the skirt of my dress: that was already dirty anyway. Then after a little time sitting there being terrified and more terrified, while nothing at all happened, I got up and crept timidly down the hallway. I'd have taken any way out of the room but the one he had used, if there had been any other way. There wasn't.

He'd already gone on, though. The short hallway was empty. It had the same cold hard marble underfoot, illuminated with an unfriendly pale white light from hanging lamps. They weren't real lamps, just big chunks of clear polished stone that glowed from inside. There was only one door, and then an archway at the end that led to stairs.

I pushed the door open and looked in, nervously, because that was better than going past it without knowing what was inside. But it only opened into a small bare room, with a narrow bed and a small table and a wash-basin. There was a large window across from me, and I could see the sky. I ran to it and leaned out over the sill.

The Dragon's tower stood in the foothills on the western border

of his lands. All our long valley lay spread out to the east, with
its villages and farms, and standing in the window I could trace
the whole line of the Spindle, running silver-blue down the middle
with the road dusty brown next to it. The road and the river ran
together all the way to the other end of the Dragon's lands, dipping into stands of forest and coming out again at villages, until the
road tapered out to nothing just before the huge black tangle of the
Wood. The river went on alone into its depths and vanished, never
to come out again.

There was Olshanka, the town nearest the tower, where the
Grand Market was held on Sundays: my father had taken me there,
twice. Beyond that Poniets, and Radomsko curled around the shores
of its small lake, and there was my own Dvernik with its wide green
square. I could even see the big white tables laid out for the feasting
the Dragon hadn't wanted to stay for, and I slid to my knees and
rested my forehead on the sill and cried like a child.

But my mother didn't come to rest her hand on my head; my
father didn't pull me up and laugh me out of my tears. I just sobbed
myself out until I had too much of a headache to go on crying, and
after that I was cold and stiff from being on that painfully hard floor,
and I had a running nose and nothing to wipe it with.

I used another part of my skirt for that and sat down on the bed,
trying to think what to do. The room was empty, but aired-out and
neat, as if it had just been left. It probably had. Some other girl had
lived here for ten years, all alone, looking down at the valley. Now
she had gone home to say good-bye to her family, and the room
was mine.

A single painting in a great gilt frame hung on the wall across
from the bed. It made no sense, too grand for the little room and not
really a picture at all, just a broad swath of pale green, grey-brown
at the edges, with one shining blue-silver line that wove across the
middle in gentle curves and narrower silver lines drawn in from the
edges to meet it. I stared at it and wondered if it was magic, too. I'd
never seen such a thing.

But there were circles painted at places along the silver line, at familiar distances, and after a moment I realized the painting was the valley, too, only flattened down the way a bird might have looked down upon it from far overhead. That silver line was the Spindle, running from the mountains into the Wood, and the circles were villages. The colors were brilliant, the paint glossy and raised in tiny peaks. I could almost see waves on the river, the glitter of sunlight on the water. It pulled the eye and made me want to look at it and look at it. But I didn't like it, at the same time. The painting was a box drawn around the living valley, closing it up, and looking at it made me feel closed up myself.

I looked away. It didn't seem that I could stay in the room. I hadn't eaten a bite at breakfast, or at dinner the night before; it had all been ash in my mouth. I should have had less appetite now, when something worse than anything I'd imagined had happened to me, but instead I was painfully hungry, and there were no servants in the tower, so no one was going to get my dinner. Then the worse thought occurred to me: what if the Dragon expected me to get his?

And then the even worse thought than that: what about *after* dinner? Kasia had always said she believed the women who came back, that the Dragon didn't put a hand on them. "He's taken girls for a hundred years now," she always said firmly. "*One* of them would have admitted it, and word would have got out."

But a few weeks ago, she'd asked my mother, privately, to tell her how it happened when a girl was married—to tell her what her own mother would have, the night before she was wed. I'd overheard them through the window, while I was coming back from the woods, and I'd stood there next to the window and listened in with hot tears running down my face, angry, so angry for Kasia's sake.

Now that was going to be *me*. And I wasn't brave—I didn't think that I could take deep breaths, and keep from clenching up tight, like my mother had told Kasia to do so it wouldn't hurt. I found myself imagining for one terrible moment the Dragon's face so close to mine, even closer than when he'd inspected me at the choosing—his black eyes cold and glittering like stone, those iron-hard fingers, so strangely warm, drawing my dress away from my skin, while he smiled that sleek satisfied smile down at me. What if all of him was fever-hot like that, so I'd feel him almost glowing like an ember, all over my body, while he lay upon me and—

I shuddered away from my thoughts and stood up. I looked down at the bed, and around at that small close room with nowhere to hide, and then I hurried out and went back down the hall again. There was a staircase at the end, going down in a close spiral, so I couldn't see what was around the next turn. It sounds stupid to be afraid of going down a staircase, but I was terrified. I nearly went back to my room after all. At last I kept one hand on the smooth stone wall and went down slowly, putting both my feet on one step and stopping to listen before I went down a little more.

After I'd crept down one whole turn like that, and nothing had jumped out at me, I began to feel like an idiot and started to walk more quickly. But then I went around another turn, and still hadn't come to a landing; and another, and I started to be afraid again, this time that the stairs were magic and would just keep going forever, and—well. I started to go quicker and quicker, and then I skidded three steps down onto the next landing and ran headlong into the Dragon.

I was skinny, but my father was the tallest man in the village and I came up to his shoulder, and the Dragon wasn't a big man. We nearly tumbled down the stairs together. He caught the railing with one hand, quick, and my arm with the other, and somehow managed to keep us from landing on the floor. I found myself leaning heavily on him, clutching at his coat and staring directly into his startled face. For one moment he was too surprised to be thinking, and he looked like an ordinary man startled by something jumping out at him, a little bit silly and a little bit soft, his mouth parted and his eyes wide.

I was so surprised myself that I didn't move, just stayed there gawking at him helplessly, and he recovered quick; outrage swept over his face and he heaved me off him onto my feet. Then I realized what I'd just done and blurted in a panic, before he could speak, "I'm looking for the kitchen!"

"*Are* you," he said silkily. His face didn't look at all soft anymore, hard and furious, and he hadn't let go of my arm. His grip was clenching, painful; I could feel the heat of it through the sleeve of my shift. He jerked me towards him and bent towards me—I think he would have liked to loom over me, and because he couldn't was even more angry. If I'd had a moment to think about it, I would have bent back and made myself smaller, but I was too tired and scared. So instead his face was just before mine, so close his breath was on my lips and I felt as much as heard his cold, vicious whisper: "Perhaps I'd better show you there."

"I can—I can—" I tried to say, trembling, trying to lean back from him. He spun away from me and dragged me after him down the stairs, around and around and around again, five turns this time before we came to the next landing, and then another three turns down, the light growing dimmer, before at last he dragged me out into the lowest floor of the tower, just a single large bare-walled dungeon chamber of carven stone, with a huge fireplace shaped like a downturned mouth, full of flames leaping hellishly.

He dragged me towards it, and in a moment of blind terror I realized he meant to throw me in. He was so strong, much stronger than he ought to have been for his size, and he'd pulled me easily stumbling down the stairs after him. But I wasn't going to let him put me in the fire. I wasn't a lady-like quiet girl; all my life I'd spent running in the woods, climbing trees and tearing through brambles, and panic gave me real strength. I screamed as he pulled me close to it, and then I went into a fit of struggling and clawing and squirming, so this time I really did trip him to the floor.

I went down with him. We banged our heads on the flagstones together, and dazed lay still for a moment with our limbs entwined. The fire was leaping and crackling beside us, and as my panic

faded, abruptly I noticed that in the wall beside it were small iron
oven doors, and before it a spit for roasting, and above it a huge
wide shelf with cooking-pots on it. It was only the kitchen.

After a moment, he said, in almost marveling tones, "Are you
deranged?"

"I thought you were going to throw me in the oven," I said, still
dazed, and then I started to laugh.

It wasn't real laughter—I was half-hysterical by then, wrung
out six ways and hungry, my ankles and knees bruised from being
dragged down the stairs and my head aching as though I'd cracked
my skull, and I just couldn't stop.

But *he* didn't know that. All he knew was the stupid village girl
he'd picked was laughing at him, the Dragon, the greatest wizard
of the kingdom and her lord and master. I don't think anyone had
laughed at him in a hundred years, by then. He pushed himself
up, kicking his legs free from mine, and getting to his feet stared
down at me, outraged as a cat. I only laughed harder, and then he
turned abruptly and left me there laughing on the floor, as though
he couldn't think what else to do with me.

After he left, my giggles tapered off, and I felt somehow a little
less hollow and afraid. He hadn't thrown me into the oven, after all,
or even slapped me. I got myself up and looked around the room: it
was hard to see, because the fireplace was so bright and there were
no other lights lit, but when I kept my back to the flames I could
start to make out the huge room: divided after all, into alcoves and
with low walls, with racks full of shining glass bottles—wine, I realized. My uncle had brought a bottle once to my grandmother's
house, for Midwinter.

There were stores all over: barrels of apples packed in straw,
potatoes and carrots and parsnips in sacks, long ropes of onions
braided. On a table in the middle of the room I found a book standing with an unlit candle and an inkstand and a quill, and when I
opened it I found a ledger with records of all the stores, written
in a strong hand. At the bottom of the first page there was a note

written very small; when I lit the candle and bent down to squint I could just make it out:

Breakfast at eight, dinner at one, supper at seven. Leave the meal laid in the library, five minutes before, and you need not see him—no need to say who—*all the day. Courage!*

Priceless advice, and that *Courage!* was like the touch of a friend's hand. I hugged the book against me, feeling less alone than I had all day. It seemed near midday, and the Dragon hadn't eaten at our village, so I set about dinner. I was no great cook, but my mother had kept me at it until I could put together a meal, and I did do all the gathering for my family, so I knew how to tell the fresh from the rotten, and when a piece of fruit would be sweet. I'd never had so many stores to work with: there were even drawers of spices that smelled like Midwinter cake, and a whole barrel full of fresh soft grey salt.

At the end of the room there was a strangely cold place, where I found meat hanging up: a whole venison and two great hares; there was a box of straw full of eggs. There was a fresh loaf of bread already baked wrapped in a woven cloth on the hearth, and next to it I discovered a whole pot of rabbit and buckwheat and small peas all together. I tasted it: like something for a feast day, so salty and a little sweet, and meltingly tender; another gift from the anonymous hand in the book.

I didn't know how to make food like that at all, and I quailed thinking that the Dragon would expect it. But I was desperately grateful to have the pot ready nonetheless. I put it back on the shelf above the fire to warm—I splashed my dress a little as I did—and I put two eggs in a dish in the oven to bake, and found a tray and a bowl and a plate and a spoon. When the rabbit was ready, I set it out on the tray and cut the bread—I had to cut it, because I had torn off the end of the loaf and eaten it myself while I waited for the rabbit to heat up—and put out butter. I even baked an apple, with the spices: my mother had taught me to do that for our Sunday supper in winter, and there were so many ovens I could do that at the same time as everything else cooked. I even felt a little proud of myself, when everything was assembled on the tray together: it looked like a holiday, though a strange one, with just enough for one man.

I took it up the stairs carefully, but too late I realized I didn't know where the library was. If I'd thought about it a little, I might have reasoned out that it wouldn't be on the lowest floor, and indeed it wasn't, but I didn't find that out until I'd wandered around carrying the tray through an enormous circular hall, the windows draped with curtains and a heavy throne-like chair at the end. There was another door at the far end, but when I opened that I found only the entry hall and the huge doors of the tower, three times the height of my head and barred with a thick slab of wood in iron brackets.

I turned and went back through the hall to the stairs, and up another landing, and here found the marble floor covered in soft furry cloth. I'd never seen a carpet before. That was why I hadn't heard the Dragon's footsteps. I crept anxiously down the hall, and peered through the first door. I backed out hastily: the room was full of long tables, strange bottles and bubbling potions and unnatural sparks in colors that came from no fireplace; I didn't want to spend another moment inside there. But I managed to catch my dress in the door and tear it, even so.

Finally the next door, across the hall, opened on a room full of books: wooden shelves up and up from floor to ceiling crammed with them. It smelled of dust, and there were only a few narrow windows throwing light in. I was so glad to find the library that I didn't notice at first that the Dragon was there: sitting in a heavy chair with a book laid out on a small table across his thighs, so large each page was the length of my forearm, and a great golden lock hanging from the open cover.

I froze staring at him, feeling betrayed by the advice in the book. I'd somehow assumed that the Dragon would conveniently keep out of the way until I'd had a chance to put down his meal. He hadn't raised his head to look at me, but instead of just going quietly with the tray to the table in the center of the room, laying it

out, and scurrying away, I hung in the doorway and said, "I've—
I've brought dinner," not wanting to go in unless he told me to.

"Really?" he said, cuttingly. "Without falling into a pit along the
way? I'm astonished." He only then looked up at me and frowned.
"Or *did* you fall into a pit?"

I looked down at myself. My skirt had one enormous ugly stain,
from the vomit—I'd wiped it off best as I could in the kitchen, but
it hadn't really come out—and another from where I'd blown my
nose. There were three or four dripping stains from the stew, and
some more spatters from the dish-pan where I'd wiped the pots.
The hem was still muddy from this morning, and I'd torn a few
other holes in it without even noticing. My mother had braided and
coiled my hair that morning and pinned it up, but the coils had slid
mostly down off my head and were now a big snarled knot of hair
hanging half off my neck.

I hadn't noticed; it wasn't anything out of the usual for me, except that I was wearing a nice dress underneath the mess. "I was—I
cooked, and I cleaned—" I tried to explain.

"The dirtiest thing in this tower is *you*," he said—true, but unkind
anyway. I flushed and with my head low went to the table. I laid
everything out and looked it over, and then I realized sinkingly that
with all the time I'd taken wandering around, everything had gone
cold, except the butter, which was a softened runny mess in its dish.
Even my lovely baked apple was all congealed.

I stared down at it in dismay, trying to decide what to do; should
I take it all back down? Or maybe he wouldn't mind? I turned to
look and nearly yelped: he was standing directly behind me peering
over my shoulder at the food. "I see why you were afraid I might
roast you," he said, leaning over to lift up a spoonful of the stew,
breaking the layer of cooling fat on its top and dumping it back in.
"You would make a better meal than this."

"I'm not a splendid cook, but—" I started, meaning to explain
that I wasn't quite so terrible at it, I'd only not known my way, but
he snorted, interrupting me.

UPROOTED 23

"Is there anything you *can* do?" he asked, mockingly.

If only I'd been better trained to serve, if only I'd ever really thought I might be chosen and had been more ready for all of it; if only I'd been a little less miserable and tired, and if only I hadn't felt a little proud of myself in the kitchen; if only he hadn't just twitted me for being a rag, the way everyone who loved me did, but with malice instead of affection—if any of those things, and if only I hadn't run into him on the stairs, and discovered that he *wasn't* going to fling me into a fire, I would probably have just gone red, and run away.

Instead I flung the tray down on the table in a passion and cried, "Why did you take me, then? Why didn't you take Kasia?"

I shut my mouth as soon as I'd said it, ashamed of myself and horrified. I was about to open my mouth and take it back in a rush, to tell him I was sorry, I didn't mean it, I didn't mean he should go take Kasia instead; I would go and make him another tray—

He said impatiently, "Who?"

I gaped at him. "Kasia!" I said. He only looked at me as though I was giving him more evidence of my idiocy, and I forgot my noble intentions in confusion. "You were going to take her! She's—she's clever, and brave, and a splendid cook, and—"

He was looking every moment more annoyed. "Yes," he bit out, interrupting me, "I do recall the girl: neither horse-faced nor a slovenly mess, and I imagine would not be yammering at me this very minute: enough. You village girls are all tedious at the beginning, more or less, but you're proving a truly remarkable paragon of incompetence."

"Then you needn't keep me!" I flared, angry and wounded—*horse-faced* stung.

"Much to my regret," he said, "that's where you're wrong."

He seized my hand by the wrist and whipped me around: he stood close behind me and stretched my arm out over the food on the table. *"Lirintalem,"* he said, a strange word that ran liquidly off his tongue and rang sharply in my ears. "Say it with me."

"What?" I said; I'd never heard the word before. But he pressed closer against my back, put his mouth against my ear, and whispered, terrible, *"Say it!"*

I trembled, and wanting only for him to let me go said it with him, *"Lirintalem,"* while he held my hand out over the meal.

The air rippled over the food, horrible to see, like the whole world was a pond that he could throw pebbles in. When it smoothed again, the food was all changed. Where the baked eggs had been, a roast chicken; instead of the bowl of rabbit stew, a heap of tiny new spring beans, though it was seven months past their season; instead of the baked apple, a tartlet full of apples sliced paper-thin, studded with fat raisins and glazed over with honey.

He let go of me. I staggered with the loss of his support, clutching at the edge of the table, my lungs emptied as if someone had sat on my chest; I felt like I'd been squeezed for juice like a lemon. Stars prickled at the edge of my sight, and I leaned over half-fainting. I only distantly saw him looking down at the tray, an odd scowl on his face as though he was at once surprised and annoyed.

"What did you do to me?" I whispered, when I could breathe again.

"Stop whining," he said dismissively. "It's nothing more than a cantrip." Whatever surprise he might have felt had vanished; he flicked his hand at the door as he seated himself at the table before his dinner. "All right, get out. I can see you'll be wasting inordinate amounts of my time, but I've had enough for the day."

I was glad to obey that, at least. I didn't try to pick up the tray, only crept slowly out of the library, cradling my hand against my body. I was still stumbling-weak. It took me nearly half an hour to drag myself back up all the stairs to the top floor, and then I went into the little room and shut the door, dragged the dresser before it, and fell onto the bed. If the Dragon came to the door while I slept, I didn't hear a thing.

TWO

I didn't see the Dragon for another four days. I spent them in the kitchen morning until night: I had found a few cook-books there and was working through every recipe in them one after another, frantically, trying to become the most splendid cook anyone had ever heard of. There was enough food in the larder that I didn't care what I wasted; if anything was bad, I ate it myself. I followed the advice and got his meals to the library ex-actly five minutes to the hour, and I covered the dishes and hurried. He was never there again when I came, so I was content, and I heard no complaints from him. There were some homespun clothes in a box in my room, which fit me more or less—my legs were bare from the knee down, my arms from the elbow down, and I had to tie them around my waist, but I was as tidy as I had ever been.

I didn't want to please him, but I did want to keep him from ever doing that to me again, whatever that spell had been. I'd woken from dreams four times a night, feeling the word *lirintalem* on my lips and tasting it in my mouth as though it belonged there, and his hand burning hot on my arm.

Fear and work weren't all bad, as companions went. They were both better than loneliness, and the deeper fears, the worse ones that I knew would come true: that I wouldn't see my mother and my father for ten years, that I'd never live again in my own home, never run wild in the woods again, that whatever strange alchemy acted on the Dragon's girls would soon begin to take hold of me, and make me into someone I wouldn't recognize at the end of it. At least while I was chopping and sweltering away in front of the ovens, I didn't have to think about any of that.

After a few days, when I realized that he wouldn't come and use that spell on me at every meal, I stopped my frenzy of cooking. But then I found I had nothing else to do, even when I went looking for work. As large as the tower was, it didn't need cleaning: no dust had gathered in the corners or the window-sills, not even on the tiny carved vines on the gilt frame.

I still didn't like the map-painting in my room. Every night I imagined I heard a faint gurgle coming from it, like water running down a gutter, and every day it sat there on the wall in all its excessive glory, trying to make me look at it. After scowling at it, I went downstairs. I emptied out a sack of turnips in the cellar, ripped the seams, and used the cloth to cover it up. My room felt better at once with the gold and splendor of it hidden away.

I spent the rest of that morning looking out the window across the valley again, lonely and sick with longing. It was an ordinary work-day, so there were men in the fields gathering in the harvest and women at the river doing their washing. Even the Wood looked almost comforting to me, in its great wild impenetrable blackness: an unchanged constant. The big herd of sheep that belonged to Radomsko was grazing on the lower slopes of the mountains at the northern end of the valley; they looked like a wandering white cloud. I watched them roam awhile, and had a small weep, but even grief had its limits. By dinner-time I was horribly bored.

My family weren't either poor or rich; we had seven books in our house. I'd only ever read four of them; I had spent nearly every day of my life more out-of-doors than not, even in winter and rain. But I didn't have many other choices anymore, so when I brought the dinner tray to the library that afternoon, I looked over at the shelves. Surely there could be no harm in my taking one. The other girls must have taken books, since everyone always said how well read they were when they came out of service.

So I boldly went to a shelf and picked out a book that nearly called out to be touched: it was beautifully bound in a burnished leather the color of wheat that glowed in the candle-light, rich and inviting. Once I'd taken it out, I hesitated: it was bigger and heavier than any of my family's books, and besides that the cover was engraved with beautiful designs painted in gold. But there was no lock on it, so I carried it away with me up to my room, half-guilty and trying to convince myself I was being foolish for feeling that way.

Then I opened it and felt even more foolish, because I couldn't understand it at all. Not in the usual way, of not knowing the words, or not knowing what enough of them meant—I *did* understand them all, and everything that I was reading, for the first three pages, and then I paused and wondered, what was the book about? And I couldn't tell; I had no idea what I'd just read.

I turned back and tried again, and once more I was sure that I was understanding, and all of it made perfect sense—better than perfect sense, even; it had the feeling of truth, of something that I'd always known and just hadn't ever put into words, or of explaining clearly and plainly something I'd never understood. I was nodding with satisfaction, going along well, and this time I got to the fifth page before I realized again that I couldn't have told anyone what was on the first page, or for that matter the page before.

I glared down at the book resentfully, and then I opened it to the first page again and started to read out loud, one word at a time. The words sang like birds out of my mouth, beautiful, melting like sugared fruit. I still couldn't keep the train of it in my head, but I kept reading, dreamily, until the door smashed open.

I'd stopped barring my door with furniture by then. I was sitting on my bed, which I'd pushed under the window for the light, and the Dragon was directly across the room from me framed in the doorway. I froze in surprise and stopped reading, my mouth hanging open. He was furiously angry: his eyes were glittering and terrible, and he held out a hand and said, *"Tualidetal."*

The book tried to jump out of my hands, to fly across the room to him. I blindly clutched after it from some badly misguided instinct. It wriggled against me, trying to go, but stupidly obstinate I gave it a jerk and managed to yank it back into my arms. He gaped at me and grew even more wildly angry; he stormed across the tiny chamber, while I belatedly tried to scramble up and back, but there was nowhere for me to go. He was on me in an instant, thrusting me flat down against my pillows.

"So," he said, silkily, his hand pressed down upon my collarbone, pinning me easily to the bed. It felt as though my heart was thumping back and forth between my breastbone and my back, each beat shaking me. He plucked the book away with a hand—at least I wasn't stupid enough to *keep* trying to hold on to it anymore—and tossed it with an easy flip so it landed upon the small table. "Agnieszka, was it? Agnieszka of Dvernik."

He seemed to want an answer. "Yes," I whispered.

"Agnieszka," he murmured, bending low towards me, and I realized he meant to kiss me. I was terrified, and yet half-wanting him to do it and have it over with, so I wouldn't have to be so afraid, and then he didn't at all. He said, bent so close I could see my eyes reflected in his, "Tell me, dear Agnieszka, where are you really from? Did the Falcon send you? Or perhaps even the king himself?"

I stopped staring in terror at his mouth and darted my eyes towards his. "I—what?" I said.

"I *will* find out," he said. "However skillful your master's spell, it will have holes in it. Your—*family*—" He sneered the word. "—may think they remember you, but they won't have all the things of a child's life. A pair of mittens or a worn-out cap, a collection of broken toys—I won't find those things in your house, will I?"

"All my toys were broken?" I said helplessly, seizing on the only part of this I even understood at all. "They're—yes? All my clothes were always worn out, our rag-bag is all them—"

He shoved me hard against the bed and bent low. "Don't dare lie to me!" he hissed. "I will tear the truth out of your throat—"

His fingers were resting on my neck; his leg was on the bed, between mine. In a great gulp of terror I put my hands on his chest and shoved with all my body against the bed, and heaved us both off it. We fell heavily together to the ground, him beneath me, and I was up like a rabbit scrambling off him and running for the door. I fled for the stairs. I don't know where I thought I was going: I couldn't have gotten out the front door, and there was nowhere else to go. But I ran anyway: I scrambled down two flights, and as his steps pursuing me came on, I flung myself into the dim laboratory, with all its hissing fumes and smoke. I crawled away desperately under the tables into a dark corner behind a high cabinet, and pulled my legs in towards me.

I'd closed the door behind me, but that didn't seem to keep him from knowing where I'd gone. He opened it and looked into the room, and I saw him over the edge of one table, his cold and angry eye between two beakers of glass, his face painted in shades of green by the fires. He came with a steady unhurried step around the table, and as he rounded the end I darted forward scrambling the other way, trying for the door—I had some thought of locking him in. But I jarred the narrow shelf against the wall. One of the stoppered jars struck my back, rolled off, and smashed on the floor at my feet.

Grey smoke billowed up around me and into my nose and mouth, choking me, stilling me. It stung in my eyes, and I couldn't blink, I couldn't reach up to rub them, my arms refusing to answer. The coughs caught in my throat and stopped; my whole body froze slowly into place, still in a crouch on the floor. But I didn't feel afraid anymore, and after a moment not even uncomfortable. I was somehow at once endlessly heavy and weightless, distant. I heard the Dragon's footsteps very faintly and far-off as he came and stood over me, and I didn't care what he would do.

He stood there looking down at me with cold impatience. I didn't try to guess what he would do; I could neither think nor wonder. The world was very grey and still.

"No," he said after a moment, "—no, you can't possibly be a spy."

He turned and left me there, for some time—I couldn't have told you how long, it could have been an hour or a week or a year, though later I learned it had been only half a day. Then at last he returned, with a displeased set look to his mouth. He held up a small raggedy thing that had once been a piglet, knitted of wool and stuffed with straw, before I had dragged it behind me through the woods for the first seven years of my life. "So," he said, "no spy. Only a witling."

Then he laid his hand on my head and said, *Tezavon tahozh, tezavon tahozh kivi, kanzon lihush.*

He didn't so much recite the words as chant them, almost like a song, and as he spoke color and time and breath came back into the world; my head came free and I shied out from under his hand. The stone was slowly fading out of my flesh. My arms came loose, flailing for a grip on anything while my still-stone legs held me locked in place. He caught my wrists, so when I finally came loose all the way I was held by his hand, with no chance of flight.

I didn't try to run, though. My suddenly free thoughts ran around in a dozen directions, as though they were catching up with lost time, but it seemed to me he might have just left me stone, if he'd wanted to do something terrible to me, and at least he had stopped thinking me some sort of spy. I didn't understand why he thought anyone would have wanted to spy on him, much less the king; he was the king's wizard, wasn't he?

"And now you'll tell me: what were you doing?" he said. His eyes were still suspicious and cold and glittering.

"I only wanted a book to read," I said. "I didn't—I didn't think there was any harm—"

"And you happened to take *Luthe's Summoning* off the shelf for a little reading," he said, cuttingly sarcastic, "and merely by chance—" until perhaps my alarmed and blank look convinced him, and he halted and looked at me with unconcealed irritation. "What an unequaled gift for disaster you have."

Then he scowled down, and I followed his look to the shards of the glass jar around our feet: he hissed his breath out between his teeth and said abruptly, "Clean that up, and then come to the library. And *don't* touch anything else."

He stalked away, leaving me to go hunt out some rags from the kitchens to pick up the glass with, and a bucket: I washed the floor as well, though there wasn't a trace of anything spilled, as though the magic had burned off like the liquor on a pudding. I kept stopping and lifting my hand up from the stone floor to turn it over front and back, making sure the stone wasn't creeping back up my fingertips. I couldn't help but wonder why he had a jar of that on his shelf, and whether he'd ever used it on someone else—someone who had become a statue somewhere, standing with fixed eyes, time eddying past them; I shuddered.

I was very, very careful not to touch anything else in the room.

The book I'd taken was back upon the shelf when at last I girded myself and went into the library. He was pacing, his own book on its small table thrust aside and neglected, and when I came in he scowled at me again. I looked down: my skirt was marked with wet tracks from the mopping, and it had been too short to begin with, barely covering my knees. The sleeves of my shift were worse: I'd got some egg on the ends that morning, making his breakfast, and had singed the elbow a little getting the toast off before it burned.

"We'll begin with *that*, then," the Dragon said. "I needn't be offended every time I have to look at you."

I shut my mouth on apologies: if I began to apologize for being untidy, I'd be apologizing the rest of my life. I could tell from only a few days in the tower that he loved beautiful things. Even his legions of books were none of them exactly alike: their leather bindings in different colors, their clasps and hinges of gold and sometimes even dotted with small chips of jewels. Anything that anyone might rest their eyes on, whether a small blown-glass cup upon the window-sill here in the library, or the painting in my room, was beautiful, and set aside in its own place where it might shine without distractions. I was a glaring blot on the perfection. But I didn't care: I didn't feel I owed him beauty.

He beckoned me over, impatiently, and I took a wary step towards him; he took my hands and crossed them over my chest, fingertips on each opposite shoulder, and said, "Now: *vanastalem.*"

I stared at him in mute rebellion. The word when he said it rang in my ears just like the other spell he'd used me for. I could feel it wanting to come into my mouth, to drain away my strength.

He caught me by the shoulder, his fingers gripping painfully hard; I felt the heat of each one penetrating through my shirt. "I may have to put up with incompetence; I won't tolerate spinelessness," he said. "*Say it.*"

I remembered being stone; what else could he do to me? I trembled and said, very soft, as if whispering could keep it from taking hold of me, "*Vanastalem.*"

My strength welled up through my body and fountained out of my mouth, and where it left me, a trembling in the air began and went curling down around my body in a spiraling path. I sank to the ground gasping in strangely vast skirts of rustling silk, green and russet brown. They pooled around my waist and swamped my legs, endless. My head bowed forward on my neck under the weight of a curved headdress, a veil spilling down my back, lace picked out with flowers in gold thread. I stared dully at the Dragon's boots, the tooled leather of them: there were curling vines embossed upon them.

"Look at you, and over a nothing of a spell again," he said over me, sounding exasperated with his own handiwork. "At least your appearance is improved. See if you can keep yourself in a decent state from now on. Tomorrow, we'll try another."

The boots turned and walked away from me. He sat down in his chair, I think, and went back to his reading; I don't know for certain. After a while I crawled out of the library on my hands and knees, in that beautiful dress, without ever lifting my head.

The next few weeks blurred into one another. Every morning I woke a little before dawn and lay in my bed while my window brightened, trying to think of some way to escape. Every morning, having failed, I carried his breakfast tray to the library, and he cast another spell with me. If I hadn't been able to keep myself neat enough—usually I hadn't—he used *vanastalem* upon me first, and then a second spell, too. All my homespun dresses were vanishing one after another, and the unwieldy elaborate dresses dotted my bedroom like small mountains, so heavy with brocade and embroidery that they half stood up without me inside them. I could barely writhe my way out from under the skirts at bedtime, and the awful boned stays beneath them squeezed in my breath.

The aching fog never left me. After each morning, I crept shattered back to my chamber. I suppose the Dragon got his own dinner, because I certainly did nothing for him. I lay on my bed until supper-time, when usually I was able to creep back downstairs and get a simple meal, driven more by my own hunger than any concern for his needs.

The worst of it was not understanding: why was he using me this way? At night, before drowning in sleep, I imagined all the worst out of tales and fairy-stories, vampyrs and incubi drinking the life out of maidens, and swore in terror that in the morning I would find a way out. Of course, I never did. My only comfort was that I wasn't the first: I told myself he'd done this to all those other girls before me, and they had come through it. It wasn't much comfort: ten years seemed to me forever. But I grasped at any thought that could ease my misery even a little.

He gave me no comfort himself. He was irritated with me every time I came into his library, even on the few days that I managed to keep myself in good order: as though I were coming to annoy and interrupt him, instead of him tormenting and using me. And when he had finished working his magic through me and left me crumpled on the floor, he would scowl down at me and call me useless.

One day I tried to keep away entirely. I thought if I left his meal early, he might forget about me for a day. I laid his breakfast as dawn broke, then hurried away and hid in the back of the kitchens. But promptly at seven, one of his wisp-things, the ones I'd sometimes seen floating down the Spindle towards the Wood, came gliding down the stairs. Seen close, it was a misshapen soap-bubble thing, rippling and shifting, almost invisible unless the light caught on its iridescent skin. The wisp went bobbing in and out of corners, until at last it reached me and came to hover over my knees insistently. I stared up at it from my huddle and saw my own face looking back in ghostly outline. Slowly I unfolded myself and followed the wisp back up to the library, where he set aside his book and glared at me.

"As happy as I would be to forgo the very doubtful pleasure of watching you flop about like an exhausted eel over the least cantrip," he bit out, "we've already seen the consequences of leaving you to your own devices. How much of a slattern have you made yourself today?"

I'd been making a desperate effort to keep myself tidy so I could at least avoid the first spell. Today I had only acquired a few small smudges making breakfast, and one streak of oil. I held a fold of my dress shut around that. But he was looking at me with distaste anyway, and when I followed the line of his gaze I saw to my dismay that while I had been hiding in the back of the kitchens, I had evidently picked up a cobweb—the one cobweb in all the tower, I suppose—which was now trailing from the back of my skirt like a thin ragged veil.

"*Vanastalem,*" I repeated with him, dully resigned, and watched a riotously beautiful wave of orange and yellow silk come sweeping up from the floor to surround me, like leaves blown down an autumn path. I swayed, breathing heavily, as he sat down again.

"Now then," he said. He had set a stack of books upon the table, and with a shove he toppled them over into a loose and scattered heap. "To order them: *darendetal*."

He waved his hand at the table. *"Darendetal,"* I mumbled along with him, and the spell came strangling out of my throat. The books on the table shuddered, and one after another lifted and spun into place like unnatural jeweled birds in their bindings of red and yellow and blue and brown.

This time, I didn't sink to the floor: I only gripped the edge of the table with both hands and leaned against it. He was frowning at the stack. "What idiocy is this?" he demanded. "There's no order here—look at this."

I looked at the books. They were piled into a single stack neatly enough, with like colors next to each other—

"—*color?*" he said, his voice rising. "By *color?* You—" He was as furious with me as if it had been my fault. Maybe it did something to his magic, when he pulled strength from me to fuel it? "Oh, get out!" he snarled, and I hurried away full of resentful secret delight: oh, I was *glad* if I was spoiling his magic somehow.

I had to stop halfway up the stairs to catch my breath inside the stays, but when I did, I realized abruptly that I wasn't crawling. I was still tired, but the fog hadn't descended. I even managed to climb the rest of the way to the top of the stairs without another pause, and though I fell onto my bed and drowsed away half of the day, at least I didn't feel like a mindless husk.

The fog lifted more and more as the next few weeks passed, as though practice was making me stronger, better able to bear whatever he was doing to me. The sessions began little by little to be—not pleasant, but not terrifying; only a tiresome chore, like having to scrub pots in cold water. I could sleep at night again, and my spirit began to recover, too. Every day I felt better, and every day more angry.

I couldn't get back into the ridiculous gowns in any kind of reasonable way—I'd tried, but I couldn't even reach the buttons and laces in the back, and I usually had to burst threads and crumple the skirts even to get out of them. So every night I shoved them into a piled-up heap out of the way, and every morning I would put on another of the homespun ones and try and keep as tidy as I could, and every few days he would lose patience with my untidiness and change that one, too. And now I had reached the last of my homespun gowns.

I held that last gown of plain undyed wool in my hands, feeling like it was a rope I was clinging to, and then in a burst of defiance I left it on my bed, and pulled myself into the green-and-russet gown.

I couldn't fasten the buttons in back, so I took the long veil from the headdress, wound it twice around my waist and made a knot, just barely good enough to keep the whole thing from falling off me, and marched downstairs to the kitchens. I didn't even try to keep myself clean this time: I carried the tray up to the library defiantly bespattered with egg and bacon-grease and splotches of tea, my hair in snarls, looking like some sort of mad noblewoman who'd run off to the woods from a ball.

Of course, it didn't last long. As soon as I resentfully said *vanastalem* along with him, his magic seized me and shook off my stains, squashed me back into stays, piled my hair back upon my head, and left me once again looking like a doll for some princess to play with.

But I felt happier that morning than I had in weeks, and from then on it became my private defiance. I wanted him to be bitterly annoyed every time he looked at me, and he rewarded me with every incredulous scowl. "How do you do this to yourself?" he asked me, almost marveling, one day when I wandered in with a clump of rice pudding on top of my head—I had accidentally hit a spoon with my elbow and flung some into the air—and a huge red streak of jam going all the way down my front of beautiful cream silk.

The last homespun dress, I kept in my dresser. Every day after he had done with me, I went upstairs. I would wrestle my way out of the ballgown, drag my hair out of the nets and headdresses, scattering jeweled pins on the floor, and then I would put on the soft

well-worn letnik and the homespun smock, which I kept washed
and clean by hand. And then I went down to the kitchens to make
my own bread, and I rested by the warm fireplace while it baked,
careless of a few smudges of ash and flour on my skirts.

I began to have enough energy for boredom once again. I didn't
even think of taking another book from the library, though. Instead, I went for a needle, much as I loathed to sew. As long as I was
going to be drained to the belly every morning to make dresses, I
thought I might as well tear them apart and make something less
useless of them: sheets, perhaps, or handkerchiefs.

The mending-basket had stood untouched inside the box in my
room: there was nothing in the castle to mend but my own clothes,
which until now I had been sullenly glad to leave torn. But when
I opened it, I found tucked inside a single scrap of paper, written
on with a bit of stubby charcoal: the hand of my friend from the
kitchen.

> *You are afraid: don't be! He won't touch you. He will only want you
> to make yourself handsome. He won't think to give you anything,
> but you can take a fine dress from one of the guest chambers and
> make it over to fit you. When he summons you, sing to him or tell
> him a story. He wants company but not much of it: bring his meals
> and avoid him when you can, and he will ask nothing more.*

How priceless those words would have been to me, if I had
opened the mending-basket and found them that first night. Now
I stood holding the note, shaking with the memory of his voice
overlaid on my halting one, dragging spells and strength out of me,
draping me in silks and velvet. I had been wrong. He hadn't done
any of this to the other women at all.

THREE

I huddled in my bed all that night without sleeping, desperate all over again. But getting out of the tower didn't become easier just because I wanted it more. I did go to the great doors the next morning, and tried for the first time to lift the enormous bar across them, no matter how ridiculous the attempt. But of course I couldn't budge it a quarter of an inch.

Down in the pantry, using a long-handled pot for a lever, I pried up the great iron cap that covered the refuse-pit and looked down. Deep below a fire gleamed; there was no escape there for me. I pushed the iron lid back into place with an effort, and then I searched all along the walls with both my palms, into every dark corner, looking for some opening, some entry. But if there was one, I didn't find it; and then morning was spilling down the stairs behind me, an unwelcome golden light. I had to make the breakfast and carry the tray up to my doom.

As I laid the food out, the plate of eggs, the toast, the preserves, I looked over and looked over again, at the long steel-gleaming butcher's knife with its handle jutting out of the block towards me. I had used it to cut meat; I knew how quick it was. My parents raised a pig every year. I'd helped at butchering-time, held the bucket for the pig's blood, but the thought of putting a knife into a man was something else, unimaginable. So I didn't imagine it. I only put the knife on the tray, and went upstairs.

When I came into the library, he was standing by the window-sill with his back to me and his shoulders stiff with irritation. I mechanically put out the dishes, one after another, until there was nothing left but the tray, the tray and the knife. My dress was splattered with oatmeal and egg; in a moment he would say—

"Finish with that," he said, "and go upstairs."

"What?" I said, blankly. The knife was still under its napkin, drowning out all my other thoughts, and it took a moment for me to understand I'd been reprieved.

"Are you grown suddenly deaf?" he snapped. "Stop fussing with those plates and take yourself off. And keep to your rooms until I summon you again."

My dress was stained and crumpled, a ruin of tangled ribbons, but he hadn't even turned to look at me. I snatched up the tray and fled the room, needing no more excuse. I ran up the stairs, feeling almost as if I were flying without that terrible weariness dragging at my heels. I went into my room and shut the door and tore off my silken finery, put back on my homespun, and sank down on the bed, hugging myself with relief like a child who'd escaped a whipping.

And then I saw the tray discarded on the floor, the knife lying bare and gleaming. Oh. Oh, what a fool I'd been, even to think about it. He was my lord: if by some horrible chance I *had* killed him, I would surely be put to death for it, and like as not my parents along with me. Murder was no escape at all; better to just throw myself out the window.

I even turned and looked out the window, miserably, and then I saw what the Dragon had been watching with such distaste. There was a cloud of dust on the road coming to the tower. It wasn't a wagon but a great covered carriage almost like a house on wheels:

harnessed to a team of steaming horses, with two horsemen riding before the driver, all of them in coats of grey and brilliant green. Four more horsemen followed it, in similar coats.

The carriage drew up outside the great doors: there was a green crest on it, a monster with many heads, and all the outriders and guards came rolling down off their horses and went into an enormous bustle of work. They all flinched away a little when the tower doors swung lightly open, those huge doors I couldn't even shift. I craned my head to peer down and saw the Dragon step out from the doors alone, onto the threshold.

A man came ducking out of the belly of the carriage: tall, golden-haired, broad-shouldered, with a long cloak all of that same brilliant green; he jumped down over the steps which had been put out for him, took with one hand the sword which another of his servants held across the palms, and strode quickly between his men and up to the door even as he belted it on, with no hesitation.

"I loathe a coach more than a chimaera," he said to the Dragon, clear enough that I heard his voice rising to my window, over the snorting stamping horses. "A week shut up in the thing: why can't you ever come to court?"

"Your Highness will have to forgive me," the Dragon said, coldly. "My duties here occupy me."

I was leaning out far enough by then I might have easily fallen out just by accident, with all my fear and misery forgot. The king of Polnya had two sons, but Crown Prince Sigmund was nothing but a sensible young man. He had been well educated and had married the daughter of some reigning count in the north, which had brought us an ally and a port. They had already assured the succession with a boy and a girl for spare; he was supposedly an excellent administrator, and would be an excellent king, and no one cared anything about him.

Prince Marek was enormously more satisfying. I had heard at least a dozen stories and songs of how he had slain the Vandalus Hydra, none of them alike but all of them, I was assured, true in every particular; and besides that he had killed at least three or four or nine giants in the last war against Rosya. He had even ridden out to try and kill a real dragon once, only it had turned out to be some peasants pretending to have been attacked by a dragon and hiding the sheep they claimed it had eaten, to get out of tax. And he hadn't even executed them, but had chastised their lord for levying too high a tax.

He went into the tower with the Dragon, and the doors closed behind them; the prince's men began encamping on the level field before the doors. I turned back into my small room and paced the floor in circles; at last I went and crept down the stairwell to try and listen, edging down until I heard their voices drifting out of the library. I couldn't catch more than one word in five, but they were speaking of the wars with Rosya, and of the Wood.

I didn't try very hard to eavesdrop; I didn't much care what they were talking about. Far more important to me was the faint hope of rescue stirring: whatever the Dragon was doing to me, this horror of life-draining, it was surely against the king's law. He'd told me to keep away, to keep out of sight; what if that wasn't only because I was a discreditable mess, which he could have repaired with a word, but because he didn't want the prince to know what he was doing? What if I threw myself on the prince's mercy, and he took me away—

"Enough," Prince Marek said, his voice breaking in on my thoughts: the words had come clearer as if he was moving closer to the door. He sounded angry. "You and my father and Sigmund, all of you bleating like sheep—no, enough. I don't mean to let this rest."

I hastily flew back up the stairwell on bare feet as noiseless as I could make them: the guest chambers were on the third floor, the one between mine and the library. I sat at the top of the stairwell listening to their boots on the steps below until the sounds died away. I wasn't sure I had it in me to disobey the Dragon directly: if he caught me trying to go knock on the prince's door, he'd surely do something terrible to me. But he was already doing something terrible to me. Kasia would have seized the chance, I was sure—if she'd been here, she would go and open the door and kneel at the prince's feet and beg him for rescue, not like a frightened blubbering child but like a maiden out of the stories.

I went back to my room and practiced the scene, murmuring words under my breath, while the sun sank down. And when at last it was dark and late, I crept down the stairs with my heart pounding. But I was still afraid. First I went down and looked to make sure the lights were out in the library and in the laboratory: the Dragon wasn't awake. On the third floor, a dim fire's glow showed orange beneath the first guest chamber, and I couldn't see anything of the Dragon's bedroom door at all; it was lost in the shadows at the end of the hall. But still I hesitated on the landing—and then I went down to the kitchens instead.

I told myself I was hungry. I ate a few mouthfuls of bread and cheese to fortify myself, while I stood shivering in front of the fire, and then I went back upstairs. All the way upstairs, back to my room.

I couldn't make myself really imagine it, me at the prince's door, me kneeling and making a graceful speech. I wasn't Kasia, wasn't anyone special. I'd only burst into tears and look like a lunatic, and he'd probably throw me out or, worse, call the Dragon to have me properly chastised. Why would he believe me? A peasant girl in a homespun smock, a low servant in the Dragon's house, waking him in the middle of the night with a wild story of the great wizard tormenting me?

I went desolately back into my room and stopped short. Prince Marek was standing in the middle of the chamber, studying the painting: he'd pulled down the cover I'd put over it. He turned around and looked me over with a doubtful expression. "My lord, Highness," I said, but not really. The words came out in such a whisper he couldn't have heard them except as an inarticulate noise.

He didn't seem to care. "Well," he said, "you aren't one of his beauties, are you." He crossed the room, barely two steps needed: he made it seem smaller by being there. He put his hand under my chin, turned my face side-to-side inspecting it. I stared up at him dumbly. He was strange to be so close to, overwhelming: taller than I was, broad with the weight of a man who nearly lived in armor, handsome as a portrait and clean-shaven, freshly bathed; his golden hair was dark and damply curling at the base of his neck. "But perhaps you've some particular skill, sweet, that makes up for it? That's his usual line, isn't it?"

He didn't sound cruel, only teasing, and his smile down at me was conspiratorial. I didn't feel wounded at all, only dazed from so much attention, as though I'd already been saved without having to say a word. And then he laughed, and kissed me, and reached efficiently for my skirts.

I startled like a fish trying to jump out of a net and struggled against him. It was like struggling against the tower doors, impossible; he scarcely even noticed me trying. He laughed again and kissed my throat. "Don't worry, he can't object," he said, as though that was my only reason to protest. "He's still my father's vassal, even if he likes to stay out here in the hinterlands lording it over you all alone."

It's not that he was taking pleasure in overcoming me. I was still mute and my resistance was more confused batting at him, half-wondering: surely he couldn't, Prince Marek couldn't, the hero; surely he couldn't even really want me. I didn't scream, I didn't plead, and I think he scarcely imagined that I would resist. I suppose in an ordinary noble house, some more-than-willing scullery maid would already have crept into his bedchamber and saved him the trouble of going looking. For that matter, I'd probably have been willing myself, if he'd asked me outright and given me enough time to get over my surprise and answer him: I struggled more by reflex than because I wanted to reject him.

But he did overcome me. Then I began to be really afraid, wanting only to get away; I pushed at his hands, and said, "Prince, I don't, please, wait," in disjointed bursts. And though he might not have wanted resistance, when he met it, he cared nothing: he only grew impatient.

"There, there; all right," he said, as though I were a horse to be reined in and made calm, while he pinned my hand by my side. My homespun dress was tied up with a sash in a simple bow; he already had it loose, and then he dragged up my skirts.

I was trying to thrust my skirts back down, push him away, drag myself free: useless. He held me with such casual strength. And then he reached for his own hose, and I said aloud, desperate, without thinking, *"Vanastalem."*

Power shuddered out of me. Crusted pearls and whalebone closed up beneath his hands like armor, and he jerked his hands off me and stepped back as a wall of velvet skirts fell rustling between us. I caught myself on the wall trembling and struggling to get my breath while he stared at me.

And then he said, in a very different voice, a tone I couldn't understand, "You're a witch."

I backed from him like a wary animal, my head spinning: I couldn't get my breath properly. The gown had saved me but the stays were strangling-tight, the skirts dragging and heavy, as though they'd deliberately made themselves impossible to remove. He came towards me more slowly, a hand outstretched, saying, "Listen to me—" but I hadn't the least intention of listening. I snatched up the breakfast tray, still sitting atop my dresser, and swung it wildly at his head. The edge of it clanged loudly against his skull and knocked him staggering sideways. I gripped it with both hands and lifted it up and swung again and again, blindly, desperate.

I was still swinging when the door burst open and the Dragon was there, in a long magnificent dressing-gown flung over his night-shift, his eyes savage. He took one step into the room and halted, staring. I halted too, panting, the tray still upraised mid-swing. The prince had sunk to his knees before me. A maze of blood was running down over his face, bloody bruises across his forehead. His eyes were closed. He fell over onto the floor before me unconscious with a thump.

The Dragon took in the scene, looked at me, and said, "You idiot, what have you done *now?*"

We heaved the prince onto my narrow bed together. His face was already blackening with bruises: the tray upon the floor was dented badly with the curve of his skull. "Splendid," the Dragon said through his teeth, inspecting him—the prince's eyes were staring and strange, dull, when he lifted their lids, and his arm, lifted, fell limply back to the cot and dangled off the side.

I stood watching, panting against the bodice, my desperate fury gone and only horror left. As strange as it may sound, I wasn't only afraid of what would happen to me; I didn't want the prince to die. He was still half in my head as the shining hero of legend, all confusedly tangled up with the beast who'd just been pawing at me. "He's not—he's not—"

"If you don't want a man dead, don't bludgeon him over the head repeatedly," the Dragon snapped. "Go down to the laboratory and bring me the yellow elixir in the clear flask from the shelf in the back. *Not* the red one, and *not* the violet one—and try if possible not to break it as you bring it up the stairs, unless you want to try and persuade the king that your virtue was worth the life of his son."

He laid his hands on the prince's head and began to chant softly, words that shivered along my spine. I ran for the stairs clutching my skirts up against me. I brought the elixir back up in only moments, panting with haste and the confinement of my stays, and found the Dragon still working: he didn't interrupt his chanting, only held a hand out towards me impatiently, beckoning sharply; I lay the flask in his hand. With the fingers of one hand, he worked out the cork and tipped a swallow into the prince's mouth.

The smell of it was horrible, like rotting fish; I nearly choked with nausea just from standing nearby. The Dragon shoved the flask and cork back at me without even looking, and I had to hold my breath to close it. He was clamping the prince's jaw shut with both hands. Even unconscious and wounded, the prince jerked and tried to spit. The elixir was glowing somehow from inside his mouth, so bright that I could see his jaw and teeth outlined like a skull.

I managed to shut the flask again without retching, and then sprang to help: I pinched the prince's nose shut, and after a moment he finally swallowed. The brilliant glow went down his throat and into his belly. I could make it out still traveling all throughout his body, a light underneath his clothes, thinning out as it branched away into his arms and legs, until at last it died away too dim to see.

The Dragon let go of the prince's head and stopped chanting the spell. He sagged back against the wall with his eyes shut: he looked drained as I had never seen him before. I stood hovering anxiously over the bed, over both of them, and finally I blurted, "Will he—"

"No thanks to you," the Dragon said, but that was good enough: I let myself sink to the ground in my heap of cream velvet, and buried my head on the bed in my arms sheathed in embroidered golden lace.

"And now you're going to blubber, I suppose," the Dragon said over my head. "What were you thinking? Why did you put yourself into that ludicrous dress if you didn't want to seduce him?"

"It was better than staying in the one he tore off me!" I cried, lifting my head: not in tears at all; I had spent all my tears by then, and all I had left was anger. "*I* didn't choose to be in this—"

I stopped, a heavy fold of silk caught up in my hands, staring at it. The Dragon had been nowhere near; he hadn't worked any magic, cast any spell. "What have you done to me?" I whispered. "He said—he called me a witch. You've made me a witch."

The Dragon snorted. "If I could make witches, I certainly wouldn't choose a half-wit peasant girl as my material. I haven't done anything to you but try and drum a few miserable cantrips into your nearly impenetrable skull." He levered himself up off the bed with a hiss of weariness, struggling, not unlike the way I'd struggled in those terrible weeks while he—

While he taught me magic. Still on my knees, I stared up at him, bewildered and yet unwillingly beginning to believe. "But then why would you teach me?"

"I would have been delighted to leave you moldering in your coin-sized village, but my options were painfully limited." To my blank look, he scowled. "Those with the gift must be taught: the king's law requires it. In any case, it would have been idiotic of me to leave you sitting there like a ripe plum until something came along out of the Wood and ate you, and made itself into a truly remarkable horror."

While I flinched away appalled from this idea, he turned his scowl on the prince, who had just groaned a little and stirred in his sleep: he was beginning to wake, lifting a groggy hand to rub at his face. I scrambled up to my feet and edged away from the bed in alarm, closer towards the Dragon.

"Here," the Dragon said. "*Kalikual.* It's better than beating paramours into insensibility."

He looked at me expectantly. I stared at him, and at the slowly rousing prince, and back. "If I wasn't a witch," I said, "—if I wasn't a witch, would you let me—could I go home? Couldn't you take it out of me?"

He was silent. I was used to the contradiction of his wizard's face by now, young and old together. For all his years, he only had folds at the corners of his eyes, a single crease between his brows; sharp frown lines around his mouth: nothing else. He moved like a young man, and if people grew milder or kinder with age, he certainly hadn't. But for a moment now, his eyes were purely old, and very strange. "No," he said, and I believed him.

Then he shook it off and pointed: turning, I found the prince pushing himself up onto his elbow, and blinking at us both: still dazed and unknowing, but even as I looked, the spark of recognition came back into his face, remembering me. I whispered, *"Kalikual."*

The power rushed out of me. Prince Marek sank back down

against the pillows, eyes closing back into sleep. I staggered over to the wall and slid down it to the floor. The butcher knife was still there lying on the ground where it had fallen down. I picked it up and at last used it: to cut through the dress and the laces of my stays. My dress gaped open all along my side, but at least I could breathe.

I lay back against the wall with my eyes shut for a moment. Then I looked up at the Dragon, who had turned away in impatience from my fatigue: he was looking down at the prince with irritation. "Won't his men ask for him in the morning?" I said.

"Did you imagine you were going to keep Prince Marek locked up fast asleep in my tower indefinitely?" the Dragon said over his shoulder.

"But then, when he wakes," I said, then stopped and asked, "Could you—can you make him forget?"

"Oh, certainly," the Dragon said. "He won't at all notice anything peculiar if he wakes up with a splitting headache and an enormous gap in his memory to go with it."

"What if—" I struggled back up to my feet, still clutching the knife, "—what if he remembered something else? Just going to bed in his own room—"

"Try not to be stupid," the Dragon said. "You said you didn't seduce him, so he came up here of his own intention. When was that intention formed? Merely tonight as he already lay in his bed? Or was he thinking of it along the road—a warm bed, welcoming arms—yes, I realize yours weren't; you've provided sufficient evidence to the contrary," he snapped, when I would have protested. "For all we know, he meant to do it even before he set out—a calculated sort of insult."

I remembered the prince speaking of the Dragon's "usual line"—as though he had thought of it beforehand, as though he'd planned it almost. "To insult you?" I said.

"He supposes I take women to force them to whore for me," the Dragon said. "Most of those courtiers do: they'd do as much themselves if they had the chance. So I imagine he thought of it as cuckolding me. He would have been delighted to spread it around the court, I'm sure. It's the sort of thing the Magnati waste their time caring about."

He spoke disdainfully, but he'd certainly been angry enough when he came storming into the room. "Why would he want to insult you?" I timidly asked. "Didn't he come to—to ask you for some magic?"

"No, he came to enjoy the view of the Wood," the Dragon said. "Of course he came for magic, and I sent him about his business, which is hacking at enemy knights and not meddling in things he scarcely understands." He snorted. "He's begun to believe his own troubadours: he wanted to try and get back the queen."

"But the queen is dead," I said, confused. That had been the start of the wars. Crown Prince Vasily of Rosya had come to visit Polnya on an embassy, nearly twenty years ago now. He'd fallen in love with Queen Hanna and they'd run away together, and when the king's soldiers had drawn near on their trail they'd fled into the Wood.

That was the end of the story: no one went into the Wood and came out again, at least not whole and themselves. Sometimes they came out blind and screaming, sometimes they came out twisted and so misshapen they couldn't be recognized; and worst of all sometimes they came out with their own faces but murder behind them, something gone dreadfully wrong within.

The queen and Prince Vasily hadn't come out at all. The king of Polnya blamed Rosya's heir for abducting her, the king of Rosya had blamed Polnya for his heir's death, and since then we'd had one war after another, broken only by occasional truces and a few short-lived treaties.

Here in the valley, we shook our heads over the story; everyone agreed it had all been the Wood's doing from the start. The queen, with two small children, to run away? To start a war with her own husband? Their own courtship had been famous; there had been a dozen songs of their wedding. My mother had sung me one of them, the parts she remembered; none of the traveling singers would perform them anymore, of course.

The Wood had to be behind it. Perhaps someone had poisoned the two of them with water taken from the river just where it went into the Wood; perhaps some courtier traveling along the mountain pass to Rosya had accidentally spent a night under the dark trees near the edge, and gone back to the court with something else inside him. We knew it was the Wood, but that didn't make a difference. Queen Hanna was still gone, and she'd gone with the prince of Rosya, and so we were all at war and the Wood crept a little farther into both realms every year, feeding on their deaths and all the deaths since then.

"No," the Dragon said, "the queen's not dead. She's still in the Wood."

I stared at him. He sounded matter-of-fact, certain, although I'd never heard of anything like it. But it was enough of a horror for me to believe it: to be trapped in the Wood, for twenty years, imprisoned endlessly in some way—it was the kind of thing the Wood would do.

The Dragon shrugged and waved a hand at the prince. "There's no getting her out again, and he'd only start something worse by going in, but he won't hear it." He snorted. "He thinks killing a day-old hydra has made him a hero."

None of the songs had ever mentioned the Vandalus Hydra being one day old: it diminished the story more than a little.

"In any case," the Dragon said, "I suppose he does feel aggrieved; lords and princes loathe magic anyway, and all the more for how badly they need it. Yes: some petty revenge of that sort is the most likely."

I could easily believe it, and I did grasp the Dragon's point. If the prince had meant to enjoy the Dragon's companion, whoever that girl might be—I felt a surge of indignation, thinking of Kasia in my place, without even unwanted magic to save her—then he wouldn't have simply gone to bed. That memory wouldn't fit neatly into his head, like a wrong puzzle piece.

"However," the Dragon added, in a tone of mild condescension, as if I were a puppy that had managed not to chew a shoe, "it's not an entirely useless idea: I ought to be able to alter his memory in the other direction."

He raised a hand, and, puzzled, I said, "The other direction?"

"I'll give him a memory of enjoying your favors," the Dragon said. "Full of suitable enthusiasm on your part and the satisfaction of making a fool of me. I'm sure he won't have any difficulty swallowing that."

"What?" I said. "You'll have him—no! He'll—he'll—"

"Do you mean to tell me you care what he thinks of you?" the Dragon demanded, an eyebrow rising.

"If he thinks I've lain with him, what's to stop him from—from wanting it again!" I said.

The Dragon waved a dismissive hand. "I'll make it an unpleasant memory—all elbows and shrill maidenly giggling, over quickly. Or do *you* have any better notions?" he added, waspish. "Perhaps you'd rather he woke up remembering you doing your best to murder him?"

So the next morning, I had the deeply wretched experience of seeing Prince Marek stop outside the tower doors to look up to my window and blow me a cheerful and indiscreet kiss. I'd been watching only to be sure he actually left; it took nearly all the caution left in me not to throw something down at his head, and I don't mean a token of my regard.

But the Dragon hadn't been wrong to be wary: even with such a comfortable memory written into his head, the prince hesitated on the carriage steps and looked back up at me with a slight frown, as though something troubled him, before at last he ducked inside and allowed himself to be bundled off. I stood at the window watching the dust of his carriage recede along the road until it really and truly vanished behind the hills, and only then did I step away, and feel like I was safe again—an absurd feeling to have, in an enchanted tower with the dark wizard and magic lurking under my own skin.

I pulled on the gown of russet and green, and went slowly down the stairs to the library. The Dragon was back at his chair, the book open on his lap, and he turned to look at me. "Very well," he said, sour as always. "Today we'll try—"

"Wait," I interrupted him, and he paused. "Can you tell me how to make this something I can wear?"

"If you haven't grasped *vanastalem* by now, there is nothing I can possibly do to help you," he snapped. "In fact, I'm inclined to believe you mentally defective."

"No! I don't want—that spell," I said, hastily avoiding even saying the word. "I can't even move in one of these dresses, or lace it for myself, or clean anything—"

"Why wouldn't you just use the cleaning cantrips?" he demanded. "I've taught you at least five."

I'd done my best to forget them all. "It tires me less to scrub!" I said.

"Yes, I can see you'll be making a mark on the firmament," he said, irritably; but that hadn't any power to wound me: any magic was bad enough, I didn't feel the least desire to be a great and powerful witch. "What a strange creature you are: don't all peasant girls dream of princes and ballgowns? Try to degrade it, then."

"What?" I said.

"Drop part of the word," he said. "Slur it, mumble it, something of the sort—"

"Just—any part?" I said doubtfully, but tried it: *"Vanalem?"*

The shorter word felt better in my mouth: smaller and more friendly somehow, although perhaps that was just my imagination. The gown shuddered and the skirts deflated all around me into a fine letnik of undyed linen stopping at the shin, and over it a simple brown dress with a green sash to draw it snug. I pulled in a glad deep breath: no dragging weight pulling me down from shoulders to ankles, no strangling corsets, no endless train: plain and comfortable and easy. Even the magic hadn't dragged out of me so horribly. I didn't feel tired at all.

"If you've arranged yourself to your satisfaction," the Dragon said, his voice dripping sarcasm. He held out his hand, and summoned a book flying over from the shelf. "We'll begin with syllabic composition."

FOUR

As little as I liked having magic, I was glad not to be so afraid all the time. But I was no prize pupil: when I didn't just forget the spell-words he taught me, they went wrong in my mouth. I slurred and mumbled and muddled them together, so a spell that ought to have set a dozen ingredients neatly out for a pie—"I am certainly not trying to train you on potions," he had said, caustically—instead mixed them into a solid mess that couldn't even be saved for my supper. Another that should have neatly banked the fire in the library, where we were working, instead seemed to do nothing at all—until we heard a distant and ominous crackling, and we ran upstairs to find green-tinged flames leaping out of the fireplace in the guest chamber directly above, and the embroidered bedcurtains going up.

He roared at me furiously for ten minutes after he finally managed to put out the sulky and determined fire, calling me a witless muttonheaded spawn of pig farmers—"My father's a woodcutter," I said—"Of axe-swinging lummocks!" he snarled. But even so, I wasn't afraid anymore. He only spluttered himself into exhaustion and then sent me away, and I didn't mind his shouting at all, now I knew there were no teeth in it to rend me.

I was almost sorry not to be better, for now I could tell his frustration was that of the lover of beauty and perfection. He hadn't wanted a student, but, having been saddled with me, he wanted to make a great and skillful witch of me, to teach me his art. I could see, as he made me examples of higher workings, great intricate interweavings of gesture and word that went on like songs, that he loved the work: his eyes grew glittering and dazzled in the spell-light, his face almost handsome with a kind of transcendence. He loved his magic, and he would have shared that love with me.

But I was just as happy to mumble my way through a few can-trips, take my inevitable lecture, and go cheerfully downstairs to the cellars and chop onions for dinner by hand. It maddened him to no end, not without some justice. I know I was being foolish. But I wasn't used to thinking of myself as anyone important. I'd always been able to glean more nuts and mushrooms and berries than any-one, even if a patch of forest had been picked over half a dozen times; I could find late herbs in autumn and early plums in spring. Anything, my mother used to say, that involved getting as dirty as possible: if I had to dig for it or push through brambles or climb a tree to get at it, I would come back with a basketful, to bribe her into sighs of tolerance instead of cries of dismay at my clothing.

But that was as far as my gifts went, I'd always thought; nothing that mattered except to my own family. Even now it hadn't occurred to me to think of what magic might mean, besides making absurd dresses and doing small chores that I would just as soon do by hand. I didn't mind my own lack of progress, or how much it maddened him. I was even able to settle into a kind of contentment, until the days rolled past and Midwinter came.

I could look out my window and see the candle-trees lit up in the squares of every village, small shining beacons dotting the dark valley all the way to the edge of the Wood. In my house, my mother was basting the great ham with lard, and turning the potatoes in the dripping-pan beneath. My father and brothers would be hauling great loads of firewood for the holiday to every house, with fresh-cut pine boughs atop; they would have cut down our village's candle-tree, and it would be tall and straight and full-branched.

Next door, Wensa would be cooking chestnuts and dried plums and carrots, with a slab of tender beef, to bring over, and Kasia— Kasia would be there, after all. Kasia would be rolling the beautiful fine senkach cake on its spindle before the fireplace, pouring on the next layer of batter at each turn to make the pine-tree spikes. She had learned to make it when we were twelve: Wensa had traded away the lace veil she had been married in, twice her height, to a woman in Smolnik, in exchange for teaching Kasia the recipe. So that Kasia would be ready to cook for a lord.

I tried to be glad for her. I was mostly sorry for myself. It was hard to be alone and cold in my high tower room, locked away. The Dragon didn't mark the holiday; for all I knew, he didn't even know what day it was. I went to the library the same as always, and droned through another spell, and he shouted for a while and then dismissed me.

Trying to cure my loneliness, I went down to the kitchens and made myself a small feast—ham and kasha and stewed apples— but when I put together the plate, it still felt so plain and empty that for the first time, I used *lirintalem* for myself, aching for something that felt like a celebration. The air shimmered, and suddenly I had a lovely platter of roast pork, hot and pink and running with juice; my very favorite wheat porridge cooked thick with a ladleful of melted butter and browned bread crumbs in the middle; a heap of brand-new fresh peas that no one in my village would be eating until spring; and a taigla cake that I had only ever tasted once, at the headwoman's table, the year that it was my family's turn to be her guests at harvest-time: the candied fruits like colored jewels, the knots of sweet dough a perfect golden brown, the hazelnuts small and pale, and all of it glazed and shining with honey-syrup.

But it wasn't Midwinter dinner. There was no eager ache of hunger in my belly from the long day of cooking and cleaning without a pause; there was no joyful noise of too many people crammed in around the table, laughing and reaching for the platters. Looking down at my tiny feast only made me feel more desperately lonely. I thought of my mother, cooking all alone without even my clumsy pair of hands to help her, and my eyes were stinging when I put them into my pillow, with my untouched tray on my table.

I was still heavy-eyed and grieving, more awkward even than usual, two days later. That was when the rider came, an urgent scramble of hooves and a pounding on the gates. The Dragon put down the book he was attempting to teach me from, and I trailed him down the stairs; the doors swung open of their own accord before him, and the messenger nearly fell inside: he wore the dark yellow surcoat of the Yellow Marshes, and his face was streaked with sweat. He knelt, swallowing and pale, but he did not wait for the Dragon to give him permission to speak. "My lord baron begs you to come at once," he said. "There is a chimaera come upon us, out of the mountain pass—"

"What?" the Dragon said, sharply. "It's not the season. What sort of beast is it exactly? Has some idiot called a wyvern a chimaera, and been repeated by others—"

The messenger was shaking his head back and forth like a weight on a string. "Serpent's tail, bat's wings, goat's head—I saw it with my own eyes, lord Dragon, it's why my lord sent me—"

The Dragon hissed under his breath with annoyance: how dare a chimaera inconvenience him, coming out of season. For my part, I didn't understand in the least why a chimaera would *have* a season; surely it was a magic beast, and could do as it pleased?

"Try not to be a complete fool," the Dragon said as I trotted at his heels back to the laboratory; he opened a case and ordered me to bring him this vial and that. I did so unhappily, and very carefully. "A chimaera is engendered through corrupt magic, that doesn't mean it's not still a living beast, with its own nature. They're spawned of snakes, mainly, because they hatch from eggs. Their blood is cold. They spend the winters keeping still and lying in the sun as much as they can. They fly in summer."

"So why has this one come now?" I said, trying to follow.

"Most likely it hasn't, and that gasping yokel below frightened himself fleeing a shadow," the Dragon said, but the gasping yokel hadn't looked at all a fool to me, or a coward, and I thought even the Dragon didn't quite believe his own words. "*No*, not the red one, idiot girl, that's fire-heart; a chimaera would drink it up by the gallon if it had the chance, and become next kin to a real dragon, then. The red-violet, two farther on." They both looked red-violet to me, but I hastily swapped potions and gave him the one he wanted. "All right," he said, closing the case. "Don't read any of the books, don't touch anything in this room, don't touch anything in *any* room if you can help it, and try if you can not to reduce the place to rubble before I return."

I realized only then that he was leaving me here; I stared at him in dismay. "What am I going to do here alone?" I said. "Can't I— come with you? How long will you be?"

"A week, a month, or never, if I grow distracted, do something particularly clumsy, and get myself torn in half by a chimaera," he snapped, "which means the answer is *no*, you may *not*. And you are to *do* absolutely nothing, so far as possible."

And then he was sweeping out. I ran to the library and stared down from the window: the doors swung shut behind him as he came down the steps. The messenger leapt to his feet. "I'm taking your horse," I heard the Dragon say. "Walk down to Olshanka after me; I'll leave it there for you and take a fresh one." And then he swung up and waved an imperious hand, murmuring words: a small fire blazed up before him in the snowbound road and rolled away like a ball, melting a clear path down the middle for him. He was trotting off at once, despite the horse's flattened-ear unease. I suppose the spell which let him leap to Dvernik and back didn't work over so long a distance, or perhaps he could only use it within his own lands.

I stood in the library and kept watching until he was gone. It wasn't as though he ever made his company pleasant for me, but the tower felt echoingly empty without him. I tried to enjoy his absence as a holiday, but I wasn't tired enough. I did a little desultory sewing on my quilt, and then I just sat by my window and looked out at the valley: the fields, the villages, and the woods I loved. I watched cattle and flocks going to water, wood-sleds and the occasional lone rider traveling the road, the scattered drifts of snow, and at last I fell asleep leaning against the window-frame. It was late when I woke with a start, in the dark, and saw the line of beacon-fires burning in the distance almost the full length of the valley.

I stared at them, confused with sleep. For a moment, I thought the candle-trees had been lit again. I had seen the beacon-fire go up in Dvernik only three times in my life: for the Green Summer; and then once for the snow mares, who came out of the Wood when I was nine; and once for the shambler vines that swallowed up four houses on the edge of the village overnight, the summer when I was fourteen. The Dragon had come all those times; he had flung back the Wood's assault, and then gone away again.

In rising panic, I counted the beacons back, to see where the message had been lit, and felt my blood run cold: there were nine in a straight line, following the Spindle. The ninth beacon-fire was Dvernik. The call had gone up from my own village. I stood looking out at the fires, and then I realized: the Dragon was gone. He would be well into the mountain pass by now, crossing to the Yellow Marshes. He wouldn't see the beacons, and even when someone brought him word, first he would have to deal with the chimaera—a week, he had said, and there was no one else—

That was when I understood how much a fool I'd been. I'd never thought of magic, of *my* magic, as good for anything, until I stood there and knew that there was no one else but *me;* that whatever was in me, however poor and clumsy and untaught, was more magic than anyone else in my village had. That they needed help, and I was the only one left who could give it.

After one frozen moment I turned and flew downstairs to the laboratory. I went in on a gulp of fear and took the grey potion, the one that had turned me to stone. I took the fire-heart potion, too, and the elixir the Dragon had used on the prince to save his life, and one green one that he'd mentioned once was for growing plants. I couldn't guess what use any of them would be, but at least I knew what they did. I didn't even know what any of the others were called, and I didn't dare touch them.

I bundled them back up to my room, and began desperately to rip apart the rest of my heap of dresses, knotting strips of silk together to make myself a rope. When it was long enough—I hoped—I flung it out the window and peered down after it. The night was dark. There was no light below to tell me if my rope reached the ground. But I didn't have a choice except to try and find out.

I had sewed a few silk bags out of dresses, among my small mending projects, and I put the glass bottles into one of them, well padded with scraps, and slung it over my shoulder. I tried not to think about what I was doing. A knot was swelling at the top of my throat. I gripped the silk rope with both hands and climbed over the sill.

I'd climbed old trees: I loved the big oaks and would scramble up into them with just a scrap of worn rope thrown over a branch. This was nothing like that. The stones of the tower were unnaturally smooth, even the cracks between them very fine and filled to the brim with mortar that hadn't been cracked or wormed away by time. I kicked off my shoes and let them fall, but even my bare toes couldn't get any purchase. All my weight was on the silken rope, and my hands were damp with sweat, my shoulders aching. I slithered and scrambled and from time to time just hung on, the sack a swaying, ungainly weight on my back and the bottles sloshing. I kept going because I couldn't do anything else. Going back up would have been harder. I began to have fantasies of letting go, which was how I knew I was close to the end of my strength, and I was halfway to convincing myself it wouldn't be so very bad a fall when unexpectedly my foot jarred painfully, coming down on solid ground straight through half a foot of soft-piled snow, against the tower's side. I dug my shoes out of the snow and ran down the cleared path the Dragon had made towards Olshanka.

They didn't know in the least what to do with me when I first got there. I came staggering into the tavern sweat-stained and frozen at the same time, my hair matted down on my head and frost built up on the loose strands near my face where my breath had gone streaming away. There was no one there I knew. I recognized the mayor, but I'd never said a word to him. They would probably have thought me just a madwoman, but Borys was there: Marta's father, one of the other girls born in my year. He'd been at the choosing. He said, "That's the Dragon's girl. That's Andrey's daughter."

None of the chosen girls had ever left the tower before her ten years were up. As desperate as a beacon-fire was, I think at first they would have been happier to be left to deal with whatever the Wood had sent than to have me come bursting in on them, a sure problem and unconvincing as any sort of help.

I told them the Dragon was gone to the Yellow Marshes; I said I needed someone to take me to Dvernik. They unhappily believed the first; very quickly I realized they hadn't the least intention of doing the second, no matter what I told them about magic lessons. "You'll come and spend the night in my house, under my wife's care," the mayor said, turning away. "Danushek, ride for Dvernik: they need to know they must hold out, whatever it is, and we must find out what help they need. We'll send a man into the mountains—"

"I'm not spending the night in your house!" I said. "And if you won't take me, I'll walk; I'll still be there quicker than any other help!"

"Enough!" the mayor snapped at me. "Listen, you stupid child—"

They were afraid, of course. They thought I had run away, that I was just trying to get home. They didn't want to hear me beg them to help me. I think more so because they felt ashamed to give a girl up to the Dragon in the first place; they knew it wasn't right, and they did it anyway, because they didn't have a choice, and it wasn't terrible enough to drive them to rebellion.

I took a deep breath and used my weapon *vanastalem* again. The Dragon would have been almost pleased with me, I think, for every syllable was pronounced with the sharpness of a fresh-honed blade. They backed from me as the magic went whirling around me, so bright the very fireplace grew dim by comparison. When it cleared I stood inches higher and ludicrously grand, in heeled court boots and dressed like a queen in mourning: a letnik made of black velvet bordered with black lace and embroidered in small black pearls, stark against my skin that hadn't seen the sun in half a year, the full sleeves caught around my arms with bands of gold. And over it, even more extravagant, a shining coat in gold and red silk, trimmed in black fur around my neck and clasped at the waist by a golden belt. My hair had been caught up in a net of gold cord and small hard jewels. "I'm *not* stupid, nor a liar," I said, "and if I can't do any good, I can at least do *something*. Get me a cart!"

FIVE

It helped, of course, that none of them knew the spell was a mere cantrip, and that none of them had seen much magic done. I didn't enlighten them. They hitched four horses to the lightest sleigh they had and sped me down the solid-packed river road in my idiotic—but warm!—dress. It was a fast drive, and an uncomfortable one, flying breathlessly over the icy road, but not fast or uncomfortable enough to keep me from thinking about how little hope I had of doing anything but dying, and not even usefully.

Borys had offered to drive me: a kind of guilt I understood without a word. I had been taken—not his girl, not his daughter. She was safe at home, perhaps courting or already betrothed. And I had been taken not four months ago, and here I was already unrecognizable.

"Do you know what's happened in Dvernik?" I asked him, huddled in the back under a heap of blankets.

"No, no word yet," he answered over his shoulder. "The beacon-fires were only just lit. The rider will be on the road, if—" He stopped. If there were a rider left to send, he had meant to say. "We'll meet him halfway, I'd guess," he finished instead.

With my father's heavy horses and his big wagon, in summertime, it was a long day's drive to Dvernik from Olshanka, with a break in the middle. But the midwinter road was packed with snow a foot deep, frozen almost solid with a thin dusting atop, and the weather was clear, the horses shod in hard ice shoes. We flew on through the night, and a few hours before dawn we changed horses at Vyosna village without stopping properly: I didn't even climb out of the sleigh. They didn't ask any questions. Borys said only, "We're on the way to Dvernik," and they looked at me with interest and curiosity but not the least doubt, and certainly no recognition. As they harnessed the fresh horses, the stableman's wife came out to me with a fresh meat pie and a cup of hot wine, clutching a thick fur cloak around herself. "Will you warm your hands, my lady?" she said.

"Thank you," I said, awkwardly, feeling like an imposter and halfway to a thief. I didn't let it keep me from devouring the pie in ten bites, though, and after that I swallowed the wine mostly because I couldn't think what else to do with it that wouldn't be insulting.

It left me light-headed and a little muzzy, the world gone soft and warm and comfortable. I felt a great deal less worried, which meant I had drunk too much, but I was grateful anyway. Borys drove faster, with the fresh horses, and an hour's drive onward with the sun lightening the sky ahead of us, we saw in the distance a man slogging down the road, on foot. And then we drew closer, and it wasn't a man at all. It was Kasia, in boy's clothes and heavy boots. She came straight for us: we were the only ones going towards Dvernik.

She grabbed onto the side of the sleigh, panting, dropped a curtsy, and without a pause said, "It's in the cattle—it's taken all the cattle, and if they get their teeth in a man, it takes him, too. We've got them mostly penned, we're holding them, but it's taking every last man—" and then I had pulled myself forward out of the heap of blankets and reached for her.

"Kasia," I said, choking, and she stopped. She looked at me, and we stared at each other in perfect silence for a long moment, and then I said, "Quick, hurry and get in, I'll tell you as we go."

She climbed in and sat next to me under the pile of sleigh blankets: we made a ridiculously unlikely pair, her in dirty rough homespun, a pig-boy's clothes, with her long hair stuffed up under a cap and a thick sheepskin jacket, and me in my finery: together we looked like the fairy godmother descending on Masha sweeping cinders from the hearth. But our hands still gripped each other tight, truer than anything else between us, and as the sleigh dashed onwards I blurted out a disjointed set of bits and scraps of the whole story—those early days grubbing miserably, the long fainting weeks when the Dragon had first begun to make me do magic, the lessons since then.

Kasia never let go my hand, and when I at last, haltingly, told her I could do magic, she said, startling the breath out of me, "I should have known," and I gawked at her. "Strange things always happened to you. You'd go into the forest and come back with fruit out of season, or flowers no one else had ever seen. When we were little, you always used to tell me stories the pines told you, until one day your brother sneered at you for playing make-believe, and you stopped. Even the way your clothes were always such a mess—you couldn't get so dirty if you tried, and I knew you weren't trying, you were never trying. I saw a branch reach out and snag your skirt once, really just reach out—"

I flinched away, made a noise of protest, and she stopped. I didn't want to hear it. I didn't want her to tell me that the magic had been there all along, and therefore inescapable. "It's not much good for anything besides keeping me a mess, if that's what it does," I said, trying to speak lightly. "I only came because *he's* gone. Now tell me, what's happened?"

Kasia told me: the cattle had sickened almost overnight. The first few had borne bite marks as if some strange enormous wolves had set teeth to them, although no wolves had been seen anywhere near, all winter. "They were Jerzy's. He didn't put them down right away," Kasia said soberly. I nodded.

Jerzy should have known better—he should have pulled them out of the herd and cut their throats at once, the moment he saw them wolf-bitten and left among the other animals. No ordinary wolf would have done anything like that. But—he was poor. He had no fields, no trade, nothing but his cows. His wife had come and quietly begged flour of us more than once, and whenever I'd come home from the woods with gleanings enough to spare, my mother would send me to their house with a basket. He had struggled for years to save enough to get a third cow, which would mean an escape from poverty, and only two years ago he had managed it. His wife Krystyna had worn a new red kerchief trimmed in lace at the harvest, and he a red waistcoat, both of them with pride. They'd lost four children before their namings; she was expecting another one. So he hadn't put the cattle down quickly enough.

"They bit him and they got into the other cattle," Kasia said. "Now they've all gone vicious, and they're too dangerous to even go near, Nieshka. What are you going to do?"

The Dragon might have known a way to purge the sickness from the cattle. I didn't. "We'll have to burn them," I said. "I hope he'll make it right, after, but I don't know anything else to do." To tell the truth, despite the horror and the waste of it, I was glad, desperately glad. At least this wasn't fire-breathing monsters or some deadly plague, and I did know *something* I could do. I pulled out the fire-heart potion, and showed Kasia.

No one argued with the idea when we got to Dvernik. Our head-woman Danka was as surprised as Kasia or the men in Olshanka when I came scrambling down from the sleigh, but she had bigger things to worry about.

Every healthy man, and the stronger women, was working in shifts to keep the poor tormented beasts penned up, using pitchforks and torches, slipping on ice and their hands going numb with cold. The rest of our village were trying to keep them from freezing or starving. It was a race whose strength would give out the first, and our village was losing. They had already tried a burning themselves, but it was too cold. The wood hadn't caught quickly enough before the cattle tore apart the piles. As soon as I told Danka what the potion was, she was nodding and sending everyone not already working around the pen to get ice-picks and shovels, to make a firebreak.

Then she turned to me. "We'll need your father and brothers to haul in more firewood," she said bluntly. "They're at your house: they worked all night. I could send you for them, but it may hurt you and them worse, when you have to go back to the tower after. Do you want to go?"

I swallowed. She wasn't wrong, but I couldn't say anything but yes. Kasia still gripped my hand, and as we ran across the village to my house together, I said, "Will you go in first, and warn them?"

So my mother was already crying when I came through the door. She didn't see the gown at all, only me, and we were crumpled into a heap of velvet on the floor, hugging each other, when my father and brothers came staggering out of the back rooms, confused with sleep, and found us. We wept all together even while we told each other there was no time for weeping, and through my tears I told my father what we were going to do. He and my brothers went dashing out to hitch up our horses, which had thankfully been safe in their own heavy stable next to the house. I snatched those last few moments and sat at the kitchen table with my mother. She smoothed her hands over my face over and over, her own tears still running. "He hasn't touched me, Mamusha," I told her, and didn't say anything about Prince Marek. "He's all right." She didn't answer, just stroked my hair again.

My father put his head in and said, "We're ready," and I had to go. My mother said, "Wait a moment," and vanished into the bedroom. She came out with a bundle made up, my own clothes and things. "I thought someone from Olshanka might take it to the tower for you," she said, "in the spring, when they bring him gifts from the festival." She kissed me again and held me once more, and let me go. It did hurt more. It did.

My father went to every house in the village, and my brothers leapt down and robbed every woodshed of every last stick they'd once hauled in, heaving great armloads onto the sled with its tall poles. When it was full, they drove out to the pens, and I saw the poor cattle at last.

They didn't even look like cows anymore, their bodies swollen and misshapen, horns grown huge and heavy and twisted. Here and there one of them sprouted arrows or even a couple of spears, thrust deep into their bodies and jutting out like horrible spikes. Things that came out of the Wood often couldn't be killed, except with fire or beheading; wounds only maddened them worse. Many of them had forelegs and chests blackened where they had stamped out the earlier fires. They were lunging against the heavy wooden fence of the pen, swinging their heavy unnatural horns and lowing in their deep voices, a dreadfully ordinary sound. There was a knot of men and women gathered to meet them, a bristling forest of pitchforks and spears and sharpened stakes, prodding the cattle back.

Some women were already hacking at the ground, mostly bare of snow here near the pens, raking away the dead matted grass. Danka was overseeing the work; she waved my father over, our horses whuffling uneasily as they drew nearer and smelled the corruption on the wind. "All right," she said. "We'll be ready before noon. We'll heave wood and hay over, in among them, and then light torches with the potion and throw them in. Save as much of it as you can, in case we have to try a second time," she added to me. I nodded.

More hands were coming as people were woken from their rest early to help in the final great effort. Everyone knew the cattle would try and stampede out when they were burning: everyone who could hold even a stick took a place in the line to hold them back. Others began to heave over bales of hay into the pen, the bindings broken so they smashed apart as they landed, and my brothers began throwing over the bundles of firewood. I stood anxiously beside Danka, holding the flask and feeling the magic in it swirling and hot beneath my fingers, pulsing as though it knew soon it would be set loose to do its work. Finally Danka was satisfied with the preparations, and held out to me the first bundle to be fired: a long dry log split halfway down the center, twigs and hay stuffed inside the crack and tied around it.

The fire-heart tried to roar up and out of the bottle as soon as I broke the seal: I found I had to hold the stopper in place. The potion fell back sullenly, and I whipped out the stopper and poured a drop—the least, the slightest drop—on the very end of the bundled log. The log went up in flames so quickly that Danka had scarcely a moment to throw it over the fence, hastily, and afterwards turned and thrust her hand into a snowbank, wincing: her fingers were already blistered and red. I was busy jamming the stopper back in, and by the time I looked up, half the pen was engulfed, the cattle bellowing furiously.

We were all taken aback by the ferocity of the magic, though we'd all heard tales of fire-heart—it figured in endless ballads of warfare and siege, and also in the stories of its making, how it required a thousandweight of gold to make a single flask, and had to be brewed in cauldrons made of pure stone, by a wizard of surpassing skill. I carefully hadn't mentioned to anyone that I didn't have *permission* to take the potions from the tower: if the Dragon was going to be angry with anyone, I meant for him to be angry with me alone.

But hearing stories about it wasn't the same as seeing it in front of our faces. We were unprepared, and the sickened cattle were already in a frenzy. Ten of them clumped together and bore down on the back wall, smashing against it heedless of the waiting stakes and prods. And all of us were terrified of being gored or bitten, even of touching them; the Wood's evil could spread so easily. The handful of defenders fell back, and Danka was shouting furiously as the fence began to give way.

The Dragon had taught me, with endless labor and grim determination, several small spells of mending and fixing and repair, none of which I could cast very well. Desperation made me try: I climbed up onto my father's empty sled and pointed at the fence and said, *"Paran kivitash farantem, paran paran kivitam!"* I had missed a syllable somewhere, I knew it, but I must have been close enough: the largest bar, splintering, jumped back whole into place and suddenly put out twigs with new leaves, and the old iron cross-braces straightened themselves out.

Old Hanka, who alone had held her ground—"I'm too sour to die," she said afterwards, by way of dismissing credit for her bravery—had been holding only the stump of a rake, the head of it already broken off and jammed between the horns of one of the oxen. Her stubby stick turned into a long sharpened rod of bright metal, steel, and she jabbed it at once straight into the open bellowing maw of the cow pushing on the fence. The spear pierced through and through and came out the back of the cow's skull, and the huge beast fell heavily against the fence and sagged dead to the ground, blocking the others from coming at it.

That proved to be the worst of the fight. We held them everywhere else, for a few minutes longer, and the task grew easier: they were all on fire by then, a terrible stink going up that twisted the stomach. They lost their cunning in panic and became merely animals again, throwing themselves futilely against the fence walls and one another until the fire brought them down at last. I used the mending charm twice more, and by the end was sagging against Kasia, who had climbed into the wagon to hold me up. The older children were running everywhere breathless with buckets of half-melted snow to put out any sparks that fell on the ground. Every last man and woman labored to exhaustion with their prods, faces red and sweaty with heat, backs freezing in the cold air, but together we kept the beasts penned, and neither the fire nor their corruption spread.

Finally the last cow fell. Hissing smoke and fat crackled on inside the fire. We all sat exhausted in a loose ring around the pen, keeping out of the smoke, watching as the fire-heart settled down and burned low, consuming everything down to ashes. Many coughed. No one spoke or cheered. There was no cause for celebration. We were all glad to see the worst danger averted, but the cost was immense. Jerzy wasn't the only one who would be impoverished by the fire.

"Is Jerzy still alive?" I asked Kasia softly.

She hesitated, and then nodded. "I heard he was taken badly," she said.

The Wood-sickness wasn't always incurable—the Dragon had saved others, I knew. Two years ago an easterly wind had caught our friend Trina on the riverbank while she was doing some washing. She came back stumbling and sick, the clothing in her basket coated with a silver-grey pollen. Her mother stopped her coming in. She threw the clothes on the fire and took Trina down to the river and dunked her over and over, while Danka sent a fast rider to Olshanka immediately.

The Dragon had come that night. I remembered I had gone over to Kasia's house and we'd watched together from her backyard. We didn't see him, only a cold blue light, flaring from the upstairs window of Trina's house. In the morning, Trina's aunt told me at the well that she was going to be all right: two days later Trina was up and about, herself again, only a little tired like someone who'd had a bad cold, and even pleased because her father was digging a well by their house, so she wouldn't ever have to go all the way to the river to do the washing again.

But that had only been a single malicious gust of wind, a drift of pollen. This—this was one of the worst takings I remembered. So many cattle sickened, so horribly, and able to spread their own corruption onward so quickly: that was a sure sign that it was very bad.

Danka had heard us speaking about Jerzy. She came over to the wagon and looked in my face. "Is there anything you can do for him?" she asked bluntly.

I knew what she was really asking. It was a slow and dreadful death, if the corruption wasn't purged. The Wood consuming you like rot eating away at a fallen tree, hollowing you out from the inside, leaving only a monstrous thing full of poison, which cared for nothing but to spread that poison onward. If I said there was nothing I could do, if I admitted I knew nothing, if I confessed that I was spent—with Jerzy so badly taken and the Dragon a week and more from coming—Danka would give the word. She would lead a few men to Jerzy's house. They would take Krystyna away to the other side of the village. The men would go inside, and come out again with a heavy shroud, and bring his body back here. They would throw it on the pyre with the burning cattle.

"There are things I can try," I said.

Danka nodded.

I clambered slowly and heavily down from the wagon. "I'll come with you," Kasia said, and linked her arm in mine to support me: she could tell I needed the help, without a word said. We walked slowly together towards Jerzy's house.

Jerzy's house was inconvenient, near the edge of the village farthest from the pens, with the forest crowding close to his small garden. The road was unnaturally quiet for afternoon, with everyone still back at the pens. Our feet crunched in the last snow that had fallen overnight. I floundered awkwardly through the corner drifts in my dress, but I didn't want to spare any strength to change it for something more sensible. As we came near the house we heard him, a snarling gurgled moan that never stopped, louder and louder the closer we came. It was hard to knock on the door.

It was a small house, but there was a long wait. Krystyna finally opened the door a crack, peering out. She stared at me without recognition, herself almost unrecognizable: there were dark purple circles under her eyes, and her belly was enormously swollen with the baby. She looked at Kasia, who said, "Agnieszka's come from the tower to help," and then she looked back at me.

After a long slow moment Krystyna said, "Come in," hoarsely.

She had been sitting in a rocking chair by the fire, right next to the door. She'd been waiting, I realized: waiting for them to come and take Jerzy away. There was only one other room, with just a curtain hanging in the doorway. Krystyna went back to the rocking chair and sat down again. She didn't knit or sew, didn't offer us a cup of tea, only stared at the fire and rocked. The moaning was louder inside the house. I gripped Kasia's hand tight and we went to the curtain together. Kasia reached out and drew it aside.

Jerzy was lying in their bed. It was a heavy clumsy thing made of small logs jointed together, but in this case that was all to the better. He had been tied hand and foot to the posts, and ropes were bound over his middle and under the whole bedframe. The ends of his toes were blackened and the nails were peeling off, and there were open sores across him where the ropes rubbed his body. He was pulling on them and making the noise, his tongue swollen and dark and almost filling his mouth, but he stopped when we came in. He lifted his head up and looked straight at me and smiled with his teeth bloody and his eyes stained yellow. He started to laugh. "Look at you," he said, "little witch, look at you, look at you," in an awful singsong voice jangling up and down. He jerked his body against the ropes so the whole bed jumped an inch across the floor towards me, while he grinned and grinned at me. "Come closer, come come come," he sang, "little Agnieszka, come come *come*," like the children's song, horrible, the bed hopping across the floor one lurch at a time, while I pulled open my bag of potions with shaking hands, trying not to look at him. I had never been so close to anyone taken by the Wood before. Kasia kept her hands on my shoulders, standing straight and calm. I think if she hadn't been there I would have run away.

I didn't remember the spell the Dragon had used on the prince, but he'd taught me a charm for healing small cuts and burns when

I cooked or cleaned. I thought it couldn't do any harm. I started singing it softly while I poured out one swallow of the elixir into a big spoon, wrinkling my nose against the rotten-fish smell of it, and then Kasia and I went cautiously towards Jerzy. He snapped at me with his teeth and twisted his hands bloody against the ropes to try and scratch at me. I hesitated. I didn't dare let him bite me.

Kasia said, "Hold on." She went out to the other room and came back with the poker and the heavy leather glove for stirring up the coals. Krystyna watched her come and go with a dull, incurious expression.

We laid the poker across Jerzy's throat and pressed him down flat to the bed from either side, and then my fearless Kasia put on the glove and reached out and pinched his nose from above. She held on even as he whipped his head back and forth, until finally he had to open his mouth for breath. I tipped in a swallow of the elixir and jumped back just in time; he heaved his chin up and managed to close his teeth on a bit of trailing lace from my velvet sleeve. I ripped free and backed away, still singing my charm in a wavering voice, and Kasia let go and came back to my side.

There wasn't that same blazing glow I remembered, but at least Jerzy's awful chanting stopped. I saw the gleam of the elixir go traveling down his throat. He fell back and lay jerking from side to side, emitting thick groans of protest. I kept on singing. Tears were leaking from my eyes: I was so *tired*. It was as bad as those early days in the Dragon's tower—it was worse, but I kept singing the charm because I couldn't bear to stop when I thought it might change the horror before me.

Hearing the chanting, Krystyna slowly stood up in the other room and came to the door, a terrible hope in her face. The glow of the elixir was sitting in Jerzy's belly like a hot coal, shining out, and a few of the bloody weals across his chest and wrists were closing. But even as I sang on, dark wisps of green drifted over the light, like clouds crossing the face of a full moon. More of them and more drew around it, thickening until the glow was lost. Slowly he stopped jerking about and his body relaxed into the bed. My chanting trailed off into silence. I edged a little closer, still hoping, and then—and then he lifted his head, eyes yellow-mad, and cackled at me again. "Try again, little Agnieszka," he said, and snapped at the air like a dog. "Come and try again, come here, come here!"

Krystyna moaned aloud and slid down the doorframe into a heap on the floor. Tears were stinging my eyes: I felt sick and hollow with failure. Jerzy was laughing horribly and thrashing the bed forward again, thump-thump of the heavy legs on the wooden floor: nothing had changed. The Wood had won. The corruption was too strong, too far advanced. "Nieshka," Kasia said softly, unhappily, a question. I dragged the back of my hand across my nose, and then I dug into my satchel again, grimly.

"Take Krystyna out of the house," I said, and waited until Kasia had helped Krystyna up and out: she was wailing softly. Kasia threw me one last anxious look, and I tried to give her a little smile, but I couldn't make my mouth work properly.

Before I edged closer to the bed, I took off the heavy velvet overskirt of my dress and wound it about my face, covering my nose and mouth three and four times over, until I had nearly smothered myself. Then I drew a deep breath and held it while I broke the seal upon the grey churning flask, and I poured out a little of the stone-spell onto Jerzy's grinning, snarling face.

I thrust the stopper back in and jumped back as quickly as I could. He had drawn in a breath already: the smoke was sliding into his nostrils and his mouth. A look of surprise crossed his face, and then his skin was greying, hardening. He fell silent as his mouth and eyes fixed open, his body stilled, his hands locked into place. The stink of corruption was fading. Stone rolled over his body like a wave, and then it was done, and I was shaking with relief and horror mingled: a statue lay tied down upon the bed, a statue only a madman would have carved, the face twisted with inhuman rage.

I made sure the bottle was sealed again, and put it back into my sack before I went and opened the door. Kasia and Krystyna were standing in the yard, in the ankle-deep snow. Krystyna's face was wet and hopeless. I let them back in: Krystyna went to the narrow doorway and stared at the statue in the bed, suspended out of life.

"He doesn't feel any pain," I said. "He doesn't feel time moving: I promise you. And this way, if the Dragon does know a way to purge the corruption . . ." I trailed off; Krystyna had sat down limply in her chair, as if she couldn't support her weight anymore, her head bent. I wasn't sure if I'd done her any real kindness, or only spared myself pain. I had never heard of anyone taken so badly as Jerzy being healed. "I don't know how to save him," I said softly. "But—but perhaps the Dragon will, when he comes back. I thought it was worth the chance."

At least the house was quiet now, without the howling and the stink of corruption. The terrible blank distance had left Krystyna's face, as if she hadn't even been able to bear thinking, and after a moment she put her hand on her belly and looked down at it. She was so close to her time that I could even see the baby move a little, through her clothes. She looked up at me and asked, "The cows?"

"Burned," I said, "all of them," and she lowered her head: no husband, no cattle, a child coming. Danka would try and help her, of course, but it would be a hard year in the village for everyone. Abruptly I said, "Do you have a dress you could give me, in trade for this one?" She stared up at me. "I can't bear to walk another step in it." She very doubtfully dug out an old patched homespun dress for me, and a rough woolen cloak. I gladly left the huge velvet and silk and lace confection heaped up next to her table: it was surely worth at least the price of a cow, and milk would be worth more in the village for a while.

It was growing dark when Kasia and I finally went outside again. The bonfire at the pens was burning on, raising a great orange glow on the other side of the village. All the houses were still deserted. The cold air bit through my thinner clothes, and I was drained to the dregs. I stumbled doggedly along behind Kasia, who broke the snow for me, and turned now and then to hold my hand and give me some support. I had one happier thought to warm me: I couldn't get back into the tower. So I would go home to my mother, and stay until the Dragon came for me again: what better place was there for me to go? "He'll be at least a week," I said to Kasia, "and maybe he'll be fed up with me, and let me stay," which I shouldn't have said even inside my own head. "Don't tell anyone," I said hastily, and she stopped and turned and threw her arms around me and squeezed me tight.

"I was ready to go," she said. "All those years—I was ready to be brave and go, but I couldn't bear it when he took you. It felt like it had all been for nothing, and everything going on the same, just as if you had never been here—" She stopped. We stood there together, holding hands and crying and smiling at each other at the same time, and then her face changed; she jerked on my arm and pulled me backwards. I turned.

They came out of the woods slowly, with measured paces and wide-spread paws that stepped without breaking the crust on the snow. Wolves hunted in our woods, quick and lithe and grey; they would take a wounded sheep but fled from our hunters. These were not our wolves. Their heavy white-furred backs rose to the height of my waist, and pink tongues lolled out of their jaws: huge jaws full of teeth crammed in on one another. They looked at us—they looked at *me*—with pale yellow eyes. I remembered Kasia telling me that the first cattle to fall sick had been wolf-bitten.

The wolf in the lead was a little smaller than the rest. He sniffed the air towards me, and then jerked his head sideways without ever taking his eyes off me. Two more came padding out of the trees. The pack spread out as if he had signaled them, fanning out to either side of me, to block me in. They were hunting; they were hunting *me*. "Kasia," I said, "Kasia, *go*, run now," with my heart stuttering. I dragged my arm out of her grip and fumbled in my bag. "Kasia, go!" I shouted, and I pulled the stopper and flung the stone potion at the lead wolf as he sprang.

The grey mist rose up around him, and a great stone statue of a

wolf fell like a boulder by my feet, the snarling jaws snapping at my
ankle even as they stilled. One other wolf was caught in the edge
of the mist, a wave of stone creeping more slowly over its body as
it pawed the snow with its front feet for a moment, trying to escape.

Kasia didn't run. She grabbed me by the arm and pulled me
up and back towards the nearest house—Eva's house. The wolves
howled with one terrible voice in protest, nosing cautiously at the
two statues, and then one of them yelped and they fell in. They
turned and came loping at us together.

Kasia pulled us through the gate of Eva's front garden, and
slammed it: the wolves leapt the fence as lightly as springing deer.
I didn't dare throw fire-heart with no protection against its spreading, not after what I'd seen that day: it would have burned all our
village, and maybe all our valley, and certainly the two of us. I drew
out the small green vial instead, hoping for enough distraction to
get us inside the house. "It grows grass," the Dragon had said, dismissively, when I'd asked: the warm healthy color of it had looked
friendly to me, like none of the other strange cold enchantments in
his laboratory. "And an inordinate number of weeds; it's useful only
if you've had to burn a field clean." I'd thought I might use it after
the fire-heart to renew our grazing meadow. I wrenched open the
stopper with shaking hands, and the potion spilled over my fingers:
it smelled wonderful, good and clean and fresh, pleasantly sticky
like crushed grass and leaves in spring full of juice, and I threw it
out of my cupped hands over the snowbound garden.

The wolves were running at us. Vines erupted like leaping snakes
out of the dead vegetable beds, brilliant green, and flung themselves onto the wolves, wrapping thick coils around their legs, and
pulled them to the ground scarcely inches away from us. Everything
was suddenly growing like a year crammed into a minute, beans
and hops and pumpkins sprawling out across the ground and growing absurdly huge. They blocked the way towards us even while
the wolves fought and snapped and tore at them. The vines kept
growing even larger, sprouting thorns the size of knives. One wolf

was crushed in a swelling green twist as thick around as a tree, and a pumpkin fell smashing onto another, so heavy it struck the wolf down to the ground as it burst.

Kasia reached for me as I gawked, and I turned and stumbled on with her. The front door of the house wouldn't open, though Kasia wrenched on it. We turned for the small empty stable, really only a shelter for pigs, and slammed inside. There was no pitchfork there; it had been taken to the pens. The only thing left like a weapon was a small axe for chopping wood. I seized it in desperation while Kasia braced the door. The rest of the wolves had fought their way out of the bursting garden, and they were coming at us again. They reared up and clawed at the door, snapping at it, and then ominously they stopped. We heard them moving, and then one of them howled on the other side of the stable, outside the small high window. As we turned in alarm, three of them came flowing through it, one after another leaping. And others howled back, on the other side of the door.

I was empty. I tried to think of any charm, any spell I'd been taught, anything that might help against them. Maybe the potion had renewed me, like the garden, or else panic had done it: I didn't feel fainting-weak any longer, and I could imagine casting some spell again, if I could only have thought of one that would be of any use. I wondered wildly whether *vanastalem* could summon up armor, and then I said, *"Rautalem?"*—groping, muddling it up with a spell for sharpening kitchen knives—as I grabbed up the old water-dish made of battered tin. I had no very good idea what it would do, but I hoped. Perhaps the magic was trying to save me and itself, because the dish flattened out and turned into an enormous shield, of heavy steel. Kasia and I crouched behind it into a corner as the wolves leapt for us.

She grabbed the axe from me and chopped at their claws and muzzles as they scrabbled around the edges, trying to tear it down or away from us. We were both hanging on to the shield's handles for life, desperate, and then to my horror one of the wolves—a wolf!—went deliberately to the barred door of the stable, and with its nose it nudged the bar up and open.

The rest of the pack crowded in towards us. There was nowhere else to run, no trick left in my satchel. Kasia and I clung to each other, held on to our shield, and then abruptly the entire wall of the shed ripped away from behind us. We fell backwards into the snow at the Dragon's feet. The wolf pack leapt for him as one, howling, but he raised a hand and sang out a long impossible line without a pause for breath. All at the same time the wolves *broke*, in midair, a dreadful sound like snapping twigs. They fell huddled dead into the snow.

Kasia and I were still clinging to each other as the wolf corpses thumped down around us one after another. We stared up at him, and he glared down at me, stiff and furious, and snarled, "Of all the idiotic things you might have done, you monstrously half-witted lunatic of a girl—"

"Look out!" Kasia cried, too late: one last limping wolf, its fur stained orange with pumpkin, flung itself over the garden wall, and though the Dragon snapped out a spell even as he turned, the beast caught his arm with one raking claw as it fell dying. Three bright drops of blood stained the snow crimson at his feet.

He sank to his knees, gripping his arm at the elbow. The black wool of his jerkin was torn and gaping. His flesh was already turning green with corruption around the scratch. The sickly color halted where his fingers gripped the arm, a faint glow of light limning his fingers, but the veins of his forearm were swelling. I fumbled for the elixir in my satchel. "Pour it on," he said with clenched teeth, when I would have given it to him to drink. I poured the liquid on, all of us holding our breath, but the black stain didn't recede: it only stopped spreading as quickly.

"The tower," he said. Sweat had sprung out across his forehead. His jaw was locked almost beyond speech. "Listen: *Zokinen valisu, akenezh hinisu, kozhonen valisu.*"

I stared: he couldn't mean to trust me to do it, to spell us back?

But he didn't say anything else. All his strength was too plainly going to hold back the corruption, and I remembered too late what he'd told me, how if the Wood had taken me, untrained and useless witch though I was, it could have made some truly dreadful horror out of me. What would it make of *him*, the foremost wizard of the realm?

I turned to Kasia and dug out the bottle of fire-heart and pressed it into her hands. "Tell Danka she has to send someone to the tower," I said, flat and desperate. "If we don't both come out and say everything's all right, if there's any doubt—burn it to the ground."

Her eyes were full of worry for me, but she nodded. I turned to the Dragon and knelt in the snow beside him. "Good," he said to me, very briefly, with a quick dart of his eyes towards Kasia. I knew then that my worst fears weren't wrong. I gripped his arm and closed my eyes and thought of the tower room. I spoke the words of the spell.

SIX

I helped the Dragon stagger down the hall the short distance to my small bedroom, the rope of silk dresses still dangling out the window. There was no hope of getting him down to his own room; he was deadweight even as I lowered him to the bed. He was still gripping his arm, holding back the corruption somehow, but the glow about his hand was growing ever fainter. I eased him back on the pillows and stood anxiously hovering over him a moment, waiting for him to say something, to tell me what to do, but he didn't speak; his eyes saw nothing, fixed on the ceiling. The small scratch had swollen up like the worst kind of spider bite. He was breathing in quick pants, and his forearm below where he gripped it was all that dreadful sickly green—the same color that had stained Jerzy's skin. The fingernails at the end of his hand were blackening.

I ran down to the library skidding down the steps badly enough to scrape my shin bloody. I didn't even feel it. The books stood in their neat elegant rows as always, placid and untroubled by my need. Some of them had become familiar to me by now: old enemies I would have called them, full of charms and incantations that would invariably go wrong inside my mouth, their very pages tingling unpleasantly when I touched the parchment. I went up the ladder and pulled them off the shelves anyway, opened them one after another, paging through lists, all for nothing: the distillation of essence of myrtle might be highly useful in all sorts of workings, but it wouldn't do me any good now, and it was enraging to spend even a moment looking at six recipes for forming a proper seal upon a potion-bottle.

But the uselessness of the effort slowed me long enough to let me think a little better. I realized I couldn't hope to find the answer to something this dreadful in the spellbooks he had tried to teach me from: as he'd told me himself, repeatedly, they were full of cantrips and trivialities, things that any witling wizard should have been able to master almost at once. I looked uncertainly at the lower shelves, where he kept the volumes he read himself, and which he had stringently warned me away from. Some were bound in new unbroken leather, tooled in gold; some were old and nearly crumbling; some tall as the length of my arm, others small enough for the palm of my hand. I ran my hands over them and on impulse pulled out a smaller one that bristled with inserted sheets of paper: it had a worn-smooth cover and plain stamped letters.

It was a journal written in a tiny crabbed hand, almost impossible to read at first and full of abbreviations. The sheets were notes in the Dragon's hand, one or more of them inserted between almost every leaf, where he had written out different ways to cast each spell, with explanations of what he was doing: that at least seemed more promising, as if his voice might speak to me from the paper.

There were a dozen spells for healing and for cleansing wounds—of sickness and gangrene, not of enchanted corruption, but at least worth the trying. I read over one spell, which advised lancing the poisoned wound, packing it with rosemary and lemon-peel, and doing something which the writer called *putting breath on it*. The Dragon had written four crammed-close pages on the subject and drawn up lines in which he noted down nearly five dozen variations: this much rosemary, dry or fresh; that much lemon, with pith on or without; a steel knife, an iron one, this incantation and another.

He hadn't written down which of the attempts had worked better and which worse, but if he had gone to so much effort, it had to be good for something. All I needed right now was to do him enough good to let him speak even a handful of words to me, give me some direction. I flew down to the kitchens and found a great bundle of hanging rosemary and a lemon. I took a clean paring knife and some fresh linens and hot water in a pot.

Then I hesitated: my eye had fallen on the great cleaver, lying on its chopping stone. If I couldn't do anything else, if I couldn't give him the strength to speak—I didn't know if I could do it, if I could cut off his arm. But I saw Jerzy on his bed, cackling and monstrous, far away from the quiet, sad man who had always nodded to me in the lane; I saw Krystyna's hollowed-out face. I swallowed and picked up the cleaver.

I honed both the knives, resolutely thinking of nothing, and then I carried my things upstairs. The window and door stood open, but even so the terrible stink of corruption had begun to gather in my small room. It turned my stomach with dread as much as physically. I didn't think I could bear to see the Dragon corrupted, all his crisp edges rotted away, his sharp tongue reduced to howling and snarls. His breath was coming shorter, and his eyes were half-closed. His face was terribly pale. I lay the linens under his arm and tied them on with some twine. I peeled off wide strips of the lemon's skin, tore rosemary leaves off the stems, crushing them all and throwing them into the hot water so that the sweet strong smell rose up and drove out the stink. Then I bit my lip, and, steeling myself, slashed open the swollen wound with the paring knife. Green tarry bile spurted out of it. I poured cup after cup of the hot water over the wound until it was clean. I caught fistfuls of the steeped herbs and lemon and packed them down tight.

The Dragon's notes said nothing of what it meant to put breath on the wound, so I bent down and breathed out the incantations over it, trying one and then another, my voice breaking. They all felt wrong in my mouth, awkward and hard-edged, and nothing was happening. Wretched, I looked back at the crabbed original writing again: there was a line that said *Kai and tihas, sung as seems good, will have especial virtue.* The Dragon's incantations all had variants of those syllables, but strung round with others, built up into long elaborate phrases that tangled on my tongue. Instead I bent down and sang *Tihas, tihas, kai tihas, kai tihas,* over and over, and found myself falling into the sound of the birthday song about living a hundred years.

That sounds absurd, but the rhythm of it was easy and familiar, comforting. I stopped having to think about the words: they filled my mouth and spilled over like water out of a cup. I forgot to remember Jerzy's mad laughter, and the green vile cloud that had drowned the light inside him. There was only the easy movement of the song, the memory of faces gathered around a table laughing. And then finally the magic flowed, but not the same way as when the Dragon's spell-lessons dragged it in a rush out of me. Instead it seemed to me the sound of the chanting became a stream made to carry magic along, and I was standing by the water's edge with a pitcher that never ran dry, pouring a thin silver line into the rushing current.

Under my hands, the sweet fragrance of rosemary and lemon was rising strong, overpowering the stench of corruption. More and more of the bile began to flow from the wound, until I would have worried except that the Dragon's arm kept looking better: the dreadful greenish cast was fading, the darkened and swollen veins shrinking back.

I was running out of breath; but besides that, I felt somehow that I was finished, that my work was done. I brought my chanting to a simple close, going up and down a note: I had only really been humming anyway by the end. The shining glow where he held his arm at the elbow was growing stronger now, brighter, and abruptly thin lines of light shot away from his grip, running down his veins and spreading out through them like branches. The rot was disappearing: the flesh looked healthy, his skin restored—to his usual unhealthy sunless pallor, but nevertheless his own.

I watched it holding my breath, hardly daring to hope, and then his whole body shifted. He drew one longer, deeper breath, blinking at the ceiling with eyes that were aware again, and his fingers one after another let go their iron grip around his elbow. I could have sobbed with relief: incredulous and hopeful, I looked up at his face, a smile working its way onto my mouth, and found him staring at me with an expression of astonished outrage.

He struggled up from the pillows. He stripped his arm clean of the rosemary and lemon packing and held it in his fist with a look of incredulity, then leaned over and seized the tiny journal from the coverlet over his legs: I had put it there so I could look at it while I worked. He stared at the spell, turned the book to see the spine as if he didn't quite believe his own eyes, and then he spluttered at me, "You impossible, wretched, nonsensical contradiction, what on earth have you done *now*?"

I sat back on my heels in some indignation: *this*, when I had just saved not only his life, but everything he might be, and all the kingdom from whatever the Wood might have made from him. "What ought I have done?" I demanded. "And how was I to know to do it? Besides, it worked, didn't it?"

For some reason, this only made him nearly incoherent with fury, and he levered himself up from my cot, threw the book across the room, all the notes flying everywhere, and flung himself out into the hallway without another word. "You might *thank* me!" I shouted after him, outraged myself, and his footsteps had vanished before I recalled that he had been wounded at all in saving my life—that he had surely pressed himself to terrible lengths to come to my aid at all.

That thought only made me feel more sulky, of course. So, too, did the slogging work of cleaning my poor little room and changing my bed; the stains wouldn't come out, and everything smelled foul, though without the terrible wrongness. Finally I decided, for this, I would use magic after all. I began to use one of the charms the Dragon had taught me, but then I instead went and dug up the journal from the corner. I was grateful to that little book and the past wizard or witch who had written it, even if the Dragon wasn't to me, and I was happy to find, near the beginning, a charm for freshening a room: *Tishta, sung up and down, with work to show the way.* I warbled it half in my head while I turned out all the damp, stained ticking. The air grew cold and crisp around me, but without any unpleasant bite; by the time I had finished, the bedclothes were clean and bright as though they were new-washed, and my ticking smelled like it was fresh from a summer haystack. I assembled my bed again, and then I sat down upon it very heavily, almost surprised, as the last dregs of desperation left me, and with them all my strength. I fell down on the bed and barely managed to drag my coverlet over me before I slept.

I woke slowly, peacefully, serenely, with sunlight coming in the window over me, and only gradually became aware that the Dragon was in my room.

He was sitting by the window, in the small work-chair, glaring at me. I sat up and rubbed my eyes and glared back. He held up the tiny book in his hand. "What made you pick *this* up?" he demanded.

"It was full of notes!" I said. "I thought it must be important."

"It is *not* important," he said, although for how angry he seemed over it, I didn't believe him. "It is *useless*—it has *been* useless, for all five hundred years since it was written, and a century of study has not made it anything other than useless."

"Well, it wasn't useless *today*," I said, folding my arms across my chest.

"How did you know how much rosemary to use?" he said. "How much lemon?"

"You used all sorts of amounts, in those tables!" I said. "I supposed it didn't much matter."

"The tables are of *failures*, you blundering imbecile!" he shouted. "None of them had the least effect—not in any parts, not in any admixture, not with any incantation—what did you *do*?"

I stared at him. "I used enough to make a nice smell, and steeped them to make it stronger. And I used the chant on the page."

"There is no incantation here!" he said. "Two trivial syllables, with no power—"

"When I sang it long enough, it made the magic flow," I said. "I sang it to 'Many Years,'" I added. He went even more red and indignant.

He spent the next hour interrogating me as to every particular of how I had cast the spell, growing ever more upset: I could scarcely answer any of his questions. He wanted exact syllables and repetitions, he wanted to know how close I had been to his arm, he wanted the number of rosemary twigs and the number of peels. I did my best to tell him, but I felt even as I did so that it was all wrong, and finally I blurted out, as he wrote angrily on his sheets, "But none of that matters at all." His head raised to stare balefully at me, but I said, incoherent yet convinced, "It's just—a way to go. There isn't only one way to go." I waved at his notes. "You're trying to find a road where there isn't one. It's like—it's gleaning in the woods," I said abruptly. "You have to pick your way through the thickets and the trees, and it's different every time."

I finished triumphantly, pleased to have found an explanation which felt so satisfyingly clear. He only flung down his pen and slumped angrily back in his chair. "That's nonsense," he said, almost plaintively, and then stared down at his own arm with an air of frustration: as though he would rather have the corruption back, instead of having to consider that he might be wrong.

He glared at me when I said as much—I was beginning to be in something of a temper by then myself, thirsty and ravenously hungry, still wearing Krystyna's ragged homespun dress that hung off my shoulder and didn't keep me warm. Fed up, I stood, ignoring his expression, and announced, "I'm going down to the kitchen."

"Fine," he snapped, and stormed off to his library, but he couldn't bear an unanswered question. Before my chicken soup had even finished cooking, he appeared at the kitchen table again, carrying a new volume of pale blue leather tooled in silver, large and elegant. He set it down on the table next to the chopping block and said firmly, "Of course. It's that you've an affinity for healing, and it led you to intuit the true spell—even though you can't remember the particulars accurately anymore. That would explain your general incompetence: healing is a particularly distinct branch of the magical arts. I expect you will progress considerably better going forward, once we devote our attention to the healing disciplines. We'll begin with Groshno's minor charms." He lay a hand on the tome.

"Not until I've eaten lunch, we won't," I said, not pausing: I was chopping carrots.

He muttered something under his breath about recalcitrant idiots. I ignored him. He was happy enough to sit down, and to eat the soup when I gave him a bowl, with a thick slice of peasant bread that I'd made—*the day before yesterday*, I realized; I had only been out of the tower for a day and a night. It seemed a thousand years. "What happened with the chimaera?" I asked around my spoon as we ate.

"Vladimir's not a fool, thankfully," the Dragon said, wiping his mouth with a conjured napkin. It took me a moment to realize he was speaking of the baron. "After he sent his messenger, he baited the thing close to the border by staking out calves and having his pikemen harry it from every other direction. He lost ten of them, but he managed to get it not an hour's ride from the mountain pass. I was able to kill it quickly. It was only a small one: scarcely the size of a pony."

He sounded strangely grim about it. "Surely that's good?" I said.

He looked at me in annoyance. "It was a *trap*," he bit out, as though that was obvious to any sensible person. "I was meant to be kept away until the corruption had overrun all of Dvernik, and worn down before I came." He looked down at his arm, opening and closing his fist. He'd changed his shirt for one of green wool, clasped with gold at the wrist. It covered his arm; I wondered if there were a scar beneath.

"Then," I ventured, "I did well to go?"

His expression was as sour as milk left out in midsummer. "If anyone could say so when you've poured out fifty years' worth of my most valuable potions in less than a day. Did it never occur to you that if they could be so easily spent, I would give half a dozen flasks to every village headman, and save myself the trouble of ever setting foot in the valley?"

"They can't be worth more than people's lives," I fired back.

"A life before you in the moment isn't worth a hundred else-where, three months from now," he said. "Listen, you simpleton, I have one bottle of fire-heart in the refining now: I began it six years ago, when the king could afford to give me the gold for it, and it will be finished in another four. If we spend all my supply before then, do you suppose Rosya will generously refrain from firing our fields, knowing that we'll have starved and sued for peace before we can return the favor? And there are likewise costs for every other vial you spent. All the more because Rosya has three master-wizards who can brew potions, to our two."

"But we're not at war!" I protested.

"We will be in the spring," he said, "if they hear a song of fire-heart and stone-skin and profligacy, and think they might have gained a real advantage." He paused, and then he added heavily, "Or if they hear a song of a healer strong enough to purge corrup-tion, and think that soon the balance will tip in our favor, instead, when you are trained."

I swallowed and looked down at my bowl of soup. It was unreal when he spoke of Rosya declaring war because of *me*, because of things I'd done or what they would imagine I might do. But I re-membered again the terror I'd felt on seeing the beacons lit with him gone, knowing just how little I could do to help those I loved. I still wasn't at all sorry to have taken the potions, but I couldn't pretend anymore that it mattered nothing whether I ever learned a single spell.

"Do you think I could help Jerzy, once I've been trained?" I asked him.

"Help a man already fully corrupted?" The Dragon scowled at me. But then he said, a grudging admission, "You shouldn't have been able to help me."

I picked up my bowl and drank the rest of the soup down, and then I put it aside and looked at him across the scarred and pitted kitchen table. "All right," I said, grimly. "Let's get on with it."

Unfortunately, the willingness to learn magic wasn't the same thing as being any good at it. Groshno's minor charms stymied me thoroughly, and the conjurations of Metrodora remained resolutely unconjured. After another three days of letting the Dragon set me at healing spells, all of which felt as awkward and wrong as ever, I marched down to the library the next morning with the little worn journal in my hand and put it down on the table before him as he scowled. "Why won't you teach me from *this*?" I demanded.

"Because it's unteachable," he snapped. "I've barely managed to codify the simplest cantrips into any usable form, and none of the higher workings. Whatever her notoriety, in practice it's worth almost nothing."

"What do you mean, notoriety?" I said, and then I looked down at the book. "Who wrote this?"

He scowled at me. "Jaga," he said, and for a moment I stood cold and still. Old Jaga had died a long time ago, but there weren't very many songs about her, and bards mostly sang them warily, only in summer, at midday. She had been dead and buried five hundred years, but that hadn't stopped her turning up in Rosya only forty years ago, at the baptism of the newborn prince. She'd turned six guards who tried to stop her into toads, put two other wizards to sleep, then she'd gone over to the baby and peered frowning down at him. Then she'd straightened up and announced in irritation, "I've fallen out of time," before vanishing in a great cloud of smoke.

So being dead wasn't a bar to her sudden return to claim her spellbook back, but the Dragon only grew even more annoyed at my expression. "Stop looking like a solemn six-year-old. Contrary to popular imagination, she is *dead,* and whatever time-wandering she may have done beforehand, I assure you she would have had a larger purpose than to run around eavesdropping on gossip about herself. As for that book, I spent an inordinate amount of money and trouble to get it, and congratulated myself on the acquisition until I realized how infuriatingly incomplete it was. She plainly used it only to jog her memory: it has no details of real spellwork."

"The four I've tried have all worked perfectly well," I said, and he stared at me.

He didn't believe me until he'd made me throw half a dozen of Jaga's spells. They were all alike: a few words, a few gestures, a few bits of herbs and things. No particular piece mattered; there was no strict order to the incantations. I did see why he called her spells unteachable, because I couldn't even remember what I did when I cast them, much less explain why I did any one step, but for me they were an inexpressible relief after all the stiff, overcomplicated spells he'd set me. My first description held true: I felt as though I was picking my way through a bit of forest that I had never seen before, and her words were like another experienced gleaner somewhere ahead of me calling back to say, *There are blueberries down on the northern slope,* or *Good mushrooms by the birches over here,* or *There's an easy way through the brambles on the left.* She didn't care how I got to the blueberries: she only pointed me in the proper direction and let me wander my way over to them, feeling out the ground beneath my feet.

He hated it so very much I almost felt sorry for him. He finally resorted to standing over me while I cast the final spell, noting down every small thing I did, even the sneeze from breathing in too deep over the cinnamon, and when I was finished he tried it again himself. It was very strange watching him, like a delayed and flattering mirror: he did everything exactly the way I had done, but more gracefully, with perfect precision, enunciating every syllable I had slurred, but he wasn't halfway through before I could tell it wasn't working. I twitched to interrupt him. He shot me a furious look, so I gave up and let him finish working himself into a thicket, as I thought of it, and when he was done and nothing whatsoever had happened, I said, "You shouldn't have said *miko* there."

"*You* did!" he snapped.

I shrugged helplessly: I didn't doubt that I had, though to be perfectly honest I didn't remember. But it hadn't been an important thing to remember. "It was all right when I did it," I said, "but when you did it, it was wrong. As though—you were following a trail, but a tree had fallen down in the meantime, or some hedge grew up, and you insisted on continuing on anyway, instead of going around it—"

"There are no *hedges!*" he roared.

"It comes, I suppose," I said thoughtfully, speaking to the air, "of spending too much time alone indoors, and forgetting that living things don't always stay where you put them."

He ordered me from the room in stiff fury.

I must give him this credit: he sulked for the rest of the week, and then he dug out a small collection of other spellbooks from his shelves, dusty and unused, full of untidy spells like the ones in Jaga's book. They all came to my hands like eager friends. He picked through them and consulted dozens of references in his other books, and with that knowledge laid out a course of study and practice for me. He warned me of all the dangers of higher workings: of the spell slipping out of your hands midway and thrashing around wild; of losing yourself in magic, and wandering through it like a dream you could touch, while your body died of thirst; of attempting a spell past your limits and having it drain away strength you didn't have. Though he still couldn't understand how the spells that suited me worked at all, he made himself a ferocious critic of my results, and demanded that I tell him beforehand what I meant to happen, and when I couldn't properly predict the outcome, he forced me to work that same spell over and over again until I could.

In short, he tried to teach me as best he could, and to advise me in my blundering through my new forest, though it was foreign country to him. He did still resent my success, not from jealousy but as a matter of principle: it offended his sense of the proper order of things that my slapdash workings *did* work, and he scowled as much when I was doing well as when I had made some evident mistake.

A month into my new training, he was glaring at me while I struggled to make an illusion of a flower. "I don't understand," I said—whined, if I tell the truth: it was absurdly difficult. My first three attempts had looked like they were made of cotton rags. Now I had managed to put together a tolerably convincing wild rose, as long as you didn't try to smell it. "It's far easier just to *grow* a flower: why would anyone bother?"

"It's a matter of scale," he said. "I assure you it is considerably easier to produce the illusion of an army than the real thing. How is that even *working*?" he burst out, as he sometimes did when pressed past his limits by the obvious dreadfulness of my magic. "You aren't maintaining the spell at all—no chanting, no gesture—"

"I'm still giving it magic. A *great deal* of magic," I added, unhappily.

The first few spells that didn't yank magic out of me like pulling teeth had been so purely a relief that I had half-thought that was the worst of it over: now that I understood how magic *ought* to work—whatever the Dragon said on that subject—everything would be easy. Well, I soon learned better. Desperation and terror had fueled my first working, and my next few attempts had been the equivalent of the first cantrips he'd tried to teach me, the little spells he had expected me to master effortlessly. So I had indeed mastered those effortlessly, and then he had unmercifully set me at real spells, and everything had once again become—if not unbearable in the same way, at least exceedingly difficult.

"*How* are you giving it magic?" he said, through his teeth.

"I already found the path!" I said. "I'm just staying on it. Can't you—feel it?" I asked abruptly, and held my hand cupping the flower out towards him; he frowned and put his hands around it, and then he said, *"Vadiya rusha ilikad tuhi,"* and a second illusion laid itself over mine, two roses in the same space—his, predictably, had three rings of perfect petals, and a delicate fragrance.

"Try and match it," he said absently, his fingers moving slightly, and by lurching steps we brought our illusions closer together until it was nearly impossible to tell them one from another, and then he said, "Ah," suddenly, just as I began to glimpse *his* spell: almost exactly like that strange clockwork on the middle of his table, all shining moving parts. On an impulse I tried to align our workings: I envisioned his like the water-wheel of a mill, and mine the rushing stream driving it around. "What are you—" he began, and then abruptly we had only a single rose, and it began to grow.

And not only the rose: vines were climbing up the bookshelves in every direction, twining themselves around ancient tomes and reaching out the window; the tall slender columns that made the arch of the doorway were lost among rising birches, spreading out long finger-branches; moss and violets were springing up across the floor, delicate ferns unfurling. Flowers were blooming everywhere: flowers I had never seen, strange blooms dangling and others with sharp points, brilliantly colored, and the room was thick with their fragrance, with the smell of crushed leaves and pungent herbs. I looked around myself alight with wonder, my magic still flowing easily. "Is this what you meant?" I asked him: it really wasn't any more difficult than making the single flower had been. But he was staring at the riot of flowers all around us, as astonished as I was.

He looked at me, baffled and for the first time uncertain, as though he had stumbled into something, unprepared. His long narrow hands were cradled around mine, both of us holding the rose together. Magic was singing in me, through me; I felt the murmur of his power singing back that same song. I was abruptly too hot, and strangely conscious of myself. I pulled my hands free.

SEVEN

I avoided him all the next day, stupidly, and realized too late that my success in doing so meant he had avoided *me*, too, when he had never let me miss a lesson before. I didn't care to think why. I tried to pretend it meant nothing, that we had both simply wanted a holiday from my laborious training. But I passed a restless night, and went down to the library the next morning sandy-eyed and nervous. He didn't look at me as I came in; he said shortly, "Begin with *fulmkea*, on page forty-three," a wholly different spell, and he kept his head bent over his own book. I gladly dived for the safety of my work.

We lasted four days in near-silence and might have gone a month without exchanging more than a few words a day, I suppose, left to our own devices. But on the morning of the fourth day, a sledge drew up to the tower, and when I looked out of the window it was Borys, but not alone; he was driving Kasia's mother Wensa, and she was huddled small in the sleigh, her pale round face looking up at me from under her shawl.

I hadn't seen anyone from Dvernik since the beacon night.

Danka had sent the fire-heart back to Olshanka, with an escort gathered grimly from every village of the valley as it passed through with the message. They had come in force to the tower four days after I had transported the Dragon and myself back. It was brave of them, farmers and craftsmen, coming to face a worse horror than any of us could even have imagined; and they had been wary of believing that the Dragon was healed.

The mayor of Olshanka had even had the courage to demand that the Dragon show the wound to the town physician: he grudgingly obliged, rolling up his sleeve to show the faint white scar, all that was left of the wound, and even told the man to draw some blood from his fingertip: it sprang out clean red. But they had also brought the old priest in his full purple gown to say a blessing over him, which infuriated him to no end. "What on earth are you lending yourself to this nonsense for?" he demanded of the priest, whom he evidently knew a little. "I've let you shrive a dozen corrupted souls: did any of them sprout the purple rose, or suddenly announce themselves saved and purified? What possible good do you imagine saying a blessing over me would do, if I *were* corrupted?"

"So you are well, then," the priest had said dryly, and they at last allowed themselves to believe, and the mayor had handed over the fire-heart with great relief.

But of course my father and brothers hadn't been allowed to come; nor had anyone from my village, who would have grieved to see me burn. And the men who *had* come, they'd looked at me standing beside the Dragon, and I didn't know how to name what was in their faces. I was back in comfortable plain skirts again, but they looked at me anyway as they went away, not with hostility, but not the way any of them would ever have looked at a woodcutter's girl from Dvernik. It was the way I had looked at Prince Marek, at first. They looked at me and saw someone out of a story, who might ride by and be stared at, but didn't belong in their lives at all. I flinched from those looks. I was glad to go back into the tower.

That was the day I had taken Jaga's book down to the library, and demanded that the Dragon stop pretending I had any more gift for healing than I did for any other sort of spell, and let me learn the kind of magic that I could do. I hadn't tried to write a letter, even though I suppose the Dragon would have let me send one. What would I say? I had gone home, and I had even saved it, but it wasn't my place anymore; I couldn't go and dance in the village square among my friends, any more than six months ago I could have marched into the Dragon's library and sat down at his table.

When I saw Wensa's face, though, even from the library window, I didn't think of any of that. I left my working hanging in the air, unfinished, as he'd so often ordered me never to do, and flung myself down the stairs. He shouted after me, but his voice couldn't reach me: because Wensa wouldn't be here if Kasia could have come. I jumped down the last few steps into the great hall, and at the doors I halted only a moment: *"Irronar, irronar,"* I cried: it was only a charm for untying snarled knots of thread, and slurred besides, but I flung profligate magic behind it, as though I'd determined to hack my way through a thicket with an axe instead of taking the time to find a way around. The doors jumped as if startled and opened for me.

I fell through them onto suddenly weak knees—as the Dragon delighted in telling me, caustically, there was good reason that the more powerful spells were also the more complicated—but I staggered up and caught Wensa's hands as she raised them to knock. Her face, seen close, was wrung with weeping; her hair was hanging down her back, clouds of it pulling out of the long thick plait, and her clothing was torn and stained with dirt: she was wearing her nightshift and a smock flung over it. "Nieshka," she said, gripping my hands too hard, strangling the feeling out of them and her nails digging into my skin. "Nieshka, I had to come."

"Tell me," I said.

"They took her this morning, when she went for water," Wensa said. "Three of them. Three walkers," her voice breaking.

It was a bad spring when even one of the walkers came out of the Wood, and went plucking people out of the forests like fruit. I'd seen one once, a long way off through the trees: like an enormous twig-insect, at once almost impossible to see among the underbrush and jointed wrong and dreadful, so when it moved I had shuddered back from it, queasy. They had arms and legs like branches, with long twiggy stalk-fingers, and they would pick their way through the woods and find places near foot-paths and near water, near clearings, and wait in silence. If someone came in arm's reach, there was no saving them, unless you had a great many men with axes and fire nearby. When I was twelve, they caught one half a mile past Zatochek, the tiny village that was the last in the valley, the last before the Wood. The walker had taken a child, a little boy, bringing a pail of water to his mother for the washing; she'd seen him snatched and screamed. There had been enough women nearby to raise the alarm, and slow it down.

They had halted it at last with fire, but it had still been a day's work to hack it to pieces. The walker broke the child's arm and legs where it gripped it, and never let go until they finally cut through the trunk of its body and severed the limbs. Even then it took three strong men to break the fingers off the boy's body, and he had scars around his arms and legs patterned like the bark of an oak-tree.

Those the walkers carried into the Wood were less lucky. We didn't know what happened to them, but they came back out sometimes, corrupted in the worst way: smiling and cheerful, unharmed. They seemed almost themselves to anyone who didn't know them well, and you might spend half a day talking with one of them and never realize anything was wrong, until you found yourself taking up a knife and cutting off your own hand, putting out your own eyes, your own tongue, while they kept talking all the while, smiling, horrible. And then they would take the knife and go inside your house, to your children, while you lay outside blind and choking and helpless even to scream. If someone we loved was taken by the walkers, the only thing we knew to hope for them was death, and it could only be a hope. We could never know for certain, until one of them came out and proved they weren't dead, and then had to be hunted down.

"Not Kasia," I said. "Not Kasia."

Wensa had bent her head. She was weeping into my hands, which she still clenched on like iron. "Please, Nieshka. Please." She spoke hoarsely, without hope. She would never have come to ask the Dragon for help, I knew; she would have known better. But she had come to me.

She couldn't stop weeping. I brought her inside, into the small entry hall, and the Dragon impatiently stalked into the room and held her out a draught, though she shrank from him and hid her face until I gave it to her. She relaxed heavily almost as soon as she had drunk it, and her face smoothed: she let me help her upstairs to my own little room, and she lay down on the bed quietly, though with her eyes open.

The Dragon stood in the doorway watching us. I held up the locket from around Wensa's neck. "She has a lock of Kasia's hair." I knew she'd cut it from Kasia's head the night before the choosing, thinking she would have nothing left to remember her daughter by. "If I use *loytalal*—"

He shook his head. "What do you imagine you're going to find, besides a smiling corpse? The girl is gone." He jerked his chin at Wensa, whose eyes had drifted shut. "She'll be calmer after she sleeps. Tell that driver to come back in the morning to take her home."

He turned and left, and the worst of it was how matter-of-factly he'd spoken. He hadn't snapped at me, or called me a fool; he hadn't said the life of a village girl wasn't worth the chance the Wood might take me to add to its host. He hadn't told me I was an idiot drunk on success in throwing potions, in pulling flowers from the air, to suddenly think I could save someone the Wood had taken.

The girl is gone. He'd even sounded sorry, in his abrupt way.

I sat with Wensa, numb and cold, holding her hard red callused hand in my lap. It was growing dark outside. If Kasia was still alive, she was in the Wood, watching the sun go down, light dying through the leaves. How long did it take, to hollow someone out from the inside? I thought of Kasia in the grip of the walkers, the long fingers curled around her arms and legs, knowing all the while what was happening, what would happen to her.

I left Wensa sleeping and went downstairs to the library. The Dragon was there, looking through one of the vast ledgers he made records in. I stood in the doorway staring at his back. "I know you held her dear," he said over his shoulder. "But there's no kindness in offering false hope."

I didn't say anything. Jaga's book of spells was lying open on the table, small and worn. I'd been studying only spells of earth this week: *fulmkea, fulmedesh, fulmishta,* solid and fixed, as far from the air and fire of illusion as magic could get. I took the book and slipped it into my pocket behind the Dragon's back, and then I turned around and went silently down the stairs.

Borys was still outside, waiting, his face long and bleak: he looked up from his blanketed horses when I came out of the tower. "Will you drive me to the Wood?" I asked him.

He nodded, and I climbed into his sleigh and drew the blankets around me as he made the horses ready again. He climbed aboard and spoke to them, jingling his reins, and the sleigh leapt out over the snow.

The moon was high that night, full and beautiful, blue light on the shining snow all around. I opened Jaga's book as we flew, and found a spell for the quickening of feet. I sang it softly to the horses, their ears pricking back to listen to me, and the wind of our passage grew muffled and thick, pressing hard on my cheeks and blurring my sight. The Spindle, frozen over, was a pale silver road running alongside, and a shadow grew in the east ahead of us, grew and grew until the horses, uneasy, slowed and came to a halt without any word or any movement of reins. The world stopped moving.

We were stopped under a small ragged cluster of pine-trees. The Wood stood ahead of us across an open stretch of unbroken snow.

Once a year, when the ground thawed, the Dragon took all the unmarried men older than fifteen out to the borders of the Wood. He burned a swath of ground along its edge bare and black, and the men followed his fire, sprinkling the ground with salt so nothing could grow or take root. In all our villages we saw the plumes of smoke rising. We saw them going up also on the other side of the Wood, far away in Rosya, and knew they were doing the same. But the fires always died when they reached the shadow beneath the dark trees.

I climbed down from the sleigh. Borys looked down at me, his face tense and afraid. But he said, "I'll wait," although I knew he couldn't: Wait how long? For what? Wait here, in the Wood's very shadow?

I thought of my own father, waiting for Marta, if our places had been changed. I shook my head. If I could bring Kasia out, I thought I could get her to the tower. I hoped the Dragon's spell would let us in. "Go home," I said, and then I asked him, wanting suddenly to know, "Is Marta well?"

He nodded slightly. "She's married," he said, and then he hesitated and said, "There's a child coming."

I remembered her at the choosing, five months ago: her red dress, her beautiful black braids, her narrow pale frightened face. It didn't seem possible we'd ever stood next to each other, just the same: her and me and Kasia in a row. It took my breath, hard and painful, to imagine her sitting at her own hearth, already a young matron, getting ready for childbed.

"I'm glad," I said, with an effort, refusing to let my mouth close up with jealousy. It wasn't that I wanted a husband and a baby; I didn't, or rather, I only wanted them the way I wanted to live to a hundred: someday, far off, never thinking about the particulars. But they meant *life:* she was living, and I wasn't. Even if I came somehow out of the Wood alive again, I'd never have what she had. And Kasia—Kasia might already be dead.

But I wouldn't go into the Wood with ill-wishing. I took a deep hard breath and made myself say, "I wish her an easy birth and a healthy child." I even managed to mean it: childbirth was frightening enough, even if it was a more familiar terror. "Thank you," I added, and turned away to cross over the barren ground, to the wall of great dark trunks. I heard the jingle of the harness behind me as Borys turned the horses and trotted away, but the sound was muffled, and soon faded. I didn't look around, taking step after step until I stopped just beneath the first boughs.

A little snow was falling, soft and quiet. Wensa's locket was cold in my hand as I opened it. Jaga had half a dozen different finding spells, small and easy—it seemed she'd had a habit of misplacing things. *"Loytalal,"* I said softly, to the small coiled braid of Kasia's hair: *good for finding the whole, from a part,* the scribbled note on the spell had said. My breath fogged into a small pale cloud and drifted away from me, leading the way into the trees. I stepped between two trunks, and followed it inside the Wood.

I expected it to be more dreadful than it was. But at first it seemed only an old, old forest. The trees were great pillars in a dark endless hall, well apart from one another, their twisting gnarled roots blanketed in dark green moss, small feathery ferns curled up close for the night. Tall pale mushrooms grew in hosts like toy soldiers marching. The snow hadn't reached the ground beneath the trees, not even now in the deep of winter. A thin layer of frost clung to the leaves and fine branches. I heard an owl calling somewhere distantly as I picked my way carefully through the trees.

The moon was still above, clear white light coming through the bare branches. I followed my own faint breath and imagined myself a small mouse hiding from owls: a small mouse hunting for a piece of corn, a hidden nut. When I went gleaning in the forest, I often daydreamed as I walked: I lost myself in the cool shady green, in the songs of birds and frogs, in the running gurgle of a stream over rocks. I tried to lose myself the same way now, tried to be only another part of the forest, nothing worthy of attention.

But there was something watching. I felt it more and more with every step the deeper I went into the Wood, a weight laid heavily across my shoulders like an iron yoke. I had come inside half-expecting corpses hanging from every bough, wolves leaping at me from the shadows. Soon I was wishing for wolves. There was something worse here. The thing I had glimpsed looking out of Jerzy's eyes was here, something *alive*, and I was trapped inside an airless room with it, pressed into a small corner. There was a song in this forest, too, but it was a savage song, whispering of madness and tearing and rage. I crept on, my shoulders hunched, trying to be small.

Then I came stumbling to a small stream—barely a rivulet, frost thick on both banks and black water running between them, the moonlight coming through the break in the trees. And there was a walker on the other side, its strange narrow stick-head bent to the water to drink, its mouth like a crack open in its face. It lifted its head and looked straight at me, dripping. Its eyes were knots in wood, round dark pouched holes that some small animal might have lived in. There was a scrap of green woolen cloth dangling from one of its legs, caught on a jutting spar at the joint.

We stared at each other across the narrow running thread of the river. *"Fulmedesh,"* I said, my voice shaking, and a crack in the ground opened beneath the walker and swallowed up its back legs. It scrabbled at the bank with the rest of its long stick-limbs, thrashing silently, throwing up sprays of water, but the earth had closed up around the middle of its body, and it couldn't pull itself out.

But I folded in on myself and swallowed a cry of pain. It felt like someone had hit me with a stick across my shoulders: the Wood had felt my working. I was sure of it. The Wood was looking for me now. It was looking, and soon it would find me. I had to force myself to move. I sprang over the stream and ran after my faint cloudy spell, which still drifted on ahead of me. The walker tried to catch at me with its long cracked-wood fingers as I skirted around it, but I ran past. I came through a ring of larger trunks and found myself in an open space around a smaller tree, the ground here heavy with snow.

There was a fallen tree stretching across the space, a giant, its trunk taller across than I was. Its fall had opened up this clearing, and in the middle of it, a new tree had sprung up to take its place. But not the same kind of tree. All the other trees I'd seen in the Wood had been familiar kinds, despite their stained bark and the twisted unnatural angles of their branches: oaks and black birch, and tall pines. But this was no kind of tree I had ever seen.

It was already larger around than the circle my arms could make, even though the giant tree couldn't have fallen very long ago. It had smooth grey bark over a strangely knotted trunk, with long branches in even circles around it, starting high up the trunk like a larch. Its branches weren't bare with winter, but carried a host of dried-up silvery leaves that rustled in the wind, a noise that seemed to come from somewhere else, as though there were people just out of sight speaking softly together.

The trail of my breath had dissolved into the air. Looking down at the deep snow, I could see the marks where the walkers' legs had poked through and the lines their bellies had drawn, all going to the tree. I took a wary step through the snow towards it, and then another, and then I stopped. Kasia was bound to the tree. Her back was against the trunk and her arms drawn backwards around it.

I hadn't seen her at first because the bark had already grown over her.

Her face was turned up a little, and beneath the skim of the covering bark I could see her mouth had been open, screaming while the bark closed over her. I made a choked cry, helplessly, and staggered forward and put out my hands to touch her. The bark was hard beneath my fingers already, the grey skin smooth and hard, as though she had been swallowed into the trunk whole, all of her made a part of the tree, of the Wood.

I couldn't get a hold on the bark, though I tried frantically to claw and peel it away. But I managed at last to scrape off a little thin piece over her cheek, and beneath I found her own soft skin— still warm, still alive. But even as I touched it with my fingertip, the bark crept quickly over it, and I had to draw back my hand, not to be caught myself. I covered my mouth with my hands, even more desperate. I still knew so little: no spell came to my mind, nothing that could get Kasia out, nothing that would even put an axe in my hands, a knife, even if there had been time to carve her free.

The Wood knew I was here: even now its creatures were moving towards me, stealthy padding feet through the forest, walkers and wolves and worse things still. I suddenly was sure that there were things that never left the Wood at all, things so dreadful no one had ever seen them. And they were coming.

With bare feet in the dirt, fulmia, ten times with conviction, will shake the earth to its roots, if you have the strength, Jaga's book had told me, and the Dragon had believed it enough not to let me try it anywhere near the tower. I had felt doubtful, anyway, about *conviction:* I hadn't believed I had any business shaking the earth to its roots. But now I fell to the ground and dug away the snow and the fallen leaves and rot and moss until I came to the hard-frozen dirt. I pried up a large stone and began to smash at the earth, again and again, breaking up the dirt and breathing on it to make it softer, pounding in the snow that melted around my hands, pounding in the hot tears that dripped from my eyes as I worked. Kasia was above me with her head flung up, her mouth open in its soundless cry like a statue in a church.

"Fulmia," I said, my fingers deep in the dirt, crushing the solid clods between my fingers. *"Fulmia, fulmia,"* I chanted over and over, bleeding from broken nails, and I felt the earth hear me, uneasily. Even the earth was tainted here, poisoned, but I spat on the dirt and screamed, *"Fulmia,"* and imagined my magic running into the ground like water, finding cracks and weaknesses, spreading out beneath my hands, beneath my cold wet knees: and the earth shud-

dered and turned over. A low trembling began where my hands drove into the ground, and it followed me as I started prying at the roots of the tree. The frozen dirt began to break up into small chunks all around them, the tremors going on and on like waves.

The branches above me were waving wildly as if in alarm, the whispering of the leaves becoming a muted roaring. I straightened up on my knees. "Let her out!" I screamed at the tree; I beat on its trunk with my muddy fists. "Let her out, or I'll bring you down! *Fulmia!*" I cried out in rage, and threw myself back down at the ground, and where my fists hit, the ground rose and swelled like a river rising with the rain. Magic was pouring out of me, a torrent: every warning the Dragon had ever given me forgotten and ignored. I would have spent every drop of myself and died there, just to bring that horrible tree down: I couldn't imagine a world where I lived, where I left this behind me, Kasia's life and heart feeding this corrupt monstrous thing. I would rather have died, crushed in my own earthquake, and brought it down with me. I tore at the ground ready to break open a pit to swallow us all.

And then with a sound like ice breaking in the spring, the bark cracked open, running up and down the length of Kasia's body. I lunged up from the dirt at once and dug my fingers into the crack, prying the sides wide and reaching in for her. I caught her wrist, her arm limp and heavy, and pulled. She fell out of the horrible dark gap bending at the waist like a rag doll, and I backed away dragging her deadweight free into the snow, both my hands wrapped around her wrist. Her skin was fish-pale, sickly, like all the sun had been drunk out of her. Sap smelling like spring rain ran over her in thin green rivulets, and she didn't move.

I fell to my knees beside her. "Kasia," I said, sobbing. "Kasia." The bark had already closed itself up like a seam around the hole where she had been. I caught Kasia's hands in my wet dirty ones and pressed them to my cheeks, to my lips. They were cold, but not as cold as my own: there was a trace of life in them. I bent down and heaved her onto my shoulders.

EIGHT

I came staggering out of the Wood at dawn, with Kasia slung across my shoulders like a bundle of firewood. The Wood had drawn back from me as I went, as if it feared driving me back to the spell. *Fulmia* rang in my head like a deep bell sounding with every heavy step I took, Kasia's weight on top of mine, dirt still covering my hands on her pale arm and leg. Finally I floundered out of the trees into the deep snow at the border and fell. I crawled out from under Kasia and pushed her over. Her eyes were still closed. Her hair was matted and sticky around her face where sap had soaked it. I heaved her head up against my shoulder and closed my eyes, and spoke the spell.

The Dragon was waiting for us in the high tower room. His face was hard and grim as ever I had seen it, and he gripped me by the chin and jerked my head up. I looked back at him, exhausted and empty, while he studied my face and searched my eyes. He was holding a bottle of some cordial in his hands; after he'd looked at me a long while he jerked out the stopper and thrust it at me. "Drink it," he said. "The whole thing."

He went over to where Kasia sprawled on the floor, still unmoving: he held his hands out over her and glared down at me when I made a note of protest and reached out. "*Now*," he snapped, "unless you want to force me to incinerate her at once, so I can deal with you." He waited until I began drinking, then murmured a quick spell, sprinkling some crushed dust over her body: a shining amber-golden net sprang out over her, like a birdcage, and he turned to watch me drink.

The first taste was inexpressibly good: like a swallow of warm honey with lemon down a sore throat. But as I kept drinking, my stomach began to turn from too much sweetness. I had to halt halfway through. "I can't," I said, choking.

"All of it," he said. "And then a second one, if I think it necessary. *Drink*," and I forced down another swallow, and another, and another, until I drained the glass. Then he seized me by the wrists and said, *"Ulozishtus sovjenta, megiot kozhor, ulozishtus megiot,"* and I screamed: it felt like he'd set fire to me from the inside. I could see light shining through my own skin, making a blazing lantern of my body, and when I held up my hands, I saw to my horror faint shadows moving there beneath the surface. Forgetting the feverish pain, I caught at my dress and dragged it off over my head. He knelt down on the floor with me. I was shining like a sun, the thin shadows moving through me like fish swimming beneath the ice in winter.

"Get them out," I said. Now that I saw them, I suddenly felt them, also, leaving a trail inside me like slime. I'd thought, stupidly, that I was safe because I hadn't been scratched, or cut, or bitten. I'd thought he was only taking precautions. Now I understood: I'd breathed in corruption with the very air, under the boughs of the Wood, and I hadn't noticed the creeping feeling of them because they'd slipped in, small and subtle. "Get them out—"

"Yes, I'm trying," he bit out, gripping me by the wrists. He shut his eyes and began to speak again, a long slow chanting that went on and on, feeding the fire. I fixed my eyes on the window, on the sunlight coming in, and tried to breathe while I burned. Tears ran down my face in rivulets, scorching hot against my cheeks. His grip on my arms felt cool by comparison, for once.

The shadows beneath my skin were growing smaller, their edges burning away in the light, sand wearing away in water. They darted around, trying to find places to hide, but he didn't let the light fade anywhere. I could see my bones and my organs as glowing shapes inside me, one of them my very heart thumping in my breast. It was slowing, each beat heavier. I understood dimly that the question was whether he could burn the corruption out of me quicker than my body could bear. I swayed in his hands. He shook me abruptly and I opened my eyes to find him glaring at me: he didn't break the course of his spell even for a moment, but he didn't need to say a word: *Don't you dare waste my time, you outrageous idiot,* his furious eyes said, and I set my teeth in my lip and held on a little longer.

The last few shadow-fish were being worn away to wriggling threads, and then they vanished, grown so thin they couldn't be seen. He slowed the chant, and paused it. The fire banked a little, an inexpressible relief. He demanded, grimly, "Enough?"

I opened my mouth to say *yes,* to say *please.* "No," I whispered, horribly afraid now. I could feel the faint quicksilver trace of the shadows still inside me. If we stopped now, they would curl up deep, hiding in my veins and my belly. They would take root and grow and grow and grow, until they strangled all the rest of me.

He nodded once. He held out his hand, murmured a word, and another flask appeared. I shuddered; he had to help me tip a swallow into my open mouth. I choked it down, and he took up the chant again. The fire rose in me again, endless, blinding, burning.

After three more swallows, each one stoking the fire back up to full height, I was almost sure. I forced myself to one more after that, to be certain, and then finally, almost sobbing, I said, "Enough. It's enough." But then he took me by surprise and forced another swallow on me. As I spluttered, he put his hand over my mouth and nose, and used a different chant, one that didn't burn but closed my lungs. For five horrible heartbeats I couldn't breathe at all, clawing at him and drowning in the open air: it was worse than everything else had been. I was staring at him, seeing his dark eyes fixed on me, implacable and searching. They began to swallow up all the world; my sight was closing, my hands were going weak; then at last he stopped and my frantic lungs swelled open like a bellows dragging in a rush of air. I yelled with it, a furious wordless shout, and shoved him away from me so he went sprawling back across the floor.

He twisted up, managing to keep the flask from spilling, and we glared at each other, equally angry. "Of all the extraordinary stupidities I have ever seen you perform," he snarled at me.

"You could have told me!" I shouted, arms wrapped around my body, still shaking with the horror of it. "I stood all the rest, I could have stood that, too—"

"Not if you were corrupted," he said flatly, breaking in. "If you were taken deep, you would have tried to evade it, if I'd told you."

"Then you would have known, anyway!" I said, and he pressed his mouth hard, into a thin line, and looked away from me with an odd stiffness.

"Yes," he said shortly. "I would have known."

And then—would have had to kill me. He would have had to slay me while I pleaded, maybe; while I begged him and pretended to be—perhaps even thought myself, as I had—untainted. I fell silent, catching my breath in slow, measured, deep drafts. "And am I—am I clean?" I asked finally, dreading the answer.

"Yes," he said. "No corruption could have hidden from that last spell. If we'd done it sooner, it would have killed you. The shadows would have had to steal the breath from your blood to live."

I sagged limply in on myself and covered my face. He pulled himself to his feet and stoppered the flask. He murmured, "*Vanastalem,*" moving his hands, and stepped over to me: he thrust out a neatly folded cloak, heavy silk-lined velvet, deep green, embroidered in gold. I looked at it blankly, and stared up at him, and only when he looked away from me with an annoyed, stiff expression did

I realize that the last glowing embers were dying beneath my skin, and I was still naked.

Then I staggered up to my feet abruptly, holding the cloak clutched against me, forgotten. "Kasia," I said urgently, and turned towards her where she lay beneath the cage.

He didn't say anything. I looked back at him desperately. "Go and dress," he said finally. "There's no urgency."

He'd seized me the instant I came into the tower: he hadn't let a moment pass. "There must be a way," I said. "There has to be a way. They'd only just taken her—she couldn't have been in the tree for long."

"What?" he said sharply, and listened with his brows drawing as I spilled out the horror of the clearing, of the tree. I tried to tell him about the dreadful weight of the Wood, watching me; the feeling of being hunted. I stumbled over it all: words didn't seem enough. But his face grew more dark, until at last I finished with that last staggering rush out into the clean snow.

"You've been inexpressibly lucky," he said finally. "And inexpressibly mad, although in your case the two seem to be the same thing. No one has gone into the Wood as deep as you and come out whole: not since—" He halted, and I somehow knew without his saying her name that it was Jaga: that Jaga had walked in the Wood, and come out again. He saw my realization, and glared at me. "And at the time," he said, icily, "she was a hundred years old, and so steeped in magic that black toadstools would spring up where she walked. And even she wasn't stupid enough to start a great working in the middle of the place, although I will grant that in this case, it's the only thing that saved you." He shook his head. "I should have chained you to the wall as soon as that peasant woman came here to weep on your shoulder, I suppose."

"Wensa," I said, my dull, exhausted mind latching on to one thing. "I have to go tell Wensa." I looked towards the hallway, but he cut in.

"Tell her *what*?" he said.

"That Kasia's alive," I said. "That she's out of the Wood—"

"And that she will surely have to die?" he said, brutally.

Instinctively I backed towards Kasia, putting myself between them, holding my hands up—futile, if he had meant to overcome me, but he shook his head. "Stop mantling at me like a rooster," he said, more weary than irritated: the tone made my chest clench in dismay. "The last thing we need is any further demonstrations that you'll go to fool's lengths for her sake. You can keep her alive as long as we can keep her restrained. But you'll find it a mercy by the end."

I did tell Wensa, when she woke a little later that morning. She clutched my hands, wild-eyed. "Let me see her," she demanded, but that much, the Dragon had flatly forbidden.

"No," he said. "You can torment yourself if you want to; that's as far as I'll go. Make that woman no false promises, and don't let her come anywhere near. If you'll take my advice, you'll tell her the girl is dead, and let her get on with her life."

But I steeled myself and told her the truth. Better, I thought, to know that Kasia was out of the Wood, that there was an end to her torment, even if there wasn't a cure. I wasn't sure if I was right. Wensa wailed and wept and begged me; if I could have, I would have disobeyed and taken her. But the Dragon didn't trust me with Kasia: he had already taken her away and put her in a cell some-where, deep beneath the tower. He'd told me he wouldn't show me the way down until I'd learned a spell of protection, something to guard myself from the Wood's corruption.

I had to tell Wensa that I couldn't; I had to swear it to her on my heart, over and over, before she would believe me. "I don't know where he's put her," I cried out finally. "I *don't!*"

She stopped begging and stared at me, panting, her hands grip-ping my arms. Then she said, "Wicked, jealous—you always hated her, always. You wanted her to be taken! You and Galinda, you knew he'd take her, you knew and you were glad, and now you hate her because he took you instead—"

She was shaking me, in jerks, and for a moment I couldn't stop her. It was too horrible, hearing her say these things to me, like poison spilling out where I'd looked for clean water. I was so desperately tired, ill from the purging and all my strength spent in bringing Kasia out. I wrenched myself loose at last and ran from the room, unable to bear it, and stood in the hallway leaning against the wall crying messily, too spent even to wipe my face. Wensa crept out after me in a moment, weeping herself. "Forgive me," she said. "Nieshka, forgive me. I didn't mean it. I didn't."

I knew she hadn't meant it, but it was also true, a little, in twisted ways. It dredged up my own secret guilt, my cry: *Why didn't you take Kasia instead?* We *had* been glad all those years, my mother and I, to think I wouldn't be taken, and I *had* been miserable afterwards, even if I'd never hated Kasia for it.

I wasn't sorry when the Dragon sent Wensa home. I didn't even argue very much when he refused to try and teach me the spell of protection that very day. "Try not to be more of a fool than you can help," he snapped. "You need rest, and if you don't, I certainly do before facing the undoubtedly torturous process of drumming the necessary protections into your head. There's no need for haste. Nothing is going to change."

"But if Kasia's infested, as I was," I started, and stopped: he was shaking his head.

"A few shadows slipped between your teeth; purging you at once kept them from getting a hold on you," he said. "This isn't anything like that, nor even some thirdhand infestation, like that luckless cowherder you turned to stone for no good reason. Do you understand that the tree you saw is one of the heart-trees of the Wood? Where they take root, its borders spread, the walkers are fed on their fruit. She was as deep in the Wood's power as any person can be. Go to sleep. A few hours won't make a difference to her, and it may keep you from committing some new folly."

I *was* too tired, and I knew it, reluctantly, though I felt argument coiling in my belly. I put it away for later. But if I'd listened to him and his caution in the first place, Kasia would still be there inside the heart-tree, being devoured and rotted away; if I'd swallowed everything he told me of magic, I'd still have been chanting cantrips to my exhaustion. He had told me himself no one had ever been brought out of a heart-tree, no one had ever come out of the Wood—but Jaga had done it, and now I had, too. He could be mistaken; he was mistaken about Kasia. He *was*.

I was up before first light. In Jaga's book I found a spell *for smelling out rot;* a simple chant, *Aish aish aishimad,* and I worked it down in the kitchens, picking out a place where mold grew on the back of a barrel, a spot of rotting mortar in the walls, bruised apples and one spoiled cabbage that had rolled away under a shelf of winebottles. When sunlight finally brightened the stairway, I went up to the library and started banging books off the shelves loudly until he appeared, tired-eyed and irritable. He didn't chide me; he only looked a brief frown, and then turned away without saying a word. I would have preferred it if he'd shouted.

But he took a small gold key and unlocked a closed cabinet of black wood on the far side of the room. I peered into it: it was full of thin flat sheets of glass in a rack, pieces of parchment pressed between them. He took one and brought it out. "I've preserved it mostly as a curiosity," he said, "but that seems to suit you best."

He laid it on the table still in its glass: a single page in sprawling messy script, many of the letters oddly shaped, with rough illustrations of a branch of pine needles, the smoke going into the nostrils of a face. There were a dozen different variations listed: *suoltal videl, suoljata akorata, videlaren, akordel, estepum,* more besides. "Which one do I use?" I asked him.

"What?" he said, and prickled up indignantly when I told him they were separate incantations, not all one long chant, in the way that meant he hadn't realized it before. "I haven't the least idea," he said shortly. "Choose one and try."

I couldn't help but be secretly, passionately glad: another proof that his knowledge had limits. I went to the laboratory for pine needles and made a small smudgy bonfire of them in a glass bowl on the library table, then bent my head eagerly over the parchment and tried. *"Suoltal,"* I said, feeling the shape of it in my mouth—but there was something wrong, a kind of sideways sliding to it.

"Valloditazh aloito, kes vallofozh," he said, a hard bitter sound that curled into me like fishhooks, and then he made a quick jerk of one finger, and my hands rose up from the table and clapped themselves together three times. It wasn't like having no control, the involuntary lurch of coming out of a dream of falling. I could feel the deliberation behind the movement, the puppet-strings digging into my skin. Someone had moved my arms, and it hadn't been me. I nearly reached for some spell to strike at him, and then he crooked his finger again and the fishhook came loose and the line slithered back out of me.

I was up on my feet, halfway across the room from him, panting, before I could stop myself. I glared, but he didn't offer me an apology. "When the Wood does it," he said, "you won't feel the hook. Try again."

It took me an hour to work out an incantation. None of the ones came out right, not the way they were on paper. I had to try them all on my tongue, rolling them this way and that, before I finally realized that some of the letters weren't meant to sound the same way I thought they did. I tried changing them until I stumbled over a syllable that felt right in my mouth; then another, and another, until I had put it together. He made me practice it over and over for hours more. I breathed in pine smoke and breathed out the words, and then he prodded at my mind with one unpleasant twisting of a spell and another.

He finally let me stop for a rest at noon. I crumpled into a chair, hedgehog-prickled and exhausted; the barriers had held, but I felt very much as though I'd been jabbed repeatedly with sharp sticks. I looked down at the old vellum, so carefully sealed away, with the strange-shaped letters; I wondered how old it was.

"Very old," he said. "Older than Polnya: it might even be older than the Wood."

I stared at him; it hadn't occurred to me even to think, before then, that the Wood hadn't always been here, always been what it was.

He shrugged. "For all we know, it has. It's certainly older than Polnya and Rosya: it was here before this valley was ever settled by either of us." He tapped the parchment in the glass. "These were the first people who lived in this part of the world, so far as we know, some thousand years ago. Their sorcerer-kings brought the tongue of magic west with them, from the barren lands on the far side of Rosya, when they first settled this valley. And then the Wood rolled over them, brought their fortresses low and laid their fields waste. There's little left of their work now."

"But," I said, "if the Wood wasn't here when they first settled the valley, where did it come from?"

The Dragon shrugged. "If you go to the capital, you'll find any number of troubadours who will be happy to sing you the rising of the Wood. It's a popular subject among them, at least when they have an audience that knows less about it than they do: it offers them enormous scope for creativity. I suppose there's a chance one of them has hit on the true story. Light the fire and let's begin again."

It wasn't until late that evening, as the light was failing, that he was satisfied with my work. He tried to send me to bed, but I wouldn't have it. Wensa's words still grated and scraped in the back of my head, and it occurred to me that perhaps he'd wanted me exhausted so he could put me off for another day. I wanted to see Kasia with my own eyes; I wanted to know what I was facing, this corruption I had to find a way to fight. "No," I said. "No. You said I could see her when I could protect myself."

He threw up his hands. "All right," he said. "Follow me."

He led me to the bottom of the stairs, and into the cellars past the kitchen. I remembered searching all those walls in desperation, when I'd thought he was draining my life; I had run my hands over every wall, poked my fingers into every crack, and tugged on every worn brick, trying to find a way out. But he led me to a smooth-polished part of the wall, a single entire slab of pale white stone unbroken by any mortar. He touched it lightly with the fingers of one hand and crooked them up like a spider; I felt the faint thrill of his magic working. The whole slab swung back into the wall, revealing a stairwell of the same pale stone, shining dimly, that bent steeply downwards.

I followed him down the passage. It was different from the rest of the tower: older and more strange. The steps were hard-edged on either side but worn in the middle to softness, and letters had been carved in a line running along the base of both walls, a script neither ours nor Rosyan: very much like the shape of the letters on the parchment with the protection spell. We seemed to go down for a long time, and I was increasingly aware of the weight of stone around us, of silence. It felt like a tomb.

"It *is* a tomb," he said. We had reached the bottom of the stairs, coming into a small round room. The very air seemed thicker. The writing came off one wall of the stairwell, continued all around it in an unbroken line that circled to the opposite side, went up the wall in a tall curve that drew an arch, and then came back and went up the other side of stairs. There was a small patch of lighter stone inside the arch, towards the bottom—as though the rest of the wall had been built, and then had been closed up afterwards. It looked perhaps the size for a man to crawl through.

"Is—is someone still buried here?" I asked, timidly. My voice came out hushed.

"Yes," the Dragon said. "But even kings don't object to sharing once they're dead. Listen to me now," he said, turning to me. "I'm not going to teach you the spell to walk through the wall. When you want to see her, I'll take you through myself. If you try to touch her, if you let her come in arm's reach of you, I'll take you out again at once. Now lay on your protections, if you insist on doing this."

I lit the small handful of pine needles on the floor and made the chant, putting my face in their smoke, and then I put my hand in his, and let him draw me through the wall.

He'd made me fear the worst: Kasia as tormented as Jerzy, foaming-mouthed and tearing at her own skin; Kasia full of those slithering corrupted shadows, eating away at everything inside her. I was prepared for anything; I braced myself. But when he brought me through the wall, she was only sitting huddled and small in the corner on a thin pallet, her arms around her knees. There was a plate of food and water on the floor next to her, and she'd eaten and drunk; she'd washed her face, her hair was neatly plaited. She looked tired and afraid, but still herself, and she struggled up to her feet and came to me, holding out her hands. "Nieshka," she said. "Nieshka, you found me."

"No closer," the Dragon said flatly, and added, *"Valur polzhys,"* and a sudden line of hot flame leapt up across the floor between us: I'd been reaching towards her without being able to help it.

I dropped my hands to my sides and clenched them into fists— and Kasia stepped back, too, staying behind the fire; she nodded obediently to the Dragon. I stood staring at her, helplessly, full of involuntary hope. "Are you—" I said, and my voice choked in my throat.

"I don't know," Kasia said, her voice trembling. "I don't— remember. Not anything after they took me into the Wood. They took me into the Wood and they—they—" She stopped, her mouth open a little. There was horror in her eyes, the same horror I'd felt when I'd found her in the tree, buried beneath the skin.

I had to stop myself reaching out to her. I was in the Wood again myself, seeing her blind, choked face, her pleading hands. "Don't speak of it," I said, thick and miserable. I felt a surge of anger at the Dragon for holding me back this long. I had already made plans in my head: I would use Jaga's spell to find where that corruption had taken root in her; then I would ask the Dragon to show me the purging spells he'd used on me. I would look through

Jaga's book and find others like it, and drive it out of her. "Don't think of it yet, just tell me, how do you feel? Are you—sick, or cold—"

I finally looked around at the room itself. The walls were of that same polished bone-white marble, and in a deep niche at the back a heavy stone box lay, longer than the height of a man, carved along the top in the same letters and other designs on the sides: tall flowering trees and vines curling over each other. A single blue flame burned on top of it, and air flowed in from a thin slit in the wall. It was a beautiful room, but utterly cold; it wasn't a place for any living thing. "We can't keep her here," I said to the Dragon fiercely, even as he shook his head. "She needs sun, and fresh air—we can lock her into my room instead—"

"Better here than the Wood!" Kasia said. "Nieshka, please tell me, is my mother all right? She tried to follow the walkers—I was afraid they'd take her, too."

"Yes," I said, wiping my face, taking a deep breath. "She's all right. She's worried for you—she's so worried. I'll tell her you're all right—"

"Can I write her a letter?" Kasia asked.

"No," the Dragon said, and I wheeled on him.

"We can give her a stub of pencil and some paper!" I said angrily. "It's not too much to ask."

His face was bleak. "You aren't this much a fool," he said to me. "Do you think she was buried in a heart-tree for a night and a day and came out talking to you, ordinarily?"

I stopped, silent, afraid. Jaga's rot-finding spell hovered on my lips. I opened my mouth to cast it—but it *was* Kasia. It was my own Kasia, who I knew better than anyone in the world. I looked at her and she looked back at me, unhappy and afraid, but refusing to weep or cower. It was her. "They put her in the tree," I said. "They saved her for it, and I brought her out before it got a hold—"

"No," he said flatly, and I glared at him and turned back to her. She smiled at me anyway, a struggling valiant smile.

"It's all right, Nieshka," she said. "As long as Mama's all right. What—" She swallowed. "What's to happen to me?"

I didn't know how to answer her. "I'll find a way to cleanse you," I said, half-desperate, and didn't look at the Dragon. "I'll find a spell to be sure you're all right—" but those were just words. I didn't know how I could ever prove to the Dragon that Kasia was well. He plainly didn't want to be convinced. And if I couldn't persuade him somehow, he would keep Kasia down here the rest of her life if need be, entombed with this ancient king and without a scrap of sunlight—never to see anyone she loved, never to *live* at all. He was as great a danger to Kasia as the Wood—he hadn't wanted me to rescue her at all.

And even before then, it occurred to me in a flash of bitterness, he had meant to steal her for himself—he'd meant to take her as much as the Wood had, to devour her in his own way. He hadn't cared about uprooting her life before, making her a prisoner in a tower, only to serve him—why would he care now, why would he ever risk letting her out?

He stood a few steps behind me, farther from the fire and from Kasia. His face was closed, yielding nothing, his thin mouth pressed hard. I looked away and tried to smooth out my face and hide my thoughts. If I could find a spell to let me pass through the wall, I would only have to find a way to evade his notice. I could try and put a spell of sleep on him, or I could put something in his cup with his dinner: *Wormwood brewed with yew berries, cook the juice down to a paste, put in three drops of blood and speak an incantation, and it will make a quick poison with no taste—*

The sudden sharp pungent smell of burning pine needles came back into my nose, and the thought took on a strange bitter edge that made the wrongness of it leap out. I flinched away from it, startled, and I took a step back from the line of fire, trembling. On the other side, Kasia was waiting for me to speak: her face resolute, clear-eyed, full of trust and love and gratitude—and a little fear and worry, but nothing but ordinary human feeling. I looked at her, and she looked back at me anxiously, still herself. But I couldn't speak. The smell of pine was still in my mouth, and my eyes stung with smoke.

"Nieshka?" Kasia said, her voice wavering with growing fear. I still said nothing. She was staring at me across the line of fire, and her face through the haze seemed to be first smiling and then unhappy, her mouth trembling through one shape and another, trying—trying different expressions. I took another step back, and it grew worse. Her head tilted, eyes fixed on my face, widening a little. She shifted her weight, a different stance. "Nieshka," she said, not sounding afraid anymore, only confident and warm, "it's all right. I know you'll help me."

The Dragon, beside me, was silent. I dragged in a breath. I still said nothing. My throat was shut. I managed, on a whisper, *"Aishi-mad."*

A pungent, bitter smell rose in the air between us. "Please," Kasia said to me. Her voice suddenly broke on a sob, an actor in a play moving from one act to the next. She lifted her hands towards me, came a little closer to the fire, her body leaning in. She came a little too close. The smell grew stronger: like greenwood burning, full of sap. "Nieshka—"

"Stop it!" I cried. "Stop it."

She stopped. For a moment still Kasia stood there, and then it let her arms drop to her sides, and her face emptied out. A wave of rotting-wood smell rolled over the room.

The Dragon raised a hand. *"Kulkias vizhkias haishimad,"* he said, and a light shone out of his hand and onto her skin. Where it played over her I saw thick green shadows, mottled like deep layers of leaves on leaves. Something looked at me out of her eyes, its face still and strange and inhuman. I recognized it: what looked out at me was the same thing I had felt in the Wood, trying to find me. There was no trace of Kasia left at all.

NINE

He was half-supporting me as he pulled me through the wall and out into the antechamber of the tomb again. When we were through I slid to the floor next to my small heap of pine-needle ashes and stared at them, hollow. I almost hated them for stealing the lie from me. I couldn't even cry; it was worse than if Kasia were dead. He stood over me. "There's a way," I said, looking up at him. "There's a way to get it out of her." It was a child's cry, a plea. He said nothing. "That spell you used on me—"

"No," he said. "Not for this. The purging spell barely worked even on you. I warned you. Did it try to persuade you to harm yourself?"

I shivered all over horribly, remembering the ashen taste of that horrible thought creeping through my head: *Wormwood and yew berries, a quick poison.* "You," I said.

He nodded. "It would have liked that: persuade you to kill me, then find some way to lure you back to the Wood."

"What *is* it?" I said. "What is that—*thing* inside her? We say the

Wood, but those trees—" I was abruptly sure of it. "—those trees are corrupted, too, as much as Kasia. That's where it *lives,* not what it is."

"We don't know," he said. "It was here before we came. Perhaps before they were," he added, gesturing to the walls with their strange foreign inscription. "They woke the Wood, or made it, and they fought it awhile, and then it destroyed them. This tomb is all that's left. There was an older tower here. Little of it remained except bricks scattered on the earth by the time Polnya claimed this valley and roused the Wood again."

He fell silent. I remained sunk in on myself, curled up around my knees on the floor. I couldn't stop shivering. Finally he said, heavily, "Are you ready to let me end this? Most likely there's nothing left of her to rescue."

I wanted to say *yes*. I wanted that thing gone, destroyed—the thing that wore Kasia's face, that used not only her hands but everything in her heart, in her mind, to destroy those she loved. I almost didn't care if Kasia was in there. If she was, I couldn't imagine anything more horrible than to be trapped in her own body, that thing dangling her like a monstrous puppet. And I couldn't persuade myself to doubt the Dragon anymore when he said that she was gone, beyond the reach of any magic he knew.

But I had saved *him*, when he had thought himself beyond rescue, too. And I still knew so little, stumbling from one impossibility to another. I imagined the agony of finding a spell in a book, a month from now, a year, that might have worked. "Not yet," I whispered. "Not yet."

If I had been an indifferent student before, now I was dreadful in a wholly different way. I turned ahead in books and took ones he didn't give me down from the shelves if he didn't catch me. I looked into anything and everything I could find. I would work spells out halfway, discard them, and go onward; I would throw myself into workings without being sure I had the strength. I was running wild through the forest of magic, pushing brambles out of my way, heedless of scratches and dirt, paying no attention where I was going.

At least every few days I would find something with enough faint promise that I would convince myself it was worth trying. The Dragon took me down to Kasia to try whenever I asked, which was far more often than I managed to find anything really worth trying. He let me tear apart his library, and said nothing when I spilled oils and powders across his table. He didn't press me to let Kasia go. I hated him and his silence ferociously: I knew he was only letting me convince myself there was nothing to be done.

She—the thing inside her—didn't try to pretend anymore. She watched me with bird-bright eyes, and smiled occasionally when my workings did nothing: a horrible smile. "Nieshka, Agnieszka," she sang softly, over and over, sometimes, if I was trying an incantation, so I had to stumble on through it while listening to her. I would come out feeling bruised and sick to my bones, and climb the stairs again slowly, with tears dripping from my face.

Spring was rolling over the valley by then. If I looked from my window, which I did now only rarely, every day I could watch the Spindle running riotous white with melted ice, and a band of open grass widening from the lowlands, chasing the snow up into the mountains on either side. Rain swept over the valley in silver curtains. Inside the tower I was parched as barren ground. I had looked at every page of Jaga's book, and the handful of other tomes that suited my wandering magic, and any other books the Dragon could suggest. There were spells of healing, spells of cleansing, spells of renewal and life. I had tried anything with any promise at all.

They held the Spring Festival in the valley before the planting began, the great bonfire in Olshanka a tall heap of seasoned wood so large I could see it plainly from the tower. I was alone in the library when I heard a faint snatch of the music drifting on the wind, and looked out to see the celebration. It seemed to me that the entire valley had burst into life, early shoots prodding their way out of all the fields, the forests bursting into pale and misty green around every village. And far down those cold stone stairs, Kasia was in her tomb. I turned away and folded my arms on the table and put my head down on them and sobbed.

When I lifted my head again, blotchy and tearstained, he was there, sitting near me, looking out of the window, his face bleak. His hands were folded in his lap, the fingers laced, as though he had held himself back from reaching out to touch me. He had laid a handkerchief on the table before me. I took it up and wiped my face and blew my nose.

"I tried, once," he said abruptly. "When I was a young man. I lived in the capital, then. There was a woman—" His mouth twisted slightly, self-mocking. "The foremost beauty of the court, naturally. I suppose there's no harm anymore in saying her name now she's forty years in the grave: Countess Ludmila."

I nearly gaped at him, not sure what confused me the most. He was the Dragon: he had always been in the tower and always would be, a permanent fixture, like the mountains in the west. The idea that he had ever lived somewhere else, that he had ever been a young man, seemed perfectly wrong; and yet at the same time, I stumbled just as much over the idea that he'd loved a woman forty years dead. His face was familiar to me now, but I looked at him startled all over again. There were those lines at the corners of his eye and mouth, if I looked for them, but that was all that betrayed his years. In everything else, he was a young man: the still-hard edges of his profile, his dark hair untouched with silver, his pale smooth unweathered cheek, his long and graceful hands. I tried to make him a young court-wizard in my mind—he almost looked the part in his fine clothes, pursuing some lovely noblewoman—and there my imagination stumbled. He was a thing of books and alembics to me, library and laboratory.

"She—became corrupted?" I asked, helplessly.

"Oh, no," he said. "Not her. Her husband." He paused, and I wondered if he would say anything more. He had never spoken of himself to me at all, and he'd said nothing of the court but to disparage it. After a moment he went on, however, and I listened, fascinated.

"The count had gone to Rosya to negotiate a treaty, across the mountain pass. He came back with unacceptable terms and a thread of corruption. Ludmila had a wise-woman at her house, her nursemaid, who knew enough to warn her: they locked him up in the cellar and barred the door with salt, and told everyone he was ill.

"No one in the capital thought anything of a beautiful young wife making a scandal of herself while her older husband ailed out of sight; least of all myself, when she made me the object of her pursuit. I was still young and foolish enough at the time to believe myself and my magic likely to elicit admiration instead of alarm, and she was clever and determined enough to take advantage of my vanity. She had me thoroughly on a string before she asked me to save him.

"She had a particularly deft understanding of human nature," he added, dryly. "She told me that she couldn't leave him in such a state. She professed herself willing to give up her place at court, her title, her reputation, but so long as he was corrupted, honor demanded she remain chained to his side; only by saving him could I free her to run away with me. She tempted my selfishness and my pride at once: I assure you I thought of myself as a noble hero, promising to save my lover's husband. And then—she let me see him."

He fell silent. I hardly breathed, sitting like a mouse under an owl's tree so he would go on talking. His gaze was turned inward, bleak, and I felt a kind of recognition: I thought of Jerzy laughing dreadfully at me out of his sickbed, of Kasia below with the terrible brightness in her eyes, and knew that same look lived in my own face.

"I spent half a year trying," he said finally. "I was already accounted the most powerful wizard of Polnya by then; I was certain there was nothing I couldn't do. I ransacked the king's library and the University, and brewed a score of remedies." He waved towards the table, where Jaga's book lay shut. "That was when I bought that book, among other less wise attempts. Nothing served."

His mouth twisted again. "Then I came here." He indicated the tower with one finger, circling. "There was another witch here guarding the Wood then, the Raven. I thought she might have an answer. She was growing old at last, and most of the wizards at court avoided her carefully; none of them wanted to be sent to replace her when she finally died. I wasn't afraid of that: I was too strong to be sent away from court."

"But—" I said, startled into speaking, and bit my lip; he looked at me for the first time, one of those sarcastic eyebrows raised. "But you *were* sent here, in the end?" I said uncertainly.

"No," he said. "I chose to stay. The king at the time wasn't particularly enthusiastic about my decision: he preferred to keep me under his eye, and his successors have often pressed me to return. But she—persuaded me." He looked away from me again, out the window and over the valley towards the Wood. "Have you ever heard of a town called Porosna?"

It sounded only vaguely familiar. "The baker in Dvernik," I said. "Her grandmother was from Porosna. She made a kind of bun—"

"Yes, yes," he said, impatient. "And do you have any idea where it is?"

I groped helplessly: I barely knew the name. "Is it in the Yellow Marshes?" I offered.

"No," he said. "It was five miles down the road from Zatochek."

Zatochek was not two miles from the barren strip that surrounded the Wood. It was the last town in the valley, the last bastion before the Wood; so it had been all my life. "The Wood—took it?" I whispered.

"Yes," the Dragon said. He rose and went for the great ledger I had seen him write in, the day that Wensa had come to tell us about Kasia being taken, and he brought it to the table and opened it.

Each of the great pages was divided into neat lines, rows and columns, careful entries like an account-book: but in each row stood the name of a town, names of people, and numbers: this many corrupted, this many taken; this many cured, this many slain. The pages were thick with entries. I reached out and turned the pages back, the parchment unyellowed, the ink still dark: there was a faint clinging magic of preservation on them. The years grew thinner and the numbers smaller as I went back. There had been more incidents lately, and larger ones.

"It swallowed Porosna the night the Raven died," the Dragon said. He reached out and turned a thick sheaf of pages to where someone else, less orderly, had been keeping the records: each incident was merely written out like a story, the writing larger and the lines a little shaky.

> Today a rider from Porosna: they have a fever there with seven sick. He did not stop in any towns. He was sickening, too. A woodbane infusion eased his fever, and Agata's Seventh Incantation was effective at purifying the root of the sickness. Sevenweight of silver worth of saffron consumed in the incantation, and fifteen for the woodbane.

It was the last entry in that hand.

"I was on my way back to the court by then," the Dragon said. "The Raven had told me the Wood was growing—she asked me to stay. I refused, indignantly; I thought it beneath me. She told me there was nothing to be done for the count, and I resented it; I told her grandly I would find a way. That whatever the Wood's magic had done, I could undo. I told myself she was an old weak fool; that the Wood was encroaching because of her weakness."

I hugged myself as he spoke, staring down at the implacable ledger, the blank page beneath that entry. I wished now he would stop speaking: I didn't want to hear any more. He was trying to be kind, baring his own failure to me, and all I could think was *Kasia, Kasia*, a cry inside me.

"So far as I could learn, afterwards—a frantic messenger caught me on the road—she went to Porosna, taking her stores with her, and wore herself out healing the sick. That, of course, was when the Wood struck. She managed to fling a handful of children to the next town—I imagine your baker's grandmother was among them. They told a story of seven walkers coming, carrying a seedling heart-tree.

"I was still able to make it through the trees when I came, half a day later. They had planted the heart-tree in her body. She yet lived, if you can call it that. I managed to give her a clean death, but that was all I could do before I had to flee. The village was gone, and the Wood had pushed its borders out.

"That was the last great incursion," he added. "I halted the advance by taking her place, and I've held it since then—more or less. But it's always trying."

"And if you hadn't come?" I said.

"I'm the only wizard in Polnya strong enough to hold it back," the Dragon said, without any particular arrogance: a statement of fact. "Every few years it tests my strength, and once a decade or so makes a serious attempt—like this last assault on your own village. Dvernik is only one village out from the edge of the Wood. If it had managed to kill or corrupt me there, and establish a heart-tree—by the time another wizard came, the Wood would have swallowed up both your village and Zatochek, and been on the doorstep of the eastern pass to the Yellow Marshes. And it would continue on from there, if given the chance. If I'd allowed them to send a weaker wizard when the Raven died, by now the whole valley would have been taken over.

"That's what's happening on the Rosyan side. They've lost four villages in the last decade, and two before that. The Wood will reach the southern pass to Kyeva Province in the next, and then—" He shrugged. "We'll learn whether it can spread itself over a mountain pass, I suppose."

We sat in silence. In his words I saw a vision of the Wood marching slow but implacable over my home, over all the valley, over all the world. I imagined looking down from the tower windows at endless dark trees, besieged; a whispering hateful ocean in every direction, moving with the wind, not another living thing in sight. The Wood would strangle all of them, and drag them down under its roots. Like it had with Porosna. Like it had with Kasia.

Tears were sliding down my face, a slow trail, not hard weeping. I was too desolate to cry anymore. The light outside was growing dim; the witch-lanterns hadn't yet lit. His face had settled into abstraction, unseeing, and in the dusk his eyes were impossible to read. "What happened to them?" I asked to fill the silence, feeling hollow. "What happened to her?"

He stirred. "Who?" he said, surfacing from his reverie. "Oh, Ludmila?" He paused. "After I came back to the court for the last time," he said finally, "I told her there was nothing to be done for her husband. I brought two other wizards from the court to attest his corruption was incurable—they were quite appalled that I'd allowed him to live so long in the first place—and I let one of them put him to death." He shrugged. "They tried to make hay of it, as it happens—there's more than a little envy among enchanters. They suggested to the king that I ought to be sent here for punishment, for having concealed the corruption. They meant the king to refuse that punishment, but settle on something else, some small or petty wrist-slapping, I suppose. It rather deflated them when I announced I was going, no matter what anyone else thought of it.

"And Ludmila—I didn't see her again. She tried to claw my eyes out when I told her we had to put him to death, and her remarks at the time rather quickly disillusioned me as to the real nature of her feelings for me," he added, dryly. "But she inherited the estate and remarried a few years later to a lesser duke; she bore him three sons and a daughter, and lived to the age of seventy-six as a leading matron of the court. I believe the bards at court made me the villain of the piece, and her the noble faithful wife, trying to save her husband at any cost. Not even false, I suppose."

That was when I realized that I already knew the story. I had heard it sung. Ludmila and the Enchanter, only in the song, the brave countess disguised herself as an old peasant woman and cooked and cleaned for the wizard who had stolen her husband's heart, until she found it in his house locked inside a box, and she stole it back and saved him. My eyes prickled with hot tears. No one was enchanted beyond saving in the songs. The hero always saved them. There was no ugly moment in a dark cellar where the countess wept and cried out protest while three wizards put the count to death, and then made court politics out of it.

"Are you ready to let her go?" the Dragon said.

I wasn't, but I was. I was so tired. I couldn't bear to keep going down those stairs, down to the thing wearing Kasia's face. I hadn't saved her at all. She was still in the Wood, still swallowed up. But *fulmia* still shuddered in my belly deep down, waiting, and if I said *yes* to him—if I stayed here and buried my head in my arms and let him go away, and come back and tell me it was done—I thought it might come roaring out of me again, and bring the tower down around us.

I looked at the shelves, all around them, desperately: the endless books with their spines and covers like citadel walls. What if one of them still held the secret, the trick that would set her free? I stood and went and put my hands on them, gold-stamped letters meaningless beneath my blind fingers. *Luthe's Summoning* caught me again, that beautiful leather tome that I'd borrowed so long ago, and enraged the Dragon by taking, before I'd ever known anything of magic, before I'd known how much and how little I could do. I put my hands on it, and then I said abruptly, "What does it summon? A demon?"

"No, don't be absurd," the Dragon said, impatiently. "Calling spirits is nothing but charlatanry. It's very easy to claim you've summoned something that's invisible and incorporeal. The *Summoning* does nothing so trivial. It summons—" He paused, and I was surprised to see him struggling for words. "Truth," he said finally, with half a shrug, as though that was inadequate and wrong, but as close as he could come. I didn't understand how you could *summon* truth, unless he meant seeing past something that was a lie.

"But why were you so angry that I had started reading it, then?" I demanded.

He glared at me. "Does that seem to you a trivial working? I thought you'd been set on to an impossible task by some other enchanter at court—with the intention, on their part, of blasting the roof off the tower when you'd spent all your strength and your working fell in on itself, and thereby making me look an incompetent fool not to be trusted with an apprentice."

"But that would have killed me," I said. "You thought someone from court would—?"

"Spend the life of a peasant with half an ounce of magic to score a victory over me—perhaps to see me ordered back to court, humiliated?" the Dragon said. "Of course. Most courtiers set peasants one degree above cows, and somewhat below their favorite horses. They're perfectly delighted to spend a thousand of you in a skirmish with Rosya for some minor advantage on the border; they'd hardly blink at this." He waved the viciousness of it aside. "In any case, I certainly didn't expect you to succeed."

I stared at the book on the shelf under my hands. I remembered reading it, that sense of sure satisfaction, and abruptly I pulled the book off the shelf and turned to him, clutching it to my body. He eyed me warily. "Could it help Kasia?" I asked him.

He opened his mouth to deny it, I could tell; but then he hesitated. He looked at the book, frowning and silent. Finally he said, "I doubt it. But the *Summoning* is—a strange work."

"It can't hurt anything," I said, but that won me an irritated look.

"Certainly it can hurt," he said. "Didn't you listen to what I just said? The entire book must be invoked in a single sitting to make the spell, and if you haven't the strength to do it, the whole edifice of the spell will collapse, disastrously, when you exhaust yourself. I've seen it cast only once, by three witches together, each having taught the next younger, passing the book from one to another to read. It almost killed them, and they were by no means weak."

I looked down at the book, heavy and golden in my hands. I didn't doubt him. I remembered how I'd liked the taste of it on my tongue, the way it had pulled at me. I drew a deep breath and said, "Will you cast it with me?"

TEN

We chained her first. The Dragon carried down heavy iron manacles and with an incantation thrust one end of them deep into the stone walls of the chamber while Kasia—the thing inside Kasia—stood back and watched us, unblinking. I held a ring of fire around her, and when he was done, I herded her over, and with another spell he forced her arms into the manacles. She resisted, more to have the pleasure of putting us to the trouble than out of any worry, I thought—her expression remained that same inhuman blankness all along, and her eyes never left my face. She was thinner than she had been. The thing ate only sparingly. Enough to keep Kasia alive, not enough to keep me from watching her wear away, her body growing gaunt and her face hollow-cheeked.

The Dragon conjured a narrow wooden stand and set the *Summoning* upon it. He looked at me. "Are you ready?" he asked me, in stiff and formal tones. He had dressed in fine garments of silk and leather and velvet in endless layers, and he wore gloves; as though armoring himself against anything like what had happened the last time we'd cast a working together. It seemed to me as long ago as a century and as distant as the moon. I was untidy in homespun, my hair pulled into a haphazard knot just to keep it out of my eyes. I reached down and opened the cover, and began to read aloud.

The spell caught me up again almost at once, and by now I knew enough of magic to feel it drawing on my strength. But the *Summoning* didn't insist on tearing away chunks of me: I tried to feed it as I did most of my spells, with a steady measured stream of magic instead of a torrent, and it permitted me to do so. The words no longer felt so impenetrable. I still couldn't follow the story, or remember one sentence to the next, but I began to have the feeling that I wasn't meant to. If I could have remembered, at least some of the words would have been wrong: like hearing again a half-remembered favorite tale from childhood and finding it un-satisfying, or at least not as I'd remembered it. And that was how the *Summoning* made itself perfect, by living in that golden place of vague and loving memory. I let it flow through me, and when I finished the page I stopped, and let the Dragon take it up: he'd insisted grimly he would read two to my one, when I wouldn't be dissuaded from trying.

His voice sounded the words a little differently than I had, with crisper edges and less of a running rhythm, and it didn't feel quite right to me at first. The working continued to build without any difficulty as far as I could tell, and by the end of his two pages, his own reading did sound well to me after all—as though I were hear-ing a gifted storyteller tell a different version of a tale than the one I loved, and he had overcome my instinctive annoyance at hearing it told differently. But when I had to begin again myself, I struggled to pick up the thread of it, and it was a greater effort than the first page had been. We were trying to tell the story together, but pulling in different ways. I realized in dismay even as I read that it wasn't going to be enough that he was my teacher: those three witches he'd seen cast the spell must have been more like one another, in their magic and their working, than he and I were.

I kept reading, pushing onward, and I managed to reach the end of the page. When I had finished it, the story was flowing smoothly for me again—but only because it had become *my* story again, and when the Dragon began to read this time, the jarring was even worse. I swallowed against my dry parched mouth and looked up from the podium—and Kasia was looking at me from the wall where she was chained, smiling with a hideous light in her face, with *delight*. She could tell as easily as I could that it wasn't good enough—that we couldn't complete the working. I looked at the Dragon reading grimly on, intently focused on the page, his brows drawn hard together. He had warned me he would halt the working before we went too deep if he thought we couldn't succeed; he would try and collapse the spell as safely as he could, and control the damage it would do. He had only agreed to try when I had agreed to accept his judgment, and to stop my part of the working and keep out of his way if he felt it necessary to do so.

But the working was already strong, full of power. We'd both had to exert ourselves just to keep going. There might already be no safe way. I looked at Kasia's face, and remembered the feeling I'd had, that the presence in the Wood, whatever it was, was in her; that it was the *same* presence. If the Wood was here in Kasia—if it knew what we were doing, and knew that the Dragon had been injured, some great part of his strength drained—it would strike again, right away. It would come again for Dvernik, or maybe just Zatochek, settling for a smaller gain. In my desperation to save Kasia, in his pity for my grief, we had just handed the Wood a gift.

I groped for something to do, anything, and then I swallowed my own hesitation and reached out with a shaking hand to cover his where he held the page down. His eyes darted towards me, and I took a breath and began to read along.

He didn't stop, although he glared at me ferociously—*What do you think you're doing?*—but after a moment he understood and caught the idea of what I was trying to do. Our voices sounded terrible at first when we tried to bring them together, off-key and grating against each other: the working wobbled like a child's tower made of pebbles. But then I stopped trying to read *like* him and simply read *with* him instead, letting instinct guide me: I found myself letting him read the words off the page, and with my own voice almost making a song of them, choosing a single word or line to chant over again twice or three times, sometimes humming instead of words, my foot tapping to give a beat.

He resisted at first, holding for a moment to the clean precision of his own working, but my own magic was offering his an invitation, and little by little he began to read—not any less sharply, but to the beat I gave. He was leaving room for my improvisations, giving them air. We turned the page together and kept on without a pause, and halfway down the page a line flowed out of us that *was* music, his voice crisply carrying the words while I sang them along, high and low, and abruptly, shockingly, it was easy.

No—not easy; that wasn't even an adequate word. His hand had closed on mine, tightly; our fingers were interlaced, and our magic also. The spell came singing out of us, effortless as water running downhill. It would have been harder to stop than to keep going.

And I understood now why he hadn't been able to find the right words, why he hadn't been able to tell me whether the spell would help Kasia or not. The *Summoning* didn't bring forth any beast or object, or conjure up some surge of power; there was no fire or lightning. The only thing it did at all was fill the room with a clear cool light, not even bright enough to be blinding. But in that light everything began to look, to *be* different. The stone of the walls grew translucent, white veins moving like rivers, and when I gazed at them, they told me a story: a strange deep endless story unlike anything human, so much slower and farther away that it felt almost like being stone again myself. The blue fire that danced in its stone cup was in an endless dream, a song circling on itself; I looked into its flickering and saw the temple where that fire had come from, a long way from here and long since fallen into ruin. But nevertheless I knew suddenly where that temple stood, and how

I could cast that very spell and make a flame that would live on after me. The carved walls of the tomb were coming alive, the inscriptions shining. If I looked at them long enough, I would be able to read them, I was sure.

The chains were rattling. Kasia was struggling against them now, furiously, and the noise of the iron links against the wall would have been a horrible noise, if the spell had left room for it. But the scraping was muffled into a mild rattling, somewhere far away, and it didn't distract me from the spell. I didn't dare look at her, not yet. When I did—I would know. If Kasia was gone, if there was nothing left of her, I would know. I stared at the pages, too afraid to look, while we kept on chanting. He lifted each one halfway; I took it and carefully finished turning it. The sheaf of pages under my hand grew and grew, and still the spell poured out of us, and finally I lifted my head, my belly tight, to look at her.

The Wood stared back at me out of Kasia's face: an endless depth of rustling leaves, whispering hatred and longing and rage. But the Dragon paused; my hand had clenched on his. Kasia was there, too. Kasia was there. I could see her, lost and wandering in that dark forest, her hands groping ahead of her, her eyes staring without seeing as she flinched away from branches that slapped in her face, thorns that drank blood from deep scratches on her arms. She didn't even know she wasn't in the Wood anymore. She was still trapped, while the Wood tore at her little by little, drinking up her misery.

I let go of him and stepped towards her. The working didn't fail: the Dragon kept on reading, and I kept feeding my magic to the spell. "Kasia," I called, and cupped my hands before her face. The light of the spell pooled in them: a brilliant sharp terrible white light, hard to bear. I saw my own face reflected in her wide glassy eyes, and my own secret jealousies, how I *had* wanted all her gifts, if not the price she would have to pay for them. Tears crept into my eyes; it felt like Wensa haranguing me all over again, and this time there was no escape. All the times I'd felt like nothing, the girl who didn't matter, that no lord would ever want; all the times

I'd felt myself a gangly tangled mess beside her. All the ways she'd been treated specially: a place set aside for her, gifts and attention lavished, everyone taking the chance to love her while they could. There had been times I had wanted to be the special one, the one everyone knew would be chosen. Not for long, never for long, but now that seemed like cowardice: I'd enjoyed a dream of being special and nursed a secret seed of envy against her, though I'd had the luxury of putting it aside whenever I chose.

But I couldn't stop: the light was reaching her. She turned towards me. Lost in the Wood, she turned towards me, and in her face I saw her own deep anger, an anger years long. She'd known all her life she was going to be taken, whether she wanted it or not. The terror of a thousand long nights stared back out at me: with her lying in the dark, wondering what would happen to her, imagining a terrible wizard's hands on her and his breath on her cheek, and behind me I heard the Dragon draw in a sharp breath; he stumbled over the words, and halted. The light pooled in my hands flickered.

I threw a desperate look back at him, but even as I did, he took up the spell again, his voice rigidly disciplined, his eyes fixed on the page. The light shone through him entirely: as though he'd somehow made himself clear as glass, emptied himself of thought and feeling to carry on the spell. Oh, how I wanted to do that; I didn't think I could. I had to turn back to Kasia full of all my messy tangled thoughts and secret wishes, and I had to let her see them, see me, like an exposed pale squirming worm from under an overturned log. I had to see her, bare before me, and that hurt even worse: because she'd hated me, too.

She'd hated me for being safe, for being loved. My mother hadn't set me to climb too-tall trees; my mother hadn't forced me to go three hours' walk every day back and forth to the hot sticky bakery in the next town, to learn how to cook for a lord. My mother hadn't turned her back to me when I'd cried, and told me I had to be brave. My mother hadn't brushed my hair three hundred strokes a night, keeping me beautiful, as though she *wanted* me taken; as though she wanted a daughter who would go to the city, and become rich, and send back money for her brothers and sisters, the ones she let herself love—oh, I hadn't even imagined that secret bitterness, as sour as spoiled milk.

And then—and then she'd even hated me for being taken. She hadn't been chosen after all. I saw her sitting at the feast afterwards, out of place, everyone whispering; she had never imagined herself here, left behind in a village, in a house that hadn't meant to welcome her back. She'd made up her mind to pay the price, and be brave; but now there was nothing left to be brave for, no glittering future ahead. The older village boys smiled at her with a kind of strange, satisfied confidence. Half a dozen of them had spoken to her during the feast: boys who'd never said a word to her, or had only looked at her from afar as though they didn't dare to touch, now came and spoke to her familiarly, as if she had nothing to do but sit there and be chosen by someone else instead. And I'd come back in silk and velvet, my hair caught in a net of jewels, my hands full of magic, the power to do as I liked, and she'd thought, *That should be me, it should have been me*, as though I was a thief who'd taken something that belonged to her.

It was unbearable, and I saw her recoil from it, too; but somehow we had to bear it. "Kasia!" I called to her, choked out, and held the light steady for her to see. I saw her stand there hesitating a moment longer, and then she came stumbling towards me, hands reaching forward. The Wood tore at her as she came, though, branches clawing and vines tangling around her legs, and I could do nothing. I could only stand there and hold the light while she fell and struggled up again, and fell again, terror rising in her face.

"Kasia!" I cried. She was crawling now, still coming, her jaw set with determination, leaving a bloody trail on the fallen leaves and dark moss behind her. She grabbed at roots and pulled herself forward, even while the branches lashed her back, but she was still so far away.

And then I looked back up at her body, at the face inhabited by the Wood, and it smiled at me. She couldn't escape. The Wood was deliberately letting her try, feasting on her very courage, on my own hope. It could drag her back at any moment. It would let her come close enough to see me, maybe even to feel her own body, the air on her face, and then vines would spring up and lash around her, a storm of falling leaves would shroud her, and the Wood would close up around her again. I moaned a protest, and I almost lost the thread of the spell, and then the Dragon said behind me, his voice strange and remote, as though he spoke from far away, "Agnieszka, the purging. *Ulozishtus.* Try it. I can finish alone."

I carefully drew my magic back from the *Summoning,* carefully, carefully, like tipping up a bottle without letting it drip down the neck. The light held, and I whispered, *"Ulozishtus."* It was one of the Dragon's spells, not the kind that came to me easily; I didn't remember the rest of the words he'd said over me. But I let the word roll over my tongue, shaping it carefully, and remembered the feeling of it—the fire that had burned in my veins, the terrible sweetness of the potion on my tongue. *"Ulozishtus,"* I said again, drawing it out slowly, *"Ulozishtus,"* and made each syllable a small spark struck on tinder, a scrap of magic flying out. And inside the Wood, I saw a thin trail of smoke going up from one patch of the undergrowth closing around Kasia; I whispered *"Ulozishtus,"* to it, and to another thread of smoke that rose ahead of her, and when I did it to a third, a tiny struggling yellow flame bloomed near her grasping arm.

"Ulozishtus," I said to it again, giving it another bit of magic, like laying scraps of kindling to a new fire in a dead hearth. The flame grew stronger, and where it touched the vines recoiled, pulling back. *"Ulozishtus, ulozishtus,"* I chanted, feeding it, building it higher, and as it climbed I took burning branches from it and set the rest of the Wood alight.

Kasia staggered up, pulling her arms free of smoking vines, her own flesh marked pink with the heat. But she could move quicker again, and she came towards me through the smoke, through the crackling leaves, running as the trees went up, as scorching branches fell around her. Her hair was burning, and her torn clothing, tears running down her face as her skin reddened and blistered. Her body before me was jerking in the manacles, writhing in a scream of rage, and I wept and shouted, *"Ulozishtus!"* again. The fire was growing, and I knew that just as the Dragon might have killed me, purging me of the shadows, Kasia might die here now, might burn to death at my hands.

I was grateful now for the long terrible months trying to find something, anything; I was grateful for all the failures, for every minute I had spent here in this tomb with the Wood laughing at me. It gave me the strength to keep the spell going. The Dragon's voice was steady behind me, an anchor, chanting to the end of the *Summoning*. Kasia was coming nearer, and all around her the Wood was burning. I could see very little of the trees now—she was close enough that she was looking out of her own eyes, and there were flames licking at her skin, roaring, crackling. Her body arched against the stone, thrashing. Her fingers stiffened, going wide, and suddenly her veins ran brilliant green in her arms.

Drops of sap burst trickling from her eyes and nose in rivulets down her face like tears, the bright fresh sweet smell horribly wrong. Her mouth hung open in a silent round cry, and then tiny white rootlets crept out from beneath her nails, like an oak-tree growing overnight. They climbed with sudden horrible speed all over the manacles, hardening into grey wood even as they went, and with a noise like ice breaking in midsummer, the chains broke.

I did nothing. There was no time to do anything: it happened quicker than I could even see it. One moment Kasia was chained, the next she was leaping for me. She was impossibly strong, flinging me to the ground. I caught her shoulders and held her off with a scream. Sap was running from her face, staining her dress, and it fell on me with a pattering like rain. It crawled over my skin, beading up against my protection spell. Her lips peeled back from her teeth in a snarl. Her hands closed around my throat like brands, hot, burning hot, and those strangling rootlets began to crawl over me. The Dragon was chanting faster, running through the final words, racing to the end of the spell.

I strangled out, *"Ulozishtus!"* again, looking up into the Wood and into Kasia's face, twisting half in rage and half in agony, as her hands tightened. She stared down at me. The light of the *Summoning* was brightening, filling every corner of the room, impossible to evade, and we looked full into each other, every secret petty hate and jealousy laid open, and tears were mingling with the sap on her face. I was weeping, too, tears sliding from my eyes even as she pressed the air out of me and darkness started to creep in over my sight.

She said, strangled, "Nieshka," in her own voice, shuddering with determination, and one by one she forced her fingers open and away from my throat. My vision cleared, and looking into her face I saw the shame falling away. She looked at me with fierce love, with courage.

I sobbed again, once. The sap was running dry, and the fire was consuming her. The little rootlets had withered and crumbled to ash. Another purging would kill her. I knew it: I could see it. And Kasia smiled at me, because she couldn't speak again, and lowered her head in a single slow nod. I felt my own face crumpling and ugly and wretched, and then I said, *"Ulozishtus."*

I looked up into Kasia's face, hungry for one last sight of her, but the Wood looked out of her eyes at me: black rage, full of smoke, burning, roots planted too deep to uproot. Kasia still held her own hands away from my throat.

And then—the Wood was gone.

Kasia fell upon me. I screamed with joy and threw my arms around her, and she clutched at me shaking, sobbing. She was still feverish, her whole body trembling, and she vomited onto the floor even as I held her, crying weakly. Her hands hurt me: they were scorching hot and hard, and she clung to me too tight, my ribs creaking painfully under my skin. But it was her. The Dragon closed the book with a final heavy thump. The room was full of blazing light: there was nowhere for the Wood to hide. It was Kasia, and only Kasia. We had won.

ELEVEN

The Dragon was strange and silent afterwards, as we wrestled Kasia slowly and wearily up the stairs. She was almost insensible, jerking out of a daze only to claw the air before subsiding again. Her limp body was unnaturally heavy: heavy as solid oak, as though the Wood had somehow left her transmuted and changed. "Is it gone?" I said to him, desperately. "Is it gone?"

"Yes," he said shortly as we heaved her up the long spiraling stairs: even with his own peculiar strength, every step was a struggle, as though we were trying to carry a fallen log between our hands, and we were both weary. "The *Summoning* would have shown us otherwise." He said nothing more until we had taken her upstairs to the guest chamber, and then he stood by the side of the bed looking down at her, his brow drawn, and then he turned and left the room.

I had little time to think of him. Kasia lay feverish and sick for a month. She would start up half-awake and lost in nightmares, still in the Wood, and she could throw even the Dragon off her and nearly across the room. We had to tie her down in the heavy postered bed, with ropes and finally with chains. I slept curled up on the rug at the foot, leaping up to give her water whenever she cried out, and to try and press a few morsels of food into her mouth: she couldn't keep down more than a bite or two of plain bread, at first.

My days and nights ran into each other, broken with her wakings—every hour at first, and ten minutes to settle her, so I could never sleep properly, and I staggered dazed through the hours. It was only after the first week that I began to be sure she would live, and I stole a few moments to scribble a note to Wensa to let her know that Kasia was free, that she was getting well. "Will she keep it to herself?" the Dragon demanded, when I asked him to send it; and I was too drained to ask why he cared; I only opened the letter and scribbled on a line, *Tell no one yet,* and handed it to him.

I should have asked; he should have pressed me harder to be cautious. But we were both frayed like worn cloth. I didn't know what he was working on, but I saw his light burning in the library late at night, as I stumbled down to the kitchens for more broth and back up again, and loose pages covered with diagrams and inscriptions stacked into heaps on his table. One afternoon, following the smell of smoke, I found him asleep in his laboratory, the bottom of an alembic flask blackening over a candle in front of him, already run dry. He jumped when I woke him, and he knocked the whole thing over and started a fire with what for him was wholly uncharacteristic clumsiness. We had to scramble to put it out together, and his shoulders were as stiff as a cat's, disliking the insult to his dignity.

Three weeks later, though, Kasia woke after a full four hours of sleep and turned her head to me and said, "Nieshka," exhausted but herself, her dark brown eyes warm and clear. I cupped her face in my hands, smiling through tears, and she managed to close her claw-like hands around mine and smile back.

From then she began to recover quickly. Her strange new strength made her clumsy at first, even once she could stand up. She blundered into furniture and fell all the way down the stairs the first time she tried to make her own way down to the kitchens, once when I was downstairs cooking more soup. But when I whirled from the fire and flew to her calling in alarm, I found her at the foot of the stairs unhurt, not even bruised, and only struggling to get back onto her feet again.

I took her to the great hall to learn how to walk again, and tried to steady her as we went slowly around the room, although more often than not she knocked me down by accident instead. The Dragon was coming down the stairs to get something from the cellars. He stood and watched our awkward progress for a little while from the archway, his face hard and unreadable. After I got her back upstairs and she crawled carefully into bed and fell asleep again, I went down to the library to speak to him. "What's wrong with her?" I demanded.

"Nothing," the Dragon said flatly. "As far as I can tell, she is uncorrupted." He didn't sound particularly pleased.

I didn't understand. I wondered if it bothered him to have someone else staying in the tower. "She's already better," I said. "It won't be for long."

He looked at me with bright irritation. "Not for long?" he said. "What do you mean to do with her?"

I opened my mouth and shut it again. "She'll—"

"Go *home*?" the Dragon said. "Marry a farmer, if she can find one who won't mind his wife is made of wood?"

"She's still flesh, she's not made of wood!" I said, protesting, but I was already realizing, quicker than I wanted to, that he was right: there was no more place for Kasia back in our village than there was for me. I sat slowly down, my hands braced on the table. "She'll—take her dowry," I said, fumbling for some answer. "She'll have to go away—to the city, to University, like the other women—"

He had been about to speak; he paused and said, "What?"

"The other chosen ones, the other ones you took," I said, without thinking anything of it: I was too worried for Kasia: what could she do? She wasn't a witch; at least people understood what that was. She was simply changed, dreadfully, and I didn't think she could conceal it.

He broke in on my thoughts. "Tell me," he bit out, caustic, and I startled and looked up at him, "did *all* of you assume I forced myself on them?"

I only gaped at him, while he glared at me, his face hard and offended. "Yes?" I said, bewildered at first. "Yes, of course we did. Why wouldn't we? If you didn't, why wouldn't you—why *don't* you just hire a servant—" Even as I said it, I began to wonder if that other woman, the one who'd left me the letter, had been right. That he just wanted a little human company—but only a little, on his own terms; not someone who could leave him when they liked.

"Hired servants were inadequate," he said, irritable and evasive; he didn't say why. He made an impatient gesture, not looking at me; if he had seen my face, perhaps he would have stopped. "I don't take puling girls who want only to marry a village lover, or ones who cringe from me—"

I stood straight up, the chair clattering back over the floor away from me. Slow and late and bubbling, a ferocious anger had risen in me, like a flood. "So you take the ones like Kasia," I burst out, "the ones brave enough to bear it, who won't hurt their families worse by weeping, and you suppose that makes it right? You don't rape them, you only close them up for ten years, and complain that we think you worse than you are?"

He stared up at me, and I stared back, panting. I hadn't even known those words were in me to be spoken; I hadn't known they were in me to be felt. I would never have thought of speaking so to my lord, the Dragon: I had hated him, but I wouldn't have reproached him, any more than I would have reproached a bolt of lightning for striking my house. He wasn't a *person*, he was a lord and a wizard, a strange creature on another plane entirely, as far removed as storms and pestilence.

But he had stepped down from that plane; he had given me

real kindness. He'd let his magic mingle with my own again, that strange breathtaking intimacy, all to save Kasia with me. I suppose it might seem strange that I should thank him by shouting at him, but it meant more than thanks: I wanted him to be human.

"It's not right," I said loudly. "It's *not* right!"

He stood up and for a moment we faced each other across the table, both of us furious, both of us, I think, equally shocked; then he turned and walked away from me, bright angry streaks of red color in his cheeks, his hand gripping hard on the window-sill as he stared out of the tower. I flung myself out of the room and ran upstairs.

For the rest of the day, I stayed by Kasia's bedside while she slept, perched on the bed with her thin hand in mine. She was still warm and alive, but he hadn't misspoken. Her skin was soft, but beneath it her flesh was unyielding: not like stone but like a smooth-polished piece of amber, hard but flowing, with the edges rounded away. Her hair shone in the deep golden cast of the candle-glow, curling into whorls like the knots of a tree. She might have been a carved statue. I had told myself she wasn't so altered, but I knew I was wrong. My eyes were too loving: I looked and only saw Kasia. Someone who didn't know her would see a strangeness in her at once. She had always been beautiful; now she was unearthly so, preserved and shining.

She woke and looked at me. "What is it?"

"Nothing," I said. "Are you hungry?"

I didn't know what to do for her. I wondered if the Dragon would let her stay here: we could share my room, upstairs. Perhaps he would be glad of a servant who could never leave, since he disliked training a new one. It was a bitter thought, but I couldn't think of anything else. If a stranger had come into our village looking like her, we'd have thought them corrupted for sure, some new kind of monstrosity put forth by the Wood.

The next morning, I made up my mind to ask him to let her stay, despite everything. I went back to the library. He was at the window with one of his wisp-creatures floating in his hands. I stopped. Its gently undulating surface held a reflection, like a still pool of water, and when I edged around beside him I could see that it reflected not the room but trees, endless deep and dark, moving. The reflection changed gradually as we watched: showing where the wisp had been, I guessed. I held my breath as a shadow moved over the surface: a thing like a walker moving by, but smaller, and instead of the stick-like legs, it had broad silvery grey limbs, veined like leaves. It stopped and turned a strange faceless head towards the wisp. In its forelegs it held a ragged bundle of green torn-up seedlings and plants, roots trailing: for all the world like a gardener who had been weeding. It turned its head from side to side, and then continued onward into the trees, vanishing.

"Nothing," the Dragon said. "No gathering of strength, no preparations—" He shook his head. "Move back," he said over his shoulder to me. He prodded the floating wisp back outside the window, then picked up what I had imagined to be a wizard's staff from the wall, lit the end in the fireplace, and thrust it out directly into the middle of the wisp. The whole floating shimmer of it caught fire in one startling blue burst, burned up, and was gone; a faint sweet smell came through the window: like corruption.

"They can't see them?" I asked, fascinated.

"Very occasionally one doesn't come back: I imagine they catch them sometimes," the Dragon said. "But if they touch it, the sentinel only bursts." He spoke abstractly; frowning.

"I don't understand," I said. "What were you expecting? Isn't it good that the Wood isn't preparing an attack?"

"Tell me," he said, "did you think she would live?"

I hadn't, of course. It had seemed like a miracle, and one I'd longed for too badly to examine. I hadn't let myself think about it. "It let her go?" I whispered.

"Not precisely," he said. "It couldn't keep her: the *Summoning* and the purge were driving it out. But I'm certain it could have held on long enough for her to die. And the Wood is hardly inclined to be generous in such cases." He was tapping his fingers against the window-sill in a pattern that felt oddly familiar; I recognized it as the rhythm of our *Summoning* chant at the same time he did. He stilled his hand at once. He demanded stiffly, "Is she recovered?"

"She's better," I said. "She climbed all the stairs this morning. I've put her in my room—"

He made a dismissive flick of his hand. "I thought her recovery might have been meant as a distraction," he said. "If she's already well—" He shook his head.

After a moment, his shoulders went back and squared. He dropped his hand from the sill and turned to face me. "Whatever the Wood intends, we've lost enough time," he said, grimly. "Get your books. We need to begin your lessons again."

I stared at him. "Stop gaping at me," he said. "Do you even understand what we've done?" He gestured to the window. "That wasn't by any means the only sentinel I sent out. Another of them found the heart-tree that had held the girl. It was highly notable," he added dryly, "because it was *dead*. When you burned the corruption out of the girl's body, you burned the tree itself, too."

Even then, I still didn't understand his grimness, and still less when he went on. "The walkers have already torn it down and replanted a seedling, but if it were winter instead of spring, if the clearing had been closer to the edges of the Wood—if we'd only been prepared, we might have gone in with a party of axemen, to clear and burn back the Wood all the way to that clearing."

"Can we—" I blurted out, shocked, and couldn't quite make myself even put the idea into words.

"Do it again?" he said. "Yes. Which means that the Wood must make an answer, and *soon*."

I began finally to catch his urgency. It was like his worry about Rosya, I suddenly understood: we were in a war against the Wood as well, and our enemy knew that we now had a new weapon we might turn against them. He'd been expecting the Wood to attack not simply for revenge, but to defend itself.

"There's a great deal of work to do before we can hope to repeat the effects," he added, and gestured to the table, littered with still more pages. I looked at them properly and realized for the first time that they were notes about the working—our working. There was a sketched diagram: the two of us reduced to blank figures at the farthest possible corners of the *Summoning* tome, Kasia opposite us reduced to a circle and labeled CHANNEL, and a line drawn back to a neatly rendered picture of a heart-tree. He tapped the line.

"The channel will offer the greatest difficulty. We can't expect to conveniently obtain a victim ripped straight out of a heart-tree on every occasion. However, a captured walker might serve instead, or even a victim of lesser corruption—"

"Jerzy," I said suddenly. "Could we try it with Jerzy?"

The Dragon paused and pressed his lips together, annoyed. "Possibly," he said.

"First, however," he added, "we must codify the principles of the spell, and you need to practice each separate component. I believe it falls into the category of fifth-order workings, wherein the *Summoning* provides the frame, the corruption itself provides the channel, and the purging spell provides the impulse—do you remember absolutely nothing I've taught you?" he demanded, seeing me bite my lip.

It was true I hadn't bothered to remember much of his insisted-on lessons about the orders of spells, which were mostly for explaining why certain spells were more difficult than others. As far as I could see, it all came down to the obvious: if you put together two workings to make a new spell, usually it would be harder than either one of those alone; but beyond that, I didn't find the rules very useful. If you put together *three* workings, it would be harder than any one of them alone, but at least when I tried it, that didn't mean it would be harder than either *two:* it all depended on what you were trying to do, and in what order. And his rules didn't have anything to do with had happened down there in the chamber.

I didn't want to speak of it, and I knew he didn't, either. But I thought of Kasia, struggling towards me while the Wood tore at her; and of Zatochek, on the edge of the Wood, one attack away from being swallowed. I said, "None of that matters, and you know it."

His hand tightened on the papers, crumpling pages, and for a moment I thought he would start to shout at me. But he stared down at them and didn't say a word. After a moment, I went for my spellbook and dug out the illusion spell we'd cast together, in winter, all those long months ago. Before Kasia.

I pushed away the heap of papers enough to clear some room before us, and set the book down in front of me. After a moment, without a word, he went and took another volume off the shelf: a narrow black book, whose cover glimmered faintly where he touched it. He opened it to a spell covering two pages, written in crisp letters, with a diagram of a single flower and every part of it attached to a syllable of the spell somehow. "Very well," he said. "Let's begin." And he held his hand out to me across the table.

It was harder to take it this time, to make that deliberate choice, without the useful distraction of desperation. I couldn't help but think about the strength of his clasp, the long graceful lines of his fingers closed around my hand, the warm callused tips brushing my wrist. I could feel his pulse beating against my own fingers, and the heat of his skin. I stared down at my book and tried to make sense of the letters, my cheeks hot, while he began to cast his own spell, his voice clipped. His illusion started taking shape, another single perfectly articulated flower, fragrant and beautiful and thoroughly opaque, and the stem nearly covered in thorns.

I began in a whisper. I was trying desperately not to think, not to feel his magic against my skin. Nothing whatsoever happened. He didn't say anything to me: his eyes were fixed determinedly on a point above my head. I stopped and gave myself a private shake. Then I shut my eyes and felt out the shape of his magic: as full of thorns as his illusion, prickly and guarded. I started to murmur my own spell, but I found myself thinking not of roses but of water, and thirsty ground; building underneath his magic instead of trying to overlay it. I heard him draw a sharp breath, and the sharp edifice of his spell began grudgingly to let mine in. The rose between us put out long roots all over the table, and new branches began to grow.

It wasn't the jungle of the first time we'd cast the spell: he was holding back his magic, and so was I, both of us letting only a thin stream of power feed the working. But the rosebush took on a different kind of solidity. I couldn't tell it was an illusion anymore, the long ropy roots twisting together, putting fingers into the cracks of the table, winding around the legs. The blossoms weren't just the picture of a rose, they were real roses in a forest, half of them not open yet, the other half blown, petals scattering and browning at the edges. The thick fragrance filled the air, too sweet, and as we held it, a bee came hovering in through the window and crept into one of the flowers, prodding it determinedly. When it couldn't get any nectar out, it tried another, and another, small legs scrabbling at the petals, which gave way exactly as if they could bear the weight of a bee.

"You won't get anything here," I told the hovering bee, and blew at it, but it only tried again.

The Dragon had stopped staring over my head, any awkwardness falling before his passion for magic: he was studying our twined spells with the same fierce intent look he bent on his most complicated workings, the light of the spell bright in his face and his eyes; he was hungry to understand. "Can you hold it alone?" he demanded.

"I think so," I said, and he slowly eased his hand from mine, leaving me to keep up the wild sprawling rosebush. Without the rigid frame of his casting, it half-wanted to collapse like a vine with its trellis gone, but I found I could keep hold of his magic: just a corner of it, enough to be a skeleton, and feeding the spell more of my own magic to make up for its weakness.

He reached down and turned a few pages of his book until he came to another spell, this to make an insect illusion, as diagrammed as the flower one had been. He spoke quickly, the spells rolling off his tongue, and made half a dozen bees and set them loose on the rosebush, which only confused our first bee-visitor further. As he made each one, he—gave them to me, with a kind of small push; I managed to catch them and hook them into the rosebush working. Then he said, "What I intend to do now is attach the watching spell to them. The one the sentinels carry," he added.

I nodded even while I concentrated on holding the spell: what could more easily pass unnoticed in the Wood than a simple bee? He turned to the far-back pages of the book, to a sheaf of spells written in his own hand. As he began the working, though, the weight of the spell came heavily down on the bee illusions, and on me. I held them, struggling, feeling my magic draining too quickly to replenish, until I managed to make a wordless noise of distress, and he looked up from the working and reached towards me.

I grabbed back at him just as incautiously with my hand and my magic both, even as he pressed magic on me from his side as well. His breath huffed out sharply, and our workings caught on one another, magic gushing into them. The rosebush began growing again, roots crawling off the table and vines climbing out the window. The bees became a humming swarm amid the flowers, each of them with oddly glittering eyes, wandering away. If I had caught one in my hands and looked closely, I would have seen in those eyes the reflection of all the roses it had touched. But I had no room in my head for bees, or roses, or spying; no room for anything but magic, the raw torrent of it and his hand my only rock, except he was being tumbled right along with me.

I felt his shocked alarm. By instinct I pulled him with me towards where the magic was running thinner, as though I really was in a rising river, striking out for a shore. Together we managed to drag ourselves out. The rosebush dwindled little by little down to a single bloom; the false bees climbed into flowers as they closed, or simply dissolved into the air. The final rose closed itself up and vanished, and we both sat down on the floor heavily, our hands still entangled. I didn't know what had happened: he'd told me often enough of the dangers of not having enough magic for a spell, but he'd never before mentioned the risk of having too much. When I turned to demand an answer, he had his head tipped back against the shelves, his eyes as alarmed as my own, and I realized he didn't know any more than I did what had happened.

"Well," I said after a moment, inconsequentially, "I suppose it did *work*." He stared at me, outrage dawning, and I started laughing, helplessly, almost snorting: I was dizzy with magic and alarm.

"You intolerable lunatic," he snarled at me, and then he caught my face between his hands and kissed me.

I didn't properly think about what was happening even as I kissed him back, my laughter spilling into his mouth and making stutters of my kisses. I was still bound up with him, our magic snarled up into great messy tangled knots. I didn't have anything to compare that intimacy to. I'd felt the hot embarrassment of it, but I'd thought of it vaguely like being naked in front of a stranger. I hadn't connected it to sex—sex was poetic references in songs, my mother's practical instructions, and those few awful hideous moments in the tower with Prince Marek, where I might as well have been a rag doll as far as he'd cared.

But now I toppled the Dragon over, clutching at his shoulders. As we fell his thigh pressed between mine, through my skirts, and in one shuddering jolt I began to form a startled new understanding. He groaned, his voice gone deep, and his hands were sliding into my hair, freeing the loose knot around my shoulders. I held on to him with my hands and my magic both, half-shocked and half-delighted. His lean hardness, the careful art of his velvet and silk and leather lush and crumpling under my fingers, suddenly meant something entirely different. I was in his lap, astride his hips, and his body was hot against mine; his hands came gripping almost painfully tight on my thighs through the dress.

I leaned down over him and kissed him again, in a wonderful place full of uncomplicated yearning. My magic, his magic, were all one. His hand slid along my leg, up beneath my skirts, and his deft, skillful thumb stroked once over me between my legs. I made a small startled huff of noise, like I'd been shocked in winter. An involuntary glittering raced over my hands and over his body, like sunlight on a moving river, and all the endless smooth buckles running down the front of his jerkin opened themselves up and slid free, and the lacings of his shirt came undone.

I still hadn't quite realized what I was doing until then, with my hands on his bare chest. Or rather, I'd only let myself think far enough ahead to get what I wanted, and I hadn't let myself put that into words. But I couldn't avoid understanding now, with him so shockingly undone beneath me. Even the lacings of his trousers were open: I felt them loose against my thighs. He could push aside my skirts, and—

My cheeks were hot, desperate. I wanted him, I wanted to drag myself away and run, and most of all I wanted to know which of those things I wanted more. I froze and stared at him, wide-eyed, and he stared back at me, more undone than I'd ever seen him, high color in his face and his hair disheveled, his clothes hanging open off him, equally astonished and almost outraged. And then he said, half under his breath, "What am I doing?" and he caught my wrists away from him and heaved us both back to our feet.

I stumbled back and caught myself against the table, torn between relief and regret. He turned away from me already jerking his laces tight, his back straightening into a long stiff line. The unraveled threads of my magic were gradually coiling back into my skin, and his slipping away from me; I pressed my hands to my hot cheeks. "I didn't mean—" I blurted, and stopped; I didn't know what I hadn't meant.

"Yes, that's patently obvious," he snapped over his shoulder. He was buckling his jerkin shut over his open shirt. "Get out."

I fled.

In my room, Kasia was sitting up in bed, grimly struggling with my mending-basket: there were three broken needles on the table, and she was only with enormous difficulty making long sloppy stitches in a spare scrap.

She looked up as I came running in: my cheeks still red and my clothing disheveled, panting like I'd come from a race. "Nieshka!" she said, dropping the sewing as she stood up. She took a step and reached for my hands, but hesitated: she had learned to be afraid of her own strength. "Are you—did he—"

"No!" I said, and I didn't know if I was glad or sorry. The only magic in me now was mine, and I sat down on the bed with an unhappy thump.

TWELVE

I wasn't granted any time to contemplate the situation. That very night, only a little past midnight, Kasia jerked up next to me and I nearly fell out of the bed. The Dragon was standing in the doorway of the room, his face unreadably stiff, a light glowing in his hand; he wore his nightshift and a dressing-gown. "There are soldiers on the road," he said. "Get dressed." He turned and left without another word.

We both scrambled up and into our clothes and went pell-mell down the stairs to the great hall. The Dragon was at the window, dressed now. I could see the riders in the distance, a large company: two lanterns on long poles in the lead, one more in the back, light glinting off harness and mail, and two outriders leading a string of spare horses behind them. They were carrying two banners at the front, a small round globe of white magic before each one: a green three-headed beast like a dragon, on white, Prince Marek's crest, and behind it a crest of a red falcon with its talons outstretched.

"Why are they coming?" I whispered, although they were too far away to hear.

The Dragon didn't answer at once; then he said, "For her."

I reached out and gripped Kasia's hand tight in the dark. "Why?"

"Because I'm corrupted," Kasia said. The Dragon nodded slightly. They were coming to put Kasia to death.

Too late I remembered my letter: no answer had come, and I had forgotten even sending it. I learned some time after that Wensa had gone home and fallen into a sick stupor after leaving the tower. Another woman visiting her bedside opened the letter, supposedly as a kindness, and she'd carried the gossip of it everywhere: the news that we had brought someone out of the Wood. It traveled to the Yellow Marshes; it traveled to the capital, carried by bards, and there it brought Prince Marek down upon us.

"Will they believe you that she's not corrupted?" I said to the Dragon. "They must believe you—"

"As you may recall," he said dryly, "I have an unfortunate reputation in these matters." He glanced out the window. "And I doubt the Falcon has come all this way only to agree with me."

I turned to look at Kasia, whose face was calm and unnaturally still, and I drew a breath and caught her hands. "I won't let them," I told her. "I won't."

The Dragon made an impatient snort. "Do you plan to blast them, and a troop of the king's soldiers besides? And what after that—run to the mountains and be outlaws?"

"If I have to!" I said, but the press of Kasia's fingers on mine made me turn; she shook her head at me a little.

"You can't," she said. "You can't, Nieshka. Everyone needs you. Not just me."

"Then you'll go to the mountains alone," I said defiantly. I felt like an animal penned up, hearing the butchering-knife on the whetstone. "Or I'll take you, and come back—" The horses were so near I could hear the drumming of their hooves over the sound of my own voice.

Time ran out. We didn't. I gripped Kasia's hand in my own as we stood in a half-alcove of the Dragon's great hall. He sat in his chair, his face hard and remote and glittering, and waited: we heard the noise of the carriage rolling to a halt, the horses stamping and snorting, men's voices muffled by the heavy doors. There was a pause; the knock I expected didn't come, and after a moment I felt the slow insinuating creep of magic, a spell taking shape on the other side of the doors, trying to grasp them and force them open. It prodded and poked at the Dragon's working, trying to pry it up, and then abruptly a hard fast blow came: a shove of magic that tried to break through his grip. The Dragon's eyes and mouth tightened briefly, and a faint crackling of blue light traveled over the doors, but that was all.

Finally the knock came, the hard pounding of a mailed fist. The Dragon crooked a finger and the doors swung inward: Prince Marek stood on the threshold, and beside him another man, who despite being half as wide across managed to be an equal presence. He was draped in a long white cloak, patterned in black like the markings of a bird's wings, and his hair was the color of washed sheep's wool but with roots of black, as though he'd bleached it. The cloak spilled back from one shoulder, and his clothes beneath were in silver and black; his face was carefully arranged: *sorrowful concern* written on it like a book. They made a portrait together, sun and moon framed in the doorway with the light behind them, and then Prince Marek stepped into the tower, drawing off his gauntlets.

"All right," he said. "You know why we're here. Let's see the girl."

The Dragon didn't say a word, only gestured towards Kasia, where she and I stood a little concealed. Marek turned and fixed on her at once, his eyes narrowing with a speculative light. I glared at him fiercely, though he didn't get any benefit of it: he didn't have so much as a glance for me.

"Sarkan, what have you done?" the Falcon said, advancing on the Dragon's seat. His voice was a clear tenor, ringing, like a fine actor's: it filled the whole room with regretful accusation. "Have you grown completely lost to all sense, hiding yourself out here in the hinterlands—"

The Dragon was still in his chair, leaning his head against his fist. "Tell me something, Solya," he said, "did you consider what you would find here in my hall, if I really *had* let one of the corrupted out?"

The Falcon paused, and the Dragon rose deliberately from his chair. The hall darkened around him with sudden, frightening speed, shadows creeping over and swallowing the tall candles, the shining magical lights. He came down from the dais, each step striking like the deep terrible ring of some great bell, one after another. Prince Marek and the Falcon backed away involuntarily; the prince gripped the hilt of his sword. "If I had fallen to the Wood," the Dragon said, "what did you imagine you would do, here in my tower?"

The Falcon had already brought his hands together, thumb and forefingers in a triangle; he was murmuring under his breath. I felt the hum of his magic building, and thin sparkling lines of light began to flicker across the space framed by his hands. They went faster and faster, until all that triangle caught, and as if that had provided an igniting spark, a halo of white fire went up to wreath his body. He spread his hands apart, the fire sizzling and crackling over them, sparks falling like rain to the ground, as if he was making ready to throw. The working had the same hungry feeling as the fire-heart in its bottle, as if it wanted to devour the very air.

"*Triozna greszhni*," the Dragon said, the words slicing out, and the flames went out like guttering candles: a cold sharp wind whistled through the hall, chilling my skin, and was gone.

They stared at him, halted—and then the Dragon spread his arms in a wide shrug. "Fortunately," the Dragon said, in his ordinary cutting tones, "I haven't been nearly as stupid as you imagined. Much to your good fortune." He turned and went back to his chair, the shadows retreating from his feet, spilling back. The light returned. I could see the Falcon's face clearly: he didn't seem to feel particularly thankful. His face was as still as ice, his mouth pressed into a straight line.

I suppose he was tired of being thought the second wizard of Polnya. I had even heard of him a little—he was often named in songs about the war with Rosya—although of course in our valley the bards didn't talk overmuch about another wizard. We wanted to hear stories about the Dragon, about *our* wizard, proprietary, and we took pride and satisfaction in hearing, yet again, that he was the most powerful wizard of the nation. But I hadn't thought before what that really meant, and I had forgotten to fear him, from too much time spent too close. It was a forcible reminder now, watching how easily he smothered the Falcon's magic, that he was a great power in the world who could make even kings and other wizards fear.

Prince Marek, I could tell, liked that reminder as little as the Falcon had; his hand lingered on his sword-hilt, and there was a hardness in his face. But he looked at Kasia again. I flinched and made an abortive grab for her arm as she stepped away from me, out of the alcove, and went to him across the floor. I swallowed the warning I wanted to hiss, too late, as she made him a curtsy, her golden head bowed. She straightened up and looked him full in the face: exactly as I had tried to imagine doing myself, all those long months ago. She didn't stammer. "Sire," she said, "I know you must doubt me. I know I look strange. But it's true: I am free."

There were spells running in the back of my head, a litany of desperation. If he drew his sword against her—if the Falcon tried to strike her down—

Prince Marek looked at her: his face was hard and downturned, intent. "You were in the Wood?" he demanded.

She inclined her head. "The walkers took me."

"Come look at her," he said over his shoulder, to the Falcon.

"Your Highness," the Falcon began, coming to his side. "It is plain to any—"

"Stop," the prince said, his voice sharp as a knife. "I don't like him any better than you do, but I didn't bring you here for politics. *Look* at her. Is she corrupted or not?"

The Falcon paused, frowning; he was taken aback. "One held overnight in the Wood is invariably—"

"Is she corrupted?" the prince said to him, every word bitten out crisp and hard. Slowly the Falcon turned and looked at Kasia— really looked at her, for the first time, and his brow slowly gathered with confusion. I looked at the Dragon, hardly daring to hope and hoping anyway: if they were willing to listen—

But the Dragon wasn't looking at me, or at Kasia. He was looking at the prince, and his face was grim as stone.

The Falcon began testing her at once. He demanded potions from the Dragon's stores and books from his shelves, all of which the Dragon sent me running after, without argument. The Dragon ordered me to stay in the kitchens the rest of the time; I thought at first that he meant to spare me watching the trials, some of them as dreadful as the breath-stealing magic he had used on me after I had come back from the Wood. Even in the kitchens, I could hear the chanting and the crackle of the Falcon's magic running overhead. It sounded in my bones, like a large drum played far away.

But the third morning I caught sight of myself in the side of one of the big copper kettles and noticed I was an untidy mess: I hadn't thought to mutter up some clean clothes for myself, not with the rumbling above and all my worry for Kasia. I didn't wonder that I'd accumulated spots, stains, tears, and I didn't mind it, either; but the Dragon hadn't said anything. He'd come down to the kitchens more than once, to tell me what to go and fetch. I stared at the reflection, and the next time he came down I blurted, "Are you keeping me out of the way?"

He paused, not even off the bottom step, and said, "Of course I'm keeping you out of the way, you idiot."

"But he doesn't remember," I said, meaning Prince Marek. It came out an anxious question.

"He will, given half a chance," the Dragon said. "It matters too much to him. Keep out of the way, behave like an ordinary serving-girl, and don't use magic anywhere he or Solya can see you."

"Kasia's all right?"

"As well as anyone would be," he said. "Make that the least of your concerns: she's a good deal harder to harm now than an ordinary person, and Solya isn't egregiously stupid. In any case, he knows very well what the prince wants, and all being equal he'd prefer to give it to him. Go get three bottles of milk of fir."

Well, I didn't know what the prince wanted, and I didn't like the idea of him getting it, either, whatever it was. I went up to the laboratory for the milk of fir: it was a potion the Dragon brewed out of fir needles, which somehow under his handling became a milky liquid without scent, although the one time he'd tried to teach me to do it, I'd produced only a wet stinking mess of fir needles and water. Its virtue was to fix magic in the body: it went into every healing potion and into the stone-skin potion. I brought the bottles down to the great hall.

Kasia stood in the center of the room, inside an elaborate double ring drawn on the floor in herbs crushed in salt. They had put a heavy collar around her neck like a yoke for oxen, of black-pitted iron engraved with spell-writing in bright silvery letters, with chains that hung from it to her manacled wrists. She didn't have so much as a chair to sit on, and it should have bowed her double, but she stood straight up underneath it, easily. She gave me a small smile when I came into the room: *I'm all right.*

The Falcon looked more weary than she did, and Prince Marek was rubbing his face through an enormous yawn, though he was only sitting in a chair watching. "Over there," the Falcon said in my direction, waving a hand to his heaped worktable, paying me no more attention than that. The Dragon sat on his high seat, and threw me a sharp look when I hesitated. Mutinous, I put the bottles on the table, but I didn't leave the room: I retreated to the doorway and watched.

The Falcon infused spells of purification into the bottles, three different ones. He worked with a kind of sharp directness: where the Dragon folded magic into endless intricacies, the Falcon drew a straight line across. But his magic worked in the same sort of way: it seemed to me he was only choosing a different road of many, not wandering in the trees as I did. He handed the bottles across the line to Kasia with a pair of iron tongs: he seemed to have grown more rather than less cautious as he went along. Each one glowed through her skin as she drank it, and the glow lingered, held; by the time she had drunk all three, she lit up the whole room. There was no hint of shadow in her, no small feathery strand of corruption lingering.

The prince sat slouched in his chair, a large goblet of wine at his elbow, careless and easy, but I noticed now that the wine was untouched, and his eyes never left Kasia's face. It made my hands itch to reach for magic: I would have gladly slapped his face just to keep him from looking at her.

The Falcon stared at her a long time, and then he took a blind-fold out of a pocket of his doublet and tied it over his eyes: thick black velvet ornamented with silver letters, large enough that it covered his forehead. He murmured something as he put it on; the letters glowed, and then an eyehole opened in the mask just over the center of his forehead. A single eye was looking out of it: large and oddly shaped, roundish, the ring around the enormous pupil dark enough to make it seem almost entirely black, shot through with small flickers of silver. He came to the very edge of the circle and stared at Kasia with it: up and down, and walking in a circle around her three times.

At last he stepped back. The eye closed, then the eyehole, and he raised shaking arms to take off the blindfold, fumbling at the knot. He took it off. I couldn't help staring at his forehead: there wasn't any sign of another eye there, or any mark at all, although his own eyes were badly bloodshot. He sat down heavily into his chair.

"Well?" the prince said, sharply.

The Falcon said nothing for a moment. "I can find no signs of corruption," he said finally, grudging. "I won't swear there is none present—"

The prince wasn't listening. He'd stood up and picked up a heavy key from the table. He crossed the room to Kasia. The shining light was fading from her body, but it had not yet gone; his boots smeared the ring of salt open as he crossed it and unlocked the heavy collar and the manacles. He lifted them off her and to the ground, and then held out his hand, as courtly as if she were a noblewoman, his eyes devouring her. Kasia hesitated—I knew she was worried she would break his hand by accident; myself, I hoped she *would*—and carefully put her hand in his.

He gripped it tight and turning led her forward, to the foot of the Dragon's dais. "And now, Dragon," he said softly, "you will tell us how this was done," with a shake of Kasia's arm, raised up in his own. "And then we will go into the Wood: the Falcon and I, if you're too much a coward to come with us, and we will *bring my mother out*."

THIRTEEN

"I'm not going to give you a sword to fall on," the Dragon said. "If that's what you insist on doing, you can do so with considerably less damage to anyone else by using the one you already have."

Prince Marek's shoulders clenched, the muscles around his neck knotting visibly; he let go of Kasia's hand and took a step onto the dais. The Dragon's face stayed cold and unyielding. I think the prince would have struck him, gladly, but the Falcon pushed himself up from his chair. "I beg your pardon, Your Highness, there's no need for this. If you recall the enchantment I used in Kyeva, when we captured General Nichkov's camp—that will serve just as well here. It will show me how the spell was done." He smiled at the Dragon without teeth, lips drawn tight. "I think Sarkan will admit that even he can't hide things from *my* sight."

The Dragon didn't deny it, but bit out, "I'll admit that you're a far more extravagant fool than I gave you credit for being, if you intend to lend yourself to this lunacy."

"I would hardly call it *extravagant* to make every reasonable attempt to rescue the queen," the Falcon said. "We've all bowed our heads to your wisdom before now, Sarkan: there was certainly no sense in taking risks to bring out the queen only to have to put her to death. Yet now here we are," he gestured to Kasia, "with evidence of another possibility plain before us. Why have you been concealing it so long?"

Just like that, when the Falcon had so plainly come here in the first place expressly to insist that there *was* no other possibility, and to condemn the Dragon for letting Kasia live at all! I nearly gawked at him, but he showed not the least consciousness of having altered his position. "If there is any hope for the queen, I would call it treason not to make the attempt," the Falcon added. "What was done, can be done again."

The Dragon snorted. "By you?"

Well, even I could tell that was hardly the way to induce the Falcon to hesitate. His eyes narrowed, and he turned coldly and said to the prince, "I will retire now, Your Highness; I must recover my strength before I cast the enchantment in the morning."

Prince Marek dismissed him with a wave of his hand: I saw to my alarm that while I'd been busy watching the sparring, he had been speaking to Kasia, gripping her hand in both of his. Her face still had that unnatural stillness, but I had learned to read it well enough by now to see that she was troubled.

I was about to go to her rescue when he let her hand go and left the hall himself, a quick wide stride, the heels of his boots ringing on the steps as he went upstairs. Kasia came to me, and I caught her hand in mine. The Dragon was scowling at the stairs, his fingers drumming on the arm of his chair in irritation.

"Can he do it?" I asked him. "Can he see how the spell was done?"

Drum, drum, drum, went his fingers. "Not unless he finds the tomb," the Dragon said finally. After a moment he added grudgingly, "Which he may be able to do: he has an affinity for sight magic. But then he'll have to find a way into it. I imagine it will take him a few weeks, at least; long enough for me to get a message to the king, and I hope forestall this nonsense."

He waved me away, and I was glad to go, pulling Kasia all the way up the stairs behind me with a wary eye on the turning up ahead. At the second landing I put my head out and made sure neither the prince nor the Falcon was in the hallway any longer before I drew Kasia across it, and when we came to my room I told her to wait outside until I had flung the door open and looked in: empty. I let her in and shut and barred the door behind us, and pushed a chair beneath the doorknob. I would have liked to seal it with magic, if the Dragon hadn't warned me against using spells, but as little as I wanted another visit from Prince Marek, I wanted him to remember what had really happened in the last one even less. I didn't know if the Falcon could notice it if I cast a tiny spell of closing up here in my room, but I had felt *his* magic from the kitchens, so I didn't mean to take chances.

I turned to Kasia: she was sitting on the bed heavily. Her back was straight—it was always straight now—but her hands were pressed flat together in her lap, and her head was bowed forward. "What did he say to you?" I demanded, a shudder of anger building in my belly, but Kasia shook her head.

"He asked me to help him," she said. "He said he would speak to me again tomorrow." She lifted her head and looked at me. "Nieshka, you saved me—*could* you save Queen Hanna?"

For a moment I was in the Wood again, deep beneath the branches, the weight of its hatred pressing on me and shadows creeping into me with every breath. Fear closed my throat. But I thought also of *fulmia*, rolling like thunder deep in my belly; of Kasia's face and another tree grown tall, a face under the bark softened and blurred by twenty years of growth, vanishing like a statue under running water.

The Dragon was in his library, writing and irritated, and not less so when I came down and asked him the same question. "Try not to borrow more folly than you already possess," he said. "Are you still incapable of recognizing a trap? This is the Wood's doing."

"You think the Wood has—Prince Marek?" I asked, wondering if that would explain it; if that was why he'd—

"Not yet it doesn't," the Dragon said. "But he'll hand himself over and a wizard to boot: a magnificent trade for a peasant girl, and how much the better if you threw yourself in as well! The Wood will plant heart-trees in you and Solya, and swallow the valley in a week. *That's* why it let her go."

But I remembered that ferocious resistance. "It didn't let her go!" I said. "It didn't *let* me take her—"

"To a point," he said. "The Wood might have done whatever it could to preserve a heart-tree, exactly as a general would to preserve a stronghold. But once the tree was lost—and it was surely already too far gone, whether the girl lived or died—then of course it would try to find a way to turn the loss to good account."

We wrangled it back and forth. It wasn't that I thought he was wrong; it seemed exactly the twisted sort of thing the Wood would do, turning love into a weapon. But that didn't mean, I thought, that it wasn't a chance worth taking. Freeing the queen could end the war with Rosya, could strengthen both nations, and if we destroyed another heart-tree in doing it, might be the chance to break the power of the Wood for a long time.

"Yes," he said, "and if a dozen angels would only sweep down from above and lay waste to the entire Wood with flaming swords, the situation would be infinitely improved as well."

I huffed in annoyance and went for the big ledger: I thumped it down on the table between us and opened it to the last pages, full of entries in his careful narrow hand, and put my hands down on it. "It's been *winning*, hasn't it, with all you can do?" His cold silence was enough answer. "We can't wait. We can't keep the secret of this locked up in the tower, waiting until we're perfectly ready. If the Wood is trying to strike, we should strike back, and quickly."

"There's a considerable distance between seeking perfection and irretrievable haste," he said. "What you really mean is you've heard too many clandestine ballads of the sad lost queen and the grief-stricken king, and you think you're living in one of them with the chance to be the hero of the piece. What do you think will even be left of her, after twenty years being gnawed by a heart-tree?"

"More than will be left after twenty and one!" I flared back at him.

"And if there's enough left of her to know when they put her child into the tree with her?" he said, unsparing, and the horror of the thought silenced me.

"That is my concern, and not yours," Prince Marek said. We both jerked around from the table: he was standing in the doorway, silent on bare feet in his nightshift. He looked at me, and I could see the spell of false memory crumbling: he remembered me, and abruptly I, too, remembered the way his face had changed when I'd used magic in front of him, his voice when he'd said, "You're a *witch*." All along, he'd been looking for someone who would help him.

"You did this, didn't you?" he said to me, his eyes gleaming. "I should have known this desiccated old serpent would never have put his neck out, even for so lovely a piece of work. *You* freed that girl."

"We—" I stammered, darting a desperate look at the Dragon, but Marek snorted.

He came into the library, came towards me. I could see the faint scar at his hairline, where I'd battered him senseless with the heavy tray; there was a tiger of magic in my belly, ready to come out roaring. But my chest still seized up with involuntary fear. My breath came short as he neared me: if he'd come closer, if he'd touched me, I think I would have screamed—some kind of curse: a dozen of Jaga's nastier ones were flitting through my head like fireflies, waiting to be snatched up by my tongue.

But he stopped at arm's length and only leaned towards me. "That girl's condemned, you know," he said, looking at my face.

"The king takes a dim view of letting wizards claim they've cleansed the corrupted: too many of them turn up corrupted themselves in no short order. The law says she must be put to death, and the Falcon certainly won't testify on her behalf."

I betrayed myself and knew it, but I couldn't help flinching anyway. "Help me save the queen," he added, soft and sympathetic, "and you'll save the girl into the bargain: once the king has my mother back, he can't fail to spare them both."

I understood perfectly well that it was a threat, not a bribe: he was telling me he'd have Kasia put to death if I refused. I hated him even more, and yet at the same time I couldn't hate him entirely. I had lived three dreadful months with that desperation scrabbling at me from inside; he'd lived with it since he was a child, mother torn from him, told she was gone and worse than dead and forever beyond his reach. I didn't feel sorry for him, but I understood him.

"And once the world is spun the other way around, the sun can't fail to rise in the west," the Dragon snapped. "The only thing you'd accomplish is to get yourself killed, and her with you."

The prince wheeled to face him and struck the table between them with his clenched fists, a rattling thump of candlesticks and books. "And yet you'd save some useless peasant while you leave the queen of Polnya to rot?" he snarled, the veneer cracking. He stopped and drew a deep breath, forcing his mouth back into a parody of a smile that wavered in and out on his lips. "You go too far, Dragon; even my brother won't listen to all your whispering counsels after this. For years we've swallowed everything you've told us about the Wood—"

"Since you doubt me, take your men with you and go inside," the Dragon hissed back. "See for yourself."

"I will," Prince Marek said. "And I'll take this witch-girl of yours, and your lovely peasant, too."

"You'll take no one who doesn't wish to go," the Dragon said. "Since you were a child, you've imagined yourself a hero out of legend—"

"Better than a deliberate coward," the prince said, grinning at him with all his teeth, violence like a living thing in the room taking shape between them, and before the Dragon could answer, I blurted out, "What if we could weaken the Wood *before* we went in?" and they broke their locked gaze and looked at me, startled, where I stood.

Krystyna's weary face went wide and frozen when she looked past me and saw the crowd of men and wizards, gleaming armor and stamping horses. I said softly, "We're here about Jerzy." She gave a jerky nod without looking at me, and backed into the house to let me in.

Knitting lay on the rocking chair, and the baby was sleeping in a cot by the fireplace: big and healthy and ruddy-faced, with a gnawed wooden rattle clutched in one fist. I went to look at it, of course. Kasia came in behind me and looked over at the cradle. I almost called her over, but she turned away, keeping her face out of the firelight, and I didn't speak. Krystyna didn't need any more to fear. She huddled into the corner with me, darting looks over my shoulder as the Dragon came in, and she told me in a bare whisper that the baby's name was Anatol. Her voice died at Prince Marek ducking into the cottage, and the Falcon with his cloak of brilliant white, which showed not a speck of dirt. None of them paid the least attention to the baby, or to Krystyna herself. "Where's the corrupted man?" the prince said.

Krystyna whispered to me, "He's in the barn. We put him in the—I thought to have the room back, we didn't want—I didn't mean any harm—"

She didn't need to explain why she hadn't wanted that tormented face in her house, every night. "It's all right," I said. "Krystyna, Jerzy might—what we can try, it might not—it will work. But he might die of it."

Her hands were gripping the side of the cradle, but she only nodded a little. I think he was already gone in her mind by then: as though he'd been at a battle that had been lost, and she only waited to hear the final word.

We went outside. Seven small rooting pigs and their big-bellied mother looked up snuffling incuriously at our horses from a new-built pen by the side of the house, the wood of the fence still pale brown and unweathered. We rode around it and single-file down a narrow path through the trees, already almost overgrown, to the small grey barn. It stood in tall grass full of eager saplings springing up, a few ragged holes in the thatch where birds had picked it apart for nests and the bar across the door rusted in its hooks. It already had the feeling of a long-abandoned place.

"Open it up, Michal," the captain of the guard said, and one of the soldiers slid down and went tramping ahead through the grass. He was a young man, and like most of the soldiers he wore his brown hair long and straight, with a long dangling mustache and beard, braided, all of them like pictures in the Dragon's history books of the old days, the founding of Polnya. He was as strong as a young oak, tall and broad even among the other soldiers; he slid the bar over with one hand and pushed open both of the doors with an easy shove, letting the afternoon sunlight into the barn.

Then he jerked back with a wordless choked noise in his throat, hand moving towards his sword-belt, and almost stumbled over his own feet backing away. Jerzy was propped against the back wall, and the light had shone full onto the snarl of his twisted face. The statue's eyes were looking straight out at us.

"What a hideous grimace," Prince Marek said in an offhand tone. "All right, Janos," he added to the chief of his guard, sliding off his horse, "Take the men and the horses to the village green, and get them under some sort of cover. The beasts won't sit still for a lot of magic and howling, I imagine."

"Yes, Your Highness," Janos said, and jerked his head to his second.

The soldiers were as happy as the horses to be out of it. They took our mounts, too, and went eagerly, a few of them glancing sidelong through the barn doors. I saw Michal look back over his hunched shoulders several times, the ruddy color gone out of his face.

None of them understood, really, about the Wood. They weren't men from the valley—as I've said, the Dragon didn't need to levy a troop to send to the king's army—and they weren't from any-where nearby, either. They carried shields marked with a crest of a knight upon a horse, so they were all from the northern provinces around Tarakai, where Queen Hanna had come from. Their idea of magic was a lightning-strike on a battlefield, deadly and clean. They didn't know what they were riding to face.

"Wait," the Dragon said, before Janos turned his own horse to follow the rest of them. "While you're there: buy two sacks of salt and divide it into pouches, one for each man; then find scarves to cover all their mouths and noses, and buy every axe that anyone will spare you." He looked at the prince. "There won't be any time to waste. If this even works, the best we'll have won is the briefest opportunity—a day, two at most, while the Wood recovers from the blow."

Prince Marek nodded to Janos, confirming the orders. "See to it everyone gets a little rest, if they can," he said. "We'll ride straight for the Wood as soon as we're done here."

"And pray that the queen isn't deep inside it," the Dragon added, flatly; Janos darted a glance at him and back to the prince, but Marek only slapped the flank of Janos's horse and turned away, a dismissal; Janos followed the other men away, down the narrow path and out of sight.

We were left alone just inside the barn, the five of us. Dust floated through the sunlight, the warm sweet smell of hay, but with a faint choking undercurrent of rotting leaves beneath. I could see a broken jagged-edged hole gaping in the side of the wall: where the wolves had come through, not to eat the cattle but to savage and corrupt them. I hugged myself. The day was growing late: we'd ridden straight across the valley to Dvernik since before the morning light, only stopping long enough to let the horses rest. Wind stirred through the doors and blew against my neck, a cold touch. The sun was orange on Jerzy's face, his wide unseeing stone eyes. I remembered the cold, still feeling of being stone: I wondered if Jerzy could see out of his own fixed gaze, or if the Wood had closed him into darkness.

The Dragon looked at the Falcon and made a wide mocking sweep of his arm towards Jerzy. "Perhaps you'd care to be of some assistance?"

The Falcon gave him a thin, smiling bow and went to stand before the statue with upraised hands. The words to lift the stone spell came ringing off his tongue, beautifully enunciated, and as he spoke Jerzy's fingertips curled in with a twitch as the stone drained out of them. The stiffened claws of his hands were still outstretched to either side of him, and the rusting chains hanging from his wrists had been nailed to the wall. The metal links scraped against one another as he started to move. The Falcon backed away a little, still smiling, as the stone retreated slowly down from the crown of Jerzy's head and his eyes began to roll and dart from side to side. A shrill faint thread of laughter wheezed out of him as his mouth came loose; then the stone freed his lungs, and the smile slid off the Falcon's face as it rose and rose to a shrieking pitch.

Kasia moved against me, clumsily, and I gripped her hand. She stood beside me like a statue herself, rigid and remembering. Jerzy howled and laughed and howled, over and over, as though he was trying to make up for all the howls that had been closed up inside his stone chest. He howled until he was out of breath, and then he lifted his head and grinned at us all with his blackened and rotting teeth, his skin still mottled green. Prince Marek was staring at him, his hand clenched on his sword; the Falcon had backed away to his side.

"Hello, princeling," Jerzy crooned to him, "do you miss your mother? Would you like to hear her scream, too? *Marek!*" Jerzy shrilled suddenly, in a woman's voice, high and desperate. *"Marechek, save me!"*

Marek flinched bodily as if something had struck him in the gut, three inches of his sword-blade coming out of its sheath before he stopped. "Stop it!" he snarled. "Make it be *silent!*"

The Falcon raised a hand and said, *"Elrekaduht!"* still staring and appalled. Jerzy's wide-mouthed cackles went muffled as if he'd been closed up inside a thick-walled room, only a faint distant whine of *"Marechek, Marechek"* still coming through.

The Falcon whirled towards us. "You can't possibly mean to cleanse *this* thing—"

"Ah, so *now* you're feeling squeamish?" the Dragon said, cold and cutting.

"Look at him!" the Falcon said. He turned back and said, *"Leh-leyast palezh!"* and swept his opened hand down through the air as though he were wiping down a pane of glass covered in steam. I recoiled, Kasia's hand clenching painfully on mine; we stared in horror. Jerzy's skin had gone translucent, a thin greenish onion-skin layer, and beneath it nothing but black squirming masses of corruption that boiled and seethed. Like the shadows I'd seen beneath my own skin, but grown so fat they'd devoured everything there was inside him, even coiling beneath his face, his stained yellow eyes barely peering out of the grotesque, seething clouds.

"And yet you were prepared to ride blithely into the Wood," the Dragon said. He turned. Prince Marek was staring at Jerzy, grey as a mirror; his mouth was a narrow bloodless line. The Dragon said to him, "Listen to me. *This?*" He gestured at Jerzy. "This is nothing. His corruption is thrice-removed, less than three days old thanks to the stone spell. If it were only four times removed instead, I could have cleansed him with the usual purgative. The queen's been held in a heart-tree for twenty years. If we can find her, if we can bring her out, if we can purge her, none of which is remotely certain, she'll still have lived twenty years in the worst torment the Wood can devise. She won't embrace you. She won't even know you.

"We have a true chance against the Wood here," he added. "If we succeed in purging this man, if we destroy another heart-tree doing it, we shouldn't use that opening to make a foolish headlong charge deep into the bowels of the Wood, risking everything. We should begin at the nearest border, cut a road into the Wood as deep as we can from sunrise to sunset, and then set fire-heart in the forest behind us before we retreat. We could reclaim twenty miles of this valley, and weaken the Wood for three generations."

"And if my mother burns with it?" Prince Marek said, wheeling on him.

The Dragon nodded towards Jerzy. "Would *you* rather live like that?"

"Then if she *doesn't* burn!" Marek said. *"No."* He heaved a breath like there were iron bands around his chest. "No."

The Dragon's mouth compressed. "If we were able to so weaken the Wood, our chances of finding her—"

"No," Marek said, a slash of his hand, cutting him off. "We'll bring my mother out, and as we go we'll lay waste as much of the Wood as we can. *Then*, Dragon, when you've purged her and burned the heart-tree that held her, I swear you'll have every man and axe that my father can spare you, and we won't just burn the Wood back twenty miles: we'll burn it all the way to Rosya, and be rid of it for good."

He straightened as he spoke, his shoulders going back; he'd planted himself still more firmly. I bit my own lip. I trusted Prince Marek not at all, except to please himself, but I couldn't help feeling that he had the right of it. If we cut the Wood back even twenty miles, it would be a great victory, but only a temporary one. I wanted all of it to *burn*.

I'd always hated the Wood, of course, but distantly. It had been a hailstorm before harvest, a swarm of locusts in the field; more horrible than those things, more like a nightmare, but still just acting according to its nature. Now it was something else entirely, a living thing deliberately reaching out the full force of its malice to hurt me, to hurt everyone I loved; looming over my entire village and ready to swallow it up just like Porosna. I wasn't dreaming of myself as a great heroine, as the Dragon had accused me, but I did want to ride into the Wood with axe and fire. I wanted to rip the queen out of its grasp, call up armies on either side, and raze it to the ground.

The Dragon shook his head after a moment, but silently; he didn't argue any further. Instead it was the Falcon who made a protest, now; he didn't look nearly as certain as Prince Marek. His eyes still lingered on Jerzy, and he had a corner of his white cloak pressed over his mouth and nose, as though he saw more than we did, and feared to breathe in some sickness. "I hope you'll forgive my doubts: perhaps I'm merely woefully inexperienced in these matters," he said, the tense sarcastic edge of his voice coming clearly even through the cloak. "But I would have called this a truly remarkable case of corruption. He's not even safe to behead before burning. Perhaps we'd best make sure you *can* free him, before you choose among grandiose plans none of which can even be begun."

"We agreed!" Prince Marek said, wheeling around to him in urgent protest.

"I agreed it was a risk worth taking, *if* Sarkan had really found some way to purge corruption," the Falcon said to him. "But *this*—?" He looked again at Jerzy. "Not until I've seen him do it, and I'll look twice even then. For all we know, the girl was never corrupted in the first place, and he put the rumor about himself, to add still more luster to his reputation."

The Dragon snorted disdainfully and didn't offer him any other answer. He turned and pulled a handful of hay stalks from one of the old falling-apart bales and began to murmur a charm over them as his fingers quickly bent them together. Prince Marek seized the Falcon's arm and dragged him aside, whispering angrily.

Jerzy was still singing to himself behind the muffling spell, but he had begun to swing himself in the chains, running forward until his arms were stretched as far as they could go behind him, held taut by the chains and straining, flinging himself against them and lunging his head forward to snap and bite at the air. He let his tongue hang out, a grossly swollen blackened thing as though a slug had crawled into his mouth, and waggled it and rolled his eyes at us all.

The Dragon ignored him. In his hands, the hay stalks thickened and grew into a small, knobbly-legged table, barely a foot wide, and then he took the leather satchel he'd brought with him and opened it up. He drew the *Summoning* out carefully, the sunset making the golden embossed letters blaze, and he laid it upon the small table. "All right," he said, turning to me. "Let's begin."

I hadn't really thought about it until then, with the prince and the Falcon turning towards us, that I would have to take the Dragon's hand in front of all of them, join my magic to his while they watched. My stomach shriveled like a dried plum. I darted a look at the Dragon, but his face was deliberately aloof, as though he was only mildly interested by anything we were doing.

I reluctantly went to stand beside him. The Falcon's eyes were on me, and I was sure there was magic in his gaze, predatory and piercing. I hated the thought of being exposed before him, before Marek; I hated it almost worse to have Kasia there, who knew me so well. I hadn't told her much about that night, about the last time the Dragon and I had tried a working together. I hadn't been able to put it into words; I hadn't wanted to *think* about it that much. But I couldn't refuse, not with Jerzy dancing on his chains like the toy my father had whittled me long ago, the funny little stick-man who jumped and somersaulted between two poles.

I swallowed and put my hand on the cover of the *Summoning*. I opened it, and together the Dragon and I began to read.

We were stiff and awkward beside each other, but our workings joined as though they knew the way by now without us. My shoulders eased, my head lifted, I drew a deep glad breath into my lungs. I couldn't help it. I couldn't care if all the world was watching. The *Summoning* flowed around us easily as a river: his voice a rippling chant that I filled with waterfalls and leaping fish, and the light dawned bright and brilliant as an early sunrise around us.

And in Jerzy's face, the Wood looked out, and snarled at us with soundless hatred.

"Is it working?" Prince Marek asked the Falcon, behind us. I didn't hear his answer. Jerzy was lost in the Wood just as Kasia had been, but he had given up: he was sitting slumped against the trunk of a tree, his bleeding feet stretched out in front of him, the muscles of his jaw slack, staring blankly down at his hands in his lap. He didn't move when I called him. "Jerzy!" I cried. Dully he lifted his head, dully looked at me, and then put it down again.

"I see—there *is* a channel," the Falcon said; when I glanced at him, I saw he'd put his blindfold mask on again. That strange hawk's-eye was peering out of his forehead, its black pupil wide. "That's the way the corruption travels out from the Wood. Sarkan, if I cast the purging-fire down along it now—"

"No!" I said in quick protest. "Jerzy will die." The Falcon threw me a dismissive look. He didn't care anything if Jerzy lived or died, of course. But Kasia turned and dashed out of the barn, down the pathway, and a little while later she brought a wary Krystyna back to us, the baby cuddled in her arms. Krystyna shrank back from the magic, from Jerzy's writhing, but Kasia whispered to her urgently. Krystyna clutched the baby tighter and slowly took one step closer, then another, until she could look into Jerzy's face. Her own changed.

"Jerzy!" she called, "Jerzy!" and stretched her hand towards him. Kasia held her back from touching his face, but deep within, I saw him lift his head again, and then, slowly, push up onto his feet.

The light of the *Summoning* was no more forgiving to him. I felt it at a distance this time, not something that touched me directly, but he was bared to us, full of anger: the small graves of all the children, and Krystyna's mutely suffering face; the pinch of hunger in his belly and his sour resentment of the small baskets of charity he pretended not to see in the corners of his house, knowing she'd gone begging. The simple raw desperation of seeing the cows turned, his last grasping clutch at a way out of poverty torn away. He'd half *wanted* the beasts to kill him.

Krystyna's face was vivid with her own sluggish desperation, helpless dark thoughts: her mother had told her not to marry a poor man; her sister in Radomsko had four children and a husband who wove cloth for a living. Her sister's children had lived; her sister's children had never been cold and starving.

Jerzy's mouth pulled wide with shame, trembling, teeth clenched. But Krystyna sobbed once and reached for him again, and then the baby woke and yelled: an awful noise but somehow wonderful by comparison, so ordinary and uncomplicated, nothing but a raw demand. Jerzy took one step.

And then it was suddenly much easier. The Dragon was right: this corruption was weaker than Kasia's had been, for all it had looked so dreadful. Jerzy wasn't deep in the Wood, as she had been. Once he began moving, he came stumbling towards us quickly, and though branches threw themselves in his way, they were only thin slapping things. He put his arms in front of his face and began to run towards us, pushing through them.

"Take the spell," the Dragon said to me as we came to the very end, and I set my teeth and held the *Summoning* with all my might while he drew his magic free from mine. "Now," he said to the Falcon, "as he emerges," and as Jerzy began to crowd forward into his own face they raised their hands side by side and spoke at the same time: *"Ulozishtus sovjenta!"*

Jerzy screamed as he pushed forward through the purging fire, but he did come through: a few tarry stinking drops squeezed out of the corners of his eyes and ran out of his nostrils and fell to the ground, smoking, and his body fell limply sagging in his chains.

Kasia kicked some dirt over the drops, and the Dragon stepped forward to grip Jerzy's face by the chin, holding him up as I finished reading the *Summoning* at last. "Look now," he said to the Falcon.

The Falcon put his hands to either side of Jerzy's face and spoke:

a spell like an arrow. It snapped away from him in the final terrible blaze of light from the *Summoning*. On the wall between the chains, above Jerzy's head, the Falcon's spell opened a window, and we all saw for one moment a tall old heart-tree, twice the size of the one Kasia had been inside. Its limbs were thrashing wildly in a crackling blaze of fire.

FOURTEEN

The soldiers were laughing to one another gaily as we left Dvernik in the hush before dawn the next morning. They had armed themselves, and were all very splendid looking in their bright mail, their nodding plumed helms and long green cloaks, their painted shields hung on their saddles. They knew it, too; they marched their horses proudly through the dark lanes, and even the horses held their necks arched. Of course thirty scarves weren't easily come by out of a small village, so most of the men were wearing thick itchy woolen ones meant for winter, wrapped haphazardly around their necks and faces as the Dragon had ordered. They kept breaking their careful poise and involuntarily reaching beneath to scratch every so often, surreptitiously.

I'd grown up riding my father's big slow draft horses, who would only look around at me in mild surprise if I stood upside down on their broad backs, and refused to have anything to do with trotting, much less a canter. But Prince Marek had put us on spare horses his knights had brought with them, and they seemed like entirely different animals. When I accidentally tugged on the reins in some wrong way, my horse jumped up onto its hind legs and lashed out its hooves, crow-stepping forward while I clung in alarm to its mane. It came down after some time, for reasons equally impenetrable to me, and pranced along very satisfied with itself. At least until we passed Zatochek.

There wasn't a single place where the valley road ended. I suppose it had gone on much farther once—on to Porosna, and maybe to some other nameless long-swallowed village beyond it. But before the creak of the mill-house at Zatochek bridge faded behind us, the weeds and grass began to nibble at the edges, and a mile onward we could barely tell that it was still underfoot. The soldiers were still laughing and singing, but the horses were wiser than we were, maybe. Their pace slowed without any signal from their riders. They whuffed nervously and jerked their heads, their ears pricking forward and back and their skin giving nervous shivers as if flies were bothering them. But there were no flies. Up ahead, the wall of dark trees was waiting.

"Pull up here," the Dragon said, and as if they'd understood him and were glad of the excuse, the horses halted almost at once, all of them. "Get a drink of water and eat something, if you like. Let nothing more pass your lips once we're beneath the trees." He swung down from his horse.

I climbed down from my own, very cautiously. "I'll take her," one of the soldiers said to me, a blond boy with a friendly round face marred only by a twice-broken nose. He clucked to my mare, cheerful and competent. All the men were taking their horses to drink from the river, and passing around loaves of bread and flasks with liquor in them.

The Dragon beckoned me over. "Put on your protection spell, as thickly as you can," he said. "And then try to place it on the soldiers, if you can. I'll lay another on you as well."

"Will it keep the shadows out of us?" I said doubtfully. "Even inside the Wood?"

"No. But it will slow them down," he said. "There's a barn just outside Zatochek: I keep it stocked with purgatives, against a need to go into the Wood. As soon as we're out again, we'll go there and dose ourselves. Ten times, no matter how certain you are that you're clear."

I looked at the crowd of young soldiers, talking and laughing among themselves as they ate their bread. "Do you have enough for all of them?"

He turned a cold certain look over them like the sweep of a scythe. "For however many of them will be left," he said.

I shivered. "You still don't think this is a good idea. Even after Jerzy." A thin plume of smoke still rose from the Wood, where the heart-tree burned: we'd seen it yesterday.

"It's a dreadful idea," the Dragon said. "But letting Marek lead you and Solya in there without me is a still-worse one. At least I have some idea what to expect. Come: we don't have much time."

Kasia silently helped me gather bundles of pine needles for my spell. The Falcon was already building an elaborate shield of his own around Prince Marek, like a shining wall of bricks going up one after another, and when he had raised it above Marek's head, the whole thing glowed as a whole and then collapsed in on him. If I glanced at Marek sideways I could see the faint shimmer of it clinging to his skin. The Falcon put another one on himself. I noticed he didn't lay it on any of the soldiers, though.

I knelt and made a smudge-fire of my pine needles and branches. When the smoke was filling the clearing, bitter and throat-drying, I looked up at the Dragon. "Cast yours now?" I asked. The Dragon's spell settling on my shoulders felt like putting on a heavy coat in front of the fireplace: it left me itchy and uncomfortable, and thinking too much about why I was going to need it. I hummed my protection spell along with his chant, imagining that I was bundling up the rest of the way against the heart of winter: not just coat but mittens, woolen scarf, hat with the ear-covers buttoned down, knitted pants over my boots, and veils wrapped over it all, everything tucked snugly in, leaving no cracks for the cold air to wriggle through.

"All of you pull up your scarves," I said, without looking away from my smoky fire, forgetting a moment that I was talking to grown men, soldiers; and what was odder still was they did what I said. I pushed the smoke out around me, letting it sink into the wool and cotton of their wraps, carrying protection with it.

The last of the needles crumbled into ash. The fire went out. I climbed a little unsteadily up to my feet, coughing from the smoke, and rubbed my tearing eyes. When I blinked them clear again, I flinched: the Falcon was watching me, hungry and intent, even as he drew a fold of his own cloak up over his mouth and nose. I turned quickly away and went to get a drink from the river myself, and wash the smoke from my hands and face. I didn't like the way his eyes tried to pierce my skin.

Kasia and I shared a loaf of bread ourselves: the endlessly familiar daily loaf from Dvernik's baker, crusty and grey-brown and a little bit sour, the taste of every morning at home. The soldiers were putting away their flasks and wiping off crumbs and getting back on their horses. The sun had broken over the trees.

"All right, Falcon," Prince Marek said, when we were all back on our horses. He drew off his gauntlet. He had a ring sitting above the first joint of his smallest finger, a delicate round band of gold set with small blue jewels; a woman's ring. "Show us the way."

"Hold your thumb above the band," the Falcon said, and leaning over from his own horse, he pricked Marek's finger with a jeweled pin and squeezed it. A fat drop of blood fell onto the ring, painting the gold red while the Falcon murmured a finding spell.

The blue stones turned dark purple. A violet light gathered around Marek's hand, and even when he pulled his gauntlet back on, the light still limned it. He raised his fist up before him and moved it from side to side: it brightened when he held it towards the Wood. He led us forward, and one after another our horses crossed over the ash and went into the dark trees.

The Wood was a different place in spring than in winter. There was a sense of quickening and wakefulness. My skin shivered with the sense of watching eyes all around as soon as the first bough-shadows touched me. The horses' hooves fell with muffled blows on the ground, picking over moss and underbrush, edging past brambles that reached for us with long pricking thorns. Silent dark birds darted almost invisible from tree to tree, pacing us. I was sure suddenly that if I had come alone, in spring, I wouldn't have reached Kasia at all; not without a fight.

But today, we rode with thirty men around us, all of them armored and armed. The soldiers carried long heavy blades and torches and sacks of salt, as the Dragon had ordered. The ones riding in the lead hacked at the brush, widening the trails as we pushed our way along them. The rest burned back the brambles to either side, and salted the earth of the path behind us so we'd be able to retreat the way we'd come.

But their laughter died. We rode silently but for the muffled jingle of harness, the soft thuds of hooves on the bare track, a murmur of a word to one another here and there. The horses didn't even whicker anymore. They watched the trees with large eyes rimmed with white. We all felt that we were hunted.

Kasia rode next to me, and her head was bowed deeply over her horse's neck. I managed to reach out and catch her fingers with mine. "What is it?" I said softly.

She looked away from our path and pointed towards a tree in the distance, an old blackened oak struck years before by lightning; moss hung from its dead branches, like a bent old woman spreading wide her skirts to curtsy. "I remember that tree," she said. She dropped her hand and stared straight ahead through her horse's ears. "And that red rock we passed, and the grey bramble—all of them. It's as though I didn't leave." She was whispering, too. "It's as though I never left at all. I don't know if you're even real, Nieshka. What if I've only been having another dream?"

I squeezed her hand, helplessly. I didn't know how to comfort her.

"There's something nearby," she said. "Something up ahead."

The captain heard her and glanced back. "Something dangerous?"

"Something dead," Kasia said, and dropped her eyes to her saddle, her hands clenched on the reins.

The light was brightening around us, and the track widened beneath the horses' feet. Their shoes clopped hollowly. I looked down and saw cobblestones half-buried beneath moss, broken. When I looked back up, I flinched: in the distance, through the trees, a ghostly grey face stared back at me, with a huge hollow eye above a wide square mouth: a gutted barn.

"Get off the track," the Dragon said sharply. "Go around: north or south, it doesn't matter. But don't ride through the square, and keep moving."

"What is this place?" Marek said.

"Porosna," the Dragon said. "Or what's left of it."

We turned our horses and went north, picking our way through brambles and the ruins of small poor houses, sagging on their beams, thatched roofs fallen in. I tried not to look at the ground. Moss and fine grass covered it thickly, and tall young trees were stretching up for sun, already spreading out overhead and breaking the sunlight into moving, shifting dapples. But there were shapes still half-buried beneath the moss, here and there a hand of bones breaking the sod, white fingertips poking through the soft carpeting green that caught the light and gleamed cold. Above the houses, if I looked towards where the village square would have stood, a vast shining silver canopy spread, and I could hear the far-off rustling whisper of the leaves of a heart-tree.

"Couldn't we stop and burn it?" I whispered to the Dragon, as softly as I could.

"Certainly," he said. "If we used fire-heart, and retreated the way we came at once. It would be the wise thing to do."

He didn't keep his voice down. But Prince Marek didn't look around, though a few of the soldiers glanced at us. The horses stretched their necks, trembling, and we rode on quickly, leaving the dead behind us.

We stopped a little while later to give the horses a rest. They were all tired, from fear as much as effort. The path had widened around some marshy ground, the end of a spring creek that was drying up now as the snowmelt stopped running. A small trickle still came bubbling along and made a wide clear pool over a bed of rocks. "Is it safe to let the horses drink?" Prince Marek asked the Dragon, who shrugged.

"You may as well," he said. "It's not much worse than having them beneath the trees. You'd have to put them all down after this in any case."

Janos had already slid down from his horse; he had a hand on its nose, calming the animal. He jerked his head around. "These are trained warhorses! They're worth their weight in silver."

"And purging elixir is worth their weight in gold," the Dragon said. "If you felt tender towards them, you shouldn't have brought them into the Wood. But don't distress yourself overly. Chances are the question won't arise."

Prince Marek threw him a hard look, but he didn't quarrel; instead he caught Janos aside and spoke to him consolingly.

Kasia had gone to stand by the edge of the clearing where a handful of deer tracks continued on; she was looking away from the pool. I wondered if she'd seen this place, too, in her long wandering imprisonment. She stared into the dark trees. The Dragon came past her; he glanced at her and spoke; I saw her head turn towards him.

"I wonder if you know what he owes you," the Falcon said unexpectedly, behind me; I startled and turned my head around. My horse was drinking thirstily; I gripped the reins and edged a little closer to its warm side. I didn't say anything.

The Falcon only raised one narrow eyebrow, black and neat. "The kingdom hasn't a limitless store of wizards. By law, the gift places you beyond vassalage. You have a right to a place at court, now, and the patronage of the king himself. You should never have been kept here in this valley in the first place, much less treated like a drudge." He waved a hand up and down at my clothes. I had dressed myself as I would have to go gleaning, in tall mud-boots, loose work trousers sewn of sacking, and a brown smock over it all. He still wore his white cloak, although the Wood's malice was stronger than whatever charm he'd used to keep it neat in the ordinary woods; there were threads snagged along the edge of it.

He misunderstood my doubtful look. "Your father is a farmer, I suppose?"

"A woodcutter," I said.

He flicked a hand as if to say it made not the least difference. "Then you know nothing of the court, I imagine. When the gift rose in me, the king raised my father to a knighthood, and when I finished my training, to a barony. He will not be less generous to you." He leaned towards me, and my horse snorted bubbles in the water as I leaned hard against her. "Whatever you may have heard, growing up in this backwater, Sarkan is by no means the only wizard of note in Polnya. I assure you that you needn't feel bound to him, simply because he's found an—interesting way to use you. I'm certain there are many other wizards you could align yourself with." He extended his hand towards me, and raised a thin spiraling flame in the palm of his hand with a murmured word. "Perhaps you'd care to try?"

"With *you*?" I blurted, undiplomatically; his eyes narrowed a little at the corners. I didn't feel at all sorry, though. "After what you did to Kasia?"

He put on injured surprise like a second cloak. "I've done her and you a favor. Do you imagine anyone would have been willing to take Sarkan's word for her cure? Your patron might charitably be called eccentric, burying himself out here and coming to court only when he's summoned, gloomy as a storm and issuing warnings of inevitable disasters that somehow never come. He hasn't any friends at court, and the few who would stand beside him are the very doom-sayers who insisted on having your friend put to death at once. If Prince Marek hadn't intervened, the king would have sent an executioner instead, and summoned Sarkan to the capital to answer for the crime of letting her live this long."

He'd come to be exactly that executioner, but apparently he didn't mean to let that stand in the way of claiming he'd done me a kindness. I didn't know how to answer anything so brazen; the only thing I could have managed would have been an inarticulate hiss. But he didn't force me to that point. He said only, in a gentle voice that suggested I was being unreasonable, "Think a little about what I've told you. I don't blame you for your anger, but don't let it make you spurn good advice," and gave me a courtly bow. He withdrew gracefully even as Kasia rejoined me. The soldiers were getting back on their horses.

Her face was sober, and she was rubbing her arms. The Dragon had gone to mount his own horse; I glanced over at him, wondering what he'd said to her. "Are you all right?" I asked Kasia.

"He told me not to fear I was still corrupted," she said. Her mouth moved a little, the ghost of a smile. "He said if I could fear it, I probably wasn't." Then even more unexpectedly she added, "He told me he was sorry I'd been afraid of him—of being chosen, I mean. He said he wouldn't take anyone again."

I had shouted at him over that; I hadn't ever expected him to listen. I stared at her, but I didn't have any time to wonder: Janos had mounted, looked his men over, and he said abruptly, "Where's Michal?"

We counted heads and horses, and called loudly in every direction. There was no answer, and no trail of broken branches or stirred leaves to show which way he'd gone. He'd been seen only a few moments before, waiting to give his horse water. If he'd been snatched, it had been silently.

"Enough," the Dragon said at last. "He's gone."

Janos looked at the prince in protest. But after a silent moment, Marek said finally, "We go on. Ride two by two, and keep in each other's sight."

Janos's face was hard and unhappy as he wrapped the scarf closely over his nose and mouth again, but he jerked his head at the first two soldiers, and after a moment they started into motion down the path. We rode on into the Wood.

Beneath the boughs it was hard to tell what time it was, how long we'd been riding. The Wood was silent as no forest ever was: no hum of insects, not even the occasional twig-snap under a rabbit's foot. Even our own horses made very little noise, hooves coming down on soft moss and grass and saplings instead of bare dirt. The track was running out. The men in the front had to hack at the brush all the time to give us a way through at all.

A faint sound of rushing water came to us through the trees. The track abruptly widened again. We halted; I stood up in my stirrups, and over the shoulders of the soldier in front of me I could just see a break in the trees. We were on the bank of the Spindle again.

We came out of the forest nearly a foot above the river, on a soft sloping bank. Trees and brush overhung the water, willows trailing long weedy branches into the reeds that clustered thickly at the water's edge, between the pale tangle of exposed tree-roots against the wet dirt. The Spindle was wide enough that over the middle, sunlight broke through the interlaced canopy of the trees. It glittered on the river's surface without penetrating, and we could tell most of the day had gone. We sat for a long moment in silence. There was a wrongness to meeting the river like this, cutting across our path. We'd been riding east; we should have been alongside it.

When Prince Marek raised his fist towards the water, the violet gleam shone bright, beckoning us across to the other side, but the water was moving swiftly, and we couldn't tell how deep it was. Janos tossed in a small twig from one of the trees: it was dragged away downstream at once and vanished almost immediately under a little glossy swell. "We'll look for a ford," Prince Marek said.

We turned and went on riding single-file along the river, the soldiers hacking away at the vegetation to give the horses a foothold on the bank. There was never any sign of an animal track leading down to the edge, and the Spindle ran on, never narrowing. It was a different river here than in the valley, running fast and silent beneath the trees; as shadowed by the Wood as we were. I knew that the river never came out on the other side in Rosya; it vanished somewhere in the deep part of the Wood, swallowed up in some dark place. That seemed almost impossible to believe here, looking at the wide dark stretch of it.

Somewhere behind me, one of the men sighed deeply—a relieved noise, as though he were setting down a heavy weight. It was loud in the Wood's silence. I looked around. His scarf had sagged down from his face: it was the friendly young soldier with the broken nose who'd led my horse to water. He reached out with a knife drawn, sharp and bright silver, and he caught the head of the man riding in front of him and cut his throat in one deep red gash from side to side.

The other soldier died without a sound. The blood sprayed out over the animal's neck and onto the leaves. It reared wildly, crying out, and as the man sagged down off its back, it floundered into the brush and disappeared. The young soldier with the knife was still smiling. He threw himself off his own horse, into the water.

We were frozen by the suddenness of it. Up ahead of me, Prince Marek gave a shout and flung himself off his own mount and down the slope, dirt furrowing away from his boots as he slid to the water's edge. He tried to reach out and catch the soldier's hand, but the man didn't reach back. He went past the prince on his back, floating like driftwood, the ends of his scarf and cloak trailing away in the water behind him. His legs were already being dragged down as his boots filled with water, then his whole body was sinking. We had one last pale flash of his round face staring upwards in the sun. The water closed in over his head, over the broken nose; the cloak went down with a last green billowing. He was gone.

Prince Marek had climbed back up to his feet. He stood down on the bank watching, gripping the trunk of one narrow sapling for balance, until the soldier went under. Then he turned and clambered up the slope. Janos had slid down from his own mount, catching Marek's reins; he reached down an arm to help him up. Another one of the soldiers had caught the reins of the other now-riderless horse; it was trembling, its nostrils flaring, but it stood still. Everything settled back into quiet again. The river ran on, the branches hung still, the sun shone on the water. We didn't even hear any noise from the horse that had run away. It was as though nothing had happened.

The Dragon pushed his horse down the line and looked down at Prince Marek. "The rest of them will go by nightfall," he said bluntly. "If not you as well."

Marek looked up at him, his face for the first time open and uncertain; as though he'd just seen something beyond his understanding. I saw the Falcon beside them looking back along the line of the men with unblinking eyes, his piercing eyes trying to see something invisible. Marek looked at him; the Falcon looked back and nodded very slightly, confirming.

The prince hauled himself up into his saddle. He spoke to the soldiers ahead of him. "Cut us a clearing." They started to hack at the brush around us; the rest of them joined in, burning and salting it as they went, until we had cleared enough room to crowd in together. The horses were eager to push their heads in and butt up closely against one another.

"All right," Marek said to the soldiers, their gazes fixed on him. "You all know why you're here. Every one of you is hand-picked. You're men of the north, the best I have. You've followed me into Rosyan sorcery and made a wall beside me against their cavalry charges; there's not a one of you who doesn't wear the scars of battle. I asked every one of you, before we left, if you'd ride into this benighted place with me; every one of you said yes.

"Well, I won't swear to you now I'll bring you out alive; but you have my oath that every man who does come out with me will have every honor I can bestow, and every one of you made a landed knight. And we'll ford the river here, now, however best we can, and we will ride on together: to death or worse perhaps, but like men and not like frightened voles."

They must have known, by then, that Marek himself didn't know what would happen; that he hadn't been ready for the shadow of the Wood. But I could see his words lift some of that shadow from all of their faces: a brightness came into them, a deep breath. None of them asked to turn back. Marek took his hunting horn from his saddle. It was a long thing made all of brass, bright-polished and circled on itself. He put it to his mouth and blew with all his voice, an enormous martial noise that shouldn't have made my heart leap but did: brash and ringing. The horses stamped and flicked their ears back and forth, and the soldiers drew their swords and roared along with that note. Marek wheeled his horse and led us in a single headlong rush down the slope and into the cold dark water, and all the other horses followed.

The river hit my legs like a shock as we plunged into it, foaming away from my horse's broad chest. We kept going. The water climbed up over my knees, over my thighs. My horse had its head held up high, nostrils flaring as its legs beat at the riverbed, surging forward and trying to keep purchase on the bottom.

Somewhere behind me, one of the horses stumbled and lost its footing. It was tumbled over at once and carried into another soldier's horse. The river swept them away and swallowed them whole. We didn't stop: there was no way to stop. I groped for a spell, but I couldn't think of anything: the water was roaring at me, and then they were gone.

Prince Marek sounded another blast from his horn: he and his horse were lurching up on the other side of the river, and he was kicking it onward into the trees. One by one we came up out of the river, dripping wet, and kept going without a pause: all of us crashing through the brush, following the purple blaze of Marek's light up ahead, following the sound of his calling horn. The trees were whipping by us. The underbrush was lighter on this side of the river, the trunks larger and farther apart. We weren't riding in a single line anymore: I could see some of the other horses weaving through the trees beside me as we flew, as we fled, running away as much as running towards. I had given up all hope of the reins and just clung to my own horse with my fingers woven into the mane, bent over its neck away from lashing branches. I could see Kasia near me, and the bright flash of the Falcon's white cloak ahead.

The mare was panting beneath me, shuddering, and I knew she couldn't last; even strong, trained warhorses would founder, ridden like this after swimming a cold river. *"Nen elshayon,"* I whispered to her ears, *"nen elshayon,"* and let her have a little strength, a little warmth. She stretched out her fine head and tossed it, gratefully, and I closed my eyes and tried to widen it to all of them, saying, *"Nen elshayine,"* pushing out my hand towards Kasia's horse as though throwing it a line.

I felt that imagined line catch; I flung more of them out, and the horses drew closer together, running more easily again. The Dragon threw a brief look back at me over his shoulder. We kept on, riding behind the blowing horn, and now I started to see something moving through the trees at last. Walkers, many walkers, and they were coming towards us rapidly, all their long stick-legs moving in unison. One of them stretched out a long arm and caught one of the soldiers off his horse, but they were falling behind us, as if they hadn't expected our pell-mell speed. We burst together through a wall of pines into a vast clearing, the horses leaping to clear a stand of brush, and before us stood a monstrous heart-tree.

The trunk of it was broader than the side of a horse, towering up into an immensity of spreading branches. Its boughs were laden with pale silver-green leaves and small golden fruits with a horrible stink, and beneath the bark looking at us was a human face, overgrown and smoothed out into a mere suggestion, with two hands crossed across the breast like a corpse. Two great roots forked at its feet, and in the hollow between them lay a skeleton, almost swallowed by moss and rotting leaves. A smaller root twisted out through one open eye socket, and grass poked through ribs and scraps of rusted mail. The remains of a shield lay across the body, barely marked with a black double-headed eagle: the royal crest of Rosya.

We pulled up our snorting, heaving horses just short of its branches. Behind me I heard a sudden snapping noise like the door of an oven slamming shut, and at the same moment I was struck by a heavy weight out of nowhere, thrown out of my saddle. I hit the bare ground painfully, the air knocked out of my lungs, my elbow scraped and legs bruised.

I twisted. Kasia was on top of me: she'd knocked me off my horse. I stared up past her. My horse was in the air above us, headless. A monstrous thing like a praying mantis was holding it up in two forelegs. The mantis blended against the heart-tree: narrow golden eyes the same shape as the fruits, and a body of the same silvery green as the leaves. It had bitten the horse's head off with a single snap, in the same lunging movement. Behind us, another of the soldiers had fallen headless, and a third was screaming, his leg gone, thrashing in the grip of another mantis: there were a dozen of the creatures, coming out of the trees.

FIFTEEN

The silver mantis dropped my horse to the ground and spat out the head. Kasia was scrambling up, dragging me away. We were all caught in horror for a moment, and then Prince Marek shouted wordlessly and flung his horn at the head of the silver mantis. He dragged out his sword. "Fall in! Get the wizards behind us!" he roared, and spurred his horse onward, getting between us and the thing, slashing at it. His sword skidded down the carapace, peeling up a long translucent strip as though he'd been paring a carrot.

The warhorses showed they really were worth their weight in silver: they weren't panicking now, as any ordinary beast would have done, but rearing and lashing out, their voices shrilling. Their hooves struck with hollow thumps against the mantis shells. The soldiers made a loose circle around me and Kasia, the Dragon and the Falcon pulling their horses in on either side of us. All the soldiers were putting their reins in their teeth; half of them had already drawn swords, making a bristling wall of points to protect us, while the others settled their shields on their arms first.

The mantis creatures were coming out of the trees to surround us. They were still hard to see in the dappled light with the trees moving, but no longer invisible. They didn't move like the walkers, slow and stiff; they ran lightly forward on four legs, the wide spiked jaws of their front legs quivering. *"Suitah liekin, suitah lang!"* the Falcon was shouting, summoning that blazing white fire he'd used in the tower. He flung it out like a lash to curl around the forelegs of the nearest mantis as it reared up to snatch for another man. He jerked on the line like a man pulling in a resisting calf, and dragged the mantis forward: there was a crackling bitter smell of burning oil where the fire pressed against its shell, thin plumes of white smoke curling away. Off-balance, the mantis snapped its terrible mandibles on thin air. The Falcon pulled its head into the line, and one of the soldiers hacked at its neck.

I didn't have much hope: in the valley, our ordinary axes and swords and scythes barely scraped the skin of the walkers. But this sword somehow bit deep. Chips of chitin flew into the air, and the man on the other side worked the point of his sword into the joint where the neck met the head. He put his weight against the hilt and shoved it through. The mantis's shell cracked loudly like a crab's leg, and its head sagged, the jaws going limp. Ichor oozed out of its body over the sword-blade, steaming, and I briefly saw letters gleam golden through the haze before they faded again into the steel.

But even as the mantis died, its whole body lurched forward, pushing through the ring and nearly knocking into the Falcon's horse. Another mantis leaned in through the opened space, reaching for him, but he seized the reins in a fist and controlled his mount as it tried to rear, then pulled his lash of fire back and cracked it into the second mantis's face.

On the ground with Kasia, I could barely see anything else of the fighting. I heard Prince Marek and Janos shouting encouragement to the soldiers, and the harsh scraping noise of metal meeting shell. Everything was confusion and noise, happening so quickly I almost couldn't breathe, much less think. I looked up wildly at the

Dragon, who was fighting his own alarmed horse; I saw him snarl something under his breath and kick his feet loose from the stirrups. He threw the reins to one of the soldiers, a man whose horse was sagging with a terrible gaping cut to its chest, and slid down to the ground beside us.

"What should I do?" I cried to him. I groped helplessly for a spell. *"Murzhetor—?"*

"No!" he shouted at me, over the cacophony, and seizing my arm turned me around, facing the heart-tree. "We're here for the queen. If we spend ourselves fighting a useless battle, all of this has been for nothing."

We had stayed back from the tree, but the mantises were herding us towards it little by little, forcing us all beneath the boughs, and the smell of the fruit was burning in my nostrils. The trunk was hideously vast. I had never seen a tree so large, even in the deepest forest, and there was something grotesque about its size, like a swollen tick full of blood.

This time a threat alone wouldn't work, even if I could have summoned up the rage to call *fulmia:* the Wood wasn't going to hand over the queen to save even so large a heart-tree, not now that it knew we could kill the tree afterwards, purging her. I couldn't imagine what we could do to this tree: the smooth bark shone with a hard luster like metal. The Dragon was staring at it narrowly, muttering as he worked his hands, but even before the leaping current of flame splashed against the bark, I knew instinctively it would do no good; and I didn't believe even the soldiers' enchanted swords could bite into that wood at all.

The Dragon kept trying: spells of breaking, spells of opening, spells of cold and lightning, systematic even while the fighting raged around us. He was looking for some weakness, some crack in the armor. But the tree withstood everything, and the smell of the fruit grew stronger. Two more of the mantis creatures had been killed; four more soldiers were dead. Kasia made a muffled cry as something rolled to a thump against my foot, and I looked down at Janos's head, his clear blue eyes still fixed in an intent frown. I jerked away from it in horror and tripped to my knees, sickened all at once and helplessly: I vomited on the grass. "Not *now!*" the Dragon shouted at me, as though I could help it. I had never seen fighting before, not like this, this slaughter of men. They were being killed like cattle. I sobbed on my hands and knees, tears falling in the dirt, and then I put out my hands and gripped the widest roots near me, and said, *"Kisara, kisara, vizh,"* like a chant.

The roots twitched. *"Kisara,"* I said again, over and over, and droplets of water slowly collected on the surface of the roots, oozing out of them and rolling down to join the tiny damp spots, one after another after another. The dampness spread, became a circle between my hands. The thinnest branching rootlets in the open air were shriveling in on themselves. *"Tulejon vizh,"* I said, whispering, coaxing. *"Kisara."* The roots began to writhe and squirm in the ground like fat earthworms as the water squeezed out of them, thin rivulets running. There was mud between my hands now, spreading and running away from the bigger roots, exposing more of them.

The Dragon knelt beside me. He took up the song of an enchantment that rang vaguely familiar in my ears, something I had heard once long before: the spring after the Green Year, I remembered, when he'd come to help the fields recover. He'd brought us water from the Spindle, then, with channels that dug themselves from the river all the way to our burned and barren fields. But this time the narrow channels ran away from the heart-tree instead, and as I chanted the water out of the roots, they carried the water far away, and the ground around the roots began to parch into desert, mud cracking into dust and sand.

Then Kasia caught us both by the arms and nearly levered us up from the ground, pulling us stumbling forward. The walkers we'd passed in the trees were coming into the clearing now, a whole host of them: as though they'd been lying in wait for us. The silver mantis had lost a limb but still pressed the attack, darting side-to-side and lashing out with spiked arms wherever an opening afforded.

The horses Janos had worried about were nearly all down or fled by now. Prince Marek fought on foot, shoulder-to-shoulder with sixteen men in a row, their shields overlapping into a wall and the Falcon still lashing fire from behind them, but we were being crowded in, ever closer to the trunk. The heart-tree's leaves were rustling in the wind, louder and louder, a dreadful whispering, and we were nearly at the foot of the tree. I dragged in a breath and almost vomited again from the sweet dreadful stink of the fruit.

One of the walkers tried edging around the side of the line, craning its head around sideways to see us. Kasia snatched a sword from the ground, fallen from some soldier's hand, and swung it in a wild sideways arc. The blade struck the walker's side and splintered through it with a crack like a breaking twig. It fell into a twitching heap.

The Dragon was coughing beside me from the stench of the fruit. But we took up our chant again, desperately, and dragged more water from the roots. Here close to the tree, the thicker roots resisted at first, but together our spells pulled the water from them, from the earth, and the dirt began to crumble in around the tree. Its branches were shivering: water was beginning to come rolling down the trunk in thick green-stained droplets, too. Leaves were beginning to dry up and shed like rain from above us, but then I heard a terrible scream: the silver mantis had seized another one of the men from out of the line, and this time it did not kill him. It bit off the hand that held the sword, and flung him to the walkers.

The walkers reached up and plucked fruits off the tree and crammed them into his mouth. He screamed around them, choking, but they pressed more upon him and forced his jaw shut around them, juice spilling in rivulets down his face. His whole body arched, thrashing in their grip. They held him upside down over the earth. The mantis jabbed him in the throat with one sharp point of its claw, and the blood came spurting out of him and watered the dry parched roots like rain.

The tree made a sighing, shivering sound as thin lines of red flushed down the roots and faded into the silver of its trunk. I was sobbing in horror, watching the life drain out of his face—a knife took him in the chest, sinking into his heart: Prince Marek had thrown it.

But much of our work had already been undone, and the walkers were ringing us all around, waiting, hungrily it now seemed: the men drew closer together, panting. The Dragon cursed under his breath; he turned back to the tree and used another spell, one I had seen him use before to form his potion-bottles. He cast it now and reached down into the desiccated sand around our feet and began to pull out ropes and skeins of glowing glass. He flung them in swooping heaps onto the exposed roots, the falling leaves. Small fires began to catch around us, putting up a haze of smoke.

I was shaking, dazed with horror and blood. Kasia pushed me behind her, the sword in her hand, sheltering me even while tears were sliding down her face, too. "Look out!" she shouted, and I turned to see a great branch above the Dragon's head crack. It came falling heavily onto his shoulder and knocked him forward.

He caught himself instinctively on the trunk, dropping the rope of glass he was holding. He tried to pull away, but the tree was already seizing him, bark growing over his hands. "No!" I screamed, reaching for him.

He managed to drag one arm free at the cost of the other, silver bark climbing to the elbow, roots whipping themselves out of the ground and twining about his leg, dragging him in closer. They were tearing at his clothes. He seized a pouch at his waist, jerked the strap loose, and thrust something into my hands: it gurgled, a vial glowing fierce red-violet. It was fire-heart, a dram of it, and he shook me by the arm. "Now, you fool! If it takes me, you're all dead! Burn it and *run*!"

I looked up from the bottle and stared at him. He meant me to fire the tree, I realized; he meant me to burn the tree—and him with it. "Do you think I'd rather live like this?" he said to me, his voice tight and clenched, as though he was speaking past horror:

the bark had already swallowed one of his legs, and climbed nearly to the shoulder.

Kasia was next to me, her face pale and stricken; she said, "Nieshka, it's worse than dying. It's worse."

I stood with the vial clutched in my hand, glowing between my fingers, and then I put my hand on his shoulder and said to him, "*Ulozishtus*. The purging spell. Cast it with me."

He stared at me. Then he gave one short jerk of a nod. "Give her the vial," he said, between his clenched teeth. I gave Kasia the fire-heart and gripped the Dragon's hand, and together we said the spell: I whispered, *"Ulozishtus, ulozishtus,"* a steady drumbeat, and then he joined in with me, reciting all the long careful song of it. But I didn't let the purging magic flow: I held it back. In my mind I built a dam before the power of it, let our joined spell fill up a vast lake within me as the working built and built.

The swelling heat of it filled me, burning bright, almost unbearable. I couldn't breathe, my lungs crushed against my rib cage; my heart strained to beat. I couldn't see: the fighting went on somewhere behind me, a distant clamoring only: shouts, the eerie clatter of the walkers, the hollow ring of swords. It was coming closer and closer still. I felt Kasia's back pressed to mine; she was making herself a final shield. The fire-heart was singing cheerful and hungry in the vial she held, hoping to be let out, hoping to devour us all, almost comforting.

I held the working as long as I could, until the Dragon's voice failed, and then I opened my eyes again. The bark had climbed over his neck, up his cheek. It had sealed over his mouth, it was creeping around his eye. He squeezed my hand once, and then I poured the power through him, down the half-formed channel to the devouring tree.

He stiffened, his eyes going wide and unseeing. His hand clenched on mine in silent agony. Then the bark over his mouth withered away, flaking like the shed skin of some monstrous snake, and he was screaming aloud. I clutched his hand with both of mine, biting my lip against the pain of his brutal grip while he cried out, the tree blackening and charring away around him, leaves above us crackling into flames. They were falling, stinging bits of ash, the hideous smell of the fruit cooking and liquefying. Juice ran down the limbs, and sap came bursting in boiling-hot gouts from the trunks and the bark.

The roots caught as quickly as well-seasoned firewood: we'd pulled so much water out of them. The bark was loosening and peeling off in great strips. Kasia grabbed the Dragon's arm and wrestled his limp body away from the tree, blistered and seared. I helped her pull him away through the gathering smoke, and then she turned and plunged through the haze again. Dimly I saw her gripping a slab of bark, pulling it away in a thick sheet; she hacked at the tree with her sword and pried at it, and more of the sides broke away. I laid the Dragon down and stumbled to help her: the tree was too hot to touch, but I put my hands over it anyway and after a groping moment I blurted, *"Ilmeyon!"* Come out, come out, as if I were Jaga calling a rabbit out of a burrow for dinner.

Kasia hacked at it again, and then the wood split with a crack, and I saw through it a sliver of a woman's face, blank, a staring blue eye. Kasia reached into the edges of the broken gap and started pulling away more of the wood, breaking it away, and suddenly the queen came falling out, her whole body bending limply forward out of a hollow of wood and leaving a woman's shape behind, scraps of desiccated cloth falling away from her body and catching fire even as she tipped through the broken opening. She stopped, hanging: her head wouldn't come free, held by a net of golden hair, impossibly long and embedded in the wood all around her. Kasia slashed the sword down through the cloud, and the queen came loose and fell into our arms.

She was as heavy and inert as a log. Smoke and fire wreathed us, and above us the moaning and thrashing of the branches: the tree had become a pillar of fire. The fire-heart was clamoring so loudly in its vial it seemed to me I could hear it with my ears, eager to come out and join the blaze.

We staggered forward, Kasia all but dragging the three of us: me, Queen Hanna, and the Dragon. We fell out from beneath the branches into the clearing. The Falcon and Prince Marek alone of the soldiers remained, fighting back-to-back with ferocious skill, Marek's sword lit with the same white fire the Falcon held. The last four walkers crowded close. They made a sudden rush; the Falcon whipped them back with a circling lash of fire, and Marek chose one and leapt for it through the blaze: he caught its neck in one mailed fist and wrapped his boots about the body, one foot hooked underneath one of the forelimbs. He drove his sword down hard between the base of the neck and the body and twisted himself: almost exactly the motion of pulling a twig away from a living branch, and the long narrow head of the walker splintered and cracked.

He let its twitching body drop, then dived back through the dying ring of fire before the other walkers could close in on him. Four other dead walkers lay sprawled in the exact same way on the ground: he'd worked out a method, then, for killing them. But the walkers had almost caught him at the end, and he was staggering with fatigue. He had thrown aside his helm. He ducked his head and wiped his tabard across his dripping forehead, panting. The Falcon was sagging beside him, also. Though his lips never stopped moving, the silver fire around his hands was burning low; the white cloak had been discarded across the dirt, smoking where burning leaves were falling upon it. The three walkers backed away, making ready for another rush; he drew himself up.

"Nieshka," Kasia said, spurring me out of dull staring, and I stumbled forward, opening my mouth. Only a ragged croak came out, smoke-hoarsened. I struggled for another breath, and managed to whisper, *"Fulmedesh,"* or at least enough of a suggestion of the word to give my magic form, even as I fell forward and put my hands on the ground. The earth cracked along a line running away from me, opening beneath the walkers. As they fell into it thrashing, the Falcon flung fire into the crevice, and it closed up around them.

Marek turned, and then he suddenly came running towards me as I staggered up. He slid into the dirt heels-first and kicked my legs back out from under me. The silver mantis had lunged out of the burning cloud of the heart-tree, its wings alight and crackling with fire, seeking some last vengeance. I stared up into its golden, inhuman eyes; its dreadful claws drew back for another lunge. Marek was flat on the ground beneath its belly. He set his sword against a seam of the carapace and kicked its leg out from under it, one of only three remaining. It fell, impaling itself, even as he heaved up: it thrashed wildly, going over, and he pushed it off his sword with one final kick to join the raging blaze of the heart-tree. It lay still.

Marek turned and dragged me up to my feet. My legs were shaking; my whole body trembling. I couldn't hold myself upright. I had always been dubious of war stories, songs of battle: the occasional fights between boys in the village square had always ended in mud and bloody noses and clawing, snot and tears, nothing graceful or glorious, and I didn't see how adding swords and death to the mix could make it any better. But I couldn't have imagined the horror of this.

The Falcon was stumbling over to another man lying curled in the dirt. He had a vial of some elixir in his belt: he fed the man a swallow of it and helped him up. Together they went to a third with one arm only left: he had cauterized the stump in the fire, and lay dazed on the ground, staring up. Two men left, of thirty.

Prince Marek didn't seem stricken. He absently wiped an arm across his forehead again, smearing more soot across his face. He had already caught his breath, nearly; his chest rose and fell, but easily, not in the struggling heaves I could barely get as he easily pulled me with him, away from the flames to the cooler shelter of the trees beyond the clearing's edge. He didn't speak to me. I don't know if he even knew me: his eyes were half-glazed. Kasia joined us, the Dragon heaved over her shoulders; she stood incongruously easily beneath his deadweight.

Marek blinked a few more times while the Falcon gathered the two men towards us, and then he seemed to finally become aware of the spreading bonfire of the tree, the blackening branches falling. His grip on my arm tightened into bruising pain, the edges of the gauntlet digging into my flesh as I tried to pry at it. He turned to me and shook me, his eyes widening with rage and horror. "What have you done?" he snarled at me, harsh with smoke, and then he went suddenly very still.

The queen was standing in front of us, unmoving, lit golden in the light of the blazing tree. She stood like a statue where Kasia had propped her onto her feet, and her arms dangled by her sides. Her cropped hair was as yellow as Marek's, thin and fine; it floated around her head like a cloud. He stared at her, his face open as the beak of a hungry bird. He let go of me and reached out a hand.

"Don't touch her!" the Falcon said sharply, hoarse with smoke. "Get the chains."

Marek halted. He didn't take his eyes off her. For a moment I thought he wouldn't listen; then he turned and stumbled across the ruin of the battlefield to the corpse of his horse. The chains the Falcon had put on Kasia, while he'd examined her, were bundled up in cloth on the back of his saddle. Marek dragged them down and brought them back to us. The Falcon took the yoke from him with the cloth and cautiously, as wary as if he'd been approaching a mad dog, went towards the queen.

She didn't stir, her eyes didn't blink; it was as though she didn't even see him. He hesitated even so, and then he spoke the protection spell over himself again, and he put the yoke over her neck in one swift movement and backed away. She still didn't move. He reached out again, still with the cloth, and clasped the manacles onto her wrists one after another; then he draped the cloth over her shoulders.

There was a loud terrible crack behind us. We all jumped like rabbits. The heart-tree had split down its trunk, one whole massive half leaning away. It came down with a roaring crash, smashing through the hundred-year oaks on the edge of the clearing; a cloud of orange sparks roared up out of the heart of the trunk. The second half suddenly burst entirely into flames: consumed and roaring, and the branches thrashed once more and were still.

The queen's body came alive with one jerky, clenched motion; the chains scraped and clanked as she moved within them, a whine of metal, and she staggered away from us, putting her hands up in front of her. The cloth slid off her shoulders; she didn't notice it. She was groping at her own face with her curling, too-long nails, clawing at herself, with a low incoherent moan.

Marek sprang forward and caught her by the manacled wrists; she convulsively flung him off her with unnatural strength. Then she stopped and fixed a stare on him. He staggered back and caught his balance, straightened. Bloodstained, smeared with soot and sweat, he still looked a warrior and a prince; the green crest was still visible on his chest, the crown above the hydra. She looked at it and then at his face. She didn't speak, but her eyes didn't leave him.

He drew one quick harsh breath and said, "Mother."

SIXTEEN

She didn't answer him. Marek stood with his hands clenched, waiting, his eyes fixed on her face. But she didn't answer.

We stood silent and oppressed, still breathing the smoke of the heart-tree, the burning corpses of men and the Wood's creatures. Finally the Falcon gathered himself and limped forward. He raised his hands towards her face, hesitating a moment, but she didn't flinch from him. He put his hands on her cheeks and turned her towards him. He looked into her, his pupils widening and narrowing, changing shape; the color of his irises went from green to yellow to black. Hoarsely he said, "There's nothing. I can't find any corruption in her at all," and let his hands drop.

But there was nothing else, either. She didn't look at us, or if she did, that was even worse; her wide staring eyes didn't see our faces. Marek stood still panting in heaving breaths, staring at her. "Mother," he said again. "Mother, it's Marek. I've come to take you home."

Her face didn't change. The first horror had faded out of it. She was staring and empty now, hollowed out. "Once we're out of the Wood . . . ," I said, but my voice died in my throat. I felt odd and sick. Did you ever get out of the Wood, if you'd been in it for twenty years?

But Marek seized on the suggestion. "Which way?" he demanded, sliding his sword back into its sheath.

I rubbed ash away with a sleeve over my face. I looked down at my blistered and cracked hands, stained with blood. The whole from a part. "*Loytalal,*" I whispered to my blood. "Take me home."

I led them out of the Wood as best I could. I didn't know what we'd do if we met another walker, much less another mantis. We were a far distance from that shining company that had ridden into the Wood that morning. In my mind, I imagined us a gleaning-party creeping through the forest on our way home before nightfall, trying not to startle so much as a bird. I picked our way carefully through the trees. We didn't have any hope of breaking a trail, so we had to keep to the deer tracks and the thinner brush.

We crept out of the Wood half an hour before nightfall. I stumbled out from under the trees still following the glimmer of my spell: *home, home,* over and over again in my head, singsong. The glowing line ran curving towards the west and south, towards Dvernik. My feet kept carrying me after it, across the barren strip of razed dirt and into a wall of tall grass that finally became thick enough to halt me. Above the top edge of the grass, when I slowly raised my head, forested slopes rose up like a wall in the distance, hazy brown with the setting sun thrown along them.

The northern mountains. We'd come out not far from the mountain pass from Rosya. That made a certain sense, if the queen and Prince Vasily had been fleeing towards Rosya, and had been caught and taken into the Wood from there. But it meant we were miles and miles away from Zatochek.

Prince Marek came out of the Wood behind me with his head bent, his shoulders stooped as if he were dragging a heavy weight behind him. The two soldiers followed him raggedly. They'd pulled off their mail shirts and abandoned them somewhere along the way inside the Wood; their sword-belts, too. He alone was still in armor, and his sword was still in his hand, but when he reached the grass he sank in on himself, to his knees, and stayed there without moving. The soldiers came up to him and fell to either side of him, flat on their faces, as though they'd only been pulled along in his wake.

Kasia laid the Dragon down on the ground next to me, trampling the grass flat with her feet to make room. He was limp and still, his eyes closed. His right side was scorched and blistered everywhere, red and deadly glistening, his clothes torn away and burned off his skin. I'd never seen burns so dreadful.

The Falcon sagged to the ground on his other side. He held one end of a chain that reached to the yoke on the queen's neck; he tugged on it, and she halted, too, standing still and alone in the razed barren strip around the Wood. Her face had the same inhuman stillness as Kasia's, only worse, because no one was looking out of her eyes. It was like being followed by a marionette. When we tugged the chain forward, she walked, with a stiff, swinging puppet-stride as if she didn't entirely know how to use her arms and legs anymore, as if they wouldn't bend properly.

Kasia said, "We have to get farther from the Wood." None of us answered her, or moved; it seemed to me she was speaking from very far away. She carefully gripped me by the shoulder and shook me. "Nieshka," she said. I didn't answer. The sky was deepening to twilight, and the early spring mosquitoes were busy around us, whining in my ear. I couldn't even lift my hand to slap away a big one sitting right on my arm.

She straightened up and looked at us all, irresolute. I don't think she wanted to leave us there alone, in the condition we were in, but there wasn't much choice. Kasia bit her lip, then knelt in front of me and looked me in the face. "I'm going to Kamik," she said. "I think it's closer than Zatochek. I'll run all the way. Hold on, Nieshka, I'll be back as soon as I can find anyone."

I only stared at her. She hesitated, and then she reached into my skirt pocket and brought out Jaga's book. She pressed it into my hands. I closed my fingers around it, but I didn't move. She turned and plunged into the grass, hacking and pushing her way through, following the last light to the west.

I sat in the grass like a field mouse, thinking of nothing. The sound of Kasia fighting her way through the tall grass faded away. I was tracing the stitches of Jaga's book, feeling the soft ridges in the leather, mindlessly, staring at it. The Dragon lay inert beside me. His burns were getting worse, blisters rising translucent all over his skin. Slowly I opened the book and turned pages. *Good for burns, better with morning cobwebs and a little milk,* said the laconic page for one of her simpler remedies.

I didn't have cobwebs or milk, but after a little sluggish thought I put out my hand to one of the broken stems of grass around us and squeezed a few milky green drops out onto my finger. I rubbed them between my thumb and finger and hummed, *"Iruch, iruch,"* up and down, like singing a child down to sleep, and began to lightly touch the worst of his blisters one after another with my fingertip. Each one twitched and slowly began to shrink instead of swell, the angriest red fading.

The working made me feel—not better exactly, but cleaner, as though I were rinsing water over a wound. I kept singing on and on and on and on. "Stop making that *noise,*" the Falcon said finally, lifting his head on a hiss.

I reached out and grabbed his wrist. "Groshno's spell for burns," I told him: it was one of the charms the Dragon had tried to teach me when he'd still been insisting on thinking me a healer.

The Falcon was silent, and then he hoarsely began, *"Oyideh viruch,"* the start of the chant, and I went back to my humming, *"Iruch, iruch,"* while I felt out his spell, fragile as a spoked wheel built out of stalks of hay instead of wood, and hooked my magic onto it. He broke off his chant. I managed to hold the working together long enough to prod him into starting again.

It wasn't nearly the same as casting with the Dragon. This was like trying to push in harness with an old and contrary mule that I didn't like very much, with savage hard teeth waiting to bite me. I was trying to hold back from the Falcon even while I drove on the spell. But once he picked up the thread, the working began to grow. The Dragon's burns began fading quickly to new skin, except for a dreadful shiny scar twisting down the middle of his arm and side where the worst of the blisters had been.

The Falcon's voice was strengthening beside me, and my head cleared, too. Power was coursing through us, a renewed tide swelling, and he shook his head, blinking with it. He twisted his hand and caught my wrist, reaching for me, for more of my magic. Instinctively I jerked loose, and we lost the thread of the working. But the Dragon was already rolling over onto his hands, heaving for breath, retching. He coughed up masses of black wet soot out of his lungs. When the fit subsided, he sank back wearily onto his heels, wiping his mouth, and looked up. The queen was still standing on the razed ground nearby, a luminous pillar in the dark.

He pressed the heels of his hands to his eyes. "Of all the fool's errands that ever were," he rasped, so hoarse I could barely hear it, and dropped his hands again. He reached for my arm, and I helped him drag himself to his feet. We were alone in the sea of cooling grass. "We need to get back to Zatochek," he said, prodding. "To the supplies we left there."

I stared back at him dully, my strength fading again as the magic ebbed. The Falcon had already subsided back into a heap. The soldiers were beginning to shiver and twitch, their eyes staring as if they saw other things. Even Marek had gone inert, a silent slouched boulder between them. "Kasia went for help," I said finally.

He looked around at the prince, the soldiers, the queen; back to me and the Falcon, down to the dregs of ourselves. He rubbed his face. "All right," he said. "Help me lay them straight on their backs. The moon is almost up."

We wrestled Prince Marek and the soldiers flat in the grass, all three of them staring blindly at the sky. By the time we had wearily pushed down the grass around them, the moon was on their faces. The Dragon put me between him and the Falcon. We didn't have the strength for a full purging: the Dragon and the Falcon only chanted another few rounds of the shielding spell he'd used that morning, and I hummed my little cleansing spell, *Puhas, puhas, kai puhas.* A little color seemed to come back into their faces.

Kasia came back not quite an hour later, driving a woodcutter's cart with a hard expression. "I'm sorry I took so long," she said shortly; I didn't ask how she'd got the cart. I knew what someone would have thought, seeing her come from the direction of the Wood, looking as she did.

We tried to help her, but she had to do the work mostly alone. She lifted Prince Marek and the two soldiers onto the cart, then heaved the three of us up after them. We sat with our legs dangling out the back. Kasia went to the queen and stepped between her and the trees, breaking the line of her gaze. The queen looked at her with the same blankness. "You aren't in there anymore," Kasia said to the queen. "You're free. We're free."

The queen didn't answer her, either.

We were a week in Zatochek, all of us laid out on pallets in the barn on the edge of town. I don't remember any of it from the moment I fell asleep in the cart until I woke up three days later in the warm quieting smell of hay, with Kasia at my bedside wiping my face with a damp cloth. The dreadful honey-sweet taste of the Dragon's purging elixir coated my mouth. When I was strong enough to stagger up from my cot, later that morning, he put me through another round of purging, and then made me do another for him.

"The queen?" I asked him, as we sat on a bench outside afterwards, both of us rag-limp.

He jerked his chin forward, and I saw her: she was in the shade on the other side of the clearing, sitting quietly on a stump beneath a willow-tree. She still wore the enchanted yoke, but someone had given her a white dress. There wasn't a stain or smudge anywhere on it; even the hem was clean, as if she hadn't moved from the spot since she'd been put into it. Her beautiful face was blank as an unwritten book.

"Well, she's free," the Dragon said. "Was it worth the lives of thirty men?"

He spoke savagely, and I hugged my arms around myself. I didn't want to think about that nightmarish battle, about the slaughter. "Those two soldiers?" I said, a whisper.

"They'll live," he said. "And so will our fine princeling: more fortune than he deserves. The Wood's grip on them was weak." He pushed himself up. "Come: I'm purging them by stages. It's time for another round."

Two days later, Prince Marek was himself again with a speed that made me feel dull and sourly envious: he rose from his bed in the morning and by dinnertime he was wolfing down an entire roast chicken and doing exercises. I could barely taste the few mouthfuls of bread I forced down. Watching him pull himself up and down on a tree-branch made me feel even more like a cloth that had been washed and wrung out too many times. Tomasz and Oleg were awake, too, the two soldiers; I'd learned their names by then, ashamed that I didn't know any of the ones we'd left behind.

Marek tried to take some food to the queen. She only stared at the plate he held out to her, and wouldn't chew when he put slivers of meat in her mouth. Then he tried a bowl of porridge: she didn't refuse, but she didn't help. He had to work the spoon into her mouth like a mother with an infant just learning how to eat. He kept at it grimly, but after an hour, when he'd barely managed to get half a dozen swallows into her, he got up and hurled the bowl and spoon savagely against a rock, porridge and pottery-shards flying. He stormed away. The queen didn't even blink at that, either.

I stood in the doorway of the barn, watching and wretched. I couldn't be sorry to have got her out—at least she wasn't being tormented by the Wood anymore, devoured to the scraps of herself. But this awful half-life left to her seemed worse than dying. She wasn't ill or delirious, the way Kasia had been those first few days after the purging. There just didn't seem to be enough left of her to feel or think.

The next morning, Marek came up behind me and caught me by the arm as I trudged back to the barn with a bucket of wellwater; I jumped in alarm and sloshed water over us both, trying to jerk out of his grip. He ignored both the water and my efforts and snapped at me, "Enough of this! They're soldiers; they'll be fine. They'd already be fine, if the Dragon didn't keep emptying potions into their bellies. Why haven't you done anything for *her*?"

"What do you imagine there is to do?" the Dragon said, coming out of the barn.

Marek wheeled on him. "She needs healing! You haven't even dosed her, when you have flasks to spare—"

"If there was corruption in her to purge, we'd purge it," the Dragon said. "You can't heal absence. Consider yourself lucky she didn't burn with the heart-tree; if you want to call it luck, and not a pity."

"A pity *you* didn't, if that's all the advice you have," Marek said.

The Dragon's eye glittered with what looked to me like a dozen cutting replies, but he compressed his lips and shut them in. Marek's teeth were moving against each other, and through his gripping hand I could feel strung-hard tension, a trembling like a spooked horse, though he'd been as steady as a rock in that terrible glade with death and danger all around him.

The Dragon said, "There's no corruption left in her. For the rest, only time and healing will help. We'll take her back to the tower as soon as I've finished purging your men and it's safe for them to go among other people. I'll see what else can be done. Until then, sit with her and talk of familiar things."

"*Talk?*" Marek said. He shoved my arm out of his grip; more water sloshed out over my feet as he stalked away.

The Dragon took the bucket from me, and I followed him back into the barn. "Can we do anything for her?" I asked.

"What is there to be done with a blank slate?" he said. "Give her some time and she may write something new on it. As for bringing back whatever she was—" He shook his head.

Marek sat by the queen the rest of the day; I had glimpses of his hard, downturned face a few times when I came out of the barn. But at least he seemed to accept there wasn't going to be a sudden miraculous cure. That evening he got up and walked to Zatochek to speak to the village headman; the next day, when Tomasz and Oleg could finally walk as far as the well and back on their own, he gripped them hard by the shoulders and said, "We'll light a fire for the others tomorrow morning, in the village square."

Men came from Zatochek to bring us horses. They were wary of us, and I couldn't blame them. The Dragon had sent word we would come out of the Wood, and he'd told them where to keep us and what signs of corruption to look for, but even so I wouldn't have been surprised if they'd come with torches instead, to burn us all inside the barn. Of course, if the Wood had taken possession of us, we'd have done worse things than sit in a barn quietly exhausted for a week.

Marek himself helped Tomasz and Oleg up into their saddles before he lifted the queen up to her own, a steady brown mare some ten years old. She sat stiff and inflexible; he had to put her feet one by one into the stirrups. He paused, looking up at her from the ground: the reins hung slack in her manacled hands where he'd given them to her. "Mother," he tried again. She didn't look at him. After a moment, his jaw hardened. He took a rope and made a leading rein for her horse, hooked it to his own saddle, and led her on.

We rode behind him to the square and found a tall bonfire assembled and waiting, full of seasoned wood, and all the village in their holiday best standing on the far side. They held torches in their hands. I didn't know anyone from Zatochek well, but they came occasionally to our market days in spring. A handful of distantly familiar faces looked out at me from the crowd, like ghosts from another life through the faint grey haze of smoke, while I stood opposite them with a prince and wizards.

Marek took a torch himself: he stood by the wood pile with his brand lifted into the air and named every man we had lost, one after another, and Janos at the last. He beckoned to Tomasz and Oleg, and together the three of them stepped forward and thrust their torches into the heaped wood. The smoke came smarting into my eyes and barely-healed throat, and the heat was dreadful. The Dragon watched the fire catch with a hard face and then turned away: I know he didn't think much of the prince honoring the men he'd led to their deaths. But it loosened something in me to hear all their names.

The bonfire kept burning a long time. The villagers brought out food and beer, whatever they had, and pressed it on us. I crept away into a corner with Kasia and drank too many cups of beer, washing misery and smoke and the taste of the purging-elixir out of my mouth, until finally we leaned against each other and wept softly; I had to hold on to her, because she didn't dare grip me tight.

The drink made me lighter and more dull at the same time, my head aching, and I snuffled into my sleeves. Across the square, Prince Marek was speaking to the village headman and a wide-eyed young carter. They were standing beside a handsome green wagon, fresh-painted, with a team of four horses, their manes and tails clumsily braided in green ribbons also. The queen was already sitting in the wagon bed, cushioned on straw, with a wool cloak draped over her shoulders. The golden chains of the enchanted yoke caught the sunlight and glittered against her shift.

I blinked a few times at the sun-dazzle, and by the time I began to make sense of what I was looking at, the Dragon was already striding across the square, demanding, "What are you doing?" I climbed to my feet and went to them.

Prince Marek turned even as I came. "Arranging for passage to take the queen home," he said, pleasantly.

"Don't be absurd. She needs healing—"

"Which she can get in the capital as easily as here," Prince Marek said. "I don't choose to let you lock my mother up in your tower until it pleases you to let her out again, Dragon. Don't imagine that I've forgotten how unwillingly you came with us."

"You seem ready to forget a great many other things," the Dragon bit out. "Such as your vows to raze the Wood all the way to Rosya, if we succeeded."

"I've forgotten nothing," Marek said. "I haven't the men to help you now. What better way to get you the men you need than by going back to the court to ask my father for them?"

"The only thing you can do at court is parade around that hollow puppet and call yourself a hero," the Dragon said. "*Send* for the men! We can't simply go now. Do you think the Wood won't make answer for what we've done, if we ride away and leave the valley defenseless?"

Marek kept his fixed smile, but it trembled on his face, and his hand worked open and shut upon his sword-hilt. The Falcon smoothly inserted himself between them, laying a hand on Marek's arm, and said, "Your Highness, while Sarkan's tone is objectionable, he isn't mistaken."

For a moment I thought perhaps he understood, now; perhaps the Falcon had felt enough of the malice of the Wood for himself to realize the threat it made. I looked at the Dragon with surprised hope, but his face was hardening, even before the Falcon turned to him with a graceful inclination of his head. "I think Sarkan will agree that despite his gifts, the Willow exceeds him in the healing arts, and she will be able to aid the queen if anyone can. And it is his sworn duty to hold back the Wood. He cannot leave the valley."

"Very well," Prince Marek said at once, even though he was talking through his clenched teeth: a rehearsed answer. They had worked it out between them, I realized in dawning outrage.

Then the Falcon added, "And you in turn must realize, Sarkan, that Prince Marek cannot possibly let you just keep Queen Hanna and your peasant girl here." He gestured to Kasia, standing beside me. "Of course they must both go to the capital, at once, and face their trial for corruption."

"A clever piece of maneuvering," the Dragon said to me afterwards, "and an effective one. He's right: I don't have the right to abandon the valley without the king's leave, and by the law, strictly speaking, they must both stand trial."

"But it doesn't have to be this instant!" I said. I darted a look at the queen, sitting listless and silent in the wagon while the villagers piled too many supplies and blankets in around her, more than we would have needed if we'd been going to the capital and back again three times without a stop. "What if we just took her back to the tower, now—her and Kasia? Surely the king would understand—"

The Dragon snorted. "The king's a reasonable man. He wouldn't have minded in the least if I'd discreetly whisked away the queen for a convalescence out of anyone's sight, before anyone had seen her or even knew for certain that she was rescued. But now?" He waved an arm at the villagers. Everyone had gathered in a loose ring near the wagon, at a safe distance, to stare at the queen and whisper bits of the story to each other. "No. He would object greatly to my openly defying the law of the realm before witnesses."

Then he looked at me and said, "And I can't go, either. The king might allow it, but not the Wood."

I stared back at him, hollow. "I can't let them just take Kasia," I said, half a plea. I knew this was where I belonged, where I was needed, but to let them drag Kasia off to the capital for this trial, where the law said they might put her to death—and I didn't trust Prince Marek at all, except to do whatever suited him best.

"I know," the Dragon said. "It's just as well. We can't strike another blow against the Wood without soldiers, and a great number of them. And you're going to have to get them from the king. Whatever he says, Marek isn't thinking of anything but the queen, and

Solya may not be wicked, but he likes to be too clever for everyone's good."

I said finally, a question, "Solya?" The name felt strange on my tongue, moving, like the high shadow of a bird, circling; even as I said it, I felt the brush of a piercing eye.

"It means *falcon*, in the spell-tongue," the Dragon said. "They'll put a name on you, too, before you're confirmed to the list of wizards. Don't let them put that off until after the trial; otherwise you won't have the right to testify. And listen to me: what you've done here carries power with it, of a different sort. Don't let Solya take all the credit, and don't be shy of using it."

I had no idea how to carry out any of the instructions he was firing at me: how was *I* supposed to persuade the king to give us any soldiers? But Marek was already calling for Tomasz and Oleg to mount up, and I didn't need the Dragon to tell me I was going to have to work it out for myself. I swallowed and nodded instead, and then I said, "Thank you—Sarkan."

His name tasted of fire and wings, of curling smoke, of subtlety and strength and the rasping whisper of scales. He eyed me and said stiffly, "Don't land yourself into a boiling-pot, and as difficult as you may find it, try and present a respectable appearance."

SEVENTEEN

I didn't do very well at following his advice.

We were a week and a day riding to the capital, and my horse jerked her head the entire way: step, step, step, and a sudden nervous thrust forward against the bit, pulling my reins and my arms forward, until my neck and my shoulders were hard as stone. I always lagged to the back of our little caravan, and the big iron-bound wagon-wheels kicked up a fine cloud of dust in front of me. My horse added regular sneezing pauses to her gait. Even before we passed Olshanka I was coated in pale grey, sweat clumping the dust into thick brown lines under my fingernails.

The Dragon had written me a letter for the king in the last few minutes we'd had together. It was only a few lines hastily scribbled on cheap paper with thin ink borrowed from the villagers, telling him I was a witch, and asking him for men. But he had folded it over, and cut his thumb with a knife and wiped a little blood across the edge, and then he'd written his name through the smear: *Sarkan* in strong black letters that smoked at the edges. When I took it out of my skirt pocket and touched the letters with my fingers, the whisper of smoke and beating wings came near. It was a comfort and a frustration at the same time, as every day's miles took me farther from where I should have been, helping to hold back the Wood.

"Why are you insisting on taking Kasia?" I said to Marek, one last try as we camped the first night at the foot of the mountains, near the shallow eddy of a stream hurrying off to join the Spindle. I could see the Dragon's tower to the south, lit orange by the last of the sunset. "Take the queen if you insist on it, and let us go back. You've seen the Wood, you've seen what it is—"

"My father sent me here to deal with Sarkan's corrupted village girl," he said. He was sluicing his head and neck down with water. "He's expecting her, or her head. Which would you prefer I took with me?"

"But he'll understand about Kasia once he sees the queen," I said.

Marek shook off the water and raised his head. The queen still sat blank and unmoving in the wagon, staring ahead, as the night closed around her. Kasia was sitting next to her. They were both changed, both strange and straight and unwearied even by a full day of travel; they both shone like polished wood. But Kasia's head was turned back looking towards Olshanka and the valley, and her mouth and her eyes were worried and alive.

We looked at them together, and then Marek stood up. "The queen's fate is hers," he said to me flatly, and walked away. I hit at the water in frustration, then I cupped water and washed my face, rivulets black with dirt running away over my fingers.

"How dreadful for you," the Falcon said, popping up behind me without warning and making me come spluttering up out of my hands. "To be escorted to Kralia by the prince, acclaimed as a witch and a heroine. What misery!"

I wiped my face on my skirt. "Why do you even want me there? There are other wizards at court. They can see the queen isn't corrupted for themselves—"

Solya was shaking his head as if he pitied me, silly village girl, who didn't understand anything. "Do you really think it's so trivial? The law is absolute: the corrupted must die by the flame."

"But the king will pardon her?" I said. It came out a question.

Solya looked thoughtfully over at the queen, almost invisible now, a shadow among shadows, and didn't answer. He glanced back at me. "Sleep well, Agnieszka," he said. "We have a long road yet to go." He went to join Marek by the fire.

After that, I didn't sleep well at all, that night or any of the others.

Word raced ahead of us. When we passed through villages and towns, people stopped work to line the road and stare at us wide-eyed, but they didn't come near, and held their children back against them. And on the last day a crowd was waiting for us, at the last crossroads before the king's great city.

I had forgotten hours and days by then. My arms ached, my back ached, my legs ached. My head ached worst of all, some part of me tethered back to the valley, stretched out of recognizable shape and trying to make sense of myself when I was so far from anything I knew. Even the mountains, my constants, had disappeared. Of course I'd known there were parts of the country with no mountains, but I'd imagined I would still see them somewhere in the distance, like the moon. But every time I looked behind me, they were smaller and smaller, until finally they disappeared with one final gasp of rolling hills. Wide rich fields planted with grain seemed to go on forever in every direction, flat and unbroken, the whole shape of the world gone strange. There were no forests here.

We climbed one last hill, and at the summit found ourselves overlooking the vast sprawl of Kralia, the capital: yellow-walled houses with orange-brown roofs blooming like wildflowers around the banks of the wide shining Vandalus, and in the midst of them Zamek Orla, the red-brick castle of the kings, rearing up on a high outcropping of stone. It was larger than any building I could have imagined: the Dragon's tower was smaller than the smallest tower of the castle, and there seemed to be a dozen of them jutting up to the sky.

The Falcon looked around at me, I think to see how I took the view, but it was so large and strange that I didn't even gawk. I felt I was looking at a picture in a book, not something real, and I was so tired that I was nothing but my body: the steady dull throb in my thighs, the tremor all along my arms, the thick grime of dust muffling my skin.

A company of soldiers waited for us below at the crossroads, arrayed in ranks around a large platform that had been raised over the center. Half a dozen priests and monks stood upon it, flanking a man in the most astonishing priest's robes I had ever seen, deep purple embroidered all over with gold. His face was long and severe, made longer by his tall, double-coned hat.

Marek pulled up, looking down at them, and I had time to catch my plodding horse up to him and the Falcon. "Well, my father's trotted out the old prosy," Marek said. "He'll put the relics on her. Is this going to cause difficulties?"

"I wouldn't imagine so," the Falcon said. "Our dear archbishop can be a little tedious, I'll grant you, but his stiff neck is all to the good at the moment. He'd never permit anyone to substitute in a false relic, and the real ones won't show anything that's not there."

Caught in indignation at their impiety—calling the archbishop *old prosy!*—I missed the chance to ask for an explanation: why would anyone *want* to show corruption if it wasn't there? Marek was already spurring his horse onward. The queen's wagon rattled down the hill behind him, and even though their faces were avid and bright with curiosity, the crowd of onlookers drew back from it like a wave washing back out from the shore, keeping well clear of the wheels. I saw many of them wearing cheap little charms against evil and crossing themselves as we passed.

The queen sat without looking to either side or fidgeting, only rocking back and forth with the wagon's roll. Kasia had drawn close to her side, darting a look back at me that I returned, equally wide-eyed. We'd never seen so many people in our life. People were press-

ing in close enough around me to brush against my legs, despite my
horse's big iron-shod hooves.

When we drew up to the platform, the soldiers let us through
their ranks and then circled round, leveling their pikes at us. I
realized in alarm that there was a tall thick stake raised up in the
middle of the platform, and beneath it a heap of straw and tinder.
I reached forward and caught a corner of the Falcon's sleeve in
alarm.

"Stop looking like a frightened rabbit, sit up straight, and *smile*,"
he hissed at me. "The last thing we need to do right now is give
them any excuse to imagine something's wrong."

Marek behaved as though he didn't even see the sharp steel
points not two feet from his head. He dismounted with a flourish of
the cape he'd bought, a few towns back, and went to lift the queen
down from the wagon. Kasia had to help her along from the other
side, and then at Marek's impatient beckoning, she climbed down
after her.

I'd never known it before, but a crowd so large had a steady
running noise to it like a river, a murmuring that rose and ebbed
without turning into separate voices. But now a complete hush descended. Marek led the queen up the steps onto the platform, the
golden yoke still on her, and drew her before the priest in the tall
hat.

"My Lord Archbishop," Marek said, his voice rolling out clear
and loud. "At great peril, my companions and I have freed the
queen of Polnya from the evil grasp of the Wood. I charge you now
to examine her to the utmost, to prove her with all your relics and
the power of your great office: be sure that she bears no sign of
corruption, which might spread and infect other innocent souls."

Of course that was exactly what the archbishop was here for, but
I don't think he liked Marek making it seem as though it was all his
idea. His mouth pressed down to a thin line. "Be sure that I will,
Your Highness," he said coldly, and turned and beckoned. One of

the monks stepped up beside him: a short, anxious-looking man
in plain brown linen, with brown hair cut in a round cap around
his head. His eyes were enormous and blinking behind large gold-
rimmed spectacles. He held a long wooden casket in his hands. He
opened it, and the archbishop reached in and lifted out with both
hands a fine shining mesh of gold and silver, almost like a net. The
whole crowd murmured approvingly, wind rustling in spring leaves.

The archbishop held up the net and prayed long and sonorously,
and then he turned and flung the net over the queen's head. It
settled over her gently and the edges unrolled, draping to her feet.
Then to my surprise the monk stepped forward and put his hands
on the mesh and spoke. *"Yilastus kosmet, yilastus kosmet vestuo palta,"* he
began, and went on from there: a spell that flowed into the lines of
the net and lit them up.

The light filled the queen's whole body from every side, illuminating her. She shone atop the platform, head up straight, blazing.
It wasn't like the light of the *Summoning*. That was a cold clear bril-
liance, hard and painful. This light felt like coming back home late
in midwinter to find a lamp shining out of the window, beckoning
you into the house: it was a light full of love and warmth. A sighing
went around the crowd. Even the priests drew back for a moment
just to look at the shining queen.

The monk kept his hand on the net, steadily pouring in magic. I
kicked my horse until she grudgingly moved in closer to the Falcon's
and leaned from my saddle to whisper, "Who is he?"

"Do you mean our gentle Owl?" he said. "Father Ballo. He's
the archbishop's delight, as you might imagine: it's not often you
can find a meek and biddable wizard." He sounded disdainful, but
the monk didn't look so very meek to me: he looked worried and
displeased.

"And that net?" I asked.

"You've heard of Saint Jadwiga's veil, surely," the Falcon said,
so offhanded I gawked at him. It was the holiest relic of all Polnya.

I had heard the veil was only brought out when they crowned the kings, to prove them free of any influence of evil.

The crowd was jostling the soldiers now to come nearer, and even the soldiers were fascinated, the tips of their pikes rising into the air as they let themselves be pushed up close. The priests were going over the queen inch by inch, bending down to squint at her toes, holding each arm out to inspect her fingers, staring at her hair. But we could all see her shining, full of light; there was no shadow in her. One after another the priests stood up and shook their heads to the archbishop. Even the severity in his face was softening, the wonder of the light in his face.

When they had finished their examination, Father Ballo gently lifted the veil away. The priests brought other relics, too, and now I recognized them: the plate of Saint Kasimir's armor still pierced with a tooth from the dragon of Kralia that he had slain; the arm bone of Saint Firan in a gold-and-glass casket, blackened from fire; the golden cup Saint Jacek had saved from the chapel. Marek lifted the queen's hands onto each, one after another, and the archbishop prayed over her.

They repeated each trial on Kasia, but the crowd wasn't interested in her. Everyone hushed to watch the queen, but they all talked noisily while the priests examined Kasia, more unruly than any crowd I'd ever seen, even though they were in the presence of so many holy relics and the archbishop himself. "Little more to be expected from the Kralia mob," Solya told my half-shocked expression. There were even bun-sellers going around the crowd hawking fresh rolls, and from atop my horse I could see a couple of enterprising men had set up a stand to sell beer just down the road.

It was beginning to have the feeling of a holiday, of a festival. And finally the priests filled Saint Jacek's golden cup with wine, and Father Ballo murmured over it: a faint curl of smoke rose up from the wine, and it went clear. The queen drank it all when they put it to her lips, and she didn't fall down in a fit. She didn't change her expression at all, but that didn't matter. Someone in the crowd raised up a cup of sloshing beer and shouted, "God be praised! The queen is saved!" People all began to cheer madly and press in on us, all fear forgotten, so loudly I could barely hear the archbishop giving his grudging permission for Marek to take the queen into the city.

The crowd's ecstasy was almost worse than the soldiers' pikes had been. Marek had to shove people out of the way to get the wagon up next to the platform, and lift the queen and Kasia back into it bodily. He abandoned his own horse and jumped into the cart and took the reins. He liberally lashed people away from the heads of the horses with the carter's whip to make room, and Solya and I had to bring our horses right up to the back of the wagon as the mob closed in again behind us.

They stayed with us all the five miles left towards the city, running alongside and after us, and when any fell off the pace, more came to swell the ranks. By the time we reached the bridge over the Vandalus, grown men and women had abandoned their day's work to follow, and by the time we reached the outer gates of the castle we were barely moving through a wildly cheering crowd that pressed in on us from all sides, a living thing with ten thousand voices, all of them shouting with joy. The news had traveled already: the queen was saved, the queen was uncorrupted. Prince Marek had saved the queen at last.

We were all living in a song: that was how it felt. I felt it myself, even with the queen's golden head swaying back and forth with the rocking wagon and making no effort to resist the motion, even knowing how small our real victory had been and how many men had died for it. There were children running beside my horse, laughing up at me—and probably not in any complimentary way, because I was one enormous smudge with tangled hair and a torn skirt—but I didn't mind. I looked down and laughed with them, too, forgetting my stiff arms and my numb legs.

Marek rode at our head with a nearly exalted expression. I suppose it must have felt to him, too, like his life had become a song. Right then, nobody was thinking about the men who hadn't come back. Oleg had the stump of his arm still bound up tightly, but he waved the other to the crowd with vigor, and kissed his hand to every pretty girl in sight. Even when we had gone through the gates of the castle, the crowd didn't abate: the king's soldiers had come out of their barracks and the noblemen out of their houses, throwing flowers in our path, and the soldiers clashing their swords on their shields in a clamoring applause.

Only the queen paid no attention to it all. They had taken the yoke and chains off her, but she sat no differently, still next thing to a carven figure.

We had to fall into single file to come through the final archway into the inner courtyard of the castle itself. The castle was dizzyingly large, arches rising in three tiers from the ground around me, endless faces leaning over the balconies, smiling down at us. I stared dazzled back up at them, at the embroidered banners in their riot of color everywhere, at the columns and the towers all around. The king himself was standing at the head of a staircase at one side of the courtyard. He wore a mantle of blue clasped at the throat with a great jewel, a red stone in gold with pearls.

The dull roar of cheering was still coming from outside the walls. Inside, the whole court hushed around us like the start of a play. Prince Marek had lifted the queen down from the wagon. He led her forward and up the stairs, courtiers ebbing like a tide before him, and brought her to the king. I found I was holding my own breath.

"Your Majesty," Marek said, "I restore to you your queen." The sun was shining brilliantly, and he looked like a warrior saint in his armor and his green cloak, his white tabard. The queen beside him was a tall stiff figure in her plain white shift, her short cloud of golden hair, and her transmuted skin lustrous.

The king looked down at them, his brow drawn. He seemed more worried than jubilant. We were all silent, waiting. At last he drew breath to speak, and only then the queen stirred. She slowly lifted up her head to look him in the face. He stared at her. She blinked her eyes once, and then she sighed a little and sank in on herself as limply as a sack: Prince Marek had to drag her forward by the arm he held and catch her, or she would have fallen down the stairs.

The king let out his breath, and his shoulders straightened a little as if let off a string, relaxing. His voice carried strongly across the courtyard. "Take her to the Grey Rooms, and let the Willow be sent for." Servants were already swooping in. They carried her away from us and into the castle as if on a wave.

And just like that—the play was ended. The noise inside the court-yard climbed back up to a roar to match the crowd outside, every-one talking to everyone else, across all three stories of the courtyard. The bright heady feeling ran out of me like I'd been unstoppered and turned over. Too late I remembered I wasn't here for a tri-umph. Kasia sat in the wagon in her white prisoner's shift, alone, condemned; Sarkan was a hundred leagues away, trying to hold the Wood off from Zatochek without me; and I had no idea how I was going to fix either of those things.

I shook my feet out of my stirrups, heaved my leg over, and slith-ered to the ground inelegantly. My legs wobbled when I put my weight on them. A groom came for my horse. I let him take her away, a little reluctantly: she wasn't a good horse, but she was a familiar rock in this ocean of strangeness. Prince Marek and the Falcon were going into the castle along with the king. I had already lost sight of Tomasz and Oleg in the crowd, surrounded by others in uniform.

Kasia was climbing out of the back of the wagon, a small com-pany of guards waiting for her. I pushed through the tide of ser-vants and courtiers and got between them and her.

"What are you going to do with her?" I demanded, shrill with worry. I must have looked absurd to them in my dusty ragged peasant clothes, like a sparrow piping at a pack of hunting tomcats; they couldn't see the magic in my belly, ready to come roaring out of me.

But however insignificant I looked, I was still part of the triumph, of the queen's rescue, and anyway they weren't inclined to cruelty. The chief guard, a man with the most enormous mustaches I had ever seen, the tips waxed into stiff curls, said to me kindly enough, "Are you her maid? Don't fret; we're to take her to be with the queen herself, in the Grey Tower, with the Willow to look after them. Everything's to be done right and by the law."

That wasn't much comfort: by the law, Kasia and the queen should both have been put to death at once. But Kasia whispered, "It's all right, Nieshka." It wasn't, but there wasn't anything else to do. The guards put her among them, four men before and four men after, and marched her away into the palace.

I stared after them hollowly for a moment, and then I realized I'd never find her again in this enormous place if I didn't see where they took her. I jumped and darted after them. "Here, now," a door guard said to me as I tried to follow them inside, but I told him, "*Param param,*" humming it like the song about the tiny fly that no one could catch, and he blinked and I was past him.

I trailed after the guards like a dangling thread, keeping my hum going to tell everyone I passed that I was too small to notice, nothing important. It wasn't hard. I felt as small and insignificant as could be imagined. The corridor went on and on. There were doors everywhere, heavy wood and hung with iron. Servants and courtiers bustled in and out of enormous rooms hung with tapestries, full of carven furniture and stone fireplaces bigger than my front door. Glittering lamps full of magic hung from the ceilings, and in the hallways, racks of tall white candles stood, burning without melting.

Finally the corridor ended in a small iron door, guarded again. The guards nodded to Kasia's escort, and let them and rag-tag me through into a narrow circling stairway, their eyes sliding over me. We climbed and climbed, my tired legs struggling to push me up each step, until at last we came crowding onto a small round land-ing. It was dim and smoky: there wasn't any window, and only an ordinary oil lamp stood set in a rough niche in the wall. It shone on the dull grey of another heavy iron door, a big round knocker upon it shaped like the head of a hungry imp, the knocker's ring held in its wide open mouth. A strange chill came off the iron, a cold wind lapping at my skin, even though I was pressed up against the wall in the corner behind the tall guards.

The chief guard knocked, and the door swung inward. "We've brought the other girl, milady," he said.

"All right," a woman's voice said, crisply. The guards parted to let Kasia through. A tall slim woman stood in the doorway, yel-low coiled braids and a golden headdress atop her head, wearing a blue silk gown delicately jeweled at the neck and waist, with a train sweeping the floor behind her, although her sleeves were practical, laced snug from the elbow to the wrist. She stood to one side and waved Kasia in past her with two impatient flicks of her long hand. I had a brief glimpse of a large room beyond, carpeted and com-fortable, and the queen sitting upright in a straight-backed chair. She was looking blankly out a window down at the glitter of the Vandalus.

"And what's this?" the lady said, turning to look at me. All the guards turned and stared, seeing me. I froze.

"I—" the chief guard stammered, going a little red in the face, with a darted look at the two men who'd been last in their party, a look that promised them trouble for not noticing me. "She's—"

"I'm Agnieszka," I said. "I came with Kasia and the queen."

The lady gave me one incredulous stare that saw every snagged thread and every mud-spatter on my skirts, even the ones in back, and was astonished to find that I had the gall to speak. She looked at the guard. "Is this one suspected of corruption as well?" she de-manded.

"No, milady, not as I know," he said.

"Then why are you bringing her to me? I've enough to do here."

She turned back into the room, her train swashing along after her, and the door slammed shut. Another cold wave washed over me and back to the imp with its greedy mouth, licking away the last of my concealing spell. It devoured magic, I realized: that must have been why they brought corrupted prisoners here.

"How did you get in here?" the chief guard demanded suspiciously, all of them looming around me.

I would have liked to hide myself away again, but I couldn't with that hungry mouth waiting. "I'm a witch," I said. They looked even more suspicious. I brought out the letter I still clutched in my skirt pocket: the paper was more than a little grubbier for wear, but the charred letters of the seal still smoked faintly. "The Dragon gave me a letter for the king."

EIGHTEEN

They took me downstairs and put me into a small unused stateroom, for lack of anyplace better. The guards kept watch outside the door while their captain went off, my letter in hand, to find out what ought to be done with me. My legs were ready to give out on me, but there was nothing to sit on but a few alarming chairs pushed up against the wall, delicate fragile-looking confections of white paint and gilt and red velvet cushions. I would have thought any one of them a throne, if there hadn't been four in a row.

I leaned against the wall for a while instead, and then I tried sitting on the hearth, but the fire hadn't been lit in here for a long time. The ashes were dead and the stone was cold. I went back to the wall. I went back to the hearth. Finally I decided that no one could put a chair in a room and not mean anyone to sit on it, and I gingerly perched on the edge of one of the chairs, holding my skirts close against me.

The moment I sat, the door opened and a servant came in, a

woman in a crisp black dress, something like Danka's age with a small pursed mouth of disapproval. I sprang up guiltily. Four long gleaming red threads followed me unraveling from the cushion, caught on a burr on my skirt, and a long sharp white-painted splinter snagged in my sleeve and broke off. The woman's mouth pursed harder, but she only said, "This way, please," stiffly.

She led me out past the guards, who didn't look sorry to see the back of me, and took me back up yet another different staircase—I'd seen half a dozen in the castle already—and showed me to a tiny dark cell of a room on the second floor. It had a narrow window that looked out on the stone wall of the cathedral: a rainspout shaped like a wide-mouthed and hungry gargoyle sneered in at me. She left me there before I could think to ask her what to do next.

I sat down on the cot. I must have slept, because by the next thought I had, I was flat on the cot instead, but it wasn't a deliberate choice; I didn't even remember lying down. I struggled up still sore and weary, but too conscious that I had no time to waste, and no idea what to do. I didn't know how to make anyone pay attention to me, unless I went to the middle of the courtyard and began to lob fire spells at the walls. I doubted that would make the king any more inclined to let me speak at Kasia's trial.

I was sorry now that I'd given the Dragon's letter away, my only tool and talisman. How did I know it had even been delivered? I decided to go find it: I remembered the guard captain's face, or at least his mustache. There couldn't be many mustaches like that even in all Kralia. I stood up and pulled the door open boldly, walked out into the hallway, and nearly ran straight into the Falcon. He was just raising his hand to the latch on my door. He flowed deftly back out of my way, saving us both, and gave me a small, gentle smile that I didn't trust at all.

"I hope you're feeling refreshed," he said, and offered me his arm.

I didn't take it. "What do you want?"

He turned the gesture neatly into a long inviting sweep of his hand towards the hallway. "To escort you to the Charovnikov. The king has given orders you're to be examined for the list."

I was so relieved that I didn't quite believe him. I eyed him side-long, half-expecting a trick. But he kept standing there with his arm and smile, waiting for me. "At once," he added, "although perhaps you'd care to change first?"

I would have liked to tell him what to do with his mocking little hint, but I looked down at myself: all mud and dust and sweat-stained creases, and underneath the mess a homespun skirt that stopped just below my knee and a faded brown cotton shift, worn old clothes I'd begged off a girl in Zatochek. I didn't look like one of the servants; the servants were far better dressed than me. Mean-while Solya had exchanged his black riding clothes for a long robe of black silk with a long sleeveless coat embroidered in green and silver over it, and his white hair spilled over it in a graceful fall. If you had seen him from a mile away, you would have known him for a wizard. And if they didn't think *me* a wizard, they wouldn't let me testify.

"Try and present a respectable appearance," Sarkan had said.

Vanastalem gave me clothes to match the mood of my sullen muttering: a stiff and uncomfortable gown of rich red silk, end-less flounces edged in flame-orange ribbons. I could have used an arm to lean on, at that, trying to negotiate stairs in the enormous skirt without being able to see my feet, but I grimly ignored Solya's subtly renewed offer at the head of the staircase, and picked my way slowly down, feeling for the edges of the steps with my tight-slippered toes.

He clasped his hands behind his back instead and paced me. He remarked idly, "The examinations are often challenging, of course. I suppose Sarkan prepared you for them?" He threw me a mildly inquiring glance; I didn't answer him, but I couldn't quite keep myself from dragging my bottom lip through my teeth. "Well," he said, "if you *do* find them difficult, we might provide a—joint demonstration to the examiners; I'm sure they would find that re-assuring."

I only glared at him and didn't answer. Anything we did, I was sure he'd take the credit for. He didn't press the matter, smiling on as though he hadn't even noticed my cold looks: a circling bird high above waiting for any opening. He took me through an archway flanked by two tall young guards who looked at me curiously, and into the Charovnikov, the Hall of Wizards.

I slowed involuntarily coming into the cavernous room. The ceiling was like an opening into Heaven, painted clouds spilling over a blue sky and angels and saints stretched across it. Enormous windows poured in the afternoon sunlight. I stared up, dazzled, and almost ran myself into a table, reaching blindly to catch myself with my hands on the corner and feeling my way around it. All the walls were covered in books, and a narrow balcony ran the full length of the room, making an even taller second level of bookcases. Ladders hung down from the ceiling on little wheels all along it. Great worktables stood along the length of the room, heavy solid oak with marble topping them.

"This is only an exercise in delaying what we all know has to be done," a woman was saying, somewhere out of sight: her voice was deep for a woman, a lovely warm sound, but there was an angry edge to her words. "No, don't start bleating at me again about the relics, Ballo. Any spell can be defeated—yes, even the one on holy blessed Jadwiga's shawl, and stop looking scandalized at me for saying so. Solya's gone drunk on politics to lend himself to this enterprise in the first place."

"Come, Alosha. Success excuses all risks, surely," the Falcon said mildly as we rounded a corner and found three wizards gathered at a large round table in an alcove, with a wide window letting in the afternoon sun. I squinted against it, after the dim light of the palace hallways.

The woman he'd called Alosha was taller even than me, with ebony-dark skin and shoulders as broad as my father's, her black hair braided tightly against her skull. She wore men's clothes: full red cotton trousers tucked into high leather boots, and a leather coat over it. The coat and the boots were beautiful, embossed with gold and silver in intricate patterns, but they still looked lived-in; I envied them in my ridiculous dress.

"Success," she said. "Is that what you call this, bringing a hollow shell back to the court just in time to burn her at the stake?"

My hands clenched. But the Falcon only smiled and said, "Perhaps we'd best defer these arguments for the moment. After all, we aren't here to judge the queen, are we? My dear, permit me to present to you Alosha, our Sword."

She looked at me unsmiling and suspicious. The other two were men: one of them the same Father Ballo who'd examined the queen. He didn't have a single line creasing his cheeks, and his hair was still solidly brown, but he somehow contrived to look old anyway, his spectacles sliding over a round nose in a round face as he peered up and down at me doubtfully. "Is this the apprentice?"

The other man might have been his opposite, long and lean, in a rich wine-red waistcoat embroidered elaborately in gold and a bored expression; his narrow pointed black beard curled up carefully at the tip. He was stretched in a chair with his boots up on the table. There was a heap of short stubby golden bars on the table beside him and a small black velvet bag heaped with tiny glittering red jewels. He was working two bars in his hands, magic whispering out of him; his lips were moving faintly. He was running the ends of the gold together, the bars thinning under his fingers into a narrow strip. "And this is Ragostok, the Splendid," Solya said.

Ragostok said nothing, and didn't even lift his head save for one brief glance that took me in from head to feet and dismissed me at once and forever as beneath his notice. But I preferred his disinterest to the hard suspicious line of Alosha's mouth. "Where exactly did Sarkan find you?" she demanded.

They'd heard some version of the rescue by then, it seemed, but Prince Marek and the Falcon hadn't bothered with the parts of the story that didn't suit them, and there was more they hadn't known. I stumbled through an awkward explanation of how I'd met Sarkan, uncomfortably aware of the Falcon's eyes on me, bright and attentive. I wanted to say as little as I could about Dvernik, about my family; he already had Kasia as a tool to use against me.

I borrowed Kasia's secret fear and tried to hint that my family had chosen to offer me to the Dragon; I made sure to say my father was a woodcutter, which I already knew they would disdain, and I didn't tell them any names. I said *the village headwoman* and *one of the herdsmen* instead of *Danka* and *Jerzy,* and made it sound as though Kasia was my only friend, and not just my dearest, before I haltingly told them of her rescue.

"And I suppose you asked nicely, and the Wood gave her back to you?" said Ragostok without looking up from his work: he was pressing the tiny red jewels into the gold with his thumbs, one after another.

"The Dragon—Sarkan—" I found myself grateful for the small lift I felt, from the thunder of his name on my tongue. "—he thought the Wood gave her to me for the chance of setting a trap."

"So he hadn't lost his mind entirely by then," Alosha said. "Why didn't he put her to death at once? He knows the law as well as anyone."

"He let—he let me try," I said. "He let me try to purge her. And then it worked—"

"Or so you imagine," she said. She shook her head. "And so does pity lead straight to disaster. Well, I'm surprised to hear it of Sarkan; but better men than he have lost their heads over a girl not half their age."

I didn't know what to say: I wanted to protest, to say *That's not it, there's nothing like that,* but the words stuck in my throat. "And do you suppose that I lost my head over her as well?" the Falcon said, in amused tones. "And Prince Marek in the bargain?"

She looked at him, an edge of contempt. "When Marek was a boy of eight, he wept for a month demanding his father take the army and every wizard in all Polnya into the Wood to bring his mother back," she said. "But he's not a child anymore. He should have known better, and so should you. How many men did this crusade of yours cost us? You took thirty veterans, cavalrymen, every one of them a prime soldier, every one of them carrying blades from my forge—"

"And we brought back your queen," the Falcon said, a sudden hard bite in his voice, "if that means anything to you?"

Ragostok heaved a noisy and pointed sigh without even looking up from his golden circlet. "What difference does it make at the moment? The king wants the girl tried—so try her already and let's be done with it." His tone made clear he didn't expect it to take long.

Father Ballo cleared his throat; he reached for a pen, dipped it into an inkwell, and leaned in towards me, peering through his small spectacles. "You do seem rather young to be examined. Tell me, my dear, how long have you been studying under your master?"

"Since the harvest," I said, and stared back at their incredulous eyes.

Sarkan hadn't mentioned to me that wizards ordinarily took seven years of study before asking to be admitted to the list. And after I spent a good three hours flubbing half the spells they set me on, exhausting myself in the meantime, even Father Ballo was inclined to believe that Sarkan had gone stupidly in love with me, or was having some sort of joke at their expense, to send me to be tested.

The Falcon was of no help: he watched their deliberations from the sideline with a mild air of interest, and when they asked him what magic he had seen me use, he only said, "I don't think I can properly attest—it's always difficult to separate the workings of an apprentice from a master, and Sarkan was there all the while, of course. I should prefer you all to make your own judgments." And then he looked at me from under his lashes, a reminder of that hint he'd given me in the hallway.

I gritted my teeth and tried again to appeal to Ballo: he seemed the best chance for any sympathy, although even he was growing irritated. "Sir, I've told you, I'm no use at these kinds of spells."

"These are not any *kind* of spell," he said, peevish and purse-mouthed. "We have set you at everything from healing magic to in-scription, under every element and every quarter of affinity. There is no category which encompasses all these spells."

"But they're *your* sort of magic. Not—not Jaga's," I said, seizing upon the example they would surely know.

Father Ballo peered at me even more dubiously. "Jaga? What on earth has Sarkan been teaching you? Jaga is a folk story." I stared at him. "Her deeds are borrowed from a handful of real wizards, mixed in with fanciful additions, and exaggerated over the years into mythic stature."

I gaped at him, helplessly: he was the only one who had been polite to me at all, and now he was telling me with a straight face that Jaga wasn't real.

"Well, this has been a waste of time," Ragostok said. He hadn't any right to complain about that, though: he hadn't stopped work-ing once, and by now his jeweled piece had become a tall circlet with a large socket in the middle waiting for a larger gemstone. It hummed faintly with trapped sorcery. "Pushing out a handful of cantrips isn't enough magic to make her worthy of the list, now or ever. Alosha had it right in the first place, what's happened to Sar-kan." He eyed me up and down. "Without much excuse, but there's no accounting for taste."

I was mortified, and angry, and afraid even more than angry: for all I knew, the trial might start in the morning. I dragged in a breath against the hard whalebone grip of the corsets, pushed back my chair and stood, and under my skirts I stamped my foot on the ground and said, *"Fulmia."* My heel came down jarring against the stone, a blow that rang through me and back out on a wave of magic. All around us the castle shuddered like a sleeping giant, a tremor that made the hanging jewels on the lamp above our heads chime softly against one another, and brought books thumping down off the shelves.

Ragostok had jerked up to his feet, his chair going over, his circlet clattering out of his hands onto the table. Father Ballo stared around at the corners of the room with startled blinking confusion before he transferred his astonishment to me, as if surely there had to be some other explanation. I stood panting with my hands clenched at my sides, still ringing head-to-foot, and said, "Is *that* magic enough to put me on the list? Or do you want to see more?"

They stared at me, and in the silence I heard shouts outside in the courtyard, running feet. The guards were looking in with their hands on their sword-hilts, and I realized I'd just shaken the king's castle, in the king's city, and shouted at the highest wizards of the land.

They did, after all, put me on the list. The king had demanded an explanation for the earthquake, and been told it was my fault; after that, they couldn't very well also say I wasn't much of a witch. But they weren't very happy about it. Ragostok seemed to have taken offense enough to build a grudge on, which I thought was unreasonable: *he'd* been the one insulting *me*. Alosha regarded me with even more suspicion, as if she imagined I'd been hiding my power for some devious reason, and Father Ballo just disliked having to admit me on the grounds of my being outside his experience. He wasn't unkind, but he had all Sarkan's obsessive hunger for explanation, with none of his willingness to bend. If Ballo couldn't find it in a book, that meant it couldn't be so, and if he found it in three books, that meant it was the unvarnished truth. Only the Falcon smiled at me, with that irritating air of secret amusement, and I could have done very well without his smiles.

I had to face them in the library again the very next morning for the naming ceremony. With the four of them around me I felt lonelier than in those early days in the Dragon's tower, cut away from everything I'd known. It was worse than being alone to feel that none of them were my friend, or even wished me anything good at all. If I'd been struck by a bolt of lightning, they would have been relieved, or at least not distressed. But I was determined not to care: the only thing that really mattered was being able to speak in Kasia's defense. I knew by now that no one else here would give her a moment's thought: she didn't matter.

The naming itself seemed more like another test than a ceremony. They set me at a worktable and put out a bowl of water, three bowls of different powders in red and yellow and blue, a candle, and an iron bell inscribed around in letters of gold. Father Ballo placed the naming spell on a sheet of parchment in front of me: the incantation was nine long tangled words, with detailed annotations that gave precise instructions on the pronunciation of every syllable, and how one ought to stress each word.

I muttered it over to myself, trying to feel out the important syllables, but they sat inert on my tongue: it just didn't want to come apart. "Well?" Ragostok said, impatiently.

I slogged my awkward tongue-twisted way through the entire incantation and started to put the powder in the water, a pinch here and there. The magic of the spell gathered sluggish and reluctant. I made a brownish mess of the water, spilled some of all three kinds of powder on my skirts, and finally gave up trying to make anything better. I lit the powder, squinted through the cloud of smoke, and groped for the bell.

Then I let the magic go, and the bell clanged in my hand: a long deep note that came strangely out of so small a bell; it sounded like the great church bell in the cathedral that rang matins every morning over the city, a sound that filled the room. The metal hummed beneath my fingers as I put it down and looked around expectantly; but the name didn't write itself on the parchment, or appear in letters of flame, or anywhere at all.

The wizards were all looking annoyed, although for once not at me; Father Ballo said to Alosha in some irritation, "Was that meant for a joke?"

She was frowning; she reached out to the bell and picked it up and turned it over: there wasn't a clapper inside it at all. They all stared into it, and I stared at them. "Where will the name come from?" I asked.

"The bell should have sounded it," Alosha said shortly. She put it down; it clanged again softly, an echo of that deep note, and she glared at it.

No one knew what to do with me, after that. After they all stood in silence for a moment while Father Ballo made noises about the irregularity, the Falcon—he still seemed determined to be amused by everything to do with me—said lightly, "Perhaps our new witch should choose a name for herself."

Ragostok said, "I think it more appropriate *we* choose a name for her."

I knew better than to let him have any part in picking my name: surely I'd end up as *the Piglet* or *the Earthworm*. But it all felt wrong to me, anyway. I'd gone along with the elaborate dance of the thing, but I knew abruptly I didn't want to change my name for a new one that trailed magic around behind it, any more than I wanted to be in this fancy gown with its long dragging train that picked up dirt from the hallways. I took a deep breath and said, "There's nothing wrong with the name I already have."

So I was presented to the court as Agnieszka of Dvernik.

I half-regretted my refusal during the presentation. Ragostok had told me, I think meaning to be nasty, that the ceremony would only be a little thing, and that the king didn't have much time to spare for such events when they came out of the proper season. It seems ordinarily new wizards were put onto the list in the spring and the fall, at the same time as the new knights. If he was telling the truth, I could only be grateful for it, standing at the end of that great throne room with a long red carpet like the lolling tongue of some monstrous beast stretched out towards me, and crowds of glittering nobility on either side of it, all of them staring at me and whispering to one another behind their voluminous sleeves.

I didn't feel like my real self at all; I would almost have liked another name on me then, a disguise to go with my clumsy, wide-skirted dress. I set my teeth and picked my way down the endless hall until I came to the dais and knelt at the king's feet. He still looked weary, as he had in the courtyard when we'd come. The dark gold crown banded his forehead, and it must have been an enormous weight, but it wasn't that simple kind of tiredness. His face beneath his brown-and-grey beard had lines like Krystyna's, the lines of someone who couldn't rest for worrying about the next day.

He put his hands around mine, and I squeaked out the words of the oath of fealty, stumbling over them; he answered me with long and easy practice, took his hands back, and nodded for me to go.

A page began making little beckoning motions at me from the side of the throne, but I realized belatedly that this was the first and just as likely only chance I had to ask the king anything.

"Your Majesty, if you please," I said, trying hard to ignore the looks of puffing indignation from everyone near enough the throne to hear me, "I don't know if you read Sarkan's letter—"

One of the tall strong footmen by the throne almost at once got my arm, bowing to the king with a fixed smile on his face, and tried to tug me away. I planted my feet, muttering a sliver of Jaga's earth spell, and ignored him. "We have a real chance to destroy the Wood, now," I said, "but he hasn't any soldiers, and—yes, I'll go in a moment!" I hissed at the footman, who'd now got me by both my arms and was trying to rock me off the dais. "I only need to explain—"

"All right, Bartosh, stop breaking your back on her," the king said. "We can give our newest witch a moment." He was really looking at me now, for the first time, and sounding faintly amused. "We have indeed read the letter. It could have used a few more lines. Not least about you." I bit my lip. "What would you ask of your king?"

My mouth trembled on what I really wanted to ask. *Let Kasia go!* I wanted to cry out. But I couldn't. I knew I couldn't. That was self-ishness: I wanted that for me, for my own heart's sake, and not for Polnya. I couldn't ask that of the king, who hadn't even let his own queen go without facing trial.

I dropped my eyes from his face to the tips of his boots, gold-embossed and just curling from underneath the fur trim of his robes. "Men to fight the Wood," I whispered. "As many as you can spare, Your Majesty."

"We cannot easily spare any," he said. He held up a hand when I drew breath. "However, we will see what can be done. Lord Spytko, look into the matter. Perhaps a company can be sent." A man hovering by the side of the throne bowed acknowledgment.

I tottered away suffused with relief—the footman eyed me narrowly as I went past him—and through a door behind the dais. It let me into a smaller antechamber, where a royal secretary, a severe older gentleman with an expression of strong disapproval, stiffly asked me to spell my name. I think he had heard some of the scene I'd created outside.

He wrote my name down in an enormous leather-bound tome at the heading of a page. I watched closely to be sure he put it down right, and ignored the disapproval, too glad and grateful to care: the king didn't seem at all unreasonable. Surely he would pardon Kasia at the trial. I wondered if perhaps we might even ride out with the soldiers, and join Sarkan at Zatochek together to start the battle against the Wood.

"When will the trial begin?" I asked the secretary when he had finished writing my name.

He only gave me an incredulous stare, lifted from the letter he'd already turned his attention to. "I surely cannot say," he said, and then sent his stare from me to the door leading out of the room, the hint as pointed as a pitchfork.

"But isn't there—it must start soon?" I tried.

He had already looked back down at his letter. This time he raised his head even more slowly, as if he couldn't believe I was still there. "It will begin," he said, with awful enunciated precision, "whenever the king decrees."

NINETEEN

Three days later, the trial still hadn't begun, and I hated everyone around me.

Sarkan had told me there was power to be had here, and I suppose for someone who understood the court there would have been. I could see there was a kind of magic in having my name written down in the king's book. After speaking to the secretary, I had gone back to my tiny room, baffled and uncertain what to do next, and before I had been sitting on my bed for half an hour the maids had knocked five times carrying cards of invitation to dinners and parties. I thought the first one was a mistake. But even after I realized they couldn't all have gone astray, I still had no idea what to do with them, or why they were coming.

"I see you're already in demand," Solya said, stepping out of a shadow and through my doorway before I could close it after yet another maid, delivering yet another card.

"Is this something we're supposed to do?" I asked warily. I had begun to wonder if perhaps this was a duty of the king's wizards. "Do these people need some kind of magic done?"

"Oh, it might come to that eventually," he said. "But at the moment, all they want is the privilege of displaying the youngest royal witch ever named. There are already a dozen rumors flying about your appointment." He plucked the cards out of my hands, shuffled through them, and handed one out to me. "Countess Boguslava is by far the most useful: the count has the king's ear, and he's sure to be consulted about the queen. I'll take you to her soirée."

"No, you won't!" I said. "You mean they just want me to come and visit? But they don't even know me."

"They know enough," he said, in patient tones. "They know you're a witch. My dear, I really think you would be better off accepting my escort for your first outing. The court can be—difficult to navigate, if you're unfamiliar with its ways. You know that we want the same thing: we want the queen and Kasia acquitted."

"You wouldn't give a crust of bread to save Kasia," I said, "and I don't like the way you go about getting the things you want."

He didn't let me chase away his manners. He only politely bowed himself backwards into the shadows in the corner of my room. "I hope you'll learn to think better of me, by and by." His voice floated distantly out of the dark, even as he vanished. "Do keep in mind that I am ready to be your friend, if you find yourself at sea." I threw the card from Countess Boguslava after him. It fluttered to the ground in the empty corner.

I didn't trust him at all, though I couldn't help but worry he was telling me part of the truth. I was beginning to understand how little I understood about the life of the court. To listen to Solya, if I showed my face at a party given by a woman who didn't know me, she would be pleased, and tell her husband so, and he'd—tell the king that the queen shouldn't be put to death? And the king would listen? None of that made sense to me, but neither did strangers sending me a pile of invitations, all because a man had written my name down in a book. But here were the invitations, so plainly I was missing steps along the way.

I wished I could speak to Sarkan: half for advice, half to complain at him. I even opened up Jaga's book and hunted through it for a spell that would let me reach him, but I didn't find anything that seemed as though it could work. The closest was one called *kialmas,* with the note, *to be heard in the next village,* but I didn't think anyone would appreciate me shouting so loudly that my voice would go a week's distance across the country, and I didn't think the mountains would let the noise through anyway, even if I deafened everyone in Kralia.

In the end, I picked out the earliest dinner invitation, and went. I was hungry, anyway. The last of the bread I'd saved in my skirt pocket was so stale by now that even magic couldn't make it go down easily, or really fill my belly. There had to be kitchens somewhere in the castle, but the servants eyed me oddly when I went too far down the wrong hallway; I didn't want to imagine their faces if I went sailing into the kitchens. But I couldn't bring myself to stop one of those maids, a girl just like me, and ask her to serve me—as though I really thought myself a fine lady, instead of just dressed up pretending to be one.

I roamed up and down stairs and through hallways until I found my way back out to the courtyard, and there I girded myself and went to one of the guards on the door, and asked him the way, showing him my invitation. He gave me the same odd look the servants did, but he looked at the address and said, "It's the yellow one third in from the outer gate. Go down the road and you'll see it after you get around the cathedral. Do you want a chair? Milady?" He tacked on the last, doubtfully.

"No," I said, confused by the question, and set off.

It wasn't a very long walk: the nobles lived in houses set inside the outer walls of the citadel—or the richest ones did, anyway. The footmen at the yellow house stared at me, too, when I finally walked up to the entrance, but they opened the doors for me. I stopped on the threshold: it was my turn to stare. On my way, I had gone by more than one pair of men carrying peculiar tall boxes around the castle grounds; I hadn't known what they were for. Now one of them was being carried to the steps of the house, right behind me. A footman opened up the door in its side, and there was a *chair* inside it. A young lady climbed out.

The footman offered her a hand to step out onto the stairs of the house, but then he went back to his place. She paused on the lower step looking up at me. I asked her doubtfully, "Do you need help?" She didn't stand as though she had a bad leg, but I couldn't tell what was beneath her skirts, and I couldn't imagine any other reason she would have shut herself up into such a bizarre thing.

But she only stared at me, and then two more of the chairs came up behind her, discharging more guests behind her. It was just how they went from place to place. "Do none of you ever *walk*?" I asked, baffled.

"And how do *you* keep from getting all over mud?" she said.

We both looked down. I was a good two inches deep in mud along all the bottom of today's skirt: bigger around than a wagon-wheel and made of purple velvet and silver lace.

"I don't," I said glumly.

That was how I met Lady Alicja of Lidzvar. We walked into the house and were immediately interrupted by our hostess, who appeared in the hall between us, greeted Lady Alicja very perfunctorily, then seized my arms and kissed me on both cheeks. "My dear Lady Agnieszka," she said, "how lovely that you were able to come, and what a charming gown: you are sure to start a new fashion." I stared at her beaming face in dismay. Her name had gone completely out of my head. But it didn't seem to matter. Even while I mumbled something polite and grateful, she twined her perfumed arm around mine and drew me into the sitting-room where her guests were gathered.

She paraded me around to everyone there, while I silently and fervently hated Solya all the more, for being right. Everyone was so very glad to make my acquaintance, everyone was scrupulously polite—at first, anyway. They didn't ask me for magic. What they did want was gossip about the queen's rescue. Their manners were too nice to ask questions outright, but each of them said something like, "I've heard that there was a chimaera guarding her . . . ," letting the words trail off expectantly, inviting me to correct them.

I could have said anything. I could have passed it off in some clever way, or claimed any number of marvels: they were plainly ready to be impressed with me, to let me assume a heroic role. But I recoiled from the memory of that dreadful slaughter all around me, of blood watering the earth into mud. I flinched and blundered, answering with a flat "No" or saying nothing at all, and dropping one conversation after another into an awkward hole of silence. My disappointed hostess finally abandoned me in a corner near a tree—there was an orange tree growing inside the house, in a pot— and went to smooth over the ruffled feathers of her other guests.

It was perfectly clear to me that if there was any good I could have done Kasia here, I'd just done the opposite. I was grimly wondering if I should swallow my reluctance and go find Solya after all when Lady Alicja appeared at my elbow. "I didn't realize you were the new witch," she said, taking my arm and leaning in conspiratorially. "Of course you don't need a sedan chair. Do tell me, do you travel by turning yourself into an enormous bat? Like Baba Jaga—"

I was glad to talk about Jaga, about anything besides the Wood, and even more glad to find someone other than Solya willing to show me how to go on. By the time we finished dinner, I had agreed to go with Lady Alicja to a breakfast and a card party and a dinner the next day. I spent the next two days almost entirely in her company.

I didn't think us friends, exactly. I wasn't in a mood to make friends. Every time I trudged back and forth from the castle to yet another party, I had to pass by the barracks of the royal guard, and in the middle of their courtyard stood the stark iron block, scorched and black, where they beheaded the corrupted before they burned their corpses. Alosha's forge stood nearby, and more often than not her fire was roaring, her silhouette raising showers of orange sparks with a hammer made of shadow.

"The only mercy you can give the corrupted is a sharpened blade," she had said, when I'd tried to persuade her to at least visit Kasia once herself. I couldn't help but think maybe she was working on the headman's axe right then, while I sat in stuffy rooms and ate fish eggs on toast with the crusts cut off, and tea sweetened with sugar, and tried to talk to people I didn't know.

But I did think Lady Alicja was kind, taking a clumsy peasant girl under her wing. She was only a year or two older than me, but already married to a rich old baron who spent most of his days at card-parties. She seemed to know everyone. I was grateful, and determined to be grateful, and I felt half-guilty for not being better company or understanding the manners of the court. I didn't know what to say when Lady Alicja insisted on paying me loud and intensely fervent compliments on the excessive lace on my gown, or on the way I mangled the steps of a courtly dance when she persuaded some poor goggle-eyed young nobleman to take me on, much to the dismay of his toes and the amused stares of the room.

I didn't realize she was mocking me all the time until the third day. We'd planned to meet at an afternoon music party held at the house of a baroness. There was music at all the parties, so I didn't understand what made this one especially a music party; Alicja had just laughed when I'd asked her. But I dutifully tramped over after lunch, trying my best to hold up my long silver-frost train and balance the matching headdress, a long curved heavy swoop over my head that wanted to fall either backwards or forwards, either way as long as it didn't stay in place. Coming into the room, I caught the train in the doorway and stumbled, and the headdress went sliding back over my ears.

Alicja caught sight of me and crossed the room in a dramatic rush to clasp my hands. "Dearest," she said urgently, breathlessly, "what a brilliantly *original* angle—I've never seen anything like it before."

I blurted out, "Are you—are you trying to be rude?" As soon as the idea occurred to me, all the odd things she'd said and done came together and made a strange malicious sense. But I couldn't believe it at first; I didn't understand why she would have. No one had made her talk to me, or be in my company. I couldn't understand why she would have gone to the trouble just to be unpleasant.

Then I couldn't doubt it anymore: she put on a wide-eyed, surprised expression that plainly meant yes, she *was* trying to be rude. "Why, Nieshka," she began, as though she thought I was an idiot, too.

I pulled my hands free from hers with a jerk, staring at her. "Agnieszka will do," I said, startled and sharp, "and since you like my style so much, *katboru*." Her own curved headdress tipped backwards down her head—and took with it the elaborate lovely curls to either side of her face, which were evidently false. She gave a small scream and clutched at them, and ran out of the room.

That wasn't the worst of it, though. Worse was the titter that went all around the room, from men I'd seen her dance with and women she'd called her intimate friends. I jerked off my own headdress and hurried over to the lavish refreshments, hiding my face from the room over bowls of grapes. Even there, a young man in an embroidered coat that must have taken some woman a year of work sidled up to my side and whispered in tones of glee that Alicja wouldn't be able to show her face at court for a year—as though that should have pleased me.

I managed to duck away from him into a servants' hallway, and then in desperation I pulled out Jaga's book from my pocket until I found a spell *for a quick exit*, to let me pass through the wall of the house instead of going back inside and out the front door. I couldn't bear to hear any more poisonous congratulations.

I came out through the yellow-brick wall panting like I'd escaped from a prison. A small lion-mouthed fountain stood gurgling away in the center of the plaza, the afternoon sun dazzling and captured in the basin, and a carved flock of birds around the top singing softly. I could tell at a glance it was Ragostok's work. And there was Solya, perched on the edge of the fountain, running his fingers through the light in the water.

"I'm glad to see you've rescued yourself," he said. "Even though you walked yourself into it as determinedly as you possibly could." He hadn't been in the house at all, but I was sure he knew every detail of Alicja's mortification and mine, and for all his sorrowful expression, I was sure he'd been delighted to watch me make a fool of myself.

All the time I'd been grateful that Alicja didn't want my magic or my secrets, it had never occurred to me that she might want something else. Even if it had, I wouldn't have imagined she'd been looking for a target for malice. We weren't stupidly cruel to each other in Dvernik. Of course there were quarrels sometimes and people you liked less, and sometimes even a fight broke out, if people got angry enough. But when harvest came, your neighbors came to help you gather and thresh, and when the shadow of the Wood stole over us, we knew better than to make it any darker. And none of us would've been rude to a witch no matter what. "I would have thought even a noblewoman had more sense than that," I said.

Solya shrugged. "Perhaps she didn't believe you one."

I opened my mouth to protest that she'd seen me do magic, but I suppose she hadn't: not like Ragostok, who would burst into rooms like a thunderclap with showers of glittering silver sparks and birds calling as they flew out in every direction; not even like Solya gliding smoothly in and out of shadows in his elegant robes, with those bright sharp eyes of his that seemed to see everything that went on in the castle grounds. I shoved myself into ballgowns in my own room, and walked to parties stubbornly, and in a strangling corset that was quite enough to spend my breath on without doing tricks just to show off.

"But how did she think I got myself on the list?" I demanded.

"I imagine she thought what the rest of the wizards did, at first."

"What, that you put me on because Sarkan was in love with me?" I said, sarcastic.

"Marek, more likely," he said, entirely serious, and I stared at him appalled. "Really, Agnieszka, I would have expected you to understand that much by now."

"I don't want to understand any of this!" I said. "Those people in there, they were happy for Alicja to mock me, and then they were just as happy for me to make her miserable."

"Of course," he said. "They're delighted to learn that you were playing the yokel only to set up an elaborate mockery of the first person who took your bait. That makes you part of the game."

"I didn't set a trap for her!" I said. I wanted to add that no one would think of something like that, no one in their right mind anyway, only I had the unpleasant sticky feeling that some of these people *would*.

"No, I didn't imagine you had," Solya said judiciously. "But you may want to let people believe you did. They will anyway, no matter what you say." He stood up from the edge of the fountain. "The situation's not beyond repair. I think you'll find people much friendlier to you at the dinner tonight. Won't you let me escort you, after all?"

For answer, I turned on my pointed heel and stalked away from him and his amused huff of laughter, letting my stupid train drag along the ground behind me.

I made my thundercloud way out of the neat courtyard and into the noisy bustle of the green outer courtyard of the castle. A heap of haybales and barrels sat alongside the main road from the outer gates to the inner ones, waiting to be loaded somewhere or other. I sat down on one bale to think. I had the horrible certain feeling that Solya was right about this, too. And that meant any courtier who would speak to me now would only do so because they liked this sort of spiteful game; anyone decent wouldn't want anything to do with me.

But there wasn't anyone else I could talk to, or even ask for advice. The servants and soldiers didn't want any part of me, either, nor the officials hurrying on their appointed rounds. As they came past me now I could see them all throwing doubtful looks in my direction: a fine lady sitting on a haybale next to the road in my satin and lace finery, my dragging train full of grass and sand, a stray leaf in a well-tended garden. I didn't belong.

Worse than that, I wasn't being any use—to Kasia or to Sarkan or anyone back home. I was ready to testify, and there wasn't a trial; I'd begged for soldiers, but none had gone. I'd attended more parties in three days than in my whole life before, and I had nothing to show for it but ruining the reputation of one silly girl who'd probably never had a real friend in her life.

In a burst of frustration and anger, I called *vanastalem*, but slurred deeply, and between one passing wagon and the next, I put myself back into the clothes of a woodcutter's daughter: good plain homespun, a skirt that wasn't too long for sensible boots to show beneath it, an apron with two big pockets in it. I breathed easier at once, and found myself suddenly invisible: no one was looking at me anymore. No one cared who I was, or what I was doing.

There were hazards to invisibility, too: while I stood there on the edge of the road enjoying the pleasure of a deep breath, an enormous carriage swollen out over its wheels on all sides and four footmen hanging off it came rattling past me, and nearly knocked me over. I had to jump out of the way into a puddle, my boots squelching and mud spattering my skirts. But I didn't care. I knew myself for the first time in a week, standing on earth instead of polished marble.

I went back up the hill in the carriage track, my stride swinging wide and free in my easy skirts, and slipped into the inner court without any trouble. The fat carriage had drawn up to disgorge an ambassador in a white coat, a red sash of office brilliant across his chest. The crown prince was there to meet him, with a crowd of courtiers and an honor guard carrying the flag of Polnya and a yellow-and-red flag with the head of an ox upon it, one I'd never seen before. He must have been coming to the state dinner. I'd been meant to go there with Alicja this evening. All the guards were watching the ceremony with half an eye at least, and when I whispered to them that I wasn't worth taking any notice of, their eyes slid over me the way they wanted to, anyway.

Going back and forth from parties three times a day from my inconvenient room had been good for one thing, at least: I had learned to find my way about the castle. There were servants in the hallways, but all of them were laden under linens and silver, hurrying to make ready for the dinner party. None of them had attention to spare for a mud-spattered scullery-maid. I eeled around and through them and made my way down the long dark corridor to the Grey Tower.

The four guards on duty at the base of the tower were bored and yawning with the late hour. "You missed the stair to the kitchens, sweetheart," one of them said good-naturedly to me. "It's back down the hall."

I stored that information away for later, and then I did my best to stare at them the way that everyone had been staring at me for the last three days, as though I were perfectly astonished by their ignorance. "Don't you know who I am?" I said. "I'm Agnieszka, the witch. I'm here to see Kasia." And to have a look at the queen, more to the point. I couldn't think why the trial would be put off so long, unless the king was trying to give the queen more time to get well.

The guards all looked at each other uncertainly. Before they could decide what to do about me, I whispered, *"Alamak, alamak,"* and walked straight on through the locked doors between them.

They weren't nobles, so I suppose they weren't inclined to pick a quarrel with a witch. They didn't come after me, at least. I climbed the narrow staircase around and around until I came out onto the landing with the hungry imp knocker gaping at me. Taking the round knob felt as though my hand was being licked thoroughly by a lion that was deciding whether or not I would taste good. I held it as gingerly as I could and banged on the door.

I had a list of arguments for the Willow, and behind them flat determination. I was ready to shove my way past her if I had to;

she was too much a fine lady to lower herself to wrestling with me, I suspected. But she didn't come to the door at all, and when I pressed my ear to it, I faintly heard shouting inside. In alarm, I backed up and tried to think: would the guards be able to knock the door down, if I shouted for them? I didn't think so. The door was made of iron and riveted with iron, and there wasn't even a keyhole to be seen.

I looked at the imp, which leered back. Hunger radiated from its empty maw. But if I filled it up? I called a simple spell, just some light: the imp immediately began to suck the magic in, but I kept feeding power to the spell until finally a little candle-wavering gleam lit in my hand. The imp's hunger was an enormous pull, guzzling in nearly all the magic I could give, but I managed to divert a narrow silver stream: I let it collect into a tiny pool inside me, and then I squeezed out, *"Alamak,"* and with one desperate jump I went through the door. It took all the strength I had left: I rolled out onto the floor of the room beyond and sprawled flat on my back, emptied.

Footsteps came running across the floor to me, and Kasia was at my side. "Nieshka, are you all right?"

The shouting was from the next room: Marek, standing fists clenched in the middle of the floor and roaring at the Willow, who stood ramrod-stiff and white with anger. Neither of them paid much attention to my falling in through the door; they were too busy being furious at each other.

"Look at her!" Marek flung an arm out at the queen. She still sat by the same window as before, listless and unmoved. If she heard the shouting, she didn't so much as flinch. "Three days without a word from her lips, and you call yourself a healer? What use are you?"

"None, evidently," the Willow said icily. "All I have done is everything that could be done, as well as it could be done." She did take notice of me then, finally: she turned and looked down her nose at me on the floor. "I understand *this* is the miracle-worker of the kingdom. Perhaps you can spare her from your bed long enough to do better. Until then, tend her yourself. I am not going to stand here to be howled at for my efforts."

She marched past me, twitching her skirts to one side so they wouldn't even brush up against mine, as if she didn't care to be contaminated. The bar lifted itself at a flick of her hand. She swept out, and the heavy iron door clanged shut behind her, scraping on the stone like an axe-blade coming down.

Marek turned on me, his temper still unspent. "And you! You're meant to be the foremost witness, and you're wandering the castle looking like a kitchen slut. Do you think anyone is going to believe a word out of your mouth? Three days since I got you on the list—"

"*You* got me!" I said indignantly, wobbling up to my feet with the support of Kasia's arm.

"—and all you've done is persuade the entire court you're a useless bumpkin! Now this? Where is Solya? He was supposed to be showing you how to go on."

"I don't want to *go on*," I said. "I don't care what any of these people think of me. What they think doesn't matter!"

"Of course it matters!" He seized me by the arm and dragged me out of Kasia's hands. I stumbled with him, trying to gather together a spell to knock him away, but he pulled me to the window-sill and pointed down to the castle courtyard. I paused and looked down, puzzled. There didn't seem to be anything alarming happening. The red-sashed ambassador was just going into the building with Crown Prince Sigmund.

"That man with my brother is an envoy from Mondria," Marek said, low and savage. "Their prince consort died last winter: the princess will be out of mourning in six months. Now do you understand?"

"No," I said, baffled.

"She wants to be queen of Polnya!" Marek shouted.

"But the queen's not dead," Kasia said, and then we understood.

I stared at Marek, cold, horrified. "But the king—" I blurted. "He *loved*—" I stopped.

"He's putting the trial off to buy time, do you understand?" Marek said. "Once memories of the rescue have faded, he'll get the nobility to look the other way, and then he can put her quietly to death. Now are you going to help me, or do you want to keep blundering around the castle until the snow flies and they burn her—and your beloved friend here—once it's too cold for anyone to come out and watch?"

I curled my fingers tight around Kasia's stiff hand, as if I could protect her that way. It felt too cruel and hollow to imagine: that we could have won Queen Hanna free, brought her out of the Wood, all so the king could cut off her head and marry someone else. Just to add a principality to the map of Polnya, another jewel to his crown. "But he loved her," I said again, a protest I couldn't help making—stupidly I suppose. Yet that story, the story of the lost beloved queen, made more sense to me than the one Marek was telling me.

"And you think that would make him forgive being made a fool?" Marek said. "His beautiful wife, who ran away from him with a Rosyan boy who sang her charming songs in the garden. That's what they said of her, until I was old enough to kill men for saying it. They told me not to even mention her name to him, when I was a boy."

He was staring down at Queen Hanna in her chair, where she sat blank as waiting paper. In his face, I could see him as he'd been, a child hiding in his mother's deserted garden to escape that same crowd of poisonous courtiers—all of them smirking and whispering about her, shaking their heads and pretending at sorrow while they gossiped that they'd known it all along.

"And you think we can save her and Kasia by dancing to their music?" I said.

He lifted his gaze from the queen and looked at me. For the

first time ever, I think he really listened to me. His chest rose and fell, three times. "No," he said finally, agreeing. "They're all just vultures, and he's the lion. They'll shake their heads and agree it's a shame, and pick at the bones he throws them. Can you force my father to pardon her?" he demanded, as easily as if he wasn't asking me to ensorcell *the king*, and take someone's will away from them, as dreadful as the Wood.

"No!" I said, appalled. I looked at Kasia. She stood with a hand resting on the back of the queen's chair, straight and golden and steady, and she shook her head to me. She wouldn't ask that of me. She wouldn't even ask me to run away with her, to abandon our people to the Wood—even if it meant the king would murder her, just so he could kill the queen, too. I swallowed. "No," I said again. "I won't do that."

"Then what *will* you do?" Marek snarled, angry again, and stalked from the room without waiting for me to answer. It was just as well. I didn't know what to say.

TWENTY

The guards on the Charovnikov did recognize me,
despite my clothes. They opened the heavy wooden
doors for me and swung them closed again. I stood
with my back pressed up to them, the gilt and turning
angels overhead and the endless walls of books looming all the way
down one wall and back along the next, dipping into alcoves and
back out again. There were a handful of other people working at
the tables here and there, young men and women in robes with
their heads bent over alembics or books. They didn't pay attention
to me; they were all busy themselves.

The Charovnikov wasn't welcoming to me, colder than the
Dragon's library and too impersonal, but at least it was a place I
understood. I still didn't know how I was going to save Kasia, but
I knew I had more chance of finding a way to do it here than I did
in a ballroom.

I took hold of the nearest ladder and dragged it squeaking all
the way to the very front of the very first shelf, then I tucked up my
skirts, climbed up to the top, and began to rummage. It was a famil-

iar kind of searching. I didn't go gleaning in the forest to find something in particular; I went to find whatever there was to find, and to let ideas come to me: if I found a heap of mushrooms, we'd have mushroom soup the next day, and if I found flat stones the hole in the road near our house would get mended. I thought surely there had to be at least a few books here that would speak out to me like Jaga's book; maybe they even had another one of hers somewhere hidden away among all these fancy gold-stamped volumes.

I worked as quickly as I could. I looked at the dustiest books, the ones least-used. I ran my hands over all of them, read the titles off their spines. But it was slow going no matter what, and full of frustration. After I had gone through twelve wide bookcases, ceiling-to-floor, thirty shelves on each, I began to wonder if I would find anything here, after all: there was a dry stiff feeling to all the books beneath my hands, and nothing that invited me to keep looking.

It had grown late while I worked. The handful of other students were gone, and the magical lights had dimmed down to the faint glow of hot ash all along the library, as though they had gone to sleep. Only the one on my shelf still shone firefly-bright, and my back and ankles were complaining. I was twisted up on the ladder, my foot hooked around a rail, so I could reach out and grab the farthest books. I'd barely made it a quarter of the way down one side of the room, and that was going as quick and slipshod as I could, not a tenth of the books looked at properly; Sarkan would have muttered something uncomplimentary.

"What are you looking for?"

I nearly pitched off the ladder onto Father Ballo's head, just barely catching the side rail in time and barking my ankle painfully on a joint. There was a section of one of the bookshelves standing open halfway down the room, the door to some hidden nook; he'd come out of there. He was carrying four thick volumes in his arms, which I supposed he meant to put back on the shelves, and staring up at me doubtfully from the floor.

I was still twitching inwardly with surprise, and I spoke without thinking. "I'm looking for Sarkan," I said.

Ballo looked blankly at the shelves I'd been pawing over: did I think I was going to find the Dragon pressed between the pages of a book? But as if I'd told myself at the same time as him, I realized that was exactly what I was after. I wanted Sarkan. I wanted him to look up from among his heaped books and snap at me at the disorder I'd created. I wanted to know what he was doing, if the Wood had struck back. I wanted him to tell me how I could persuade the king to let Kasia go.

"I want to speak to him," I said. "I want to see him." I already knew there wasn't a spell in Jaga's book, and Sarkan had never shown me such a spell himself. "Father, what spell would you use, if you wanted to talk to someone in another part of the kingdom?"— but Ballo was already shaking his head at me.

"Far-speaking is a thing of fairy-tales, however convenient bards find the notion," he said, in lecturing tones. "In Venezia they have discovered the art of laying a spell of communion within a pair of mirrors made together from the same pool of quicksilver. The king has such a mirror, with the mate carried by the chief of the army at the front. But even these can speak only with one another. The king's grandfather purchased them in exchange for five bottles of fire-heart," he added, making me squeak involuntarily at the price: you might as well buy a kingdom. "Magic may extend the senses, extend sight and hearing; it may amplify the voice, or conceal it into a nut to emerge later. It cannot fling your visage across half a kingdom in an instant, or carry someone's voice back to you."

I listened to him dissatisfied, although it made unfortunate sense: why would Sarkan ever send a messenger, or write a letter, if he could simply cast a spell? It was sensible enough, the same way he could only use his transporting spell to go around the valley, his own territory, and not leap straight to the capital and back.

"Are there any other spellbooks like Jaga's here, that I might look in?" I asked, even though I knew Ballo didn't have any use for her.

"My child, this library is the heart of the scholarship of magic in Polnya," he said. "Books are not flung onto these shelves by the whim of some collector, or through the chicanery of a bookseller; they are not here because they are valuable, or painted in gold to please some noble's eye. Every volume added has been carefully reviewed by at least two wizards in the service of the crown; their virtues have been confirmed and at least three correct workings attested, and even then they must be of real power to merit a place here. I myself have spent nearly my entire life of service pruning out the lesser works, the curiosities and the amusements of earlier days; you will certainly not find anything like that here."

I stared down at him: his entire life! And he would surely have pounced instantly on anything that I could use. I took the sides of the ladder and slid myself to the foot, to his pinched disapproving look: I suppose he would have stared to see anyone climb a tree, too. "Did you burn them?" I said, hopelessly.

He recoiled as if I'd suggested burning him. "A book need not be *magical* to be of *value*," he said. "Indeed, I would have liked to move them to the University's collection for more thorough study, but Alosha insisted on their being kept here, under lock—which I cannot deny is a sensible precaution, as such books can attract the worst sort of elements of lower society; occasionally enough of the gift crops up to make a street apothecary dangerous, if they get the wrong book in their hands. However, I do believe the University archivists, who are men of excellent training, might with the proper instruction and a rigorous scheme of oversight have been entrusted with the safekeeping of lesser—"

"Where are they?" I interrupted.

The tiny room he showed me to was crammed full of old, ragged-edged books with not even an arrow-slit window for air. I had to leave the door cracked open. I was happier rummaging through these messy heaps, where I didn't have to worry about putting them back in any order, but most of the books were just as useless to me as the ones on the shelves. I pushed aside any number of dry histories of magic, and others that were tomes of elaborate small cantrips—at least half of which would have taken twice as long and made five times the mess of doing whatever they wanted to do by hand—and others that seemed perfectly reasonable formal spell-books to me, but evidently hadn't met Father Ballo's more rigorous standards.

There were stranger things in the piles. One very peculiar volume looked just like a spellbook, full of mysterious words and pictures, diagrams like those in many of the Dragon's books, and writing that made no sense. After I lost ten solid minutes to puzzling over the thing, I realized slowly that it was mad. I mean, a madman had written it, pretending he was a wizard, wanting to be one: it wasn't real spells at all, just made-up ones. There was something hopelessly sad about it. I pushed that one away into a dark corner.

Then finally my hand fell on one small thin black book. On the outside it looked like my mother's recipe-book for dishes to serve on holidays, and it felt warm and friendly to me at once. The paper was cheap, yellowing and crumbly, but it was full of small, comfortable spells, sketched out in a neat hand. I looked through the pages, smiling down at it involuntarily, and then I looked at the inside of the front cover. In that same neat hand was written, *Maria Olshankina, 1267.*

I sat looking down at it, surprised and not surprised at the same time. This witch had lived in my valley more than three hundred years ago. Not long after the valley had been settled: the big corner-stone on Olshanka's stone church, the oldest building in the valley, was engraved with the year 1214. Where had Jaga been born? I wondered, suddenly. She had been Rosyan. Had she lived in the valley on the other side of the Wood, before Polnya settled it from the other direction?

I knew it wasn't going to help me. It was a warm kind presence in my hands, but with the kindness of a friend who sits with you in comfort by the fire and can't change what's wrong. There were folk-witches who cured some kinds of sickness and dealt with crop-blight, in most big towns; I think Maria had been one of them. For a moment I saw her, a big, cheerful woman with a red apron sweeping out her front yard, children and chickens underfoot, going inside to brew up some cough-potion for an anxious young father with a sick baby at home, pouring it into his cup with a lecture on running across town without a hat on. There had been something gentle in her, a pool of magic, not a running stream that had washed away all the ordinary parts of her life. I sighed and put the book into my pocket anyway. I didn't want to leave it here thrown away and forgotten.

I found two more like that, among the thousands of tumbled books, and paged through them; they had a few useful spells between them, a little good advice. They didn't have places written in them, but somehow I knew they, too, had come from my valley. One had been written by a farmer who'd found a working that could call clouds together so they'd bring rain. On that page he had sketched a field beneath clouds, and in the distance a familiar toothy line of grey mountains.

There was a note of warning at the bottom of that spell: *Be careful when it's already grey: if you call too many, thunder comes, too.* I touched the short simple word with my fingers, *kalmoz*, and I knew I could call thunder, lightning forking down from the sky. I shivered and put that book aside. I could imagine how Solya would like to help me with *that* kind of spell.

None of them had what I needed. I cleared a space around me on the floor and kept on going, bent over reading one book while my free hand groped through the piles for the next. Without looking, my fingers caught on a scalloped edge of raised leather, and I jerked back my hand and sat up, shaking it out uneasily.

Once out gleaning in winter, still young, not quite twelve, I'd found a strange big white sac on a tree, between the roots, buried beneath wet dead leaves. I'd poked it with a stick a few times, and then I ran to where my father was working and brought him back to show him. He'd cut down the nearest trees for a fire-break, and then burned the sac and the tree with it. In the ashes we'd poked through with a stick and found a curled skeleton of some misshapen growing thing, not any beast we recognized. "You keep away from this clearing, Nieshka, you hear me?" my father had said.

"It's all right now." I'd told him that, I suddenly remembered. I'd known, somehow.

"All the same," he'd said, and we'd never spoken of it again. We'd never even told my mother. We hadn't wanted to think about what it meant, that I could find evil magic hiding in the trees.

The memory came back to me vividly now: the faint damp smell of the rotting leaves, my breath cold and white in the air, a glaze of frost along the edges of the branches and the raised bark, the heavy silence of the forest. I'd gone out looking for something else; I'd drifted into the clearing that morning with a thread of unease pulling me along. I felt the same way now. But I was in the Charovnikov, in the heart of the king's palace. How could the Wood be here?

I wiped my fingers on my skirts, braced myself, and drew the book out. The cover was painted and sculpted elaborately by hand, a raised amphisbaena of leather with every serpent-scale painted in a shimmering blue, the eyes red jewels, surrounded by a forest of green leaves with the word *Bestiare* hanging above it in golden letters joined to the branches like fruits.

I turned the pages with a finger and a thumb, holding them by the lower corner only. It was a bestiary, a strange one full of monsters and chimaeras. Not all of them were even real. I turned a few more pages slowly, only glancing at the words and pictures, and with an odd, creeping sensation began to realize that while I read, the monsters *felt* real, I believed in them, and if I went on believing in them long enough—abruptly I shut the book hard and put it down on the floor and stood up away from it. The hot stifling room had gone even more stifling, a thickness like the worst days of summer, the air hot and moist under a smothering weight of still leaves that stopped the wind from ever getting through.

I scrubbed my hands on my skirts, trying to get rid of the oily feeling of the pages against my hands, and watched the book suspiciously. I had the feeling if I took my eyes away, it would turn itself into some kind of twisted thing and come leaping for my face, hissing and clawing. Instinctively I reached for a spell of fire, to burn it, but even as I opened my mouth, I stopped, realizing how stupid that would be: I was standing in a room full of old dry books, the air so desiccated it tasted of dust when I breathed, and outside was an enormous library. But I was sure it wasn't safe to leave the book there, not even for a moment, and I couldn't imagine touching it again—

The door swung open. "I understand your caution, Alosha," Ballo was saying peevishly, "but I hardly see what harm can come from—"

"Stop!" I shouted, and he and Alosha halted in the narrow doorway and stared at me. I suppose I looked bizarre, standing there like a lion-tamer with a particularly vicious beast, and only a single book lying quietly on the floor in front of me.

Ballo stared at me, astonished, and then peered down at the book. "What on earth—"

But Alosha was already moving: she pushed him gently to one side and drew a long dagger off her belt. She crouched down and stretched her arm to its full length and prodded the book with just the tip. The blade lit silver all along its edge, and where it touched the book, the light glowed through a greenish cloud of corruption. She drew the dagger back. "How did you find that?"

"It was just here in the heap," I said. "It tried to catch me. It felt like—like the Wood."

"But how could—" Ballo started, but Alosha vanished out of the doorway. A moment later she reappeared, wearing a heavy metal gauntlet. She picked up the book between two fingers and jerked her head. We followed her out into the main part of the library, the lights coming up over our heads where we walked, and she shoved a heap of books off one of the large stone tables and laid the book down upon it. "How did this particular piece of nastiness escape you?" she demanded of Ballo, who was peering down at it over her shoulder, alarmed and frowning.

"I don't believe I even looked into it," Ballo said, with a faintly defensive note. "There was no need: I could see at a glance it wasn't a serious text of magic, and quite plainly had no place in our library. I recall I had rather strong words with poor Georg about it, in fact: he tried to insist on keeping it on the shelves even though there was not the least sign of enchantment about it."

"Georg?" Alosha said grimly. "Was this just before he disappeared?" Ballo paused and nodded.

"If I'd kept going," I said, "would it have—*made* one of those things?"

"Made *you* into one, I imagine," Alosha said, horrifyingly. "We had an apprentice go missing five years ago, the same day a hydra crawled up out of the palace sewers and attacked the castle: we thought it had eaten him. We had better take poor Georg's head off the wall in the parade-room."

"But how did it get here in the first place?" I asked, looking down at the book, the dappled leaves of pale and dark green, the two-headed serpent winking at us with its red eyes.

"Oh—" Ballo hesitated, and then he went down the hall to a shelf full of ledgers, each of them nearly half his own height: he muttered some small dusty spell over them as he drew his fingers along, and one page gleamed out far down the shelf. He lifted out the heavy book with a grunt and brought it to the table, supporting it from beneath with absent practice as he opened to the one illuminated page, with one row shining out upon it. "Bestiary, well-ornamented, of unknown origin," he read. "A gift from the court of . . . of Rosya." His voice trailed off. He was looking at the date, his ink-stained index finger resting upon it. "Twenty years ago, and one of half a dozen volumes gifted at the same time," he said, finally. "Prince Vasily and his embassy must have brought it with them."

The malevolent carved book sat in the middle of the table. We stood in silence around it. Twenty years ago, Prince Vasily of Rosya had ridden into Kralia, and three weeks later he had ridden out again in the dead of night with Queen Hanna beside him, fleeing towards Rosya. They had gone too close to the edge of the Wood, trying to evade pursuit. That was the story. But perhaps they'd been caught long before then. Maybe some poor scribe or book-binder had wandered too close to the Wood, and under the boughs pounded fallen leaves into paper, brewed ink out of oak galls and water, and wrote corruption into every word, to make a trap that could creep even into the castle of the king.

"Can we burn it here?" I said.

"What?" Ballo said, jerking up in protest as though he were on a string. I think he recoiled instinctively from burning any book at all, which I thought was all very well, but not when it came to *this* one.

"Ballo," Alosha said, and from her expression she felt just as I did.

"I will attempt a purification, to make it safe to examine," Ballo said. "If *that* should fail, then we will of course have to consider cruder methods for disposal."

"This isn't something to keep, purified or not," she said grimly. "We should take it to the forge. I'll build a white fire, and we'll close it in until it's ash."

"We cannot burn it at once, no matter what," Ballo said. "It is evidence in the queen's case, and the king must know of it."

Evidence, I realized too late, of corruption: if the queen had touched this book, if it had led her to the Wood, she had been corrupted even before she was drawn under the boughs. If this were presented at the trial—I looked at Alosha and Ballo in dismay. They hadn't come here to help me. They'd come to stop me finding anything useful.

Alosha sighed back at me. "I'm not your enemy, though you want to think me so."

"You *want* them put to death!" I said. "The queen, and Kasia—"

"What I want," Alosha said, "is to keep the kingdom safe. You and Marek: all you worry about is your own sorrows. You're too young to be as strong as you are, that's the trouble of it; you haven't let go of people. When you've seen a century of your own go by, you'll have more sense."

I'd been about to protest at her accusation, but that silenced me: I stared at her in horror. Maybe it was silly of me, but it hadn't occurred to me until that very moment that *I* was going to live like Sarkan, like her, a hundred years, two hundred—when did witches even die? I wouldn't grow old; I'd just keep *going*, always the same, while everyone around me withered and fell away, like the outer stalks of some climbing vine going up and up away from them.

"I don't want more sense!" I said loudly, beating against the silence of the room. "Not if *sense* means I'll stop loving anyone. What is there besides people that's worth holding on to?" Maybe there was some way, I wondered wildly, to give away some of that life: maybe I could give some to my family, to Kasia—if they would take it; who would want anything like that, at the price of falling out of the world, taking yourself out of *life*.

"My dear child, you are growing very distressed," Ballo said feebly, making a gesture at calming me. I stared at him and the faint fine lines at the corner of his eyes, all his days spent with dusty books, loving nothing else; him and Alosha, who spoke as easily of putting people in the fire as she did books. I remembered Sarkan in his tower, plucking girls out of the valley, and his coldness when I'd first come, as though he couldn't remember how to think and feel like an ordinary person.

"A nation is people as well," Alosha said. "More people than just the few you love best yourself. And the Wood threatens them all."

"I've lived seven miles from the Wood all my days," I said. "I don't need to be told what it is. If I didn't care about stopping the Wood, I'd have taken Kasia and run away by now, instead of leaving her to all of you to push her like a pawn from here to there, as if she doesn't even matter!"

Ballo made startled murmuring noises, but Alosha only frowned at me. "And yet you can speak of letting the corrupted live, as if you didn't know better," she said. "The Wood is not just some enclave of evil, lying in wait to catch people who are foolish enough to wander inside, and if you can get someone out of it there's an end to the harm. We aren't the first nation to face its power."

"You mean the people of the tower," I said slowly, thinking of the buried king.

"You've seen the tomb, have you?" Alosha said. "And the magic that made it, magic that's lost to us now? That should have been enough warning to make you more cautious. Those people weren't weak or unprepared. But the Wood brought their tower down, wolves and walkers hunted them, and trees choked all the valley. One or two of their weaker sorcerers fled to the north and took a few books and stories with them. The rest of them?" She waved a hand towards the book. "Twisted into nightmares, beasts to hunt their own kind. That's all the Wood left of that people. There's something worse than monsters in that place: something that makes monsters."

"I know it better than you!" I said. My hands still itched, and the book sat there on the table, malevolent. I couldn't stop thinking about that heavy, monstrous presence looking out of Kasia's face, of Jerzy's, the feeling of being hunted beneath the boughs.

"Do you?" Alosha said. "Tell me, if I said to uproot every person living in your valley, to move them elsewhere in the kingdom and abandon it all to the Wood, save them and let it all go; would you come away?" I stared at her. "Why haven't you already left, for that matter?" she added. "Why do you keep living there, in that shadow? There are places in Polnya that aren't haunted by evil."

I fumbled for an answer I didn't know how to give. The idea was simply foreign. Kasia had imagined leaving, because she'd had to; I never had. I loved Dvernik, the deep soft woods around my house, the long bright running of the Spindle beneath the sun. I loved the cup of the mountains around us, a sheltering wall. There was a peace deep in our village, in our valley; it wasn't just the Dragon's light hand on the reins. It was home.

"A home where some misshapen thing might come out of the forest at night and steal away your children," Alosha said. "Even before the Wood roused fully again, that valley was infested with corruption; there are old tales from the Yellow Marshes that speak of seeing walkers on the other side of the mountain passes, from before we ever pushed our way over the mountains and started to cut down the trees. But men still sought out that valley, and stayed there, and tried to live in it."

"Do you think we're *all* corrupted?" I said in horror: maybe she would rather burn all the valley, and all of us inside it, if given her way.

"Not corrupted," she said. "*Lured.* Tell me, where does the river go?"

"The Spindle?"

"Yes," she said. "Rivers flow to the sea, to lakes or marshland, not to forests. Where does that one go? It's fed every year by the snows of a thousand mountains. It doesn't simply sink into the earth. *Think,*" she added, with a bite, "instead of going on blindly wanting. There is some power deep in your valley, some strangeness beyond mortal magic that draws men in, plants roots in them—and not only men. Whatever thing it is that lives in the Wood, that puts out corruption, it's come to live there and drink from that power like a cup. It killed the people of the tower, and then it slumbered for a thousand years because no one was fool enough to bother it. Then along we come, with our armies and our axes and our magic, and think that *this* time we can win."

She shook her head. "Bad enough we went there at all," she said. "Worse to keep pressing on, cutting down trees, until we woke the

Wood again. Now who knows where it will end? I was glad when Sarkan went to hold it back, but now he's behaving like a fool."

"Sarkan's not a fool," I snapped out, "and neither am I." I was angry and more than that, afraid; what she was saying rang too true. I missed home like the ache of hunger, something in me left empty. I'd missed it every day since we crossed out of the valley, going over the mountains. Roots—yes. There were roots in my heart, as deep as any corruption could go. I thought of Maria Olshankina, of Jaga, my sisters in the strange magic that no one else seemed to understand, and I knew, suddenly, why the Dragon took a girl from the valley. I knew why he took one, and why she left after ten years.

We were of the valley. Born in the valley, of families planted too deep to leave even when they knew their daughter might be taken; raised in the valley, drinking of whatever power also fed the Wood. I remembered the painting, suddenly, that strange painting in my room, showing the line of the Spindle and all its little tributaries in silver, and the odd pull of it that had made me cover it up, instinctively. We were a channel. He used us to reach into the valley's power, and kept each girl in his tower until her roots had withered and the channel closed. And then—she didn't feel the tie to the valley anymore. She could leave, and so she did, getting away from the Wood like any sensible ordinary person would.

I wanted to speak to Sarkan now more than ever, to shout at him; I wanted him in front of me so I could shake him by his thin shoulders. I shouted at Alosha instead. "Maybe we shouldn't have gone in," I said, "but it's too late for that now. The Wood isn't going to let us go, even if we could. It doesn't want to drive us away, it wants to devour us. It wants to devour everything, so no one ever comes back again. We need to *stop* it, not run away."

"The Wood isn't to be defeated by wanting it so," she said.

"That's no reason not to try when we have the chance!" I said. "We've destroyed three heart-trees already, with the *Summoning* and the purging spell, and we can destroy more. If only the king would give us enough soldiers, Sarkan and I could start burning the whole thing back—"

"Whatever are you speaking of, child?" Ballo said, bewildered, breaking in. "Do you mean *Luthe's Summoning*? No one has cast that spell in fifty years—"

"All right," Alosha said, contemplating me from under her dark brows. "Tell me exactly how you've been destroying these trees, and from the beginning: we shouldn't have relied on Solya to tell it to us properly."

I haltingly told them about the first time we'd cast the *Summoning*, about the long stretch of that brilliant light reaching down to Kasia, the Wood lashing at her and trying to hold her back; about those final dreadful moments with Kasia's fingers around my throat unlocking one by one, knowing I would have to kill her to save her. I told them about Jerzy, too; and the strange inner Wood the *Summoning* had shown us, where the two of them had wandered lost.

Ballo looked distressed through my whole recitation, wavering between resistance and unwilling belief, occasionally saying faintly, "But I have never heard . . . ," and "The *Summoning* has never been reported to . . . ," only to trail off again when Alosha made impatient silencing gestures.

"Well," she said, when I was done, "I'll grant that you and Sarkan have done *something*, anyway. You're not entirely fools." She was still holding the dagger in her hand, and she tapped the tip of the blade against the stone edge of the table, tap, tap, tap, a ringing noise like a small bell. "That doesn't mean the queen was worth saving. After twenty years wandering in this shadow-place you've seen, what did any of you expect to be left of her?"

"We didn't," I said. "Sarkan didn't. But I had to—"

"Because Marek said he'd put your friend to death otherwise," Alosha finished for me. "Damn him anyway."

I didn't feel I owed Marek anything, but I said honestly, "If it were my mother—I'd try anything, too."

"Then you'd be behaving like a child instead of a prince," Alosha said. "Him and Solya." She turned to Ballo. "We should have known better, when they offered to go after the girl Sarkan had brought out." She looked back at me grimly. "I was too busy worrying that the Wood had finally got its claws into Sarkan. All I wanted was to have her put to death quickly, and Sarkan dragged back here for the rest of us to look over. And I'm still not certain that wouldn't be for the best, after all."

"Kasia's not corrupted!" I said. "And neither is the queen."

"That doesn't mean they can't still be turned to serve the Wood."

"You can't put them to death just because something dreadful *might* happen that won't even be their fault," I said.

Ballo said, "I cannot disagree with her, Alosha. When the relics have already proven they are pure—"

"Of course we can, if it'll save the kingdom from being overrun by the Wood," Alosha said, brutally, overriding us both. "But that doesn't mean I long to do it; and still less," she added to me, "to provoke *you* into some stupidity. I'm starting to understand why Sarkan indulged you as far as he has."

She tapped the blade on the table again before she spoke on, with sudden decision. "Gidna," she said.

I blinked at her. I knew about Gidna, of course, in a vague distant way; it was the great port city on the ocean, far to the north, that brought in whale oil and green woolen cloth; the crown prince's wife had come from there.

"That's far enough from the Wood, and the ocean is inimical to corruption," Alosha said. "If the king sends them both there—that might do. The count has a witch, the White Lark. Lock them up under her eyes, and in ten years' time—or if we do manage to burn down the whole rotten Wood—then I'll stop worrying so much."

Ballo was already nodding. But—ten years! I wanted to shout, to refuse. It was as though Kasia would be taken all over again. Only someone a century old could so easily throw ten years away. But I hesitated. Alosha wasn't a fool, either, and I could see she wasn't wrong to be wary. I looked at the corrupt bestiary lying on the table. The Wood had set us one trap after another, over and over. It had set a chimaera on the Yellow Marshes and white wolves on Dvernik, trying to catch the Dragon. It had taken Kasia, to lure me in. And when I'd found a way to break her out, the Wood had still tried to use Kasia to corrupt the Dragon and me both, and when that hadn't worked, it had let her live, to lure us into its hands again. We'd fought our way out of that trap, but what if there was another one, some way the Wood could turn our victory into defeat all over again?

I didn't know what to do. If I agreed, if I went along with Alosha—would the king listen to her? If I wrote to Sarkan, and he wrote back to agree? I bit my lip while she raised one cool eyebrow at me, waiting for me to answer. Then she looked over: the doors to the Charovnikov had swung open. The Falcon stood in the doorway, his snowy robes catching the light, a white figure framed in the dark opening. His eyes narrowed as he took the three of us in standing together; then he manufactured another of his smiles. "I see you've all been busy here," he said lightly. "But in the meantime, there have been developments. Perhaps you'd care to come down to the trial?"

TWENTY ONE

Outside the haven of the Charovnikov, the noise of the party filled the empty corridors. The music had stopped, but a sea of raised voices in the distance roared and fell like waves, louder and louder as the Falcon led us to the state ballroom. The footmen opened the doors for us hastily onto the staircase leading down to the vast dancing-floor. The ambassador in his white coat sat in a chair beside the king's throne, on a high dais overlooking the floor; Prince Sigmund and his wife were on the king's other side. The king was sitting with his hands clenched over the lion-clawed arms of his chair, face mottled with anger.

In the middle of the floor before him, Marek had cleared a wide-open circle, six full rows of shocked and avidly staring dancers drawn back from him, the ladies in their billowing skirts like strewn flowers in a ring. In the center of that circle stood the queen, blank-faced in a white prisoner's shift, with Kasia holding on to her arm; Kasia looked around and saw me with relief on her face, but I couldn't get anywhere near her. The crowd was packed up the stairs, hanging over the edge of the overlooking mezzanine to watch.

The royal secretary was almost crouched before Marek, speaking in a tremulous voice, holding a heavy law-book in front of himself as if it could make a shield. I couldn't blame him for cowering. Marek stood not two paces from him like a figure stepped out of a song: encased in armor of bright, polished steel, with a sword in his hand that could have cut down an ox and a helm under his arm. He stood before the secretary like a figure of avenging justice, shining with violence.

"In cases—in cases of corruption," the secretary stammered, "the right of trial by combat is not—is expressly revoked, by the law of Boguslav the—" He fell back with a choked sound. Marek had swept the sword up barely inches from his face.

Marek continued the movement, swung the sword around all the room, turning: the breathless crowd drew back from the point. "The queen of Polnya has the right to a champion!" he shouted. "Let any wizard stand forth and show any sign of corruption in her! You there, Falcon," he said, whirling and pointing up the stairs, and the whole court's eyes turned towards us, "lay a spell upon her now! Let all the court look and see if there is any spot upon her—" The whole court made a sound together, a sigh that rose and fell, ecstatic: archdukes and serving-maids as one.

I think that was why the king didn't stop it right away. The crowd on the stairs parted to make way for us, and the Falcon swept forward, his long sleeves trailing down the staircase, and coming to the floor made the king an elegant bow. He had obviously made ready for this moment: he had a large pouch full of something heavy, and he crooked his finger and brought four of the high spell-lamps down from the ceiling, to stand around the queen. And then he opened the pouch and flung a wave of blue sand up into the air over her head, speaking softly.

I couldn't hear the incantation, but a hot white light came crackling out of his fingers and ran through the falling sand. There was a smell of melting glass, thin wisps of smoke escaping: the sand dissolved away entirely as it came down, and a faintly blue distortion formed in the air instead, so that it seemed I saw the queen and Kasia through a thick pane of glass with mirrors all around them. The spell-lamps' light shone blazing through the distortion, brightening as it passed through. I could see the bones of Kasia's hand through her flesh, where it rested on the queen's shoulder, and the faint outline of her skull and her teeth.

Marek reached out and took the queen's hand, leading her in a circle on display. The nobles hadn't seen the archbishop's trial, Jadwiga's veil. They stared avidly at the queen in her white gown, her very blood vessels a faint tracework of shining lines inside her, everything glowing; her eyes were lamps and her parted lips breathing a glowing haze: no shadow, no smudge of darkness. The court was murmuring even before the light slowly faded out of her.

The glass shattered apart and fell in a chiming shower, dissolving back into blue wisps of smoke as it reached the ground. "Let her be examined further," Marek shouted over the rising noise of conversation, almost aglow himself with righteousness. "Call any witness: let the Willow come forth, and the archbishop—"

The room was plainly Marek's for the moment; even I could see a thousand rumors of murder beginning here if the king refused, if he ordered the queen taken away, and put her to death later. The king saw it, too. He looked around at all his courtiers and then gave a short, hard jerk of his chin to his chest; he sat back in the throne. So Marek had managed to force his father's hand this far, even without sorcery: whether the king had wanted to call a trial or not, the trial was effectively begun.

But I had seen the king three times now. I would have called him—not pleasant, exactly; there were too many lines drawn deep in his face, frowning, to imagine him gentle or kind. But if I'd been asked to describe him in a word, I would have said *worried*. Now I would have said *angry*, cold as a winter storm, and he was still the one who had to pass judgment in the end.

I wanted to run out and break up the trial, to tell Marek to take it back, but it was too late. The Willow had already stepped forward to testify, pillar-straight in a silver gown. "I have found no corruption, but I will not swear there is none," she said coolly, speaking directly up to the king and ignoring Marek's clenched jaw and the scrape of his gauntleted hand upon his sword-hilt. "The queen is not herself. She has spoken not a word, and she shows no signs of recognition. Her flesh is wholly changed. There is nothing left of her mortal sinew or bone. And while flesh may be turned to stone or to metal without carrying corruption, this change has certainly been carried out by a corrupt agency."

"And yet if her altered flesh *carried* corruption," the Falcon broke in, "would you not have expected to observe it beneath my spell?"

The Willow didn't even turn her head to acknowledge him; he had evidently spoken out of turn. She only inclined her head to the king, who nodded once and moved his fingers in a slight gesture to dismiss her.

The archbishop was just as equivocal. He would only say that he had tried the queen on all the holy relics of the cathedral, not that she wasn't corrupt. They neither of them cared to be proven wrong afterwards, I imagine.

Only a few other witnesses came forward to speak in the queen's favor, physicians whom Marek had brought to see her. None of them spoke about Kasia at all. She wasn't even an afterthought to them, but she would live or die on their words. And the queen stood silent and inert next to her. The glow had faded out now and left her blank-faced, empty, for all the court to see.

I looked at Alosha, standing next to me, and Ballo on her other side. I knew when it was their turn, they would stand up and tell the king about that hideous bestiary, sitting back there in the Charovnikov in a thick circle of salt and iron with all the protective spells they could layer over it and the guards posted to watch it close. Alosha would say that the chance shouldn't be taken; she would tell the king that there was too much risk to the kingdom.

And then, if he wanted to, the king could rise and say the laws against corruption were absolute; he could put on a regretful face, and send the queen to death, and Kasia along with her. And looking at him, I thought that he would. He would do it.

He'd sunk back deeply into his great carved chair as if he needed the support for the weight of his body, and his hand covered his unsmiling mouth. Decision was settling over him like snowfall, the first thin dusting that would build and build. The rest of the witnesses would speak, but he wouldn't hear them. He'd already decided. I saw Kasia's death in his heavy, grim face, and I looked desperately across the room to catch the Falcon's eye. Next to him, Marek stood as tense as his fist clenched around his sword.

Solya looked back at me and only spread his hands, subtly, as much as to say *I've done what I can.* He leaned in and murmured something to Marek, and when the last physician had stepped down, the prince said, "Let Agnieszka of Dvernik be called to witness how the queen was freed."

That's what I had wanted, after all; this was the reason I'd come and fought to have myself put on the list. Everyone was looking at me, even the king with his lowered brows. But I still didn't know what to say. What would it matter to the king, to any of these courtiers, for me to say the queen wasn't corrupt? They certainly wouldn't care what I said of Kasia.

Maybe Solya would try and cast the *Summoning* with me, if I asked him to. I thought of doing that, imagined that white light showing the whole court the truth. But—the queen had already been tested beneath Jadwiga's veil. The court had seen her beneath the Falcon's sight. The king could see she wasn't corrupted. This wasn't about truth at all. The court didn't want truth, the king didn't want truth. Any truth I could give them, they could ignore as easily as the rest. It wouldn't change their minds.

But I could give them something else entirely. I could give them what they really wanted. And then I realized I knew what that was, after all. They wanted to know. They wanted to see what it had been like. They wanted to feel themselves a part of it, of the queen's rescue; they wanted to be living in a song. That wasn't truth, anything like it, but it might convince them to spare Kasia's life.

I closed my eyes and remembered the illusion spell: *Easier than real armies*, Sarkan had said, and as I began to whisper the spell, I knew that he was right. It was no harder than making a single flower to raise up the whole of that monstrous heart-tree, and it climbed up out of the marble floor with terrible ease. Kasia dragged in a breath; a woman screamed; there was a clatter of a chair falling over somewhere in the room. I shut the noise out. I let the incantation keep rolling singsong off my tongue while I poured out magic and the sick, tight dread that had never left the back of my stomach. The heart-tree kept growing, spreading its great silver branches through the hall, the ceiling fading away into silver rustling leaves and the terrible stench of fruit. My stomach turned over once, and then Janos's head came rolling by across the grass in front of my feet, and struck against the sprawling roots.

All the courtiers cried out and jerked back against the walls, but even as they did, they were fading away, disappearing. The walls all around us were gone, too, falling away into forest and the ringing clash of steel. Marek turned in sudden startled alarm, raising his sword: the silver mantis was there, lunging towards him. When its claws struck against his shoulders, they scraped against the steel of his brilliant armor. Corpses were staring up from the grass around his feet.

A haze of smoke was drifting across my eyes, the sudden crackle of fire. I turned towards the trunk, and Sarkan was there, too, caught in the tree with silver bark trying to devour him, saying, *"Now, Agnieszka,"* while fire-heart glowed red between his fingers. Instinctively, I half-reached my hand towards him, remembering dread and anguish, and for a moment—for one brief moment, he wasn't illusion at all, not just illusion. He frowned back at me startled; his eyes said, *What are you doing, you idiot?* and it was him, somehow; really him—then the purging-fire boiled up between us, and he was gone; he was only illusion again, and burning.

I put my hands on the tree trunk as the bark curled and split apart like the skin of a too-ripe tomato. Kasia was beside me, real; the trunk was splintering open beneath her pounding hands. She was breaking open the wood of the trunk, and the queen came staggering forward out of it, her hands reaching out to meet ours, groping for help, her face suddenly alive and full of horror. We caught her and pulled her out. I heard the Falcon shouting a spell of fire—and then I realized, he was calling *real* fire, and we weren't really in the Wood. We were in the king's castle—

As soon as I let myself remember that, the illusion spell went slithering straight out of my grasp. The tree burned away into the air; the fire at its roots swept up along the trunk and took all the rest of the Wood along with it. The corpses sank down through the ground, one last glimpse of their faces, all their faces, before the white marble floor closed over them. I watched them with tears running down my face. I hadn't known I remembered the soldiers well enough to make so many of them. And then the last leaf-shadows cleared, and we were in the palace again, before the throne, with the king standing shocked upon his dais.

The Falcon whirled staring around himself, panting, fire still crackling in his hands and skittering over the marble floors; Marek also swung back looking for an enemy that wasn't there anymore. His sword was unstained again, his armor bright and undented. The queen stood in the middle of the floor trembling, her eyes wide. All the court was pressed up against the walls and one another, as far from us and the center of the room as they could go. And I, I sank to my knees shaking, my arms wrapped around my stomach, feeling sick. I had never wanted to be back there again, in the Wood.

Marek recovered first. He stepped towards the throne, his chest still heaving. "That is what we reft her from!" he shouted up at his father. "That is the evil we overcame to bring her out, that is what we paid to save her! That is the evil you serve, if you—I won't see it done! I will—"

"Enough!" the king roared back at him: he was pale beneath his beard.

Marek's face was flushed and bright with violence, battle-lust. He was still holding his sword. He took a step towards the throne. The king's eyes widened; red anger flushed into his cheeks, and he beckoned to his guards; there were six of them beside the dais.

Queen Hanna cried out suddenly, "No!"

Marek whirled back to look at her. She took a clumsy lurching step forward, her feet dragging as if she had to make an effort to move them. Marek was staring at her. She took another step and seized his arm. "No," she repeated. She pulled his arm down, when he would have kept it up. He resisted, but she had turned her eyes up at him, and his face was suddenly a boy's, looking down at her. "You saved me," she said to him. "Marechek. You already saved me."

His arm sank, and still clinging to it she turned slowly to the king. He was staring down at her. Her face was pale and beautiful framed in the cloud of her short hair. "I wanted to die," she said. "I wanted so to die." She took another dragging step and knelt on the wide dais stairs, and pulled Marek down with her; he bowed his head, staring at the floor. But she kept looking up. "Forgive him," she said to the king. "I know the law. I am ready to die." Her hand held tight when Marek would have jerked. "I am the queen of Polnya!" she said, loudly. "I am ready to die for my country. But not as a traitor.

"I am not a traitor, Kasimir," she said, stretching her other arm out. "He took me. He took me!"

A murmuring started through the room, rising fast as a river in flood. I lifted my weary head and stared around, not understanding. Alosha's face when I looked at her was drawing into a frown. The queen's voice was trembling but loud enough to rise above the noise. "Let me be put to death for corruption," she said. "But God above witness me! I did not leave my husband and my children. The traitor Vasily took me from the courtyard with his soldiers, and carried me to the Wood, and there he bound me to the tree himself."

TWENTY TWO

"I warned you," Alosha said, without looking up from her steady ringing thumps of hammer-strokes. I hugged my knees in the corner of her forge, just beyond the scorched circle of ground where the sparks fell, and didn't say anything. I didn't have an answer: she *had* warned me.

No one cared that Prince Vasily must have been corrupted himself, to do such a mad thing; no one cared that he'd died in the Wood, a lonely corpse feeding the roots of the heart-tree. No one cared that it was the fault of the bestiary. Prince Vasily had kidnapped the queen and given her to the Wood. Everyone was as angry as if he'd done it yesterday, and instead of marching on the Wood, they wanted to march on Rosya.

I'd tried to speak to Marek already: a waste of time. Not two hours after the queen had been pardoned, he was in the barracks courtyard exercising horses, already choosing which ones he'd take to the front. "You'll come with us," he said as though it was unquestioned, without even taking his eyes off the flashing legs as he sent a tall bay gelding around him in a circle, one hand on the lead and the other on the long-tailed whip. "Solya says you can double the strength of his workings, perhaps more."

"No!" I said. "I'm not going to help you kill Rosyans! It's the Wood we need to fight, not them."

"And so we will," Marek said easily. "After we take the eastern bank of the Rydva, we'll come south over their side of the Jaral Mountains and surround the Wood from both sides. All right, we'll take this one," he said to his groom, tossing over the lead; he caught up the dangling tail of the whip with an expert flick of his wrist and turned to me. "Listen, Nieshka—" I glared at him speechlessly; how dare he put a pet name on me? But only he put an arm around my shoulders, too, and sailed straight onward. "If we take half the army south to your valley, they'll come pouring over the Rydva themselves while our backs are turned, and sack Kralia itself. That's probably why they leagued with the Wood in the first place. They wanted us to do just that. The Wood doesn't have an army. It'll stay where it is until we've dealt with Rosya."

"No one would ever be in league with the Wood!" I said.

He shrugged. "If they aren't, they've still deliberately used it against us," he said. "What comfort do you think it is to my mother if that dog Vasily died, too, after he handed her over to that endless hell? And even if he *was* corrupted beforehand, you must see it doesn't matter. Rosya won't scruple to take advantage of the opening if we turn south. We can't turn on the Wood until we've protected our flank. Stop being shortsighted."

I jerked away from his hand and his condescension both. "*I'm* not the one being shortsighted," I told Kasia, fuming, as we hurried across the courtyard to seek Alosha out at her forge.

But Alosha only said, "I warned you," grim but without heat. "The power in the Wood isn't some blind hating beast; it can think and plan, and work towards its own ends. It can see into the hearts of men, all the better to poison them." She took the sword from her anvil and plunged it into the cold water; steam billowed in great gusts like the breath of some monstrous beast. "If there wasn't any corruption, you might have guessed there was something else at work."

Sitting next to me, Kasia raised her head. "Is—is there something else at work in me?" she asked, unhappily.

Alosha paused and glanced at her. I found myself holding my breath, silent; then Alosha shrugged. "Isn't this bad enough? You freed, then the queen freed, and now all of Polnya and Rosya ready to go up in flames? We can't spare the men they're sending to the front," she added. "If we could, they would already have been there. The king is stripping the kingdom bare, and Rosya will have to do the same to meet us. It'll be a bad harvest this year for all of us, win or lose."

"And that's what the Wood wanted, all along," Kasia said.

"One of the things it wanted," Alosha said. "I've no doubt it would gladly have eaten Agnieszka and Sarkan if it had the chance, and then it could have devoured the rest of the valley overnight. But a tree isn't a woman; it doesn't bear a single seed. It scatters as many of them as it can, and hopes for some of them to grow. That book was one; the queen was one. She should have been sent away at once, and you with her." She turned back to the forge. "Too late to mend that now."

"Maybe we should just go straight home," I said to Kasia, and tried to ignore the longing rising in me like a swell just at the thought, that involuntary pull. I wanted to believe myself, saying, "There's nothing more to do here. We'll go home, we can help burning the Wood. We can raise a hundred men out of the valley at least—"

"A hundred men," Alosha said to her anvil, with a snort. "You and Sarkan and a hundred men can do some damage, I've no doubt, but you'll pay for every inch of ground you get. And meanwhile the Wood will have twenty thousand men slaughtering each other on the banks of the Rydva."

"The Wood will have that anyway!" I said. "Can't *you* do something?"

"I'm doing it," Alosha said, and put the sword back into the fire again. She'd done it four times already just while we'd been sitting here with her, which I realized didn't make any sense. I hadn't seen swords made before, but I'd watched the smith at work often enough: we'd all liked to watch as children while he hammered out scythes, and pretend he was making swords; we would pick up sticks and have mock battles around the steaming forge. So I knew you weren't meant to forge a blade over and over, but Alosha took the sword out again and put it back on the anvil, and I realized she was hammering spells into the steel: her lips moved a little while she worked. It was a strange kind of magic, because it wasn't finished in itself; she was catching up a dangling spell, and she left it hanging again before she plunged it once more into the cold water.

The dark blade came out dripping, glazed with water. It had a strange and hungry feeling. When I looked into it I saw a long fall into some deep dry crack in the earth, tumbling away onto sharp rocks. It wasn't like the other enchanted swords, the ones Marek's soldiers had carried; this thing wanted to drink life.

"I've been forging this blade for a century," Alosha said, holding it up. I looked at her, glad to take my eyes away from the thing. "After the Raven died, and Sarkan went to the tower, I began it. There's less iron than spellcraft in it by now. The sword only remembers the shape it once had, and it won't last for longer than a single stroke, but that's all it will need."

She put it back in the forge again, and we watched it sitting in the bath of flames, a long tongue of shadow among them. "The power in the Wood," Kasia said slowly, her eyes on the fire. "Is it something you can kill?"

"This sword can kill anything," Alosha said, and I believed her. "As long as we can make it put out its neck. But for that," she added, "we'll need more than a hundred men."

"We could ask the queen," Kasia said suddenly. I blinked at her. "I know there are lords who owe her fealty on her own—a dozen of them tried to come and pay her homage, while we were locked up together, though the Willow wouldn't let them in. She must have soldiers she could give us, instead of sending them to Rosya."

And she, at least, would surely want the Wood struck down. Even if Marek wouldn't listen to me, or the king, or anyone else in the court, perhaps she would.

So Kasia and I went down to hover outside the great council-chamber: the queen was there again, a part of the war-council now. The guards would have let me inside: they knew who I was, now. They watched me sidelong out of the corners of their eyes, nervous and interested both, as though I might erupt with more sorcery at any moment, like contagious boils. But I didn't want to go in; I didn't want to get caught up in the arguments of the Magnati and the generals planning how best to murder ten thousand men, and harvest glory while the crops rotted in the fields. I wasn't going to put myself into their hands as another weapon to aim.

So we waited outside and held back against the wall instead while the council came pouring out, a torrent of lords and soldiers. I had thought the queen would come behind them, with servants to help her walk. But she didn't: she came out in the center of the crowd. She was wearing the circlet, Ragostok's circlet, the one he'd been working on. The gold caught the light, and the rubies shone above her golden hair. She wore red silk, too, and all of the court-iers gathered around her, sparrows around a cardinal bird. It was the king who came behind the rest, talking in low voices with Father Ballo and two councilors, an afterthought.

Kasia looked at me. We would have had to shove through the crowd to get to her—brazen, but we could have done it; Kasia could have made a way for us. But the queen looked so different. The stiffness seemed to have faded, and her silence. She was nod-ding to the lords around her, she was smiling; she was one of them again, one of the actors moving on the stage, as graceful as any of them. I didn't move. She glanced aside for a moment, almost towards us. I didn't try to catch her eye; instead I caught Kasia's arm, and pressed her farther back into the wall with me. Something held me like the instinct of a mouse in a hole, hearing the breath of the owl's wing overhead.

The guards fell in after the court with last looks at me; the hallway stood empty. I was trembling. "Nieshka," Kasia said. "What is it?"

"I've made a mistake," I said. I didn't know just what, but I'd done something wrong; I felt the dreadful certainty of it sinking down through me, like watching a penny falling away down a deep well. "I've made a mistake."

Kasia followed me through the hallways, the narrow stairs, almost running by the end, back to my small room. She was watching me, worried, while I shut the door hard behind us and leaned against it, like a child hiding. "Was it the queen?" Kasia said.

I looked at her standing in the middle of my room, firelight golden on her skin and through her hair, and for one horrible moment she was a stranger wearing Kasia's face: for one moment I'd brought the dark in with me. I whirled away from her to the table. I'd brought a few branches of pine into my bedroom, to have them nearby. I took a handful of needles and burned them on the hearth and breathed in the smoke, the sharp bitter smell, and I whispered my cleansing spell. The strangeness faded. Kasia was sitting on the bed watching me, unhappy. I looked up at her miserably: she'd seen suspicion in my eyes.

"It's no more than I've thought myself," she said. "Nieshka, I should—maybe the queen, maybe both of us, *should* be—" Her voice shook.

"No!" I said. "No." But I didn't know what to do. I sat on the hearth, panting, afraid, and then I turned abruptly to the fire, cupping my hands, and I called up my old practice illusion, the small and determinedly thorny rose, the vining branches of the rosebush climbing sluggishly over the sides of the fire-screen. Slowly, singing,

I gave it perfume, and a handful of humming bees, and leaves curling at the edges with ladybugs hiding; and then I made Sarkan on the other side of it. I called up his hands beneath mine: the long spindly careful fingers, the smooth-rubbed pen calluses, the heat of his skin radiating; and he took shape on the hearth, sitting beside me, and we were sitting in his library, too.

I was singing my short illusion spell back and forth, feeding a steady silver thread of magic to it. But it wasn't like the heart-tree had been, the day before. I was looking at his face, his frown, his dark eyes scowling at me, but it wasn't really him. It wasn't just an illusion that I needed, not just the image of him or even a smell, or a sound, I realized. That wasn't why the heart-tree had *lived*, down in that throne room. It had grown out of my heart, out of fear and memory and the churning of horror in my belly.

The rose was cupped in my hands. I looked at Sarkan on the other side of the petals, and let myself feel his hands cupped around mine, the places where his fingertips just barely brushed against my skin and where the heels of my palms rested in his. I let myself remember the alarming heat of his mouth, the crush of his silk and lace between our bodies, his whole length against me. And I let myself think about my anger, about everything I'd learned, about his secrets and everything he'd hidden; I let go of the rose and gripped the edges of his coat to shake him, to shout at him, to kiss him—

And then he blinked and looked at me, and there was fire glowing somewhere behind him. His cheek was grimy with soot, flecks of ash in his hair, and his eyes were reddened; the fire on the hearth crackled, and it was the distant crackle of fire in the trees. "Well?" he demanded, hoarse and irritated, and it was him. "We can't do this for long, whatever you *are* doing; I can't have my attention divided."

My hands clenched on the fabric: I felt stitches going ragged and flecks of stinging ash on my hands, ash in my nostrils, ash in my mouth. "What's happening?"

"The Wood's trying to take Zatochek," he said. "We've been

burning it back every day, but we've lost a mile of ground already. Vladimir has sent what soldiers he could spare from the Yellow Marshes, but it's not enough. Is the king sending any men?"

"No," I said. "He's—they're starting another war with Rosya. The queen said Vasily of Rosya gave her to the Wood."

"The queen spoke?" he said sharply, and I felt that same uneasy drumbeat of fear rise up in my throat again.

"But the Falcon put a spell of seeing on her," I said, arguing with myself as much as him. "They tried her with Jadwiga's shawl. There wasn't anything in her. There wasn't a trace, none of them could see any shadow—"

"Corruption isn't the only tool the Wood has," Sarkan said. "Ordinary torment can break a person just as well. It might have let her go deliberately, broken to its service but untainted to any magical sight. Or it might have planted something on her instead, or nearby. A fruit, a seed—"

He stopped and turned his head, seeing something I couldn't. He said sharply, "Let go!" and jerked his magic loose; I fell backwards off the hearth and struck against the floor, jarred painfully. The rosebush crumbled to ash on the hearth and vanished, and he was gone with it.

Kasia sprang to catch me, but I was already scrambling to my feet. *A fruit, a seed.* His words had sparked fear in me. "The bestiary," I said. "Ballo was going to try to purify it—" I was still dizzy, but I turned and ran from the room, urgency rising in me. Ballo had been going to tell the king about the book. Kasia ran beside me, steadying my first wobbly steps.

The screaming reached us as we plunged down the first narrow servants' staircase. *Too late, too late,* my feet told me as they slapped against the stone. I couldn't tell where the screams came from: they were far away and echoing strangely through the castle hallways. I ran in the direction of the Charovnikov, past two staring maids who'd shrunk back against the walls, crumpling the folded linens in their arms. Kasia and I wheeled to go down the second staircase to the ground level just as a white burst of fire crackled below, throwing sharp-edged shadows against the walls.

The blinding light faded, and then I saw Solya go flying across the mouth of the stairwell, smashing into a wall with a wet-sack noise. We scrambled down and saw him sprawled up against the opposite wall, not moving, his eyes open and dazed, blood running from his nose and mouth, and bloody shallow slashes dragged across his chest.

The thing that crawled out of the corridor to the Charovnikov nearly filled the space from floor to ceiling. It was less a beast than a horrible conglomeration of parts: a head like a monstrous dog, one enormous eye in the middle of its forehead and the snout full of jagged sharp edges that looked like knives instead of teeth. Six heavy-muscled legs with clawed lion's feet sprouted from its swollen body, all of it armored in scales like a serpent. It roared and came rushing towards us so quickly I almost couldn't think to move. Kasia seized me and dragged me back up the stairs, and the thing doubled on itself and thrust its head up through the opening of the stairwell, snapping and biting and howling, a green froth boiling out of its mouth. I shouted, *"Polzhyt!"* stamping its head away, and it shrieked and jerked back into the hallway as a spurt of fire burst up from the stairs and scorched across its muzzle.

Two heavy bolts flew into its side with solid, meaty thumps: it twisted, snarling. Behind it, Marek threw aside a crossbow; a terrified gawky young equerry at his side had pulled a spear down off the wall for him and was clutching it, gaping at the monster; he barely remembered to let go as Marek snatched it out of his hands. "Go raise the guard!" he shouted at the boy, who flinched and ran. Marek jabbed the spear at the monster's head.

The doors to a chamber hung crazily open behind him, white and black flagstones splattered with blood and three men sprawled dead, nobles in slashed clothes. The white, frightened face of an old man stared out from beneath the table in the room: the palace secretary. Two palace guards lay dead farther back along the hallway, as if the monster had come bounding from deeper inside the castle and had smashed open the doors to get at the men inside.

Or perhaps to get at one man, in particular: it snarled at the poking spear, but then it turned away from Marek; it swung its heavy head around, teeth baring, deliberate, towards Solya. He was staring at the ceiling still, his eyes dazed, his fingers slowly scrabbling over the stone floor as though trying to find a grip on the world.

Before the thing could pounce, Kasia flung herself past me in one enormous leap down the stairs, stumbling and thudding into the wall and righting herself. She grabbed another spear off the wall and pushed it into the beast's face. The dog-thing snapped at the spear's haft, then bellowed: Marek had sunk his spear into its flanks. There were boots, shouts coming, more guards running and the cathedral bells ringing suddenly in warning; the page had raised the alarm.

I saw all of those things, and could say afterwards that they happened, but I didn't feel them happening in the moment. There was only the hot stinking breath of the monster coming up the staircase, and blood, and my heart jumping; and knowing I had to do something. The beast howled and turned back to Kasia and Solya, and I stood up on the stairs. The bells were ringing and ringing. I heard them above my head, where a high window looked out from the stairwell onto a narrow slice of sky, the bright pearl-grey haze of a cloudy summer day.

I stretched up my hand and called, *"Kalmoz!"* Outside the clouds squeezed together into a dark knot like a sponge, a cloudburst that blew water in spattering on me, and a bolt of lightning cracked in through the window and jumped into my hands like a bright hissing snake. I clutched it, blinded, white light and a high singing whine all around me; I couldn't breathe. I flung it down the stairs towards the beast. Thunder roared around me and I went flying back, sprawling painfully across the landing, smoke and a bitter sharp smell crackling.

I lay flat, shaking all over, tears running out of my eyes. My hands were stinging and painful, and smoke was coming off them like morning fog. I couldn't hear anything. When my eyes cleared, the two maids were bending over me, terrified, their mouths moving soundlessly. Their hands spoke for them, gentle, helping me up. I staggered up to my feet. At the foot of the stairs, Marek and three guards were at the monster's head, prodding it warily. It lay smoking and still, a blasted outline charred black against the walls around its body. "Put a spear in its eye to be sure," Marek said, and one of the guards thrust his in deep into the one round eye, already milky. The body didn't twitch.

I limped down the stairs, one hand on the wall, and sank shakily down on the steps above its head. Kasia was helping Solya to his feet; he put the back of his hand to his face and wiped away the maze of blood over his mouth, panting, staring down at the beast.

"What the hell is that thing?" Marek demanded. It looked even more unnatural, dead: limbs that didn't fit with one another hanging askew from the body, as if some mad seamstress had sewn together bits of different dolls.

I stared at it from above, the dog-muzzle shape, the sprawled loose legs, the thick serpent's body, and a memory slowly crept in, a picture I'd seen yesterday, out of the corner of my eye, trying not to read. "A tsoglav," I said. I stood up again, too fast, and had to catch myself on the wall. "It's a tsoglav."

"What?" Solya said, looking up at me. "What is a—"

"It's from the bestiary!" I said. "We have to find Father Ballo—" I stopped and looked at the beast, the one last filmy staring eye, and suddenly I knew we weren't going to find him. "We have to find the book," I whispered.

I was swaying and sick. I scrambled and half-fell over the body getting into the hall. Marek caught my arm and held me up, and with the guards holding spears ready we went down to the Charovnikov. The great wooden doors were hanging askew over the opening, splintered, bloodstained. Marek tipped me against the wall like a wobbly ladder, then jerked a head to one of the guardsmen: together they seized one of the heavy broken doors and lifted it out of the way.

The library was a ruin, lamps broken, tables overturned and smashed, only a few dim lights shining. Bookcases lay toppled over on heaps of the volumes they had held, disemboweled. In the center of the room, the massive stone table had cracked down the middle both ways and fallen in on itself. The bestiary lay open in the very center atop stone dust and rubble, one last lamp shining down on the unmarred pages. There were three bodies scattered on the floor around it, broken and discarded, mostly lost in the shadows, but next to me Marek went deeply and utterly still; halted.

And then he sprang forward, shouting, "Send for the Willow! Send for—" sliding to his knees next to the farthest body; he stopped as he turned it over and the light fell on the man's face: on the king's face.

The king was dead.

TWENTY THREE

There were people everywhere shouting: guards, servants, ministers, physicians, all crowding around the body of the king as close as they could get. Marek had set the three guards to watch him and vanished. I was pushed up to the side of the room like flotsam on the tide, my eyes closing as I sagged against a bookcase. Kasia pushed through to my side. "Nieshka, what should I do?" she asked me, helping me to sit on a footstool.

I said, "Go and get Alosha," instinctively wanting someone who would know what to do.

It was a lucky impulse. One of Ballo's assistants had survived: he'd fled and pulled himself up into the stone chimney of the library's great fireplace to escape. A guard noticed the claw marks on the hearth and the ashes of the fire all raked out over the floor, and they found him still up there, shaking and terrified. They brought him out and gave him a drink, and then he stood up and pointed at me and blurted, "It was her! She was the one who found it!"

I was dizzy and ill and still shaking with thunder. They all began shouting at me. I tried to tell them about the book, how it had been hiding in the library all this time; but they wanted someone to blame more than they wanted someone to explain. The smell of pine needles came into my nostrils. Two guards seized me by the arms, and I think they would have dragged me to the dungeons in a moment, or worse: someone said, "She's a witch! If we let her get her strength back again—"

Alosha made them stop: she came into the room and clapped her hands three times, each clap making a noise like a whole troop of men stamping. Everyone quieted long enough to listen to her. "Put her down in that chair and stop behaving like fools," she said. "Take hold of Jakub instead. He was here in the middle of it. Didn't any of you have the wits to suspect he'd been touched with corruption, too?"

She had authority: they all knew her, especially the guards, who went as stiff and formal as if she were a general. They let go of me and caught poor protesting Jakub instead; they dragged him up to Alosha still bleating, "But she did! Father Ballo said she found the book—"

"Be quiet," Alosha said, taking out her dagger. "Hold his wrist," she told one of the guards, and had them pin the apprentice's arm to a table by the wrist, palm up. She muttered a spell over it and nicked his elbow, then held the blade beside the bleeding cut. He squirmed and struggled in their grip, moaning, and then thin black wisps of smoke came seeping out with the blood, and rose to catch on the glowing blade. She rotated the dagger slowly, collecting up the wisps like thread on a bobbin until the smoke stopped coming. Alosha held the dagger up and looked at it with narrowed eyes, said, *"Hulvad elolveta,"* and blew on it three times: the blade grew brighter and brighter with every breath, glowing hot, and the smoke burned off with a smell of sulfur.

The room had emptied considerably by the time she was done, and everyone left had backed away to the walls, except the pale unhappy guards still holding the apprentice. "All right, give him some bandages. Stop shouting, Jakub," she said. "I was there when she found it, you idiot: the book was here in our own library for years, lurking like a rotting apple. Ballo was going to purge it. What happened?"

Jakub didn't know: he'd been sent to fetch supplies. The king hadn't been there when he'd left; when he'd come back, carrying more salt and herbs, the king and his guards had been standing by the podium with blank faces, and Ballo was reading the book aloud, already changing: clawed legs coming from beneath his robe, and two more sprouting from his sides, tearing their way out, his face lengthening into a snout, the words still coming even as they garbled and choked in his throat—

Jakub's voice rose higher and higher as he spoke, until it broke and stopped. His hands were shaking.

Alosha poured more nalevka into a glass for him to drink. "It's stronger than we thought," she said. "We have to burn it at once."

I struggled up off my footstool, but Alosha shook her head at me. "You're overspent. Go sit on the hearth, and keep watch on me: don't try to do anything unless you see it's taking me."

The book still lay placidly on the floor between the shattered pieces of the stone table, illuminated and innocent. Alosha took a pair of gauntlets from one of the guards and picked it up. She took it to the hearth and called fire: *"Polzhyt, polzhyt mollin, polzhyt talo,"* and on further from there, a long incantation, and the dull ashes in the hearth roared up like the blaze of her forge. The fire licked at the pages and gummed them, but the book only flung itself open in the fire and its pages ruffled like flags in a high wind, snapping, pictures of beasts trying to catch the eye, illuminated with firelight behind them.

"Get back!" Alosha said sharply to the guards: a few of them had been about to take a step closer, their eyes vague and caught. She reflected firelight into their faces from the flat of her dagger, and they blinked and then startled back, pale and afraid.

Alosha watched with a wary eye until they moved farther away, then turned back and kept chanting her fire spell, over and over, her arms spread wide to hold the fire in. But the book still hissed and spat on the hearth like wet green wood, refusing to catch; the fresh smell of spring leaves crept into the room, and I could see veins standing out on Alosha's neck, strain showing in her face. She had her eyes fixed on the mantelpiece, but they kept drifting downwards towards the glowing pages. Each time, she pressed her thumb against the edge of her dagger. Blood dripped. She lifted her gaze back up.

Her voice was going hoarse. A handful of orange sparks landed on the carpet and smoldered. Sitting tired on the footstool, I looked at them and slowly I began to hum the old song about the spark on the hearth, telling its long stories: *Once there was a golden princess, loved a simple player; the king gave them a splendid wedding, and the story ends there! Once there was old Baba Jaga, house made out of butter; and in that house so many wonders—tsk! The spark is gone now.* Gone, taking the story with it. I sang it once through softly and said, *"Kikra, kikra,"* and then sang it again. The flying sparks began to drop onto the pages like rain, each one darkening a tiny spot before they went out. They fell in glowing showers, and when they fell in clusters, thin plumes of smoke went up.

Alosha slowed and stopped. The fire was catching at last. The pages were curling in on themselves at the edges like small animals huddling to die, with a burnt-sugar smell of sap in the fire. Kasia took my arm gently, and we backed away from the fire while it slowly ate the book up like someone forcing herself to eat stale bread.

"How did this bestiary come to your hands?" one minister bellowed at me, seconded by half a dozen more. "Why was the king there?" The council chamber was full of nobles shouting at me, at Alosha, at one another, afraid, demanding answers that weren't to be had. Half of them still suspected me of having set a trap for the king, and talked of throwing me in the dungeon; some others decided, on no evidence at all, that shivering Jakub was a Rosyan agent who'd lured the king to the library and tricked Father Ballo into reading the book. He began to weep and make protests, but I didn't have the strength to defend myself against them. My mouth stretched into an involuntary yawn instead, and made them angrier.

I didn't mean to be disrespectful, I just couldn't help it. I couldn't get enough air. I couldn't think. My hands were still stinging with lightning and my nose was full of smoke, of burning paper. None of it seemed real to me yet. The king dead, Father Ballo dead. I had seen them barely an hour ago, walking away from the war-conference, whole and healthy. I remembered the moment, too vividly: the small worried crease in Father Ballo's forehead; the king's blue boots.

In the library, Alosha had done a purging spell over the king's body, then the priests had carried him away to the cathedral for vigil, wrapped hastily in a cloth. The boots had been sticking out of the end of the bundle.

The Magnati kept shouting at me. It didn't help that I felt I *was* to blame. I'd known something was wrong. If I'd only been quicker, if I'd only burned the book myself when I first found it. I put my stinging hands over my face.

But Marek stood up next to me and shouted the nobles down with the authority of the bloody spear he was still holding. He slammed it down on the council table in front of them. "She slew the beast when it might have killed Solya and another dozen men besides," he said. "We don't have time for this sort of idiocy. We march on the Rydva in three days' time!"

"We march nowhere without the king's word!" one of the ministers dared to shout back. Lucky for him, he was across the table and out of arm's reach: even so he shrank back from Marek leaning across the table, mailed hand clenched into a fist, rage illuminating him with righteous wrath.

"He's not wrong," Alosha said sharply, putting a hand down in front of Marek, and making him straighten up to face her. "This is no time to be starting a war."

Half of the Magnati along the table were snarling and clawing at each other; blaming Rosya, blaming me, even blaming poor Father Ballo. The throne stood empty at the head of the table. Crown Prince Sigmund sat to the right of it. His hands were clenched around each other into a single joined fist. He stared at it without speaking while the shouting went on. The queen sat on the left. She still wore Ragostok's golden circlet, above the smooth shining satin of her black gown. I noticed dully that she was reading a letter: a messenger was standing by her elbow, with an empty dispatch bag and an uncertain face. He'd come into the room just then, I suppose.

The queen stood up. "My lords." Heads turned to look at her. She held up the letter, a short folded piece of paper; she'd broken the red seal. "A Rosyan army has been sighted coming for the Rydva: they will be there in the morning."

No one let out a word.

"We must put aside our mourning and our anger," she said. I stared up at her: the very portrait of a queen, proud, defiant, her chin raised; her voice rang clearly in the stone hall. "This is no hour for Polnya to show weakness." She turned to the crown prince: his face was turned up towards her just like mine, startled and open as a child's, his mouth loosely parted over words that weren't coming. "Sigmund, they have only sent four companies. If you gather the troops already mustering outside the city and ride at once, you will have the advantage in numbers."

"I should be the one who—!" Marek said, rousing to protest, but Queen Hanna held up her hand, and he stopped.

"Prince Marek will stay here and secure the capital with the royal guard, gathering the additional levies that are coming in," she said, turning back to the court. "He will be guided by the council's advice and, I hope, my own. Surely there is nothing else to be done?"

The crown prince stood. "We will do as the queen proposes," he said. Marek's cheeks were purpling with frustration, but he blew out a breath and said sourly, "Very well."

Just that quickly, everything seemed decided. The ministers began at once to take themselves off busily in every direction, glad of order restored. There wasn't a moment to protest, a moment to suggest any other course; there wasn't a chance to stop it.

I stood up. "No," I said, "wait," but no one was listening. I reached for the last dregs of my magic, to make my voice louder, to make them turn back. *"Wait,"* I tried to say, and the room swam away into black around me.

I woke up in my room and sat straight up in one jerk, all the hair standing on my arms and my throat burning: Kasia was sitting on the foot of my bed, and the Willow was straightening up away from me with a thin, disapproving expression on her face, a potion-bottle in her hand. I didn't remember how I'd got there; I looked out the window, confused; the sun had moved.

"You fell down in the council-room," Kasia said. "I couldn't stir you."

"You were overspent," the Willow said. "No, don't try to rise. You'd better stay just where you are, and don't try to use magic again for at least a week. It's a cup that needs to be refilled, not an endless stream."

"But the queen!" I blurted. "The Wood—"

"Ignore me if you like and spend your last dregs and die, I shan't have anything to say about it," the Willow said, dismissive. I didn't know how Kasia had persuaded her to come and see to me, but from the cold look they exchanged as the Willow swept past her and out the door, I didn't think it had been very gently.

I knuckled my eyes and lay there in the pillows. The potion the Willow had given me was a churning, glowing warmth in my belly, like I'd eaten something with too many hot peppers in it.

"Alosha told me to get the Willow to look at you," Kasia said, still leaning worried over me. "She said she was going to stop the crown prince from going."

I gathered my strength and struggled up, grabbing for Kasia's hands. The muscles of my stomach were aching and weak. But I couldn't keep to my bed right now, whether I could use magic or not. A heaviness lingered in the air of the castle, that terrible pressure. The Wood was still here, somehow. The Wood hadn't finished with us yet. "We have to find her."

The guards at the crown prince's rooms were on high alert; they half-wanted to bar us coming in, but I called out, "Alosha!" and when she put her head out and spoke to them, they let us into the skelter of packing under way. The crown prince wasn't in full armor yet, but he had on his greaves and a mail shirt, and he had a hand on his son's shoulder. His wife, Princess Malgorzhata, stood with him holding the little girl in her arms. The boy had a sword—a real sword with an edge, made small enough for him to hold. He wasn't seven years old. I would have given money that a child that young would cut off a finger within a day—his or someone else's—but he held it as expertly as any soldier. He was presenting it across his palms to his father with an anxious, upturned face. "I won't be any trouble," he said.

"You have to stay and look after Marisha," the prince said, stroking the boy's head. He looked at the princess; her face was sober. He didn't kiss her, but he kissed her hand. "I'll be back as soon as I can."

"I'm thinking of taking the children to Gidna once the funeral is over," the princess said: I knew vaguely it was the name of the city she was from, the ocean port the marriage had opened to Polnya. "The sea air will be healthy for them, and my parents haven't seen Marisha since her christening." From the words, you would have thought she'd just had the idea a moment ago, but as she said them, they sounded rehearsed.

"I don't want to go to Gidna!" the boy said. "Papa—"

"Enough, Stashek," the prince said. "Whatever you think best," he told the princess, and turned to Alosha. "Will you put a blessing on my sword?"

"I'd rather not," she said grimly. "Why are you lending yourself to this? After we spoke yesterday—"

"Yesterday my father was alive," Prince Sigmund said. "Today he's dead. What do you think is going to happen when the Magnati vote on the succession, if I let Marek go and he destroys this Rosyan army for us?"

"So send a general," Alosha said, but she wasn't really arguing; I could tell she was only saying it while she searched for another answer that she believed in. "What about Baron Golshkin—"

"I can't," he said. "If I don't ride out at the head of this army, Marek will. Do you think there's any general I could appoint who would stand in the way of the hero of Polnya right now? The whole country is ringing with his song."

"Only a fool would put Marek on the throne instead of you," Alosha said.

"Men are fools," Sigmund said. "Give me the blessing, and keep an eye on the children for me."

We stayed and watched him ride away. The two small children knelt up on a footstool, peering over the window-sill with their mother behind them, her hands on their heads, golden and dark. He went with a small troop of guards for escort, his retinue, the eagle flag in red on white billowing out behind him. Alosha watched silently beside me from the second window until they had gone out of the courtyard. Then she turned to me and said dourly, "There's always a price."

"Yes," I said, low and tired. And I didn't think we were done paying.

TWENTY FOUR

I couldn't do anything more, just then, but sleep. Alosha told me to lie down right there in the room, despite the princess's dubious looks, and I fell asleep on the soft wool rug before the fireplace: it was woven in a strange dancing pattern of enormous curved raindrop shapes, or perhaps tears. The stone floor beneath was hard, but I was too tired to care.

I slept the whole evening and night and woke in the early hours of the morning: still tired but my head less thick, and my lightning-scorched palms felt cool to the touch again. Magic ran whispering and slow over rocks, deep inside me. Kasia was sleeping on the rug at the foot of the bed; through the bedcurtains I could see the princess with the two children gathered close to her. There were two guards drowsing on either side of the door.

Alosha was sitting up in a chair by the fire with the hungry sword on her lap, sharpening it with her finger. I could feel the whisper of her magic as she ran the pad of her thumb near the edge of the blade. A thin line of blood welled up on her dark skin, even though she wasn't actually touching the steel, and it lifted in a faint red mist to sink into the blade. Her chair was turned to have full view of the doors and windows, as though she'd been watching all night.

"What do you fear?" I asked her, softly.

"Everything," she said. "Anything. Corruption in the palace— the king dead, Ballo dead, the crown prince lured off to a battle-field where anything might happen. It's late enough to start being cautious. I can miss a few nights' sleep. Are you better?" I nodded. "Good. Listen to me: we need to root out this corruption in the palace, and quickly. I don't believe we made an end of it when we destroyed that book."

I sat up and hugged my knees. "Sarkan thought it might be the queen after all. That she might have been—tortured into helping, instead of corrupted." I wondered if he was right: if the queen had smuggled out a small golden fruit somehow, plucked up off the ground in the Wood, and now in some dark corner of the palace gardens a thin silver sapling had broken the earth, scattering cor-ruption all around. It was hard for me to imagine the queen so lost to everything she'd been that she would bring the Wood with her, that she'd turn it on her own family and kingdom.

But Alosha said, "She might not have needed much torment to help see her husband dead, after he abandoned her for twenty years in the Wood. And perhaps her elder son, too," she added, as I flinched in protest. "I notice Marek is the one she kept back from the front. In any case, it's safe enough to say she's at the center of what's happening. Can you put this *Summoning* of yours on her?"

I was silent. I remembered the throne room, where I'd thought of casting the *Summoning* on the queen. Instead I'd chosen to give the court an illusion, a theatrical, to win Kasia's pardon. Maybe that had been the mistake, after all.

"But I don't think I can do it alone," I said. I had a feeling the *Summoning* wasn't really meant to be cast alone: as if truth didn't mean anything without someone to share it with; you could shout truth into the air forever, and spend your life doing it, if someone didn't come and listen.

Alosha shook her head. "I can't help you. I won't leave the princess and the royal children unguarded until I see them safely to Gidna."

Reluctantly I said, "Solya might help me." The last thing I wanted was to cast a spell with him, and give him any more reasons to keep grasping at my magic, but maybe his sight would make the spell stronger.

"Solya." Alosha loaded his name with disapproval. "Well, he's been a fool, but he's not stupid. You may as well try him. If not, go to Ragostok. He's not as strong as Solya, but he might be able to manage it."

"Will he help me?" I said doubtfully, remembering the circlet on the queen's head. He hadn't liked me much, either.

"When I say so, he will," Alosha said. "He's my great-great-grandson; if he argues, tell him to come speak to me. Yes, I know he's an ass," she added, misunderstanding my stare, and sighed. "The only child of my line to show magic, at least in Polnya." She shook her head. "It's cropped up in my favorite granddaughter's children and grandchildren, but she married a man from Venezia and went south with him. It would take more than a month to send for one of them."

"Do you have much family left, besides them?" I asked timidly.

"Oh, I have—sixty-seven great-great grandchildren, I think?" she said after a moment's thought. "Perhaps more by now; they drift away little by little. A few of them write to me dutifully every Midwinter. Most of them don't remember that they're descended from me, if they ever knew. Their skin has a little tea mixed in with the milk, but it only keeps them from burning in the sun, and my husband is a hundred and forty years dead." She said it easily, as if it didn't matter anymore; I suppose it didn't.

"And that's all?" I said. I felt almost desperate. Great-great-grandchildren, half of them lost and the rest of them so distant that she could sigh over Ragostok, and feel nothing more than a mild irritation. They didn't seem enough to keep her rooted to the world.

"I didn't have any other kin to begin with. My mother was a slave from Namib, but she died having me, so that's all I know of her. A baron in the south bought her from a Mondrian trader to give his wife consequence. They were kind enough to me, even before my gift came out, but it was the kindness of masters: they weren't kin." She shrugged. "I've had lovers now and then, mostly soldiers. But once you're old enough, they're like flowers: you know the bloom will fade even as you put them in the glass."

I couldn't help bursting out, "Then why—be here at all? Why do you care about Polnya, or—or anything?"

"I'm not dead," Alosha said tartly. "And I've always cared about good work. Polnya's had a line of good kings. They've served their people, built libraries and roads, raised up the University, and been good enough at war to keep their enemies from overrunning them and smashing everything. They've been worthy tools. I might leave, if they grew wicked and bad; I certainly wouldn't put swords in men's hands to follow that damned hothead Marek into a dozen wars for glory. But Sigmund—he's a sensible man, and good to his wife. I'm glad enough to help him hold up the walls."

She saw the misery on my face, and with rough kindness added, "You learn to feel it less, child; or you learn to love other things. Like poor Ballo," she said, with a kind of dusty, wistful regret, not strong enough to call grief. "He lived for forty years in a monastery illuminating manuscripts before anyone noticed he wasn't growing older. He was always a little surprised to find himself a wizard, I think."

She went back to her sharpening, and I went out of the room, sore and more unhappy than before I'd asked. I thought of my brothers growing old, of my little nephew Danushek bringing me his ball with his frowning little serious face; that face becoming an old man's, tired and folded and worn with years. Everyone I knew buried, and only their children's children left to love.

But better that than no one left at all. Better those children running in the forest, safe to run there. If I was strong, if I'd been given strength, I could be a shield for them: for my family, for Kasia, for those two small children sleeping in the bed and all the others who slept in the shadow of the Wood.

I told myself that, and tried to believe it would be enough, but it was still a cold and bitter thought to have, alone in the dark hallways. A few of the lower maids were just beginning to get the day's work under way, creeping quietly in and out of the nobles' rooms to stir up the fires, just the same as the day before, even though the king was dead. Life went on.

Solya said, "We don't need the fire tended, Lizbeta: just bring us some hot tea and breakfast, there's a girl," when I opened up his door. His fire was already up and mouthing a pair of fresh logs in a large stone fireplace.

No small gargoyle-haunted cell of a room for him: he had a pair of chambers, each three times as large as the one they'd crammed me into. His stone floors were covered in piled white rugs, soft and thick: he must have used magic to keep them clean. A large canopied bed, rumpled and untidy, was visible in the second room through a pair of open doors. Along the broad wooden panel at its foot, a carved falcon flew, its eye made of a single large smooth-polished golden stone with a black slitted pupil staring out of it.

A round table stood in the middle of his room, and Marek was sitting at it next to Solya, sprawled long and sulky in a chair with his boots up, in a nightshift and fur-edged dressing-gown over his trousers. A silver stand on the table held a tall oval mirror as long as my arm. After a moment I realized I wasn't looking from some peculiar angle and seeing the bedcurtains; the mirror wasn't showing a reflection at all. Like some impossible window, it looked out into a tent, the swaying pole in the middle holding up the draped sides, and a front opening in a narrow triangle-slice looking out onto a green field.

Solya was looking into the mirror intently, a hand on the frame and his eyes nothing but black wells of pupil, absorbing everything;

Marek watched his face. Neither one of them noticed me until I was at their elbows, and even then Marek barely glanced away. "Where have you been?" he said, and without waiting for an answer added, "Stop disappearing before I have to put a bell on you. Rosya must have a spy in this castle to have learned we were going for the Rydva—if not half a dozen of them. I want you by me from now on."

"I've been sleeping," I said tartly, before I remembered he'd lost his father yesterday, and felt a little sorry. But he didn't look much like he'd been mourning. I suppose being king and prince had made them something other than father and son to one another, and he'd never forgiven his father letting the queen fall into the Wood. But I still would have expected to find him a little red-eyed—from confusion if not from love.

"Yes, well, what else is there to do but sleep?" he said sourly, and glared at the mirror again. "Where the hell are all of them?"

"On the field by now," Solya said absently without drawing his eyes away.

"Where *I* should be, if Sigmund wasn't a lickspittle politician," Marek said.

"You mean if Sigmund were a perfect idiot, which he's not," Solya said. "He couldn't possibly hand you a triumph right now unless he wanted to hand you the crown along with it. I assure you he knows we've got fifty votes in the Magnati already."

"And what of it? If he can't hold the nobles, he doesn't deserve it," Marek snapped, folding his arms across his chest. "If I were only *there*—"

He looked longingly at the unhelpful mirror again while I stared at them both in rising indignation. So it wasn't just Sigmund worrying the Magnati would give Marek the throne; Marek was *trying* to take it. Suddenly I understood the crown princess, why she'd looked sidelong at me—I was Marek's ally, as far as she knew. But I swallowed the first ten remarks that came to my tongue and said shortly to Solya, "I need your help."

That won me a look from one of those pit-black eyes, at least, with an arched eyebrow to go over it. "I'm equally delighted to help you, my dear, and to hear you say so."

"I want you to cast a spell with me," I said. "We need to put the *Summoning* on the queen."

He paused, much less delighted; Marek turned and threw me a hard look. "Now what's gotten into your head?"

"Something's wrong!" I said to him. "You can't pretend not to have seen: since we came back there's been one disaster after another. The king, Father Ballo, the war against Rosya—this has all been the Wood's design. The *Summoning* will show us—"

"What?" Marek snapped, standing up. "What do you think it will show us?"

He loomed over me; I stood my ground and flung my head back. "The truth!" I said. "It's not three days since we let her out of the tower, and the king is dead, there are monsters in the palace, and Polnya's at war. We've missed something." I turned to Solya. "Will you help me?"

Solya glanced between Marek and me, calculations ticking in his eyes. Then he said mildly, "The queen is pardoned, Agnieszka; we can't simply go enchanting her with no cause, only because you're alarmed."

"You must see something's wrong!" I said to him, furiously.

"There *was* something wrong," Solya said, condescending and complacent; I could have shaken him with pleasure. Too late, I had to be sorry I *hadn't* made a friend of him. I couldn't tempt him: he knew perfectly well by now that I didn't mean to make any regular occasion of sharing magic with him, even if I'd suffer through it for something important. "Very wrong: that corrupted book you found, now destroyed. There's no need to imagine dark causes when we have one already known."

"And the last thing Polnya needs now is more black gossip flying around," Marek said, more calmly; his shoulders were relaxing as he listened to Solya, swallowing down that poisonously convenient explanation. He dropped back into his chair and put his boots up on the table again. "About my mother or about you, for that matter. The Magnati have all been summoned for the funeral, and I'll be announcing our betrothal once they're gathered."

"What?" I said. He might have been giving me some piece of mildly interesting news, which concerned me only a little.

"You've earned it, slaying that monster, and it's the sort of thing commoners love. Don't make a fuss," he added, without even looking at me. "Polnya is in danger, and I need you at my side."

I only stood there, too angry to even find my voice, but they had stopped paying attention to me anyway. In the mirror, someone was ducking into the tent. An old man in a much-decorated uniform sank heavily into the chair on the other side, his face pulled down on all sides by age: jowls sagging, mustaches sagging, pouches beneath his eyes and the corners of his mouth; there were lines of sweat running through the dust caked on his face. "Savienha!" Marek said, leaning in, fiercely intent. "What's happening? Did the Rosyans have time to fortify their positions?"

"No," the old general said, wiping a tired hand across his forehead. "They didn't fortify the crossings: they laid an ambush on the Long Bridge instead."

"Stupid of them," Marek said, intently. "Without fortifications, they can't possibly hold the crossings for more than a couple of days. Another two thousand levies came in overnight, if I ride out with them at once—"

"We overran them at dawn," Savienha said. "They are all dead: six thousand."

Marek paused, evidently taken aback: he hadn't expected that. He exchanged a look with Solya, scowling a little, as though he didn't like hearing it. "How many did you lose?" he demanded.

"Four thousand, too many horses. We overran them," Savienha repeated, his voice breaking, sagging where he sat. Not all the tracks on his face were sweat. "Marek, forgive me. Marek—your brother is dead. They killed him in the first ambush, when he went to survey the river."

I backed away from the table as if I could escape from the words. The little boy upstairs holding out his sword, *I won't be any trouble,* his round face upturned. The memory jabbed me, knife-sharp.

Marek had gone silent. His face was bewildered more than anything. Solya went on speaking with the general a little longer. I could scarcely bear to hear them go on talking. Finally Solya reached up and drew a heavy cloth down over the mirror. He turned to look at Marek.

The bewilderment was fading. "By God," Marek said after a moment, "I would rather not have it, than have it so." Solya only inclined his head, watching him with a gleam in his eye. "But that's not the choice, after all."

"No," Solya agreed softly. "It's just as well the Magnati are on their way: we'll hold the confirmation vote at once."

There was salt in my mouth: I'd been crying without knowing it. I backed up farther. The doorknob came into my hand, the hollows and bumps of its carved hawk's head pressing into my palm. I turned it and slipped out the door and shut it behind me quietly. I stood trembling in the hallway. Alosha had been right. One trap after another, long-buried under a carpet of thick leaves, finally springing shut. Tiny seedlings pushing grasping branches out of the dirt.

One trap after another.

All at once, I was running. I ran, my boots slapping on stone, past startled servants and the morning sun bright in all the windows. I was panting by the time I rounded the corner to the quarters of the crown prince. The door was shut, but unguarded. A thin grey haze trickled from underneath it into the hallway. The knob was hot under my hand as I threw the door open.

The bedhangings were aflame, and the carpet scorched; the guards were dead huddled heaps on the floor. There were ten men in a silent knot around Alosha. She was burned horribly: half her armor melted onto her skin, and somehow still fighting. Behind her, the princess lay dead, barring the door to the wardrobe with her own body; Kasia was next to her corpse, her own clothes sliced in a dozen places but her skin unmarked. She was holding a chipped sword and swinging it fiercely at two men trying to get past her.

Alosha was holding off the rest with two long knives that sang wildly in the air and left crackles of fire behind them. She'd cut them all to ribbons, blood slick on the floor, but they weren't falling down. The men wore Rosyan uniforms, but their eyes were green and lost. The room smelled like a fresh birch-tree branch broken open down the middle.

I wanted to scream, to weep. I wanted to drag my hand across the world and wipe it all away. *"Hulvad,"* I said, my hands pushing, pushing magic out with it. *"Hulvad,"* remembering how Alosha had pulled that thin cloud of corruption out of Ballo's apprentice. And wisps of black smoke came streaming out of the men, out of every slash and knife-wound. The smoke blew away through the open window into the sunlight; and then they were only men again, hurt too much to live; they fell to the ground, one after another.

With her attackers gone, Alosha turned and threw her knives at the men trying to kill Kasia. The knives sank deep into their backs, and more of that evil smoke billowed out from around the blades. They fell, one and two.

The room was strangely quiet when they were all dead. The hinges on the wardrobe door squeaked; I jumped at the noise. The door pushed open a crack and Kasia whirled towards it: Stashek was inside trying to look out, his face scared, his small sword gripped in his hand. "Don't look," she said. She pulled a cloak out of the wardrobe, long rich red velvet. She covered the children's heads with it and gathered them into her arms. "Don't look," she said, and held them huddled close against her.

"Mama," the little girl said.

"Be *quiet,*" the boy told her, his voice trembling. I covered my mouth with both my hands and crammed in a sob.

Alosha was dragging in heavy, labored breaths; blood bubbled on her lips. She sagged against the bed. I stumbled forward and reached for her, but she waved me back. She made a hooking gesture with a hand and said, *"Hatol,"* and drew the killing sword out of the air. She held the hilt out to me. "Whatever's in the Wood," she said, hoarse and whispering, her voice eaten by the fire. "Find it and kill it. Before it's too late."

I took it and held it awkwardly. Alosha was sliding to the floor even as she let it go into my hands. I knelt down beside her. "We have to get the Willow," I said.

She shook her head, a tiny movement. "Go. Get the children out of here," she said. "The castle's not safe. *Go.*" She let her head sink back against the bed, her eyes closing. Her chest rose and fell only in shallow breaths.

I stood up, shaking. I knew she was right. I felt it. The king, the crown prince; now the princess. The Wood meant to kill all of them, Alosha's good kings, and slaughter Polnya's wizards, too. I looked at the dead soldiers in their Rosyan uniforms. Marek would blame Rosya again, as he was meant to do. He'd put on his crown and march east, and after he'd spent our army slaughtering as many Rosyans as he could, the Wood would devour him, too, and leave the country torn apart, the succession broken.

I was in the Wood again, underneath the boughs, that cold hateful presence watching me. The momentary silence in the room was only its pause for breath. Stone walls and sunlight meant nothing. The Wood's eyes were on us. The Wood was here.

TWENTY FIVE

e wrapped ourselves in torn cloaks we took off the dead guards and ran for it, our hems leaving streaks of blood on the floor behind us. I had shoved Alosha's sword back into its strange waiting-place, *hatol* opening a pocket in the world for me to put it in. Kasia carried the little girl and I held Stashek's hand. We went down a tower staircase, past a landing where two men in a hallway glanced over at us, puzzled and frowning; we hurried on down another turning, fast, and came into the narrow hallway to the kitchens, servants going back and forth. Stashek tried to pull back from me. "I want my father!" he said, his voice trembling. "I want Uncle Marek! Where are we going?"

I didn't know. I was only in flight; all I knew was we had to get away. The Wood had scattered too many seeds, all around us; they'd lain quiet in fallow ground, but now they were all coming to fruit. Nowhere was safe when corruption lived in the king's castle. The princess had meant to take them to her parents, to Gidna on the northern sea. *The ocean is inimical to corruption,* Alosha had said. But trees still grew in Gidna, and the Wood would pursue the children to the shore.

"To the tower," I said. I didn't plan on saying it; the words came out of me like Stashek's cry. I wanted the stillness of Sarkan's library, the faint spice-and-sulfur smell of his laboratory; those close, narrow hallways, the clean lines and the emptiness. The tower standing tall and lonely against the mountains. The Wood had no foothold there. "We're going to the Dragon's tower."

Some of the servants were slowing, looking at us. There were footsteps on the stairs coming after us; a man called down with authority, "You, there!"

"Hold on to me," I told Kasia. I put my hand on the castle wall and whispered us through, straight out into the kitchen gardens, one staring gardener kneeling up from the dirt. I ran between rows of beanstakes with Stashek wide-eyed running with me, catching our fear; Kasia ran behind us. We reached the outer wall of heavy brick; I took us through. The castle bells began to clang alarm behind us as we scrambled in a hail of dirt all the way down the steep slope, to the Vandalus running below.

The river rushed quick and deep here around the castle, leaving the city behind, going east. A hunting bird cried high above, a falcon wheeling in wide circles around the castle: was that Solya looking down at us? I snatched up a handful of reeds from the bank, without any incantations or charms: they had all gone out of my head. Instead I pulled a thread out of my cloak and tied the reeds at two ends. I threw the bundle down on the bank, halfway in the water, and flung magic at it. It grew into a long, light boat, and we scrambled in even as the river tugged it off the bank and dragged us along, rushing, bouncing off rocks on either side. There were shouts behind us, guards appearing on the outer walls of the castle high above.

"Down!" Kasia shouted, and pushed the children down flat and covered them with her body. The guards were firing arrows at us. One tore through her cloak and hit her back. Another landed just beside me and stuck into the side of the boat, quivering. I snatched the feathers off the arrow-shaft and threw them up into the air above us. They remembered what they'd once been and turned into a cloud of half-birds that whirled and sang, covering us from view for a few moments. I held on to the sides of the boat and called up Jaga's quickening charm.

We shot forward. In one lurch, the castle and the city blurred back and away, turned into children's toys. In a second, they had vanished around a curve of the river. In a third, we struck on the empty riverbank. My boat of reeds fell apart around us and dumped us all into the water.

I nearly sank. The weight of my clothes dragged me backwards, down into the murky water, light blurring above me. The cloud of Kasia's skirts billowed next to me. I thrashed for the surface, blindly grabbing, and found a small hand grabbing back: Stashek put my hand on a tree-root. I pulled myself up coughing and managed to put my feet down in the water. "Nieshka!" Kasia was calling; she was holding Marisha in her arms.

We slogged up the soft muddy bank, Kasia's feet sinking deep with every step, gouging holes in the earth that filled slowly in with water behind her. I sank down on the mucky grass. I was trembling with magic that wanted to spill out of me in every direction, un-controlled. We'd moved too quickly. My heart was racing, still back there under the raining arrows, still in desperate flight, and not on a quiet deserted riverbank with waterbugs jumping over the ripples we'd made, mud staining my skirts. I'd been so long inside the cas-tle, people and stone walls everywhere. The riverbank almost didn't seem real.

Stashek sat down in a heap next to me, his small serious face be-wildered, and Marisha crept over to him and huddled against him. He put an arm around her. Kasia sat down on their other side. I could gladly have lain down and slept for a day, a week. But Marek knew which way we'd gone. Solya would send eyes down the river to look for us. There was no time to rest.

I shaped a pair of crude oxen out of riverbank mud and breathed a little life into them, and built a cart out of twigs. We hadn't been an hour on the road when Kasia said, "Nieshka," looking behind us, and I drove them quickly into a stand of trees some way back from the road. A small haze of dust was drifting up from the road behind us. I held the reins, the oxen standing with plodding obedience, and we all held our breath. The cloud grew, unnaturally fast. It came nearer and nearer, and then a small troop of red-cloaked riders with crossbows and bared swords went flashing past. Sparks of magic were striking from the horses' hooves, shod in steel caps that rang like bells on the hard-packed road. Some work of Alosha's hands, now being turned to serve the Wood. I waited until the cloud was out of sight again up ahead before I drove our cart back onto the road.

When we drew into the first town, we found signs already posted. They were crudely, hastily drawn: a long parchment with my face and Kasia's upon it, pinned to a tree next to the church. I hadn't thought what it meant to be hunted. I'd been glad to see the town, planning to stop and buy food: our stomachs were pinching with hunger. Instead we pulled the cloaks over our heads, and rolled onward without speaking to anyone. My hands shook on the reins, all the way through, but we were lucky. It was market day, and the town was large, so close to the city; there were enough strangers around that no one marked us out, or demanded to see our faces. As soon as we were past the buildings, I shook the reins and hurried the oxen onward, quicker, until the village disappeared entirely behind us.

We had to pull off the road twice more, packs of horsemen flying past. And then once more late that evening, when another king's messenger in his red cloak passed us going the other way, racing back towards Kralia, hoof-sparks bright in the dimming light. He didn't see us, intent on his fast pace; we were just a shadow behind a hedge. While we were hiding, I caught sight of something dark and square behind us: it was the open doorway of an abandoned cottage, half lost in a stand of trees. While Kasia held the oxen I hunted through the overgrown garden: a handful of late strawberries, some old turnips, onions; a few beans. We gave the children most of the food, and they fell asleep in the cart as we drove back onto the road. At least our oxen didn't need to eat or rest, being made out of dirt. They would march on, all night long.

Kasia climbed onto the driver's seat with me. The stars had come out in a rush, the sky wide and dark so far away from anyone living. The air was cold, still, too quiet; the cart didn't creak, and the oxen didn't huff or snort. "You haven't tried to send word to their father," Kasia said quietly.

I stared ahead, down the dark road. "He's dead, too," I said. "The Rosyans ambushed him."

Kasia carefully took my hand, and we held on to each other as the cart rocked onward. After a little while she said, "The princess died next to me. She put the children in the wardrobe, and then she stood in front of it. They stabbed her over and over, and she just kept trying to stand up in front of the doors." Her voice shook. "Nieshka, can you make a sword for me?"

I didn't want to. Of course it was only sensible to give her one, in case we were caught. I didn't fear for her: Kasia would be safe enough fighting, when blades just went dull on her skin and arrows fell away without scratching her. But she would be dangerous and terrible, with a sword. She wouldn't need a shield, or armor, or even to think. She could walk through fields of soldiers like cutting oats, steady and rhythmic. I thought of Alosha's sword, that strange hungry killing thing; it was tucked away into that magical pocket, but I could still feel its weight on my back. Kasia would be like that sword, implacable, but she wouldn't only have one use. I didn't want her to need to do things like that. I didn't want her to need a sword.

It was a useless thing to want. I took out my belt-knife, and she gave me hers. I pulled the buckles off our belts and our shoes, and the pins off our cloaks, and took a stick off a tree as we passed it, and gathered all of it together in my skirt. While Kasia drove, I told them all to be straight and sharp and strong; I hummed them the song about the seven knights, and in my lap they listened and grew together into a long curved blade with a single sharpened edge, like a kitchen-knife instead of a sword, with small bright steel posts to hold the wooden hilt around it. Kasia picked it up and balanced it across her hands, and then she nodded once and put it down, under the seat.

We were three days on the road, the mountains growing steadily overnight, comforting in the distance. The oxen made a good pace, but we still had to duck behind hedges and hillocks and abandoned cottages every time riders came by, a steady stream of them. At first I was only glad whenever we managed to hide from them, too busy with fear and relief to think anything more about it. But while we peered over a hedge, watching a cloud vanishing away ahead, Kasia said, "They keep coming," and a cold hard knot settled into the bottom of my stomach as I realized there had been too many of them just to be passing the word to look for us. They were doing something more.

If Marek had ordered the mountain passes closed, if his men had blockaded the tower; if they'd gone after Sarkan himself, taking him by surprise while he fought to hold the Wood off from Zatochek—

There wasn't anything to do but keep going, but the mountains weren't a comfort anymore. We didn't know what we would find when we got to the other side. Kasia rode in the back of the cart with the children all that day as the road began to gently climb into the foothills, her hand on the sword hidden beneath her cloak. The sun climbed high, warm golden light shining full on her face. She looked remote and strange, inhumanly steady.

We reached the top of a hill and found the final crossroads in the Yellow Marshes, a small well beside it with a watering-trough. The road was empty, although it had been trampled heavily on both sides, by feet and horses. I couldn't guess if it was only ordinary traffic or not. Kasia pulled up buckets for us to drink and wash our dusty faces, and then I mixed some fresh mud to patch up the oxen: they cracked here and there after a day's walking. Stashek silently brought me handfuls of muddy grass.

We'd told the children, as gently as we could, about their father. Marisha didn't quite understand, except to be afraid. She'd asked for her mother a few times already. Now she clung to Kasia's skirts almost all the time, like a smaller child, and didn't go out of sight of her. Stashek understood too well. He received the news in silence, and afterwards he said to me, "Did Uncle Marek try to have us killed? I'm not a child," he added, looking at my face, as if I needed him to say so, when he'd just asked me such a thing.

"No," I managed, through my tight throat. "He's only letting the Wood drive him."

I wasn't sure Stashek believed me. He'd been quiet, ever since. He was patient with Marisha, who clung to him, too, and helped with the work whenever he could. But he said almost nothing.

"Agnieszka," he said, while I finished plastering up the second oxen's hind leg, and stood up to go wash the dirt off my hands. I turned to follow his gaze. We could see a long way back behind us, miles and miles. In the west, a thick hazy cloud of dust covered the road. It seemed to move, coming onward as we stood watching. Kasia picked Marisha up. I shaded my eyes and squinted against the sun.

It was a crowd of men marching: thousands of them. A stand of tall spears glittered at the front, among riders on horses and a great banner flying white and red. I saw a bay horse leading, a silver-armored figure on its back; next to it a grey horse with a white-cloaked rider—

The world tilted askew, narrowed, rushed in on me. Solya's face leapt vividly out: he was looking right at me. I jerked my head away so hard that I fell down. "Nieshka?" Kasia said.

"Quick," I panted, scrambling up, pushing Stashek towards the back of the cart. "He saw me."

We drove into the mountains. I tried to guess how far behind us the army was. I would have whipped the oxen if that would have done any good, but they were going as fast as they could. The road was tumbled with rocks, narrow and twisting, and their legs began to crack and crumble quickly. There wasn't any mud to patch them with anymore, even if I could have brought myself to stop. I didn't dare use the quickening spell: I couldn't see beyond the next turn. What if there were men up ahead, and I whisked us straight into their arms; or worse yet I threw us into midair over a canyon?

The left ox abruptly tumbled forward, its leg crumbling away, and smashed into clods of dirt against the rocks. The second one pulled us on a little farther, and then between one step and the next just fell apart. The cart tipped forward, unbalanced, and we all came down hard on our seats in a pile of twigs and dry grass.

We were deep in the mountains by then, the trees wizened and scrubby, and high peaks on either side of the twisting road. We couldn't see far enough behind us to tell how close the army was. Usually it was a day's walk across the pass. Kasia picked up Marisha, and Stashek got to his feet. He walked beside me doggedly, uncomplaining while we hurried, feet sore and the sharp thin air painful in our throats.

We stopped to catch our breath by a jutting outcrop with a tiny summer stream trickling; just enough to cup a handful for our mouths, and as I straightened up a raucous cawing near my head made me jump. A black crow with glossy feathers stared at me from the branch of a wizened tree clinging between rocks. It cawed again, loudly.

The crow paced us as we fled, hopping from branch to rock to rock. I threw a pebble at it, trying to make it go away; it only jumped away and cawed again, a sour triumphant note. Two more joined it a little farther on. The path snaked along the crest of the ridge, green grass rolling gently away to either side down to steep slopes.

We kept running. The path dived as one mountain pulled away from it, leaving a sickening drop to the right. Maybe we were past the peak by now. I couldn't stop running long enough to think about it properly. I nearly dragged Stashek along by his arm. Somewhere behind us, I heard a horse shriek: as if it had slipped, running too fast on the narrow mountain pass. The crows lifted into the air, circling, and went to go and see; all except for our one steady companion, hopping along, its bright eyes fixed on us.

The air was thin; we struggled and gasped for air as we ran. The sun was sinking.

"Stop!" someone far behind us shouted, and an arrow sailed down, clattering against the rocks over our heads. Kasia stopped, pushed Marisha into my arms when I caught up to her, and took the place at the rear. Stashek threw a frightened look back at me.

"Keep going!" I said. "Keep going until you see the tower!" Stashek pelted on and vanished with the trail around a wall of rock. I heaved Marisha up close against me, her arms wrapping tight around my neck and her legs around my waist, clinging, and ran after him. The horses were so close we could hear pebbles crunching under their hooves.

"I can see it!" Stashek was calling from up ahead.

"Hold on tight," I told Marisha, and ran as fast as I could, her body bumping against me; she tucked her cheek down against my shoulder and didn't speak. Stashek turned anxiously as I came panting around the curve: he was standing on a ledge jutting out from the mountainside, almost wide enough to be a meadow. My legs were spent: I spilled to the ground, just barely keeping my knees long enough to put Marisha down without falling on top of her. We'd come out onto the southern slopes. Below us the path continued to snake back and forth across the mountain all the way down to Olshanka.

And on the other side of the town, in front of the western mountains, the Dragon's tower stood gleaming white in the sun, still small and far away. It was ringed around with soldiers, a small army of men in yellow surcoats. I stared at it desperately. Had they gotten inside? The great doors were still closed; there was no smoke coming from the windows. I didn't want to believe the tower had fallen. I wanted to shout Sarkan's name, I wanted to fling myself across the yawning air. I got back up on my feet.

Kasia had stopped in the narrow road behind us. She drew out the sword I'd given her even as the horses came around the curve. Marek was with them, leading; his spurs were wet with blood and he had his sword drawn, his teeth bared in a snarl. His bay came charging, and Kasia didn't move. Her hair was flying loose, streaming in the wind. She planted her feet wide in the trail and held the sword out straight, and Marek had to yank aside the horse's head or ride directly onto the blade.

He pulled up, but smashed his own sword down at her as he twisted the horse on the narrow path. Kasia caught the blow and whacked it aside with pure brute strength. She knocked the sword straight out of Marek's hand. It struck the edge of the path and fell over, disappearing down the mountainside with a wash of pebbles and dust.

"A pike!" Marek shouted, and a soldier threw him one; he caught it easily even as he wheeled his horse around on the path. He brought the pike around in a long, low sweep that nearly caught Kasia at the waist. She had to jump back: if he could knock her off the path, it wouldn't matter that she was stronger than he was. She tried to grab for the end of the pike, but Marek jerked it back too quickly; then he immediately nudged his horse forward and pulled it up into a crow-stepping rear, iron-shod hooves lashing towards her head. He was herding her back: as soon as he reached the place where the road widened, he and the other soldiers would spill out and surround her. They could come past her at us, at the children.

I groped for the Dragon's spell, the transport spell. *Valisu*, and *zokinezh*—but even while I tried to fit the words together, I knew somehow that it wasn't going to work. We weren't in the valley yet; that path wasn't open to us.

My head was light with thin air and desperation. Stashek had picked up Marisha and was holding her tight. I shut my eyes and spoke the illusion spell: I called up Sarkan's library, shelves rising up out of bare rock around us, golden-lettered spines and the smell of leather; the clockwork bird in its cage, the window looking out on the whole green length of the valley and the winding river. I even saw us in the illusion: tiny ant-figures on the mountainside, moving. There was a line of twenty men strung out on the trail behind Marek: if he could only shove his way into the wider ground, they would be on us.

I knew the Dragon wasn't there; he was in the east, in Zatochek, where the thin column of smoke rose from the edge of the Wood. But I put him in the library anyway, at the table, the hard angles of his face lit by the candles that never melted; looking at me with that annoyed, baffled expression: *Now what are you doing?*

"Help me!" I said to him, and gave Stashek a push. The Dragon put his hands out automatically and the children tumbled into them together; Stashek cried out, and I saw him stare up at the Dragon with wide eyes. Sarkan stared down at him.

I turned back, half in the library, half on the mountain. "Kasia!" I cried.

"Go!" she shouted at me. One of the soldiers behind Marek had a clear view of me and the library behind me; he slung a bow down and stretched an arrow, taking aim.

Kasia ducked under the pike and ran at Marek's horse and shoved the animal bodily back, both hands on its chest. It squealed and reared up, hopping back on its rear legs and lashing at her. Marek kicked her, snapping back her chin, and shoved the shaft of the pike down between them, just behind her ankle. He had both hands on the pike now, he'd dropped his reins, but somehow he made the horse do what he wanted anyway. The animal turned, he twisted his body as it did, gripping the pike, and he tripped Kasia up. The horse's hindquarters struck her and swept her stumbling to the edge of the path, and Marek gave a quick, massive heave. She fell over: she didn't even have time to scream, just gave a startled "Oh!" and was gone, dragging a clump of grass loose as she grabbed at it.

"Kasia!" I screamed. Marek turned towards me. The bowman let the arrow loose; the string twanged.

Hands seized my shoulders, gripping with familiar, unexpected strength; they dragged me backwards. The walls of the library rushed forward around me and closed up just before the arrow would have passed through them. The whistle of the wind, the cold crisp air, faded from my skin. I whirled, staring: Sarkan was there; he was standing right behind me. He'd pulled me through.

His hands were still on my shoulders; I was braced on his chest. I was full of alarm and a thousand questions, but he dropped his hands and stepped back, and I realized we weren't alone. A map of the valley lay unrolled on the table, and an enormous, broad-shouldered man with a beard longer than his head and a shirt of mail under a yellow surcoat stood at the far end of it, gawking at us, with four armored men behind him gripping the hilts of their swords.

"Kasia!" Marisha was crying in Stashek's arms and struggling against his grip. "I want Kasia!"

I wanted Kasia, too; I was still shaking with the memory of watching her tumble over the edge. How far could she fall, without being hurt? I ran to the window. We were far away, but I could see the thin plume of dust where she'd fallen, like a line drawn down the side of the mountain. She was a tiny dark heap of brown cloak and golden hair on the trail, a hundred feet down where it sloped back on itself down the mountain. I tried to gather my wits and my magic. My legs still shook with exhaustion.

"No," Sarkan said, coming to my side. "Stop. I don't know how you've done any of this, and I imagine I'll be appalled when I learn, but you've been too profligate with your magic for one hour." He pointed his finger out the window at the tiny huddled heap of Kasia's body, his eyes narrowing. *"Tualidetal,"* he said, and clenched his hand into a fist, jerked it quickly back, and pointed his finger to an open place on the floor.

Kasia tumbled out of the air where he pointed and spilled to the floor trailing brown dust. She rolled and got up quickly, staggering only a little; there were some bloody scrapes on her arms, but she'd kept hold of her sword. She took one look at the armed men on the other side of the table and caught Stashek by the shoulder; she pulled him behind her and held the sword out like a bar. "Hush, Marishu," she said, a quick touch of her hand to Marisha's cheek, to quiet her; the little girl was trying to reach for her.

The big man had only been staring all this while. He said suddenly, "God in Heaven; Sarkan, that's the young prince."

"Yes, I imagine so," Sarkan said. He sounded resigned. I stared at him, still half-disbelieving he was really there. He was thinner than when I'd seen him last, and almost as disheveled as I was. Soot streaked his cheek and neck, and had left a fine thin layer of grey over all his skin, enough that a line showed at the loose collar of his shirt where it gaped open, to divide clean skin from dirty. He wore a rough long coat of leather hanging open. The edges of the sleeves and the bottom hem were singed black, and the whole length of it patterned with scorch marks. He looked as though he'd come straight from burning the Wood: I wondered wildly if I'd somehow summoned him here, with my spell.

Peering from behind Kasia, Stashek said, "Baron Vladimir?" He hitched Marisha up a little in his arms, protectively, and looked at Sarkan. "Are you the Dragon?" he asked, his high young voice wavering and doubtful, as if thinking he didn't quite look the part. "Agnieszka brought us here to keep us safe," he added, even more doubtfully.

"Of course she did," Sarkan said. He looked out the window. Marek and his men were already riding down the sloping trail, and not alone. The long marching line of the army was coming out of the mountain pass, their feet raising a sunset-golden cloud of dust that rolled down towards Olshanka like a fog.

The Dragon turned back to me. "Well," he said, caustic, "you've certainly brought more men."

TWENTY SIX

"He must have scraped together every soldier in the south of Polnya," the Baron of the Yellow Marshes said, studying Marek's army. He was a big, comfortably barrel-bellied man who wore his armor as easily as cloth. He wouldn't have seemed out of place in our village tavern.

He'd just gotten the summons to come to the capital for the king's funeral when Marek's magic-sped messenger had arrived, told him that the crown prince was dead, too, and gave him his orders: to go over the mountains, seize Sarkan as corrupted and a traitor, and lay a trap for me and the children. The baron nodded, gave orders for his soldiers to gather, and waited until the messenger had left. Then he'd brought his men over the pass and gone straight to Sarkan, to tell him there was some kind of corrupt deviltry going on in the capital.

They'd come back to the tower together, and those were his soldiers encamped below; they were hastily putting up fortifications for a defense. "But we can't hold out for longer than a day, not against that," the baron said, jerking his thumb out the window at the army pouring down the mountainside. "So you'd better have something up your sleeve. I told my wife to write to Marek that I'd lost my mind and gone corrupted, so I hope he won't behead her and the children, but I'd as soon keep my own head on, too."

"Can they break down the doors?" I asked.

"If they try long enough," Sarkan said. "And the walls, for that matter." He pointed to a pair of wooden carts trundling down the mountainside, carrying the long iron barrels of cannon. "Enchantment won't hold against cannon-fire forever."

He turned away from the window. "You know we've already lost," he said to me bluntly. "Every man we kill, every spell and potion we waste, it all serves the Wood. We could take the children to their mother's family and marshal a fresh defense in the north, around Gidna—"

He wasn't saying anything I didn't know, hadn't known even when I'd come flying home like a bird to its burning nest. "No," I said.

"Listen to me," he said. "I know your heart is in this valley. I know you can't let it go—"

"Because I'm bound to it?" I said, sharply. "Me, and all the other girls you chose?" I'd tumbled into his library with an army at my heels and half a dozen people around us, and there hadn't been time for conversation, but I still hadn't forgiven him. I wanted to get him alone and shake him until answers came out, and shake him a little more for good measure. He fell silent, and I forced myself to push aside the hot anger. I knew this wasn't the time.

"That's not why," I said, instead. "The Wood could reach into the king's castle in Kralia, a week's journey from here. Do you think there's anywhere we can take the children that the Wood can't reach? At least here we have a chance of victory. But if we run, if we let the Wood take back the whole valley, we'll never raise an army anywhere that can fight all the way through to its heart."

"Unfortunately," he said, sharp, "the one we have now is pointing the wrong way."

"Then we need to persuade Marek to turn it around," I said.

Kasia and I took the children down to the cellars, the safest place, and we made up a pallet for them of straw and spare blankets from the shelves. The kitchen stores were untouched by time, and we were all hungry enough after our day of running that not even worry could stifle our appetite. I took a rabbit from the cold store in back and put it in a pot with some carrots and dried buckwheat and water and threw *lirintalem* at it, to make it into something edible. We all wolfed it down together without bothering with bowls, and almost at once the children collapsed into an exhausted sleep, curled together. "I'll stay with them," Kasia said, sitting down beside the pallet. She put her sword unsheathed next to her, and rested a hand on Marisha's sleeping head. I mixed up a simple dough in a big bowl, just flour paste and salt, and I carried it upstairs to the library.

Outside, the soldiers had put up Marek's tent, a white pavilion with two tall spell-lamps planted in the ground before it. Their blue light gave the white fabric an unearthly glow, as though the whole pavilion had descended straight from Heaven, which I imagine was the idea. The king's banner was snapping in the wind atop the highest point, the red eagle with its mouth and its talons open, crowned. The sun was sinking. The long shadow of the western mountains was creeping slowly over the valley.

A herald came out and stood between the lamps, official and stark in a white uniform with a heavy golden chain of office around his neck. Another piece of Ragostok's working: it threw his voice against the tower walls like a blast of righteous trumpets. He was recounting all our crimes: corruption, treason, murdering the king, murdering Princess Malgorzhata, murdering Father Ballo, conspiring with the traitor Alosha, the abduction of Prince Kasimir Stanislav Algirdon and Princess Regelinda Maria Algirdon—it took me a moment to realize they meant Stashek and Marisha—consorting with the enemies of Polnya, and going on from there. I was glad to hear them name Alosha a traitor: maybe that meant she was still alive.

The list finished with a demand for the return of the children and our immediate surrender. Afterwards, the herald paused for breath and to take a drink of water; then he began to recite the gruesome litany all over again. The baron's men milled uneasily around the base of the tower where they were encamped, and looked up askance towards our windows.

"Yes, Marek seems eminently persuadable," Sarkan said as he came into the room. Faint smears of oil glistened on his throat and the back of his hand and across his forehead: he had been brewing up potions of sleep and forgetfulness in his laboratory. "What do you mean to do with that? I doubt Marek is going to eat a poisoned loaf of bread, if that was your notion."

I turned my dough out onto the smooth marble top of the long table. I had the vague thought of the oxen in my head, the way I'd cobbled them together; they'd crumbled, but they'd only been made of mud. "Do you have any sand?" I asked. "And maybe some small pieces of iron?"

I kneaded iron shavings and sand into my dough while the herald chanted on outside. Sarkan sat across from me, his pen scratching out a long incantation of illusion and dismay put together from his books. An hourglass streamed sand between us, marking time while his potions brewed. A few unhappy soldiers from the baron were waiting for him while he worked, shifting from foot to foot uneasily in the corner of the room. He put down his pen just as the last few grains of sand spilled, precisely timed. "All right, come with me," he told them, and took them along to the laboratory, to give them the flasks to carry downstairs.

But I hummed my mother's baking songs while I worked, folding and folding in a steady rhythm. I thought of Alosha, forging her blade again and again, working a little more magic in each time.

When my dough was pliable and smooth, I broke off a piece, rolled it into a tower in my hands, and planted it in the middle, folding up the dough on one side to make the wall of the mountains behind us.

Sarkan came back into the room and scowled down at my work. "A charming model," he said. "I'm sure the children will be entertained."

"Come and help me," I said. I pinched up a wall around the tower out of the soft dough and started to murmur a chant of earth spells over it: *fulmedesh, fulmishta*, back and forth in a steady rhythm. I built a second wall farther out, then a third; I kept humming softly to them. A groaning sound, like trees in a high wind, came in from outside the window, and the floor trembled faintly beneath us: earth and stone, waking up.

Sarkan watched, frowning a while longer. I felt his eyes on the back of my neck. The memory curled in me of the last time we'd worked together in this room: roses and thorns sprawling furiously everywhere between us. I wanted and didn't want his help. I wanted to stay angry at him a while longer, but I wanted the connection more; I wanted to touch him, wanted the brilliant crisp bite of his magic in my hands. I kept my head down and kept working.

He turned and went to one of his cabinets; he brought over a small drawer full of chips of stone that looked like the same grey granite as the tower, of varied sizes. He began to gather the chips up and with his long fingers pressed them into the walls I'd built. He recited a spell of repairing as he worked, a spell of mending cracks and patching stone. His magic came running through the clay, vivid and bright where it brushed against mine. He brought the stone into the spell, laying the deep foundations beneath, lifting me and my working higher: like putting steps beneath me, so I could take the walls up into clear air.

I drew his magic into my working, running my hands back along the walls, my chant still marching away beneath the melody of his spell. I darted a quick glance at him. He was staring down at the dough trying to keep his scowl, and flushed at the same time with the high transcendent light that he brought to his elaborate work-ings: delighted and also annoyed, trying not to be.

Outside, the sun had gone down. A faint blue-violet glow flick-ered over the surface of the dough like strong liquor burning off in a pot. I could just barely make it out in the dim twilight of the room. Then the working went up like dry kindling. There was a jolt, a rush of magic, but this time Sarkan was ready for the dam-bursting. Even as the spell caught, he pulled abruptly back from me. Instinctively I reached after him at first, but then I pulled back, too. We fell away into our separate skins instead of spilling magic all over each other.

A cracking noise like winter ice breaking came in through the window, and shouts rose. I hurried past Sarkan, my face hot, to go and look. The spell-lamps outside Marek's tent were rolling slowly up and down as if they were lanterns on boats climbing a wave. The ground was shuddering like water.

The baron's men all backed hastily to the tower walls. Their thin fencework, little more than heaped bundles of sticks they'd gathered, was falling apart. In the spell-light, I saw Marek come ducking out of his tent, hair and armor shining brilliant and a gold chain—the gold chain the herald had been wearing—gripped in his fist. A scur-rying crowd of men and servants poured out behind him, escaping: the whole great pavilion was collapsing. "Put out the torches and the fires!" Marek bellowed, his voice unnaturally loud. The earth groaned and rumbled all around with complaining voices.

Solya came out of the pavilion with the others. He seized one of the spell-lamps out of the ground and held it up with a sharp word that brightened it. The ground between the tower and the encamp-ment was heaved and hunched up like some complaining lazy beast getting to its feet. Stone and earth began to rear themselves into three high walls around the tower, made of fresh-quarried stone laced full of white veins and jagged edges. Marek had to give orders for his men to pull the cannon back quickly, the rising walls pulling the ground out from under their feet.

The ground settled, sighing out. A few final tremors shuddered away from the tower, like ripples, and died away. Small showers of dirt and pebbles ran off the walls. Marek's face in the light was baffled and furious. For one moment he looked up straight at me, glaring; I glared right back. Sarkan dragged me away from the window.

"You won't persuade Marek to listen any sooner by provoking him into a high rage," he said when I wheeled on him, forgetting to be embarrassed in my anger.

We were standing very close. He noticed the same moment that I did. He let go of me abruptly and stepped back. He looked aside and put up his hand to wipe a trickle of sweat from the side of his forehead. He said, "We'd better go down and tell Vladimir that he needn't worry, we aren't planning to drop him and all his soldiers into the center of the earth."

"You might have warned us ahead of time," the baron said dryly when we came outside, "but I won't complain too much. We can make him pay for these walls, more than he can afford—as long as we can move between them ourselves. The stones are cutting up our ropes. We need a way through."

He wanted us to make two tunnels at opposite ends of the walls from each other, so he could make Marek fight the whole length of the walls to get through each one. Sarkan and I went to the northern end to begin. The soldiers were already laying pikes along the wall by torch-light, with the points bristling upwards; they had draped cloaks over the poles to make small tents to sleep under. A few of them were sitting around small campfires, soaking dried meat in boiling water, stirring kasha into the broth to cook up. They cleared hastily out of our way without our even having to say a word, afraid. Sarkan seemed not to notice, but I couldn't help feeling sorry and strange and wrong.

One of the soldiers was a boy my own age, industriously sharpening pike-heads one by one with a stone, skillfully: six strokes for each one and done as quick as the two men putting them along the wall could come back for them. He must have put himself to it, to learn how to do it so well. He didn't look sullen or unhappy. He'd chosen to go for a soldier. Maybe he had a story that began that way: a poor widowed mother at home and three young sisters to feed, and a girl from down the lane who smiled at him over the fence as she drove her father's herd out into the meadows every morning. So he'd given his mother his signing-money and gone to make his fortune. He worked hard; he meant to be a corporal soon, and after that a sergeant: he'd go home then in his fine uniform, and put silver in his mother's hands, and ask the smiling girl to marry him.

Or maybe he'd lose a leg, and go home sorrowful and bitter to find her married to a man who could farm; or maybe he'd take to drink to forget that he'd killed men in trying to make himself rich. That was a story, too; they all had stories. They had mothers or fathers, sisters or lovers. They weren't alone in the world, mattering to no one but themselves. It seemed utterly wrong to treat them like pennies in a purse. I wanted to go and speak to that boy, to ask him his name, to find out what his story really was. But that would have been dishonest, a sop to my own feelings. I felt the soldiers understood perfectly well that we were making sums out of them—this many safe to spend, this number too high, as if each one wasn't a whole man.

Sarkan snorted. "What good would it do them for you to roam around asking them questions, so you know that one's from Debna, and this one's father is a tailor, and the other one has three children at home? They're better served by your building walls to keep Marek's soldiers from killing them in the morning."

"They'd be better served by Marek not trying in the first place," I said, impatient with him for refusing to understand. The only way we could make Marek bargain was to make the walls too costly to breach, so he wouldn't want to pay. But it still made me angry, at him, at the baron, at Sarkan, at myself. "Have *you* got any family left?" I asked him abruptly.

"I couldn't say," he said. "I was a three-year-old beggar child when I set fire to Varsha, trying to stay warm on the street one winter's night. They didn't bother to hunt up my family before they packed me off to the capital." He spoke indifferently, as if he didn't mind it, being unmoored from all the world. "Don't make mournful faces at me," he added. "That was a century and a half ago, and five kings have breathed their last since then—six kings," he amended. "Come here and help me find a crack to open."

It was full dark by then, and no way of finding any crack except by touch. I put my hand on the wall and almost jerked it back again. The stone murmured so strangely under my fingers, a chorus of deep voices. I looked closer. We had turned up more than bare rock and earth: there were broken pieces of carved blocks jutting from the dirt, the bones of the old lost tower. Ancient words were carved upon them in places, faint and nearly worn away, but still there to be felt even if not seen. I took my hands away and rubbed them against each other. My fingers felt dusty, dry.

"They're long gone," Sarkan said, but the echoes lingered. The Wood had thrown down that last tower; the Wood had devoured and scattered all those people. Maybe it had happened like this for them, too: maybe they'd been turned and twisted into weapons against one another, until all of them were dead and the roots of the Wood could quietly creep over their bodies.

I put my hands back on the stone. Sarkan had found a narrow crack in the wall, barely wide enough for fingertips. We took hold of it on opposite sides and pulled together. *"Fulmedesh,"* I said, as he made a spell of opening, and between us the crack widened with a sound like plates breaking on a stone floor. A crumbling waterfall of pebbles came pouring out.

The soldiers dug out the loose stones with their helmets and their gauntleted hands while we pulled the crack still wider. When we were done, the tunnel was just big enough for a man in armor to get through, if he stooped. Inside the faint gleams of silvery blue letters shone here and there out of the dark. I scurried through the mouse-hole of it as quickly as I could, trying not to look at them. The soldiers began working in the trench behind us while we walked all the long curve of the wall to the southern end, to make the second opening.

By the time we finished the second tunnel, Marek's men had begun to try the outer wall, not very seriously yet: they were lobbing over burning rags soaked in lamp-oil, small thorny bits of iron with spikes pointing in every direction. But that almost made the baron's soldiers happier. They stopped watching me and Sarkan like we were poisonous snakes, and began comfortably bawling out orders and making siege-preparations, work they all plainly knew well.

There wasn't a place for us among them; we were only in their way. I didn't try to speak to any of them, after all; I silently followed the Dragon back to the tower.

He shut the great doors behind us, the thump of the bar falling into the iron braces echoing against the marble. The entry and the great hall were unchanged, the unwelcoming narrow wooden benches standing against the walls, the hanging lamps above. Everything as stiff and formal as the first day I'd come wandering through here with my tray of food, so frightened and alone. Even the baron pre-ferred to sleep outside with his men in the warm weather. I could hear their voices outside through the arrow-slit windows, but only faintly, as if they came from far away. Some of the soldiers were singing a song together, a bawdy song probably, but full of glad working rhythm. I couldn't make out the words.

"We'll have a little quiet, at least," Sarkan said, turning from the doors, towards me. He wiped a hand across his forehead, streaking a clean line through the fine layer of grey stone dust clinging to his skin; his hands were stained with green powder and iridescent traces of oil that shone in the lamp-light. He looked down at them with a grimace of distaste, at the loose sleeves of his work-shirt coming unrolled.

For a moment we might have been alone in the tower again,

just the two of us with no armies waiting outside, no royal children hiding in the cellar, with the shadow of the Wood falling across our door. I forgot I was trying to be angry at him. I wanted to go into his arms and press my face into his chest and breathe him in, smoke and ash and sweat all together; I wanted to shut my eyes and have him put his arms around me. I wanted to rub handprints through his dust. "Sarkan," I said.

"They'll most likely attack at the first light of morning," he said too quickly, cutting me off before I could say anything more. His face was as closed up as the doors. He stepped back from me and gestured at the stairs. "The best thing you can do at the moment is get some sleep."

TWENTY SEVEN

What perfectly sensible advice. It sat in my stomach, an indigestible lump. I went down to the cellars to lie down with Kasia and the children, and curled up quietly seething around it. Their small even breaths came behind me. The sound should have been comforting; instead it just taunted me: *They're asleep and you aren't!* The cellar floor couldn't cool my feverish skin.

My body remembered the endless day; I'd woken up that morning on the other side of the mountains, and I still felt the echoes of hoofbeats on stone behind me, coming closer, the strain of my panicked breaths struggling against my ribs as I'd run with Marisha in my arms. I had bruises where her heels had banged against the sides of my legs. I should have been spent. But magic was still alive and shivering in my belly, too much of it with nowhere to go, as if I were an over-ripe tomato that wanted to burst its skin for relief, and there was an army outside our doors.

I didn't think Solya had spent the evening preparing defenses and sleep spells. He'd fill our trenches with white fire, and tell

Marek where to point the cannon so they would kill the most men. He was a war-wizard; he'd been at dozens of battles, and Marek had the entire army of Polnya behind him, six thousand men to our six hundred. If we didn't stop them; if Marek came through the walls we'd built and smashed the doors, killed us all and took the children—

I threw off the covers and got up. Kasia's eyes opened just briefly to see me, and then closed again. I slipped away to sit by the ashes in the hearth, shivering. I couldn't stop thinking in circles about how easy it would be to lose, about the Wood rolling dark and terrible over the valley, a green swallowing wave. I tried not to see it, but in my mind's eye a heart-tree rose up in the square in Dvernik, sprawling and monstrous as that terrible tree in Porosna behind the borders of the Wood, and everyone I loved was tangled beneath its grasping roots.

I stood and fled from my own imagining, up the stairs. In the great hall, the arrow-slit windows were dark; there wasn't even a snatch of song outside to drift in. All the soldiers were sleeping. I kept climbing, past the laboratory and the library, green and violet and blue lights still flickering behind their doors. But they were empty; there was no one there for me to shout at, no one to snap back at me and tell me I was being a fool. I went up another flight and stopped at the edge of the next landing, near the fringed end of the long carpet. A faint gleam showed from underneath the farthest door, at the end of the hallway. I had never gone that way, towards Sarkan's private bedroom. It had been an ogre's chamber, once.

The carpet was thick and dark, with a pattern woven into it with golden-yellow thread. The pattern was all one line: it began in a tight spiral like the curl of a lizard's tail. The golden line grew thicker as it unwound, and then went twisting back and forth along the length of the rug almost like a pathway, leading into the shadows down the hallway. My feet sank deep in the soft wool. I followed the golden line as it broadened beneath my feet and took on a pattern like scales, faintly gleaming. I passed the guest chambers, two doors opposite one another, and beyond them the hallway darkened around me.

I was walking past a kind of pressure, a wind blowing against me. The pattern in the carpet was forming into clearer shapes. I walked over one great ivory-clawed limb, over the sweep of pale golden wings veined in dark brown.

The wind grew colder. The walls disappeared, fading into part of the dark. The carpet widened until it filled all the hallway I could see and stretched away beyond. It didn't feel like wool anymore. I stood on warm lapping scales, soft as leather, rising and falling beneath my feet. The sound of breathing echoed back from cavern walls out of sight. My heart wanted to hammer with instinctive terror. My feet wanted to turn and run.

I shut my eyes instead. I knew the tower by now, how long the hallway should have been. I took three more steps along the scaled back, and then I turned and put out my hand, reaching for the door I knew was there. My fingers found a doorknob, warm metal beneath my fingers. I opened my eyes again and I was back in the hallway, looking at a door. A few steps farther on, the hall and the carpet ended. The golden pattern turned back on itself, and a gleaming green eye looked up at me from a head filled with rows of silver teeth, waiting for anyone who didn't know where to turn.

I opened the door. It swung silently. The room wasn't large. The bed was small and narrow, canopied and curtained in with red velvet; a single chair stood before the fireplace, beautifully carved, alone; a single book on the small table beside it with a single cup of wine, half-drunk. The fire was banked down to glowing coals, and the lamps were out. I went to the bed and drew aside the curtain. Sarkan was sleeping stretched across the bed still in his breeches and his loose shirt; he'd only thrown off his coat. I stood holding the curtain. He blinked awake at me unguarded for a moment, too startled to be indignant, as if he'd never imagined anyone *could* barge in on him. He looked so baffled I didn't want to shout at him anymore.

"How did you," he said, pushing himself up on an elbow, indignation finally dawning, and I pushed him back down and kissed him.

He made a noise of surprise against my mouth and gripped me by the arms, holding me off. "Listen, you impossible creature," he said, "I'm a century and more older than—"

"Oh, be quiet," I said impatiently; of all the excuses he might have used. I scrambled up the tall side of the bed and climbed in on top of him, the thick featherbed yielding. I glared down. "Do you *want* me to go?"

His hands tightened on my arms. He didn't look me in the face. For a moment he didn't speak. Then harshly he said, "No."

And then he pulled me down to him instead, his mouth sweet and feverish-hot and wonderful, obliterating. I didn't have to think anymore. The heart-tree blazed up with a crackling roar and was gone. There was only the heat of his hands sliding over my chilled bare arms, making me shiver all over again. He had one arm around me, gripping tight. He caught at my waist and pulled up my loose falling-off blouse. I ducked my head through and my arms free of the sleeves, my hair spilling over my shoulders, and he groaned and buried his face into the tangled mess of it, kissing me through it: my throat, my shoulders, my breasts.

I clung to him, breathless and happy and full of uncomplicated innocent terror. It hadn't occurred to me that he would—his tongue slid over my nipple and drew it into his mouth, and I flinched a little and clutched at his hair, probably painfully. He drew away, the sudden cold a bright shock on my skin, and he said, "Agnieszka," low and deep with an almost despairing note, as if he still wanted to shout at me and couldn't.

He rolled us over in the bed and dumped me in the pillows beneath him. I gripped fistfuls of his shirt and pulled, frantic. He sat up and threw it off, over his head, and I threw my head back and stared at the canopy while he pushed up the maddening heap of my skirts. I felt desperately greedy, urgent for his hands. I'd tried not to remember that one shocking, perfect moment, the slide of his thumb between my legs, for so long; but oh, I remembered. He brushed his knuckles against me and that sweet jolting went through me again. I shuddered all over, hugely, and I closed my thighs tight around his hand, instinctive. I wanted to tell him to hurry, to go slow, to do both at the same time.

The curtain had fallen shut again. He was leaning over me, his eyes only a gleam in the dark close room of the bed, and he was ferociously intent, watching my face. He could still rub his thumb against me, just a little. He stroked just once. A noise climbed the back of my throat, a sigh or a moan, and he bent down and kissed me like he wanted to devour it, to catch it in his own mouth.

He moved his thumb again, and I stopped clenching shut. He gripped my thighs and moved them apart, lifted my leg around his waist; he was still watching me hungrily. *"Yes,"* I said, urgently, trying to move with him; but he kept stroking me with his fingers. *"Sarkan."*

"Surely it's not too much to ask a *little* patience," he said, his black eyes glittering. I glared at him, but then he stroked me again, gently, dipped his fingers into me; he drew a long line between my thighs again and again, circling at the top. He was asking me a question I didn't know the answer to, until I did; I clenched up suddenly, wrung-out and wet against his hands.

I fell back shaking against the pillows; I put my hands up into my snarled mess of hair and pressed them against my damp forehead, panting. "Oh," I said. "Oh."

"There," he said, smugly pleased with himself, and I sat up and pushed him backwards the other way on the bed.

I caught the waist of his breeches—he was still wearing his breeches!—and said, *"Hulvad."* They melted into the air with a jerk, and I flung my skirts after them. He lay naked beneath me, long and lean and suddenly narrow-eyed, his hands on my hips, the smirk fallen away from his face. I climbed onto him.

"Sarkan," I said, holding the smoke and thunder of his name

in my mouth like a prize, and slid onto him. His eyes shut tight, clenched; he looked almost in pain. My whole body felt wonderfully heavy, pleasure still going through me in widening ripples, a kind of tight ache. I liked the feeling of him deep in me. He was panting in long ragged breaths. His thumbs were pressing tight on my hips.

I held on to his shoulders and rocked against him. "Sarkan," I said again; I rolled it on my tongue, explored all the long dark corners of it, parts hiding deep, and he groaned helplessly and surged up against me. I wrapped my legs around his waist, clinging, and he put an arm tight around me and bore me over and down into the bed.

I lay curled snugly against his side to fit in the small bed, catching my breath. His hand was in my hair, and his face staring up at the canopy was oddly bewildered, as if he couldn't quite remember how all of this had happened. My arms and legs were full of sleep, heavy as if it would have taken a winch to lift them. I rested against him and finally asked, "Why did you take us?"

His fingers were carding absently through my hair, straightening out tangles. They paused. After a moment he sighed beneath my cheek. "You're bound to the valley, all of you; born and bred here," he said. "It has a hold on you. But that's a channel of its own in turn, and I could use it to siphon away some of the Wood's strength."

He raised his hand and drew it flat over the air above our heads, a fine tracery springing up silver behind the sweep of his palm: a skeletal version of the painting in my room, a map of lines of magic running through the valley. They followed the long bright path of the Spindle and all its small tributaries coming in from the mountains, with gleaming stars for Olshanka and all our villages.

The lines didn't surprise me, somehow: it felt like something I'd always known was there, beneath the surface. The splash of the water-bucket echoing up from the deep well, in the village square at Dvernik; the murmur of the Spindle running quick in summer.

They were full of magic, of power, there to be drawn up. And so he'd cut irrigation-lines to pull more of it away before the Wood could get hold of it.

"But why did you need one of us?" I said, still puzzled. "You could have just—" I made a cupping gesture.

"Not without being bound to the valley myself," he said, as if that was all the explanation in the world. I grew very still against him, confusion rising in me. "You needn't be alarmed," he added, dryly, misunderstanding dreadfully. "If we manage to survive the day, we'll find a way to untangle you from it."

He drew his palm back over the silver lines, wiping them away again. We didn't speak again; I didn't know what to say. After a while, his breath evened out beneath my cheek. The heavy velvet hangings' deep dark closed us in all around, as if we lay inside his walled heart. I didn't feel the hard grip of fear anymore, but I ached instead. A few tears were stinging in my eyes, hot and smarting, as if they were trying to wash out a splinter but there weren't enough of them to do it. I almost wished I hadn't come upstairs.

I hadn't really thought about *after*, after we stopped the Wood and survived; it seemed absurd to think about *after* something so impossible. But I realized now that without quite thinking it through, I'd half-imagined myself a place here in the tower. My little room upstairs, a cheerful rummaging through the laboratory and the library, tormenting Sarkan like an untidy ghost who left his books out of place and threw his great doors open, and who made him come to the spring festival and stay long enough to dance once or twice.

I'd already known without having to put it into words that there wasn't a place for me in my mother's house anymore. But I knew I didn't want to spend my days roaming the world on a hut built on legs, like the stories said of Jaga, or in the king's castle, either. Kasia had wanted to be free, had dreamed of all the wide world open to her. I never had.

But I couldn't belong here with him, either. Sarkan had shut himself up in this tower; he'd taken us one after another; he'd used our connection, all so he wouldn't have to make one of his own. There was a reason he never came down into the valley. I didn't need him to tell me that he couldn't come to Olshanka and dance the circle without putting down his own roots, and he didn't want them. He'd kept himself apart for a century behind these stone walls full of old magic. Maybe he would let me come in, but he'd want to close the doors up again behind me. He'd done it before, after all. I'd made myself a rope of silk dresses and magic to get out, but I couldn't make *him* climb out the window if he didn't want to.

I sat up away from him. His hand had slipped from my hair. I pushed apart the stifling bedcurtains and slid out of the bed, taking one of the coverlets with me to wrap around me. I went to the window and pushed the shutters open and put my head and shoulders out into the open night air, wanting the breeze on my face. It didn't come; the air around the tower was still. Very still.

I stopped, my hands braced on the stone sill. It was the middle of the night, still pitch-dark, most of the cooking-fires gone out or banked for the night. I couldn't see anything down on the ground. I listened for the old stone voices of the walls we'd built, and heard them murmuring, disturbed.

I hurried back to the bed and shook Sarkan awake. "Something's wrong," I said.

We scrambled into our clothes, *vanastalem* spinning clean skirts up from my ankles and lacing a fresh bodice around my waist. He was cupping a soap-bubble between his hands, a small version of one of his sentinels, giving it a message: "Vlad, rouse your men, quickly: they're trying something under cover of night." He blew it out the window and we ran; by the time we reached the library, torches and lanterns were being lit all through the trenches below.

There were almost none in Marek's camp, though, except the ones held by the handful of guards, and one lamp shining inside his pavilion. "Yes," Sarkan said. "He's doing something." He turned to the table: he'd laid out half a dozen volumes of defensive magic. But I stayed at the window and stared down, frowning. I could feel the gathering of magic that had a flavor of Solya, but there was something else, something moving slow and deep. I still couldn't see anything. Only a few guards on their rounds.

Inside Marek's pavilion, a shape passed between the lantern and the tent wall and flung a shadow against the wall, a face in profile: a woman's head, hair piled high, and the sharp peaks of the circlet she wore. I jerked back from the window, panting, as if she'd seen me. Sarkan looked back at me, surprised.

"She's here," I said. "The queen is here."

There wasn't time to think what it meant. Marek's cannon roared out with gouts of orange fire, a horrible noise, and clods of dirt went flying as the first cannon-balls smashed into the outer wall. I heard Solya give a great shout, and light blazed up all across Marek's camp: men were thrusting coals into beds of straw and kindling that they had laid down in a line.

A wall of flame leaped up to face my wall of stone, and Solya stood behind it: his white robe was stained with orange and red light, blowing out from his wide-spread arms. His face was clenched with strain, as if he were lifting something heavy. I couldn't hear the words over the roar of the fire, but he was speaking a spell.

"Try to do something about that fire," Sarkan told me, after one quick look down. He whirled back to his table and pulled out one of the dozen scrolls he'd prepared yesterday, a spell to blunt cannon-fire.

"But what—" I began, but he was already reading, the long tangled syllables flowing like music, and I was out of time for questions. Outside, Solya bent his knees and heaved up his arms as if he were throwing a large ball. The whole wall of flame jumped into the air and curved up over the wall and into the trench where the baron's men crouched.

Their screams and cries rose up with the crackling of the flames, and for a moment I was frozen. The sky was wide and too-clear above, stars from end to end, not a cloud anywhere that I could

wring rain from. I ran for the water-jug in the corner, in desperation: I thought maybe if I could make one cloud grow into a storm,
I could make a drop grow into a cloud.

I poured water into the cup of my hand and whispered the rain
spell over it, telling the drops they could be rain, they could be a
storm, a blanketing deluge, until a pool shimmered solid quicksilver
in my palm. I threw my handful of water out the window, and it
did become rain: a hiccup of thunder and a single gush of water
that went straight down into the trench, squashing the fire down in
one place.

The cannon kept roaring all the while. Sarkan was standing beside me at the window now, holding up the shield against them, but
every thump struck against him like a blow. The orange fire lit his
face from below, shone on his clenched teeth as he grunted with
impact. I would have liked to speak to him, between the cannon
rounds, to ask whether we were all right—I couldn't tell if we were
doing well, or if they were.

But the fire in the trench was still burning. I kept throwing rain,
but it was hard work making rain out of handfuls of water, and
it got harder as I went along. The air around me went dry and
parched and my skin and hair winter-crackly, as if I was stealing
every bit of moisture around me, and the torrents only struck one
part of the fire at a time. The baron's men were doing their best
to help, beating down the flames with cloaks sopped into the water
that ran off.

Then the two cannon roared together. But this time, the flying
iron balls glowed with blue and green fire, trailing them both like
comets. Sarkan was flung back hard against the table, the edge
slamming into his side. He staggered, coughing, the spell broken.
The two balls tore through his shield and sank into the wall almost
slowly, like pushing a knife into an unripe fruit. Around them the
rock seemed almost to melt away, glowing red around the edges.
They vanished inside the wall, and then, with two muffled roars,

they burst. A great cloud of earth went flying up, chips of stone flung so hard I heard them pattering against the walls of the tower itself, and a gap crumbled in right in the middle of the wall.

Marek thrust his spear up into the air and roared, "Forward!"

I couldn't understand why anyone would obey: through that ragged opening, the fire still leaped and hissed, despite all my work, and men were screaming as they burned. But men did obey him: a torrent of soldiers came charging with spears held at waist-level, into the burning chaos of the trench.

Sarkan pushed himself up from the table and came back to the window, wiping a trickle of blood from his nose and lip. "He's decided to be profligate," he said grimly. "Each of those cannon-balls was a decade in the forging. Polnya has fewer than ten of them."

"I need more water!" I said, and catching Sarkan's hand I pulled him with me into the spell. I could feel him wanting to protest: he didn't have a spell prepared to match mine. But he muttered irritation under his breath and then gave me a simple cantrip, one of the early ones he'd tried to teach me, which was meant to fill up a glass of water from the well down below us. He'd been so annoyed when I either slopped water all over his table, or barely brought up a trickle of drops. When he spoke the spell, water came rippling smoothly up to the very brim of my jug, and I sang my rain spell to the whole jug and to the well below, all that deep cold sleeping water, and then I flung the whole jug out the window.

For a moment I couldn't see: a howl of wind blew rain spattering into my face and eyes, the slap of a biting winter rain. I wiped my face with my hands. Down in the trench, a downpour had smothered the flames entirely, only small flickering pockets left, and armored men on both sides were sliding off their feet, falling in the sudden ankle-deep torrent. The gap in the wall was gushing mud, and with the fire gone, the baron's men were crowding into the breach with their pikes, filling it up with bristling points and shoving back the men who'd been trying to come in. I sagged against the sill with relief: we'd stopped Solya's fire, we'd stopped Marek's advance. He'd already spent so much magic, more than he could afford surely, and we'd still halted him; surely now he'd think better of—

"Get ready," Sarkan said.

Solya was casting another spell. He held his hands up into the air at an angle, all the fingers pointed with his eyes looking straight along them, and silver lines lanced out from each finger and split into three. The arcing lines came down over the wall, each one landing on a different target—a man's eye, a chink in his armor at the throat, the elbow of his sword-hand, the place directly over his heart.

The lines didn't seem to do anything, as far as I could see. They just hung in the air, only barely visible in the dark. Then dozens of bows twanged at once: Marek had three lines of archers ranged up behind his foot-soldiers. The arrows caught onto the silver lines and followed them straight home.

I put out a hand, a useless gesture of protest. The arrows flew on. Thirty men fell at once, cut down at a stroke, all of them defenders at the breach. Marek's soldiers shoved into the gap, spilling into the trench, and the rest of his army crowded in behind them. They began to try and push the baron's soldiers back towards the first passageway.

Every inch was hard-fought. The baron's men had put up a bristling thicket of spears and swords pointing out ahead of them, and in the narrow space, Marek's men couldn't come at them without driving themselves onto the blades. But Solya sent another flight of arrows going over the walls towards the defenders. Sarkan had turned away: he was shoving through his papers, looking for a spell to answer this new one, but he wasn't going to find it in time.

I put my hand out again, but this time I tried the spell the Dragon had used, to bring Kasia in from the mountainside. *"Tual, tual, tual,"* I called to the strings, reaching, and they caught on my fingers, thrumming. I leaned out and threw them away, down towards the top of the wall. The arrows followed them and struck against stone, clattering away in a heap.

For a moment, I thought the silver light was just lingering on my hands, reflecting into my face. Then Sarkan shouted a warning. A dozen new silver threads were pointing through the window—right at me, leading to my throat, my breast, my eyes. I only had one moment to grab up the ends in a bunch and blindly heave them away from me. Then the flight of arrows rushed buzzing in through the window and struck wherever I had thrown the lines: into the bookcase and the floor and the chair, sunk deep with the fletched ends quivering.

I stared at them all, too startled to be afraid at first, not really understanding that I'd nearly been struck by a dozen arrows. Outside, the cannon roared. I'd already begun to be used to the noise; I flinched automatically, without looking, still half-fascinated by how close the arrows were. But Sarkan was suddenly heaving the entire table over, papers flying as it smashed to the floor, heavy enough to shake the chairs. He pulled me down behind it. The high-whistling song of a cannon-ball was coming closer and closer.

We had plenty of time to know what was going to happen, and not enough to do anything about it. I crouched under Sarkan's arm, staring at the underside of the table, chinks of light showing through the heavy wooden beams. Then the cannon-ball smashed through the window-sill, the opened glass panes shattering into fragments with a crash. The ball itself rolled on until the stone wall stopped it with a heavy thud, then it burst into pieces, and a creeping grey smoke came boiling out.

Sarkan clapped his hand over my mouth and nose. I held my breath; I recognized the stone spell. As the grey fog rolled gently towards us, Sarkan made a hooking gesture to the ceiling, and one of the sentinel-spheres floated down to his hand. He pinched open its skin, made a hole, and with another wordless, peremptory gesture waved the grey smoke into the sphere, until all of it was enclosed, churning like a cloud.

My lungs were bursting before he finished. Wind was whistling noisily in through the gaping wall, books scattered, torn pages riffling noisily. We pushed the table up against the open gap, to help keep us from falling out of the window. Sarkan picked up a piece of the hot cannon-ball with a cloth and held the sentinel next to it, like giving a scent to a hound. *"Menya kaizha, stonnan olit,"* he told the sentinel, and gave it a push out into the night sky. It drifted away, the grey of it fading into just a scrap of fog.

All that couldn't have taken more than a few minutes—no longer than I could hold my breath. But more of Marek's army had already crammed into the trench, and pushed the baron's men back towards the first tunnel. Solya had flung another arrow-flight and opened more room for them, but more than that, Marek and his knights were riding just outside the wall behind them, spurring the men onward: I saw them using their horse-whips and spears against their own soldiers, driving them through the breach.

The ones in the front ranks were almost being pushed onto the defenders' blades, horribly. Other soldiers were pressing up behind them, and little by little the baron's soldiers were having to give way, a cork being forced out of a bottle. The trench was already littered with corpses—so many of them, piled on one another. Marek's soldiers were even climbing up on top of the heaps to shoot arrows down at the baron's men, as if they didn't care that they were standing on the bodies of their own dead comrades.

From the second trench, the baron's men began flinging Sarkan's potion-spheres over the wall. They landed in blue bursts, clouds that spread through the soldiers; the men caught inside the mist sank to their knees or toppled over in heaps, faces dazed and sinking into slumber. But more soldiers came on after them, climbing over them, trampling them like ants.

I felt a wild horror, looking at it, unreal.

"We've misjudged the situation," Sarkan said.

"How can he do this?" I said, my voice shaking. It seemed as if Marek was so determined to win he didn't care how expensive we made the walls; he'd pay anything, anything at all, and the soldiers would follow him to their deaths, endlessly. "He must be corrupted—" I couldn't imagine anything else that would let him spend his own men's lives like this, like water.

"No," Sarkan said. "Marek's not fighting to win the tower. He's fighting to win the throne. If he loses to us here, now, we'll have made him look weak before the Magnati. He's backed into a corner."

I understood without wanting to. Marek really would spend everything he had. No price would be too high. All the men and magic he'd used already would only make it worse, like a man throwing good money after bad because he couldn't stand to lose what he'd already spent. We couldn't just hold him off. We'd have to fight him to the last man, and he had thousands of them left to pour into the battle.

The cannon roared once more, as if to punctuate the terrible realization, and then they fell suddenly and blessedly silent. Sarkan's floating sentinel had dropped down upon them and burst against the hot iron. The dozen men working on the cannon had frozen into statues. One man stood before the left cannon with a rod thrust down the barrel; others were bent over gripping ropes, dragging the right cannon back to its place; still others held cannon-balls or sacks in their hands: a monument to a battle that wasn't over.

Marek at once ordered other men to come and get the statues clear of the cannon. They began dragging and shoving the statues away, toppling them into the dirt. I flinched when I saw one smashing the fingers off the statues to pry out the ropes: I wanted to shout down that the stone-turned men were still alive. But I didn't think Marek would care.

The statues were heavy and the work was slow, so we had a brief respite from the cannon-fire. I steadied myself and turned to Sarkan. "If we offered to surrender," I said, "would he listen?"

"Certainly," Sarkan said. "He'd put us both to death at once, and you might as well cut the children's throats yourself as hand them over, but he'd be delighted to listen." He took a turn thwarting the arrow spell: he pointed and spoke an incantation of misdirection, and another flight of silver-led arrows struck against the outer wall. He shook out his hand and wrist, looking down. "In the morning," he said finally. "Even if Marek is willing to destroy his entire army, men can't fight endlessly without a rest, and food and drink. If we can hold them until morning, he'll have to call them off for a little while. Then he might be willing to parley. If we can hold them until morning."

Morning seemed far away.

The pace of the battle ebbed for a little while. The baron's men had retreated into the second trench entirely by now, filling the passage-way in with corpses so Marek's men couldn't keep coming. Marek rode his horse back and forth outside the walls, simmering and angry and impatient, watching while his men struggled to get the cannon firing again. Near him, Solya settled into a steady rhythm of throwing arrow-flights into the second trench.

It was an easier spell for him to throw than for us to deflect. The arrow-heads were Alosha's work. They wanted to find their way to flesh, and he was only showing them the way to go. Meanwhile we were trying to twist them from their purpose, fighting not just his spell but hers: the strength of her will, the hammer-strokes that had beaten magic and determination into the iron, and even the arrows' natural flight. Pulling them aside was steady, grinding work, and meanwhile Solya threw his silver guiding lines into the air with wide easy sweeps of his arm, like a man sowing seeds. Sarkan and I had to take turns, each of us catching a flight at a time; each one an effort. We had no time or strength for any other working.

There was a natural rhythm to the work: dragging away a flight of arrows, like hauling on a heavy fishing-net, and then pausing to sip a little water and rest while Sarkan took his turn; then I would go to the window again. But Solya broke the rhythm, again and again. He kept the flights spaced apart exactly the worst amount of time: just close enough that we couldn't sit down between them without having to spring up, and then every once in a while he let a longer time go by, or threw the arrows at us instead, or sent two flights out in quick succession.

"He can't have an endless supply of them," I said, leaning against the wall, drained and aching. There were boys with the archers who were hunting for spent arrows, pulling them out of corpses and from against the walls where they'd struck, and carrying them back to be shot again.

"No," Sarkan said, a little distant and remote, also turned inward by the steady drain of magic. "But he's keeping the flights small. He'll likely have enough to last until morning."

Sarkan went briefly out of the room after finishing his next turn, and brought back a sealed glass jar from the laboratory, full of cherries in syrup. He kept a big silver samovar on a table in the back corner of the library, which never ran out of tea: it had survived the ruin of the cannon-ball, although the delicate glass cup had fallen over and smashed. He poured tea into two measuring-bowls instead, and pushed the jar of cherries over to me.

They were the deep wine-red sour cherries from the orchards outside Viosna, halfway down the valley, preserved in sugar and spirits. I stirred in two heaping spoonfuls and greedily licked the spoon clean. They tasted of home to me, and the valley's slow magic resting in them. He dipped only three of them out for himself, chary and measured, and he scraped the spoon on the edge of the jar, as though he was being careful, even now, not to take too much. I looked away and drank my own tea gladly with both hands cupped around the bowl. It was a warm night, but I felt chilled through.

"Lie down and get a little sleep," Sarkan said. "He'll likely try a final push just before morning." The cannon had fired again at last, but without doing much harm: I guessed that all the men who really knew how to work them had been caught in the stone spell.

Several of the balls had fallen short, landing among Marek's own men, or went too far and flew past the tower entirely. The walls were holding. The baron's men had covered the second trench with pikes and spear-hafts, and laid their blankets and tents on them, helping to hide themselves from the arrow-flights.

I felt thick even after the tea, tired and dulled like a knife that had been used to cut wood. I folded over the rug once to make a pallet, and it felt so very good to lie down on it. But sleep wouldn't come. The silver arrow-flares lit the top of the window-frame at long, stuttered intervals. The murmur of Sarkan's voice, turning them aside, seemed far away. His face stood in shadow, the profile sharp-outlined against the wall. The tower floor beneath my cheek and my ear trembled faintly with the fighting, like the distant heavy step of an approaching giant.

I shut my eyes and tried to think of nothing but my breath. Maybe I slept a moment; then I was sitting up with a jerk out of a dream of falling. Sarkan was looking down through the broken window. The arrow-flights had stopped. I pushed myself up and joined him.

Knights and servants were milling around Marek's pavilion like stirred-up bees. The queen had come out of the tent. She was wearing armor, a mail shirt put over a simple white shift, and in one hand she carried a sword. Marek spurred over to her, bending down, speaking; she looked up towards him with her face clear and hard as steel. "They'll give the children to the Wood as Vasily did me!" she cried out to him, her voice ringing loud enough to hear. "Let them cut me limb from limb first!"

Marek hesitated, and then he swung down from the horse and called for his shield; he drew his own sword. The rest of his knights were climbing down beside him, and Solya was at his side. I looked at Sarkan, helplessly. I almost felt that Marek deserved to die, after he'd driven so many of his men to death; but if that was what he really believed, if he thought we meant to do something dreadful to the children—"How could he believe that?" I asked.

"How could he convince himself that everything else was coincidence?" Sarkan said, already at his bookshelves. "It's a lie that matches his desire." He lifted one volume off the shelf in both his arms, a massive tome nearly three feet tall. I reached out to help him and jerked my hands away, involuntarily: it was bound in a kind of blackened leather that felt dreadful to the touch, sticky in a way that didn't want to rub off my fingers.

"Yes, I know," he said, heaving it onto his reading-chair. "It's a necromantic text; it's hideous. But I'd rather spend dead men twice than any more of the living."

The spell was written out in long old-fashioned script. I tried to help him read it, but I couldn't; I recoiled from even the first words. The root of that spell was death; it was death from beginning to end. I couldn't bear to even look at it. Sarkan frowned at my distress in irritation. "Are you being missish?" he demanded. "No, you aren't. What the devil is the matter? Never mind; go and try to slow them down."

I sprang away, eager to get far from that book, and hurried to the window. I seized bits of broken stone and rubble from the floor and tried the rain spell on them, the same way I'd used it on the water-jug. Showers of dust and pebbles rained down on Marek's soldiers. They had to take cover, wrapping their hands over their heads, but the queen didn't so much as pause. She marched through the breach in the wall; she climbed over the corpses, the hem of her shift soaking up blood.

Marek and his knights surged in front of her, holding their shields over their heads. I threw heavier rocks down at them, bigger chunks that grew into boulders, but even though a few of them staggered down to their knees, most of them stayed safe tucked under their shields. They came to the passageway, and began to seize the corpses and drag them out of the way. The baron's men stabbed at them with spears. Marek's knights caught blows on their shields and their armor. And didn't: half a dozen of them fell, bodies in full gleaming armor heaved back limp and dead. But they pressed on, forced an opening, and the queen stepped inside.

I couldn't see the fighting inside the tunnel, but it was over quickly. Blood ran out of the passageway, black in the torch-light, and then the queen was stepping through the other side. She hurled down the head of a man she'd been gripping in her free hand, the neck sliced cleanly through. The defenders began backing away from her in fear. Marek and his knights spread out around her, hacking and killing, and his foot-soldiers poured into the trench behind them. Solya lashed magic out in white crackling streams.

The baron's men began falling back quickly, stumbling over their own feet, away from the queen. I'd imagined Kasia with a sword, this same kind of horror. The queen lifted her sword again and again, stabbed and hacked with brutal practicality, and none of their swords pierced her. Marek was shouting orders. The baron's men inside the last wall had climbed up onto the top of it and were trying to shoot at the queen from above. But the arrows couldn't break her skin.

I turned and pulled one of the black-fletched arrows out of the bookcase where it had sunk in, one of the arrows Solya had fired at me, Alosha's make. I took it to the window and stopped. My hands were shaking. I didn't see what else to do. None of them could stop her. But—if I killed the queen, Marek would never listen to us, never; I might as well kill him now, too. If I killed her—I felt strange and sick at the thought. She was small and far away on the ground, a doll and not a person, her arm rising and falling.

"A moment," Sarkan said. I backed away, reprieved and glad of it, although I had to cover my ears while he recited the long shivering words of his spell. A wind breathed out through the window, brushing against my skin like a damp, oily palm, smelling of rot and iron. It kept blowing, steady and awful, and down in the trenches the endless corpses stirred, and slowly began to rise.

They left their swords on the ground. They didn't need any

weapons. They didn't try to hurt the soldiers, just reached out their empty hands and took hold of them, two and three to a man, grasping. There were already more dead men than living ones in the trenches, and all the dead served the Dragon's spell. Marek's soldiers slashed and cut at them in a frenzy, but the dead didn't bleed. Their faces were sagging and blank, uninterested.

Some of them plodded down the trench to grasp at the knights, at the queen's arms and legs, taking hold of her. But she flung them off, and the knights in their armor hacked them with their broadswords. The baron's men were as horrified by the spell as Marek's; they were scrambling back from the dead as much as from the implacable queen. And she moved forward against them. The dead were holding back the rest of the army, and the baron's men were hacking down the knights all around her, but she didn't stop.

There wasn't any white left in her shift. It was bloody from the ground to the knee; her mail shirt was dyed red. Her arms and hands were red, her face was spattered. I looked down the arrow and touched Alosha's magic: I felt the arrow's eagerness to fly again, to seek warm living flesh. There was a nick in the arrow-head; I smoothed it out with my fingers, pressing the steel flat the way I'd seen Alosha work her sword. I pushed a little more magic into it, and felt it grow heavy in my hand, full of death. "In the thigh," I told it, quailing at murder. Surely it would be enough just to stop the queen. I pointed it at her, and threw.

The arrow dived down, flying straight, whistling joyfully. It struck the queen's leg high up on the thigh, and tore through the mail shirt. And then it stuck there, hanging half through the mail. There wasn't any blood. The queen pulled the arrow out, tossed it aside. She looked up towards the window, a brief glance. I stumbled back. She returned to the slaughter.

My face ached as if she'd struck me, with a sharp hollow pressure above the bridge of my nose, familiar. "The Wood," I said out loud.

"What?" Sarkan said.

"The Wood," I said. "The Wood is in her." Every spell we'd

cast on the queen, every purging, the holy relics, every trial: none of them mattered. I was suddenly sure. That had been the Wood looking back at me. The Wood had found a way to hide.

I turned to him. "The *Summoning*," I said. "Sarkan, we have to show them. Marek and Solya, all their men. If they see that she's been taken by the Wood—"

"And you think he'll believe it?" he said. He looked out the window, though, and after a moment said, "All right. We've lost the walls in any case. We'll bring the survivors inside the tower. And hope the doors hold long enough for us to cast the spell."

TWENTY EIGHT

We ran down to the great hall and flung the doors open. The baron's men came pouring in: so horribly few of them left. A hundred maybe. They crowded into the hall and down the stairs into the cellars, all of them smudged and exhausted, faces wrung with one horror after another. They were glad to come inside, but they flinched from Sarkan and from me. Even the baron himself looked at us askance. "That wasn't them," he said, as he came to stand before Sarkan in the hall, his men eddying to either side of us, leaving a circle around us. "The dead men."

"No, and if you would have preferred to have lost the rest of the living ones, do tell me, and I'll be sure and keep your tender sensibilities in mind next time." Sarkan was drawn tight, and I felt just as spent. I wondered how long it was until morning, and didn't want to ask. "Let them get what rest they can, and share out all the stores you can find."

Soon Kasia pushed up the stairs, through the crowding soldiers;

the baron had sent the wounded and the worst-exhausted men downstairs; only his best remained with him. "They're breaking into the wine and the beer casks," she said to me in an undertone. "I don't think it's going to be safe for the children. Nieshka, what's happening?"

Sarkan had climbed the dais: he was laying out the *Summoning* across the arms of his high seat. He swore under his breath. "That's the last thing we need now. Go down there and turn it all into cider," he told me. I ran down with Kasia. The soldiers were drinking out of cupped hands and helmets, or just jabbing holes in the casks and putting their heads underneath, or tipping back bottles; some of them were quarreling already. Shouting over wine must have felt safer than shouting over horrors, over dead men and slaughter.

Kasia pushed them out of my way, and they didn't fight her when they saw me there; I got up to the biggest barrel and put my hands on it. *"Lirintalem,"* I said, with a tired shove of magic, and sagged as it ran away from me and shivered through all the bottles and casks. The soldiers kept on pushing and shoving to get a drink; it would be a while before they realized they weren't getting any drunker.

Kasia touched my shoulder, carefully, and I turned and hugged her tight for one moment, glad of her strength. "I have to go back up," I said. "Keep the children safe."

"Should I come stand with you?" she said quietly.

"Keep the children safe," I said. "If you have to—" I caught her arm and took her back to the far wall of the cellar. Stashek and Marisha were sitting up there, awake and watching the soldiers, wary; Marisha was rubbing her eyes. I put my hands on the wall and found the edges of the passageway. I put Kasia's hand on the crack, showed her where it was, and then I pulled a thin line woven of magic out of it, as a handle. "Push the door open and take them inside, and close it behind you," I said. Then I put my hand into the air and said, *"Hatol,"* pulling, and drew Alosha's sword out of the air back to me. I held it out to her. "Keep this, too."

She nodded, and slung the sword over her shoulder. I kissed her one last time and ran back upstairs.

The baron's men had all come inside. The walls still did us this much good: Marek's cannon couldn't be turned on the doors. A few of the baron's men had climbed up to the arrow-slit window seats to either side of them and were shooting down at the soldiers outside. Heavy thumps landed against the door, and once a bright flare of magic; shouts and noise came. "They're laying a fire against the doors," one of the men called from the window as I came back up into the great hall.

"Let them," Sarkan said, without looking up. I joined him on the dais. He had reshaped the grand throne-like chair into a simple bench of two seats, with a flat desk on the shared arm between them. The heavy volume of the *Summoning* lay upon it, waiting, familiar and still strange. I let myself down slowly into the seat and spread my fingers over the cover: the golden vining letters, the faint hum beneath like distant honeybees. I was so tired even my fingers felt dull.

We opened the cover and began to read. Sarkan's voice recited clear and steady, marching on precisely, and slowly the fog over my mind blew away. I hummed and sang and murmured all around him. The soldiers around us grew quiet; they settled down in corners and against the walls, listening the way you would listen in a tavern to a good singer and a sad song, late at night. Their faces were vaguely puzzled with trying to follow the story, trying to remember it, even while they were being towed onward by the spell.

The spell towed me along with them, and I was glad to lose myself inside it. All the horrors of the day didn't vanish, but the *Summoning* made them only one part of the story, and not the most important part. The power was building, running bright and clean. I felt the spell rising up like a second tower. We'd open the doors, when we were ready, and spill the irresistible light into the courtyard before the gates. Outside the windows, the sky was growing lighter: the sun was coming up.

The doors creaked. Something was coming in underneath them, over the tops, through the barely there gap between the two doors. The men nearest them shouted warning. Thin wriggling shadows were climbing through every tiny crack, narrow and quick as snakes: the squirming tendrils of vines and roots, crumbling wood and stone as they found ways inside. They spread across the wood like frost climbing a pane, gripping and grasping, and a familiar, too-sweet smell came rolling off them.

It was the Wood. Striking openly now, as if it knew what we were doing, that we were about to expose the deception. The soldiers of the Yellow Marshes were hacking at the tendrils with their swords and knives, afraid: they knew enough of the Wood to recognize it, too. But more of the vines kept coming in, through cracks and holes the first ones opened for them. Outside, Marek's battering ram struck again, and the doors shook from top to bottom. The vines caught at the iron brackets of the hinges and the bar and tore at them. Rust spread in an orange-red pool as quickly as spilling blood, the work of a century in moments. The tendrils pushed inside them, coiled around the bolts and shook them ferociously back and forth. The brackets rattled noisily.

Sarkan and I couldn't stop. We kept reading, tongues stumbling in haste, turning pages as quickly as we could. But the *Summoning* demanded its own pace. The story couldn't be rushed. The edifice of power we'd already built was wavering beneath our speed, like a storyteller about to lose the thread of her own tale. The *Summoning* had us.

With a loud splintering crack, a larger corner broke off at the bottom of the right door. More vines came spilling through, thicker ones, uncoiling long. Some of them seized the arms of the soldiers, ripped swords out of their hands, flung them bodily aside. Others found the heavy bar and curled around it and dragged it slowly aside, grating inch by inch, until it slid free of the first bracket entirely. The battering ram outside struck against the doors again, and they burst wide open, knocking men out of their way sprawling.

Marek was on the other side still on his horse, standing in his stirrups and blowing his horn. His face was bright with blood-lust and fury, so eager he didn't even look to see why the doors had opened so suddenly. The vines were rooted in the earth around the stairs, thick dark nests of woody roots hiding in the corners and in the crevices of the broken steps, barely visible in the early light of morning. Marek leaped his horse straight over them without a glance, charging up the stairs and through the broken doorway, and all his remaining knights came pouring in behind him. Their swords rose and fell in a bloody rain, and the baron's soldiers were stabbing up at them with spears. Horses screamed and fell, kicking in their death-throes as men died around them.

Tears were falling off my face onto the pages of the book. But I couldn't stop reading. Then something struck me, a hard blow that knocked out all my breath. The spell slid off my tongue. Perfect silence in my ears at first, then a hollow roaring everywhere around me and Sarkan, drowning out all other sound without touching us; like being directly in the narrow eye of a thunderstorm in the middle of a wide field, seeing the grey furious rain on every side not touching you, but knowing that in a moment—

Cracks began to open up running away from us, going through the book, through the chair, through the dais, through the floors and walls. They weren't cracks in wood and stone; they were cracks in the world. Inside them was nothing but flat dark absence. The beautiful golden volume of the *Summoning* folded up on itself and sank like a stone vanishing into deep water. Sarkan had me by the arm and out of the chair and was leading me down from the dais. The chair was falling in, too, then the whole dais, all of it collapsing into emptiness.

Sarkan was still continuing the spell, or rather holding it in place, repeating his last line over and over. I tried to join in with him again, just humming, but my breath kept disappearing. I felt so strange. My shoulder throbbed, but when I looked down at it, there didn't seem to be anything wrong. Then I looked farther down, slowly. There was an arrow-shaft jutting out of me, just below my breast. I stared at it, puzzled. I couldn't feel it at all.

The high beautiful stained-glass windows shattered outwards with faint muffled pops as the cracks reached them, showers of colored glass falling. The cracks were spreading. Men fell into them with cries that vanished as they did, swallowed up into silence. Chunks of the stone walls and floors were disappearing, too. The walls of the tower groaned.

Sarkan was holding the rest of the spell by the edge, barely, like a man trying to control a maddened horse. I tried to push him magic to do it with. He was supporting all my weight, his arm like iron around me. My legs stumbled over one another, almost dragging. My chest was beginning to hurt now, a sharp shocking pain as though my body had finally woken up and noticed something was very badly wrong. I couldn't breathe without wanting to scream, and I couldn't get enough air to scream. The soldiers were still fighting in a few places, others just fleeing the tower, trying to get away from the crumbling world. I glimpsed Marek kicking free of his dead horse, jumping over another crack that ran down the floor towards him.

Between the ruined doors the queen appeared, morning light shining behind her, and for one moment I thought instead of a woman there was a tree in the doorway, a silver-barked tree, stretching from the floor up to the ceiling. Then Sarkan drew me back with him into the stairway, and led me down. The tower was shuddering, and stones were tumbling down the stairs behind us. Sarkan chanted his last line of the spell with each step, keeping the rest of the spell from bursting free. I couldn't help him.

I opened my eyes again with Kasia kneeling next to me, anxiously. The air was full of dust, but the shuddering of the walls had stopped at least. I was leaning against the wall of the cellar; we were underground. I didn't remember coming the rest of the way down the stairs. Nearby, the baron was shouting instructions to his remaining soldiers; they were pushing over wine racks and barrels and heaping iron pots into a barricade at the bottom of the stairs, shoring it up with crumbled stone. I could see sunlight coming down from above, around the turn in the stairs. Sarkan was next to me, still chanting the same line over and over, his voice going hoarse.

He'd put me next to a locked cabinet beside us made of metal; there were scorch marks around the handles. He motioned Kasia towards the lock. She took it by the handle. Flame boiled out of the lock, lapping around her hands, but she gritted her teeth and broke it open anyway. A rack of small jars of faintly glowing liquid stood inside. Sarkan took one out and pointed at me. Kasia stared at him and then down at the arrow. "I should pull it out?" she said. He made a pushing gesture with his hand, forward—she swallowed and nodded. She knelt down next to me again and said, "Nieshka, hold on."

She took the arrow between her hands and broke off the feathered shaft that still stuck out of my chest. The arrow-head shivered inside me. My mouth opened and closed, agony silent. I couldn't breathe. Hurrying, she picked off the worst splinters and made it smooth as she could, and then she turned me to my side, against the wall, and with one horrible shove pushed the arrow the rest of the way through me. She caught the arrow-head coming out of my back and pulled it all the rest of the way through.

I moaned, and blood ran hot down my front and back. Sarkan had opened the jar. He poured the liquid into the cup of his hand and now rubbed it on my skin, pressing it into the open wound. It burned horribly. I tried to push him away with one feeble hand. He ignored me, pulling my dress aside to put on more of it; then Kasia pushed me forward, and they poured it down into the wound on my back. I screamed then, and suddenly I could scream. Kasia gave me a wad of cloth to bite on; I bit and shuddered around it.

The pain got worse instead of better. I pulled away from them and tried to press myself into the wall, the cool hard stone, as if I could make myself a part of it and be unfeeling. I dug my fingernails into the mortar, whining, Kasia's hand on my shoulder—and then the worst of it was past. The running blood slowed and stopped. I began to be able to see again, and hear: fighting on the stairs, the dull clang of swords striking each other, the stone walls, scraping metal and occasionally a ringing note. Blood was trickling down through the barricade.

Sarkan had sunk back against the wall next to me, his lips still moving but almost no sound coming anymore, his eyes clenched shut with strain. The *Summoning* was like a sand-castle with one side washed away, the rest ready to come sliding down; he was holding it up with raw strength. If the rest came down, I wondered if that nothingness would swallow up the whole tower, devour all of us and leave a blank empty hole in the world—and then close in; the mountainside tumbling to fill the eaten-away hollow in the earth, as if all of us had never existed at all.

He opened his eyes and looked at me. He gestured to Kasia, to the children huddled behind her, peering afraid over a barrel. Sarkan gestured again: *Go.* He meant me to take them and flee, to whisk us away somewhere. I hesitated, and his eyes glittered at me, angrily; he waved his hand in a sweep of the empty floor. The book was gone: the *Summoning* was gone. We couldn't finish the spell, and when his strength ran out—

I drew a breath and laced my hand with his, and went back into the spell. He resisted. I sang softly at first, in short bursts of air, feeling my way. We didn't have a map anymore, and I didn't remember the words, but we'd done this before. I remembered where we were going, what we were trying to build. I pushed up more sand against the wall, and dug a moat against the coming waves; I made it long and wide. I kept humming, bits of stories and songs. I began to heap up the sand again in my mind. He held back, baffled, not sure how to help me. I sang him something longer, putting a bit of melody like a handful of wet pebbles into his hands, and he slowly gave it back to me, chanted slow and precise and even, laying the stones one by one around along the base of the wet-sand wall, shoring our tower up.

The working was growing stronger, more solid once again. We'd stopped the slide. I kept on going, poking here and there, finding a way and showing it to him. I piled on more sand and let him smooth the wall and make it even; together we stuck a fluttering-leaf branch into the top for a flying pennant. My breath still came short. I could feel an odd puckering knot in my chest and a deep tight pain where the potion still worked away, but magic was running clear through me, bright and quick, overflowing.

Men were shouting. The last of the baron's men were scrambling over the barricade from the other side, most of them swordless and only trying to escape. A light was coming down the staircase, screams coming before it. The soldiers reached up hands, helped the fleeing men down and over. There weren't very many of them. The flow stopped, and the soldiers threw the last of the sticks and big iron cauldrons on top, blocked off the passage as much as they could. Marek's voice echoed from behind it, and I glimpsed the queen's head, golden. The baron's soldiers jabbed spears down at her that turned aside on her skin. The barricade was coming apart.

We still couldn't let the spell go. Kasia was standing up; she was pushing open the door to the tomb. "Down there, quick!" she told the children. They scrambled into the stairwell. She caught my arm and helped me up; Sarkan struggled to his feet. She pushed us inside and picked up her sword from the floor, and snatched another sealed jar from the cabinet. "This way!" she shouted to the men. They came piling in after us.

The *Summoning* came with us. I went around and around the turning steps, Sarkan just behind me, magic singing between us. I heard a grinding noise above, and the stairway grew darker: up above one of the soldiers had pushed the door shut. The line of old letters to either side shone in the dimness and murmured faintly, and I found myself changing our working a little to slide gently against their magic. Subtly my sense of our inner tower changed; it grew wider and more broad, terraces and windows forming, a gold dome at the top, walls of pale white stone, inscribed in silver like the stairway walls. Sarkan's voice slowed; he saw it, too: the old tower, the lost tower, long ago. Light was dawning all around us.

We spilled out into the round room at the bottom of the stairs. The air was stifling, not enough for all of us, until Kasia took up one of the old iron candlesticks and used the base of it to smash open the wall to the tomb, bricks tumbling in. Cool air came rushing in as she pushed the children inside, and told them to hide behind the old king's coffin.

Far above came the sound of breaking stone. The queen was leading Marek and his men in after us. A few dozen soldiers crammed themselves into the room and against the walls, their faces afraid. They wore yellow surcoats, or what was left of them, so they were with us, but I didn't recognize any of their faces. I didn't see the baron. Swords rang again distantly: the last of the Yellow Marshes soldiers still pent up on the stairs were fighting. The light of the *Summoning* was building quickly.

Marek stabbed the last man in the stairwell and kicked the body tumbling in onto the floor. Soldiers jumped forward to meet him, almost eagerly: at least he was an enemy who made sense; someone who could be defeated. But Marek met one swing on his shield, ducked under it, and thrust his sword through the man's body; he whirled and took off the head of the man on the other side; clubbed one man with his sword-hilt as he finished the swing, and stabbed forward to take another one in the eye. Kasia took a step beside me, a cry of protest, her sword rising: but they were all down before she'd even finished the sound.

But we finished the *Summoning*. I sang the last three words and Sarkan sang them after, and we sang them together once more.

Light dawned blazing through the room, glowing almost from within the marble walls. Marek pushed forward into the space he'd cleared, and the queen came down behind him.

Her sword hung, dripping blood. Her face was calm and still and serene. The light shone on her and through her, steady and deep; there was no trace of corruption. Marek was clear, and Solya behind him also; the light washing over her caught them both at the edges, and there weren't shadows in them: only a hard glittering kind of selfishness, pride like spiked citadel walls. But there wasn't even any of that in the queen. I stared at her, panting, baffled. There was no corruption inside her.

Nothing at all was inside her. The light of the *Summoning* shone straight through. She was rotted out from the inside, her body just the skin of bark around an empty space. There wasn't anything left of her to corrupt. I understood too late: we'd gone in to save Queen Hanna, so the Wood had let us find what we were looking for. But what we'd found had only ever been a hollow remnant, a fragment of a heart-tree's core. A puppet, empty and waiting until we'd finished all our trials, convinced ourselves there was nothing wrong, and the Wood could reach out and take up the strings.

The light kept pouring over her, and slowly I made out the Wood at last, as if I'd looked again at a cloud-shape and seen a tree instead of a woman's face. The Wood was there—it was the only thing there. The golden strands of her hair were the pale veins of leaves, and her limbs were branches, and her toes were long roots crawling out over the floor, roots going deep into the ground.

She was looking at the wall behind us, at the broken opening going through to the tomb with its blue flame, and for the first time her face changed, a change like the twisting of a slim willow bending in a high wind, the rage of a storm in the treetops. That animating power in the Wood—whatever it was, it had been here before.

Queen Hanna's milk-pale face was slipping away under the *Summoning*'s light, like paint washed away by running water. There was another queen beneath, all brown and green and golden, her skin patterned like alder wood and her hair a deep green nearly black, threaded with red and gold and autumn brown. Someone had picked the gold strands of her hair out and braided them into a circlet for her head, white ribbons threaded through, and she wore a white dress that sat on her wrongly; she'd put it on, though it meant nothing to her.

I saw the buried king's body take shape between her and us. He was carried by six men on a sheet of white linen, his face still and unmoving, the eyes filmed over with milk. They carried him into the tomb; they lowered him gently into the great stone coffin; they folded in the linen over his body.

In the *Summoning*-light, that other queen followed the men into the tomb-chamber. She bent over the coffin. There was no sorrow in her face, only a bewildered confusion, as if she didn't understand. She touched the king's face, touched the lids of his eyes with strangely long fingers knobbled like twigs. He didn't stir. She startled and drew her hand back, out of the way of the men. They put the lid upon the coffin, and the blue flame erupted atop it. She watched them, still baffled.

One of the attending men spoke to her, ghostly, telling her I think to stay as long as she wished; he bowed and, stooping, left the tomb through the opening, leaving her. There was something in his face as he turned away from her that the *Summoning* caught even from so long ago, something cold and determined.

The Wood-queen didn't see it. She was standing at the stone coffin, her hands spread over the top of it, uncomprehending as Marisha had been. She didn't understand death. She stared at the blue flame, watching it leap; she turned all around in the bare stone room, looking around it with a wounded, appalled face. And then she stopped and looked again. Bricks were being laid in the small opening of the wall. She was being closed up inside the tomb.

She stared for a moment, and then rushed forward and knelt before the remaining opening. The men had already pushed blocks into most of the space, working quickly; the cold-faced man was speaking sorcery while they worked, blue-silver light crackling out of his hands, over the blocks, mortaring them together. She reached a hand through in protest. He didn't answer her; he didn't look at her face. None of them looked at her. They closed up the wall with one last block, pushing her hand back into the room with it.

She stood up, alone. She was startled, angry, full of confusion; but she wasn't yet afraid. She raised a hand; she meant to do something. But behind her, the blue flame was leaping on the stone tomb. The letters around the sides were catching the light, shining out, completing the long sentence from the stairs. She whirled, and I could read them with her: REMAIN ETERNAL, REST ETERNAL, NEVER MOVING, NEVER LEAVING, and they weren't just a poem for the king's rest. This wasn't a tomb; this was a prison. A prison meant to hold *her*. She turned and beat against the wall, she tried vainly to push against it, to work her fingers into the cracks. Terror was climbing in her. Stone shut her in, cold and still. They had quarried this room out of the roots of the mountains. She couldn't get out. She couldn't—

Abruptly the Wood-queen heaved the memories away. The light of the *Summoning* broke and ran away over the stones of the tomb like water. Sarkan staggered back; I nearly fell against the wall. We were back in the round room, but the queen's fear rattled against the inside of my ribs like a bird beating itself against walls. Shut away from the sun, shut away from water, shut away from air. And she still couldn't die. She hadn't died.

She stood among us, only half-hidden behind Queen Hanna's face, and she wasn't the queen in that vision anymore, either. She'd fought her way out, somehow. She'd won free, and then she'd— killed them? She'd killed them, and not only them, but their lovers and children and all their people; she'd devoured them, become as monstrous as they had been. She'd made the Wood.

She hissed softly in the dark, not a snake's hiss but the rustling of leaves, the scrape of tree-branches rubbing in the wind, and as she stepped forward vines came boiling down the stairs behind her, grabbing all the remaining men by ankle and wrist and throat, dragging them up against the walls and ceiling, out of her way.

Sarkan and I were still struggling to our feet. Kasia put herself before us like a shield and chopped the vines away from us, keeping us free, but others snaked around behind her and into the tomb. They lashed around the children and started to drag them forward, Marisha screaming as Stashek hacked at the vines uselessly, until they seized his arm, too. Kasia took a step away from us towards the children, her face in agony, unable to protect us all.

And then Marek sprang forward. He slashed the vines apart, his own sword gleaming around the edges. He put himself between the queen and the children, and thrust them with his shield-arm back into the safety of the burial-chamber. He stood before the queen. She halted before him, and he said, *"Mother,"* fiercely, and dropped his sword to seize her by the wrists. He looked down into her face as she turned it slowly up towards him. "Mother," he said. "Fight free of her. It's Marek—it's Marechek. Come back to me."

I pulled myself up the wall. He blazed with determination, with longing. His armor was washed with blood and smoke, his face smeared with one bright red streak, but he looked for a moment like a child, or maybe a saint, pure with want. And the queen looked at him, and put her hand on his chest, and killed him. Her fingers turned into thorns and twigs and vines; she sank them through his armor, and closed her hand like a fist.

If there was anything left of Queen Hanna, any thin scraping of will, maybe she spent it then, on one small mercy: he died without knowing he'd failed. His face didn't change. His body slid easily off her hand, not much altered; only the hole in his breastplate where her wrist had gone in. He fell to the floor on his back, his armor ringing on the flagstones, still clear-eyed and certain, *certain* he would be heard, certain he would be victorious. He looked like a king.

He'd caught us all in his own certainty. For a moment we were all shocked into stillness. Solya inhaled once, stricken. Then Kasia

sprang forward, swinging her sword. The queen caught it on her
own blade. They stood fixed, pressed against each other, a few
sparks glittering away from the grinding blades, and the queen
leaned in and forced her slowly down.

Sarkan was speaking, an incantation of heat and flame rolling
off his tongue, and fire came gouting out of the ground around the
queen's legs, yellow-red and searing. The flames blackened Kasia's
skin where they licked against her; it ate up both the swords. Kasia
had to roll away. The queen's silver mail melted and ran off her in
streams of shining liquid that puddled on the floor and covered
over with blackened crust; her shift billowed into hot smoky flames.
But the fire didn't touch her body; the queen's pale limbs stayed
straight and unmarred. Solya was throwing his white lash against
her as well, the flames crackling to blue where his fire and the Dragon's met; that mingled blue fire ran twisting all over her body, trying
to seek out a weakness, find a way in.

I gripped Sarkan's hand; I fed him magic and strength, so he
could keep beating her back with flame. His fires were crisping up
the vines. The soldiers who hadn't been strangled were dragging
themselves staggering away, back up the stairs—at least they were
escaping. Other spells, one after another, came to me, but I knew
without beginning that they wouldn't work. Fire wouldn't burn her;
blade wouldn't cut her, no matter how long we hacked away. I wondered in horror if we shouldn't have let the *Summoning* fail; if that
great nothingness could have taken her. But I didn't think even that
would have done it. There was too much of her. She could have
filled in any holes we made in the world and still had more of herself left over. She was the Wood, or the Wood was her. Her roots
went too deep.

Sarkan's breath was coming in long drags, whenever he could get
it. Solya sank down onto the stairs, spent, and his white fire died.
I gave Sarkan more strength, but soon he'd fall, too. The queen
turned towards us. She didn't smile. There wasn't triumph in her
face, only an unending wrath and the awareness of victory.

Behind her, Kasia stood up. She drew Alosha's sword from over her shoulder. She swung.

The sword-blade sliced into the queen's throat and stuck there, halfway through. A hollow roaring noise began, my ear bones crackling and the whole room darkening. The queen's face stilled. The sword began to drink and drink and drink, endlessly thirsty, wanting more. The noise climbed higher.

It felt like a war between two endless things, between a bottomless chasm and a running river. We all stood, frozen, watching, hoping. The queen's expression didn't change. Where the sword stuck in her throat, a black glossy sheen was trying to take hold of her flesh, spreading from the wound like ink clouding through a glass of clean water. She put a hand slowly up and touched the wound with her fingers, and a little of the same gloss came away on her fingertips. She looked down at it.

And then she looked back up at us with sudden contempt, almost a shake of her head, as if to tell us we'd been foolish.

She sank down suddenly onto her knees, her head and body and limbs all jerking—like a marionette whose puppeteer had dropped the strings. And all at once Sarkan's flames caught in Queen Hanna's body. Her short golden hair went up in a smoky cloud, her skin blackened and split. Pale gleams showed through beneath the charred skin. For a moment I thought maybe it had worked, maybe the sword had broken the Wood-queen's immortality.

But pale white smoke came billowing out of those cracks, torrents of it, and roared away past us—escaping, just like the Wood-queen had escaped her prison once before. Alosha's sword kept trying to drink her up, to catch at the streams of smoke, but they boiled away too quickly, rushing past even the sword's hungry grasp. Solya covered his head as they fled over him and up the stairs; others twisted out through the air-channel; still more dived into the burial-chamber and up and vanished through a tiny chink in the roof I couldn't have noticed, the thinnest crack. Kasia had flung herself atop the children; Sarkan and I huddled against the wall, covering our mouths. The Wood-queen's essence dragged over our skin with the oily horror of corruption, the warm stink of old leaves and mold.

And then it was gone—she was gone.

Uninhabited now, Queen Hanna's body crumbled away all at once, like a used-up log falling into ashes. Alosha's sword fell to the floor clattering. We were alone, our rasping breaths the only sound. All the living soldiers had fled; the dead had been swallowed by the vines and the fire, leaving nothing but smoky ghosts on the white marble walls. Kasia sat up slowly, the children gathered against her. I sank to the floor on my knees, shaking with horror and despair. Marek's hand lay open near me. His face gazed up sightless from the middle of the room, surrounded by charred stone and melted steel.

The dark blade was dissolving into the air. In a moment nothing remained but the empty hilt. Alosha's sword was spent. And the Wood-queen had survived.

TWENTY NINE

We carried the children out of the tower into morning sun, pouring down bright and improbable on the silent wreckage of six thousand men. There were flies already buzzing thickly, and the crows had come in flocks; when we came out they burst up from the ground and perched on the walls to wait for us to get out of their way.

We had passed the baron in the cellar, leaning against the wall of the hearth, his eyes blank and unseeing, blood puddled beneath him. Kasia had found one of the sleep-potions still unbroken in its flask, gripped in the hand of the man-at-arms slumped dead beside him. She opened it and gave the children each a swallow, down there, before we brought them out. They'd seen more than enough already.

Now Stashek hung limp over her shoulder, and Sarkan carried a huddled Marisha in his arms. I struggled on behind them, too hollow to be sick anymore, too dry for tears. My breath was still short and painful in my chest. Solya walked with me, giving me a hand occasionally over a particularly high mound of armored corpses. We hadn't taken him prisoner; he'd just followed us out, trailing after us with a puzzled look, like a man who knew he wasn't dreaming, but felt he should have been. Down in the cellar, he'd given Sarkan what was left of his cloak to wrap around the little princess.

The tower was still standing, barely. The floor of the great hall was a maze of broken flagstones, dead roots and withered vines sprawled over them, charred up like the queen's body below. Several of the columns had collapsed entirely. There was a hole in the ceiling into the library above, and a chair had fallen partway into it. Sarkan looked up at it as we left, climbing over blocks and rubble.

We had to walk the full length of the walls we'd built to try and keep Marek out. The voices of the old stone whispered sadly to me as we came through the archways. We saw no one living until we came out into the abandoned camp. At least there were a few soldiers there, rummaging through the supplies; a couple of them burst out of the pavilion running away from us, carrying silver cups. I would have gladly paid a dozen silver cups just to hear another mortal voice, to be able to believe that not everyone was dead. But they all fled, or hid from us behind tents or supply-heaps, peering out. We stood in the silent field and after a moment I said, "The cannon-crew," remembering.

They were still there, a stone company, pushed out of the way, blank grey eyes fixed on the tower. Most of them hadn't been badly broken. We stood around them, silently. None of us had enough strength to undo the spell. Finally I reached out to Sarkan. He shifted Marisha to his other arm and let me take his hand.

We managed to pool enough magic to undo the spell. The soldiers writhed and jerked as they came loose from the stone, shaking with the sudden return of time and breath. Some of them had lost fingers, or had new pitted scars where their bodies had been chipped, but these were trained men, who managed cannon that roared as terribly as any spell. They edged back from us wide-eyed, but then they looked at Solya: they recognized him, at least. "Orders, sir?" one of them asked him, uncertainly.

He stared back blankly a moment and then looked at us, just as uncertainly.

We walked down to Olshanka together, the road still dusty from so much use yesterday. Yesterday. I tried not to think about it: yesterday six thousand men had marched over this road; today they were all gone. They lay dead in the trenches, they lay dead in the hall, in the cellars, on the long winding stairs going down. I saw their faces in the dust while we walked. Someone in Olshanka saw us coming, and Borys came out with a wagon to carry us the rest of the way. In the back we swayed with the wheels like sacks of grain. The creaking was every song I'd ever heard about war and battle; the horses clopping along, the drumbeat. All those stories must have ended this same way, with someone tired going home from a field full of death, but no one ever sang this part.

Borys's wife Natalya put me to sleep in Marta's old room, a little bedroom full of sun, with a worn rag doll sitting on the shelf and a small outgrown quilt. She'd gone to her own home now, but the room was still shaped around her, a warm welcoming place ready to receive me, and Natalya's hand on my forehead was my mother, telling me to sleep, sleep; the monsters wouldn't come. I shut my eyes and pretended to believe her.

I didn't wake again until evening, a warm summer evening with the gentle twilight falling blue. There was a familiar comfortable rising bustle in the house, someone getting supper, others coming in from the day's work. I sat at the window without moving for a long time more. They were much richer than my family: they had an upstairs part in their house just for the bedrooms. Marisha was running in the big garden with a dog and four other children, most of them older than her; she was in a fresh cotton dress marked up with grass stains, and her hair slipping out of tidy braids. But Stashek was sitting near the door watching them, though one of the others was a boy his age. Even in simple clothes he didn't look anything like an ordinary child, with his shoulders very straight and his face solemn as church.

"We have to take them back to Kralia," Solya said. Given time to rest, he'd gathered back up some of his outrageous self-assurance, sitting himself down in our company as though he'd been with us all along.

It was dark; the children had been put to bed. We were sitting in the garden with glasses of cool plum brandy, and I felt as though I were pretending to be grown-up. It was too much like my parents taking visitors to sit in the chairs and the shady swinging bench just inside the forest, talking of crops and families, and meanwhile all of us children ran cheerfully amok, finding berries or chestnuts, or just having games of tag.

I remembered when my oldest brother married Malgosia, and suddenly the two of them stopped running around with us and started sitting with the parents: a very solemn kind of alchemy, one that I felt shouldn't have been able to just sneak up on me. It didn't seem real even to be sitting here at all, much less talking of thrones and murder, quite seriously, as if those were themselves real things and not just bits out of songs.

I felt even more peculiar, listening to them all argue. "Prince Stashek must be crowned at once, and a regency established," Solya was going on. "The Archduke of Gidna and the Archduke of Varsha, at least—"

"Those children aren't going anywhere but to their grandparents," Kasia said, "if I have to put them on my back and carry them all the way myself."

"My dear girl, you don't understand—" Solya said.

"I'm not your dear girl," Kasia said, with a bite in her tone that silenced him. "If Stashek's the king now, all right; the king's asked me to take him and Marisha to their mother's family. That's where they're going."

"The capital is too close in any case." Sarkan flicked his fingers, impatient, dismissive. "I *do* understand the Archduke of Varsha won't want the king in the hands of Gidna," he added peevishly, when Solya drew breath to argue, "and I don't care. Kralia wasn't safe before; it won't be safer now."

"But nowhere will be safe," I said, breaking in on them, bewildered. "Not for long." They were all quarreling, it seemed to me, about whether to build a house on this side or that of a river, and ignoring the spring-flood mark on a tree nearby, higher than either door would be.

After a moment, Sarkan said, "Gidna is on the ocean. The northern castles will be well placed to mount a substantial defense—"

"The Wood will come anyway!" I said. I knew it. I'd looked into the Wood-queen's face, felt that implacable wrath beating against my skin. All these years, Sarkan had held the Wood back like a tide behind a dam of stone; he'd diverted its power away into a thousand streams and wells of power, scattered throughout the valley. But it was a dam that couldn't hold forever. Today, next week, next year, the Wood would break through. It would reclaim all those wells, those streams, go roaring up to the mountainside. And fueled with all that new-won strength, it would come over the mountain passes.

There wasn't going to be any strength to meet them. The army of Polnya was shattered, the army of Rosya wounded—and the Wood could afford to lose a battle or two or a dozen; it would establish its footholds and scatter its seeds, and even if it was pushed back over one mountain pass or another, that wouldn't matter in the end. It would keep coming. *She* would keep coming. We might hold the Wood off long enough for Stashek and Marisha to grow up, grow old, even die, but what about Borys and Natalya's grandchildren, running with them in the garden? Or their own children, growing up in the lengthening shadow?

"We can't keep holding the Wood back with Polnya burning behind us," Sarkan said. "The Rosyans will come over the Rydva for vengeance, as soon as they know Marek is dead—"

"We can't hold the Wood back at all!" I said. "That's what *they* tried—that's what you've been doing. We have to stop it for good. We have to stop *her*."

He glared at me. "Yes, what a marvelous idea. If Alosha's blade couldn't kill her, nothing can. What do you propose to do?"

I stared back and saw the knotting fear in my stomach reflected in his eyes. His face stilled. He stopped glaring. He sank back in his chair, still staring at me. Solya eyed us both in confusion and Kasia watched me with worry in her face. But there wasn't anything else to do.

"I don't know," I said to Sarkan, my voice shaking. "But I'll do something. Will you come into the Wood with me?"

Kasia stood with me irresolute at the crossroads outside Olshanka, unhappy. The sky was still the first pale pink-grey of morning. "Nieshka, if you think I can help you," she said softly, but I shook my head. I kissed her; she put her arms around me carefully and tightened her embrace little by little, until she was hugging me. I closed my eyes and held her close, and for a moment we were children again, girls again, under a distant shadow but happy anyway. Then the sun came down the road and touched us. We let go and stepped back: she was golden and stern, almost too beautiful to be living, and there was magic in my hands. I took her face in my hands a moment; we leaned our foreheads together, and then she turned away.

Stashek and Marisha were sitting in the wagon, watching anxiously for Kasia, with Solya next to them; one of the soldiers was driving. Some more men had come wandering back into town, those who'd run away from the fighting and the tower before the end, a mix of men from the Yellow Marshes and Marek's men. They were all going along as escort. They weren't enemies anymore; they hadn't really been enemies to begin with. Even Marek's men had thought they were saving the royal children. They'd all just been put on opposite sides of a chessboard by the Wood-queen, so she could sit to the side and watch them taken off by one another.

The wagon was loaded with supplies from the whole town, goods that would have gone to Sarkan's tribute later that year. He'd given Borys gold for the horses and the wagon. "They'll pay you to drive them as well," he'd said, handing him the purse. "And take your family along; you'd have enough to make a new start of it."

Borys looked at Natalya. She shook her head a little. He turned back and said, "We'll stay."

Sarkan muttered as he turned away, impatient with what looked to him like folly. But I met Borys's eyes. The low murmur of the valley sang beneath my feet, home. I had deliberately come outside without shoes, so I could curl my toes into the soft grass and the dirt and draw that strength into me. I knew why he wasn't going; why my mother and father wouldn't go if I went to Dvernik and asked them to leave. "Thank you," I told him.

The wagon creaked away. The soldiers fell in behind it. From the back, Kasia looked at me, her arms around the children, until the dust of marching raised up a muddy cloud behind them and I couldn't see their faces anymore. I turned back to Sarkan: he regarded me with a hard, grim face. "Well?" he said.

We walked down the road from Borys's big house, towards the wooden swish-thump of the flour mill's water-wheel, the river steadily churning it along. Under our feet, the road gradually turned into loose pebbles, then slipped beneath the clear just-foaming water. There were a handful of boats tied up on the shore. We untied the smallest one and we pushed it out into the river, my skirts hiked up and his boots thrown into the boat; we weren't very graceful about getting in, but we managed it without soaking ourselves, and he picked up the oars.

He sat down with his back to the Wood and said, "Keep time for me." I sang Jaga's quickening song in a low voice while he pulled, and the banks went blurring by.

The Spindle ran clear and straight under the rising hot sun. It sparkled on the water. We slipped quickly along it, half a mile with each oar-stroke. I had a glimpse of women doing the washing on the bank at Poniets, sitting up with heaps of white linens around them to watch us dart hummingbird-by, and when we passed Viosna for a moment we were under the cherry-trees, small fruits just forming, the water still drifted with fallen petals. I didn't catch sight of Dvernik, though I knew when we passed it. I recognized a curve of riverbank, half a mile east of the village, and looked back to see the bright brass cockerel on the church steeple. The wind was blowing at our backs.

I kept singing softly until the dark wall of trees came into view ahead. Sarkan put the oars down into the bottom of the boat. He turned and looked at the ground before the trees, and his face was grim. I realized after a moment that there wasn't a line of burnt ground visible anymore; only thick green grass.

"We had burned it back a mile all along the border," he said. He looked south towards the mountains, as if he was trying to judge the distance the Wood had already come. I didn't think it mattered now. However far was too far, and not as far as it would be, either. We'd find a way to stop it or we wouldn't.

The Spindle's current carried us along, drifting. Up ahead, the slim dark trees put up long arms and laced fingers alongside the river, a wall rising on either bank. He turned back to me, and we joined hands. He chanted a spell of distraction, of invisibility, and I took it and murmured to our boat, telling it to be an empty stray boat on the water, rope frayed and broken, bumping gently over rocks. We tried to be nothing to notice, nothing to care about. The sun had climbed high overhead, and a band of light ran down the river, between the shadows of the trees. I put one of the oars behind us as a rudder, and kept us on the shining road.

The banks became thicker and wilder, brambles full of red berries and thorns like dragon's teeth, pale white and deadly sharp. The trees grew thick and misshapen and enormous. They leaned over the river; they threw thin whips of branches into the air, clawing for more of the sky. They looked the way a snarl sounds. Our safe path dwindled smaller and narrower, and the water beneath us ran silent, as if it, too, was in hiding. We huddled in the middle of the boat.

A butterfly betrayed us, a small scrap of fluttering black and yellow that had gotten lost flying over the Wood. It sank down to rest on the prow of our boat, exhausted, and a bird like a black knife darted out of the trees and snatched it up. It perched on the prow with the crushed butterfly wings sticking out of its beak, and snapped them up, three quick clacks, staring at us with eyes like small black beads. Sarkan tried to grab it, but it darted away into the trees, and a cold wind rolled down the river at our backs.

A groaning came from the banks. One of the old massive trees leaned deeply down, roots pulling free from the earth, and fell with a roar into the water just behind our boat. The river heaved underneath us. My oar spun away. We grabbed at the sides of the boat and clung as we went spinning over the surface and plunged onward, stern-first. The boat dipped, and water came pouring in over the sides, ice-cold on my bare feet. We kept spinning, buffeted; I saw as we turned a walker clattering out on the fallen tree, from the bank. It turned its stick-head to see us.

Sarkan shouted, *"Rendkan selkhoz!"* and our boat straightened itself out. I pointed a hand at the walker, but I knew it was already too late. *"Polzhyt,"* I said, and a fire bloomed suddenly orange-bright along its twiggy back. But it turned and ran away into the woods on its four legs, smoke and orange glow trailing away behind it. We'd been seen.

The full force of the Wood's gaze came down on us like a hammer-blow. I fell back into the bottom of the boat, struck, the cold water soaking like a shock through my clothes. The trees were reaching for us, stretching thorny branches over the water, leaves coming down around us and gathering in the wake of our boat. We came around a bend and up ahead there were half a dozen walkers, a deep green mantis at their head, all of them wading out into the river like a living dam.

The water had quickened, as if the Spindle would have liked to carry us past them, but there were too many, and still more coming into the river beyond. Sarkan stood up in the boat, drawing breath for a spell, ready to strike them with fire, with lightning. I heaved myself up and caught his arm and pulled him with me over the back of the boat, into the water, feeling his startled thrash of indignation through my hand. We plunged deep into the current and came up again floating as a leaf holding on to a twig, pale green and brown, swirling with all the others. It was illusion and it wasn't; I held it with all my heart, wanting nothing more than to be a leaf, a tiny blown leaf. The river seized us in a narrow swift current and carried us on eagerly, as if it had only been waiting for the chance.

The walkers snatched up our boat, and the mantis tore it apart with its clawed forelegs, smashing it into splinters and putting its head in, as if trying to find us. It took its gleaming faceted eyes out again and looked around and around. But by then we had already shot by their legs; the river sucked us briefly down through a whirling eddy into murky green silence, out of the Wood's gaze, and spat us out again farther down into a square scrap of sunlight, another dozen leaves bursting up with us. Back farther upstream, the walkers and the mantis were churning up the water, threshing it with their limbs. We drifted away on the surface, in silence; the water took us along.

We were leaf and twig for a long time in the dark. The river had dwindled around us, and the trees had grown so monstrous and high that their branches entwined overhead into a canopy so thick that no sunlight came through, only a filtered dim glow. The underbrush had died away, starved of the sun. Thin-bladed ferns and red-capped mushrooms clustered on the banks with drowned grey reeds and snarled nests of pale exposed roots in black mud, drinking up the river. There was more room among the dark trunks. Walkers and mantises came to the banks to look for us, as did other things: one of them a great snouting boar the size of a pony with too-heavy furred shoulders and eyes like red coals, sharp teeth hooked over its upper jaw. It came closer to us than anything else, snuffling at the banks, tearing through the mud and heaped dead leaf mulch only a short way from where we drifted carefully, carefully by. *We are leaf and twig,* I sang silently, *leaf and twig, nothing more,* and as we eddied on I saw the boar shake its head and snort in dissatisfaction, going back into the trees.

That was the last beast we saw. The terrible beating rage of the Wood had lightened when we fell out of its gaze. It was looking for us, but it didn't know where to look anymore. The pressure faded still more now as we were carried onward. All the calls and whistling noises of birds and insects were dying away. Only the Spindle went on gurgling to itself, louder; it widened a little again, running quicker over a shallow bed full of polished rocks. Suddenly Sarkan moved, gasped out of human lungs, and hauled me thrashing up into the air. Not a hundred feet away the river roared over a cliff's-edge, and we weren't *really* leaves, even if I'd been careful to forget that.

The river tried to keep pulling at us, coaxingly. The rocks were as slippery as wet ice. They barked my ankles and elbows and knees, and we fell three times. We dragged ourselves to the bank barely feet from the waterfall's edge, wet and shivering. The trees around us were silent, dark; they weren't watching us. They were so tall that down here on the ground they were only long smooth towers, their hearts grown ages ago; to them we weren't anything more than squirrels, poking around their roots. An enormous cloud of mist rose up from the base of the falls, hiding the edges of the cliff and everything below. Sarkan looked at me: *Now what?*

I walked into the fog, carefully, feeling my way. The earth

breathed moist and rich beneath my feet, and the river-mist clung to my skin. Sarkan kept a hand on my shoulder. I found footholds and handholds, and we worked our way down the ragged, tumbled cliffside, until abruptly my foot slipped out from under me and I sat down hard. He fell with me, and we went slithering together down the rest of the hill, just managing to stay on our rears instead of tumbling head-over-foot, until the slope spilled us out hard against the base of a tree-trunk, leaning precariously over the churning basin of the waterfall, its roots clutching a massive boulder to keep from toppling in.

We lay there stunned out of our breath, lying on our backs staring upwards. The grey boulder frowned down at us, like nothing more than an old big-nosed man with bushy-eyebrow roots. Even bruised and scraped, I felt an immense instinctive relief; as if for a moment I'd come to rest in a pocket of safety. The Wood's wrath didn't reach here. The fog rolled in thick gusts off the water and drifted back and forth, and through it I watched the leaves gently bobbing up and down, pale yellow on silver branches, desperately glad to rest, and then Sarkan muttered half a curse and heaved himself back up, grabbing me by the arm. He dragged me almost protesting up and away, ankle-deep into the water. He stopped there, just beyond the branches, and I looked back through the fog. We'd been lying beneath an ancient gnarled heart-tree, growing on the bank.

We fled away from it down the narrow track of the river. The Spindle was barely more than a stream here, just wide enough for us to run together splashing, the bottom of grey and amber sand. The fog thinned, the last of the mist-cover blowing away, and a final gust cleared it completely. We stopped, frozen. We were in a wide glade thick with heart-trees, and they were standing in a host around us.

THIRTY

We stood with our hands clenched tight, barely breathing, as if we could keep the trees from noticing us if only we didn't move. The Spindle continued onward away from us through the trees, murmuring gently. It was so clear I could see the grains of sand in the bottom, black and silver-grey and brown, tumbled with polished drops of amber and quartz. The sun was shining again.

The heart-trees weren't monstrous silent pillars like the trees above the hill. They were vast, but only oak-tall; they spread wide instead, full of entwining branches and pale white spring flowers. Dried golden leaves carpeted the ground beneath them, last autumn's fall, and beneath them rose a faint drifting wine-scent of old fallen fruit, not unpleasant. My shoulders kept trying to unknot themselves.

There should have been endless birds singing in those branches, and small animals gathering fruits. Instead there was a deep strange stillness. The river sang on quietly, but nothing else moved here; nothing else lived. Even the heart-trees didn't seem to stir. A breeze stirred the branches a little, but the leaves only whispered drowsily a moment and fell silent. The water was running over my feet, and the sun was shining through the leaves.

Finally I took a step. Nothing came leaping from the trees; no bird shrilled the alarm. I took another step, and another. The water was warm, and the sun dappling through the trees was strong enough to begin drying my linen clothes on my back. We walked through the hush. The Spindle led us in a gently curving path between and among the trees, until it spilled at last into a small still pool.

On the far side of the pool there stood one last heart-tree: broad and towering above all the others, and in front of it a green mound rose, heaped over with fallen white flowers. On it lay the body of the Wood-queen. I recognized the white mourning-gown she'd worn in the tower: she was still wearing it, or what was left of it. The long straight skirt was ragged, torn along the sides; the sleeves had mostly rotted. The cuffs woven of pearls around her wrists were brown with old bloodstains. Her green-black hair spilled down the sides of the mound and tangled with the roots of the tree; the roots had climbed over the mound and wrapped long brown fingers gently over her body, curled around her ankles and her thighs, and her shoulders and her throat; they combed through her hair. Her eyes were closed, dreaming.

If we'd still had Alosha's sword, we might have put it down into her, through her heart, and pinned her to the earth. Maybe that might have killed her, here at the source of her power, in her own flesh. But the sword was gone.

Then Sarkan brought out the last of his vial of fire-heart instead: the red-gold hunger of it leaping with eagerness inside the glass. I looked down at it and was silent. We'd come here to make an ending. We'd come to burn the Wood; this was the heart of it. *She* was the heart of it. But when I imagined pouring fire-heart on her body, watching her limbs thrashing—

Sarkan looked at my face and said, "Go back to the falls," offering to spare me.

But I shook my head. It wasn't that I felt squeamish about killing her. The Wood-queen deserved death and horror: she'd sowed it and tended it and harvested it by the bushel, and wanted more. Kasia's soundless cry beneath the heart-tree's bark; Marek's face, shining, as his own mother killed him. My mother's terror when her small daughter brought home an apron full of blackberries, because the Wood didn't spare even children. The hollow gutted walls of Porosna, with the heart-tree squatting over the village, and Father Ballo twisted out of his own body into a slaughtering beast. Marisha's small voice, saying, "Mama," over her mother's stabbed corpse.

I hated her; I wanted her to burn, the way so many of the corrupted had burned, because she'd put her hold on them. But wanting cruelty felt like another wrong answer in an endless chain. The people of the tower had walled her up, then she'd struck them all down. She'd raised up the Wood to devour us; now we'd give her to the fire-heart, and choke all this shining clear water with ash. None of that seemed right. But I didn't see anything else we could do.

I waded across the pool with Sarkan. The water didn't come higher than our knees. Small round stones were smooth beneath our feet. Close, the Wood-queen seemed even more strange, not quite alive; her lips were parted, but her breast didn't seem to rise and fall. She might have been carved from wood. Her skin had the faint banded pattern of wood split lengthwise and smoothed, waves of light and dark. Sarkan opened the vial, and with one quick tip he poured the fire-heart directly between her lips, and then spilled the final dregs over her body.

Her eyes flew open. The dress caught, the roots of the heart-tree caught, her hair caught, fire roaring up around her like a cloud as Sarkan pulled me back. She screamed a hoarse, furious cry. Smoke and flame gouted out of her mouth, and bursts of fire were going off beneath her skin like orange stars flaring, in one part of her and another. She thrashed on the mound beneath the roots, the green grass charring swiftly away. Clouds of smoke billowed around her, over her. Within her I saw lungs, heart, liver, like shadows inside a burning house. The long tree roots crisped up, curling away, and she burst up from the mound.

She faced us, burning like a log that had been on the fire a long time: her skin charred to black charcoal, cracking to show the orange flames beneath, pale ash blowing off her skin. Her hair was a torrent of flames wreathing her head. She screamed again, a red glow of fire in her throat, her tongue a black coal, and she didn't stop burning. Fire spurted from her in places, but skin like new bark closed over it, and even as the endless heat blackened the fresh skin once more, it healed again. She staggered forward towards the pool. Watching in horror, I remembered the *Summoning*-vision and her bewilderment, her terror when she'd known she was trapped in stone. It wasn't simply that she was immortal unless slain. She hadn't known how to die at all.

Sarkan seized a handful of sand and pebbles from the floor of the stream and threw them at her, calling out a spell of increase; they swelled as they flew through the air, became boulders. They smashed into her, billows of sparks going up from her body like a fire jabbed with a poker, but even then she didn't collapse into ashes. She kept burning, unconsumed. She kept coming. She plunged to her hands and knees in the pool, steam hissing up in clouds around her.

The narrow stream came running in suddenly quicker over the rocks, as if it knew the pool needed replenishing. Even beneath the clear rippling water, she still glowed; the fire-heart gleamed deep in her, refusing to be doused. She cupped water to her mouth with both hands. Most of the water boiled away from her charred skin. Then she seized one of the boulders Sarkan had flung at her, and with a strange twisting jerk of magic she scooped the middle of it out, to give herself a bowl to drink from.

"With me, together," Sarkan shouted to me. "Keep the fire on her!" I startled; I'd been mesmerized, watching her live and burn at the same time. I took his hand. *"Polzhyt mollin, polzhyt talo,"* he chanted, and I sang about the burning hearth, about blowing gently on a flame. The burning roots crackled up again behind the Wood-queen, and within her the fire glowed fresh. She lifted her head from the bowl with a cry of rage. Her eyes were black hollowed pits glowing with fire.

Vining plants sprouted from the riverbed and wrapped themselves tangling around our legs. Barefoot, I managed to pull away from them, but they caught the laces of Sarkan's boots, and he fell into the water. Other vines at once launched themselves up his arms, reaching for his throat. I plunged my hands down and gripped them and said, *"Arakra,"* and a green fierce sparking ran along their lengths and made them dart away, my own fingers stinging. He spoke a quick charm and pulled free, leaving his boots still imprisoned in the water, and we scrambled out onto the bank.

All around us, the heart-trees had roused; they trembled and waved in shared distress, a rustling whisper. The Wood-queen had turned away from us. She was still using the bowl, to drink but also to throw water onto the burning roots of the towering heart-tree, trying to put the fire out. The Spindle-water was quenching the flames in her, little by little; already her feet deep in the pool were solid blackened cinders, no longer burning.

"The tree," Sarkan said, hoarsely, pushing himself up from the bank: there were stinging red tracks around his throat like a necklace of thorn-prickles. "She's trying to protect it."

I stood on the bank and looked up: it was late afternoon, and the air was heavy and moist. *"Kalmoz,"* I said to the sky, calling; clouds began to gather and mass together. *"Kalmoz."* A drizzle began, pattering in drops on the water, and Sarkan said sharply, "We're not trying to put it *out—*"

"Kalmoz!" I shouted, and put my hands up, and pulled the lightning out of the sky.

This time I knew what was going to happen, but that didn't mean I was ready for it: there wasn't a way to be ready for it. The lightning took away the world again, that single terrible moment of blind white silence everywhere around me, and then it jumped away from me roaring with thunder and struck the massive heart-tree, a shattering blow down the middle.

The force hurled me wildly back, spinning; I fell dazed half into the running streambed, my cheek pressed to pebbles and grass, gold-leaf-laden branches waving above me. I was dim and dazed and blank. The world was queerly silenced, but even through that cottony muffling I could hear a rising dreadful shriek of horror and rage. I managed with trembling arms to push my head up. The heart-tree was burning, all its leaves in flames, the whole trunk blackened; the lightning-bolt had struck at one of the great branchings lower on the trunk, and nearly a quarter of the tree was cracking away.

The Wood-queen was screaming. As if by instinct she put her hands on the tree, trying to push the cracked limb back, but she was still burning; where she touched the bark it caught again. She pulled her hands back. Ivy tendrils erupted from the ground and climbed the heart-tree's trunk, weaving around it, trying to hold it together in one piece. She turned and came at me through the pool, her face twisting in fury. I tried to scramble back on hands and feet, shaking, knowing that it hadn't worked. She wasn't mortally wounded herself, even though the tree was. The heart-tree wasn't a channel to her life.

The lightning had flung Sarkan back among the trees; he staggered out of them, his own clothes singed and blackened with smoke, and pointed at the stream. *"Kerdul foringan,"* he said, his voice rasping like hornets and faint in my ears, and the stream quivered. *"Tual, kerdul—"* and the riverbank crumbled away. The stream turned uncertainly, slowly, and ran into the new bed: diverting from the pool and from the burning tree. The water left standing in the pool began rising up in hot gouts of steam.

The Wood-queen whirled on him. She held out her hands and more plants came bursting up out of the water. She gripped the vine-tops in her fists and pulled them up, and then she flung them at him. The vines grew and swelled as they flew through the air, and they lashed themselves around him, arms and legs, thickening; they toppled him to the ground. I tried to push myself up. My hands were stinging, my nose was full of smoke. But she came towards me too quickly, a living coal, tangled threads of smoke and mist still thick about her body. She seized me and I screamed. I smelled my own flesh crisping, blackening where she gripped me by the arms.

She dragged me off my feet. I couldn't see or think for pain. My shift was smoldering, the sleeves burning and falling off my arms below the curl of her branding fingers. The air around her was oven-hot, rippling like water. I turned my face away from her to fight for breath. She dragged me with her through the pond and up onto the blackened ruin of her resting-mound, towards the shattered tree.

I guessed what she meant to do to me then, and even through pain I screamed and fought her. Her grip was implacable. I kicked at her with my bare feet, scorching them; I reached blindly for magic and cried out half a spell, but she shook me so furiously my teeth clacked on it in my mouth. She was a burning ember around me, fire everywhere. I tried to grab her, to pull myself against her. I would rather have burned to death. I didn't want to know what corruption she would make out of me, what she would do with my strength poured into that vast heart-tree, here in the center of the Wood.

But she kept her arms rigid. She thrust me through crisping wood and ash into the hollow my lightning had left in the shattered heart of the tree. The wrapping vines tightened. The heart-tree closed around me like a coffin-lid.

THIRTY ONE

Cool wet sap slid over me, green and sticky, drenching my hair, my skin. I pushed against the wood, frantic, choking out a spell of strength, and the tree cracked back open. I clawed wildly for the edges of the bark and got my bare foot into the bottom of the crack and heaved myself scrambling back out into the glade, sharp splinters of bark driving into my fingers and toes. Blind with terror I crawled, ran, flung myself away from the tree, until I fell into the cold water thrashing, and lifted myself out—and I realized everything was different.

There was no trace of fire or fighting. I didn't see Sarkan or the Wood-queen anywhere. Even the vast heart-tree was gone. So were most of the others. The glade was more than half-empty. I stood on the shore of the lapping quiet pool alone, in what might have been another world. It was bright morning instead of afternoon. Birds flitted between branches, talking, and the frogs sang by the rippling water.

I understood at once that I was trapped, but this place didn't feel like the Wood. It wasn't the terrible twisted shadow-place where I'd seen Kasia wandering, where Jerzy had slumped against a tree. It didn't even feel like the real glade, full of its unnatural silence. The pool lapped gently at my ankles. I turned and ran splashing down the streambed, back along the Spindle. Sarkan couldn't cast the *Summoning* alone to show me the way to escape, but the Spindle had been our way in: maybe it could be the way out.

Yet even the Spindle was different here. The stream grew wider, gently, and began to deepen, but no cloud of mist rose to meet me; I didn't hear the roaring of the waterfall. I stopped finally at a curving that felt a little familiar, and stared at a sapling on the bank: a slender heart-tree sapling, maybe ten years old, growing over that enormous grey old-man boulder we'd seen at the base of the cliff. It was the first heart-tree, the one we'd landed beneath in our mad slide down the cliff, half-lost in fog at the base of the waterfall.

But here there was no waterfall, no cliff; the ancient tree was small and young. Another heart-tree stood opposite it on the other bank of the Spindle, and beyond those two sentinels the river gradually widened, going away dark and deep into the distance. I didn't see any more heart-trees farther along, only the ordinary oaks and tall pines.

Then I realized I wasn't alone. A woman was standing on the opposite bank, beneath the older heart-tree.

For one moment I thought she was the Wood-queen. She looked so much like her that they might have been kin. She had the same look of alder and tree-bark, the same tangled hair, but her face was longer, and her eyes were green. Where the Wood-queen was gold and russet, she was simpler browns and silver-greys. She was looking down the river, just as I was, and before I could say anything a distant creaking came drifting down the river. A boat came into view, riding gently; a long wooden boat elaborately carved, beautiful, and the Wood-queen stood in it.

She didn't seem to see me. She stood in the prow smiling, flowers wreathing her hair, with a man beside her, and it took me time to recognize his face. I'd only ever seen it dead: the king in the tower.

He looked far younger and taller, his face unworn. But the Wood-queen looked much the same as she had in the tomb, the day they'd bricked her in. Behind them sat a young man with a tight look, not much more than a boy, but I could see the man he'd grow up to be in his bones: the hard-faced man from the tower. More of the tower-people were in the boat with them, rowing: men in silver armor, who glanced around themselves warily at the massive trees as they stroked their oars through the water.

Behind them came more boats, dozens of them: but these were makeshift-looking things more like overgrown leaves than real boats. They were crowded full of a kind of people I'd never seen before, all with a look of tree to them, a little like the Wood-queen herself: dark walnut and bright cherry, pale ash and warm beech. There were a few children among them, but no one old.

The carved boat bumped gently against the bank, and the king helped the Wood-queen down. She went to the wood-woman smiling, her hands outstretched. "Linaya," she said, a word that I somehow knew was and wasn't magic, was and wasn't a name; a word that meant *sister*, and *friend*, and *fellow-traveler*. The name echoed strangely away from her through the trees. The leaves seemed to whisper it back; the ripple of the stream picked it up, as if it were written into everything around me.

The Wood-queen didn't seem to notice. She kissed her sister on both cheeks. Then she took the king's hand and led him on through the heart-trees, going towards the grove. The men from the tower tied their boat up and followed the two of them.

Linaya waited silently on the bank and watched the rest of the boats unload, one after another. As each one emptied, she touched it, and the boat dwindled into a leaf floating on the water; the stream carried it tidily into a small pocket by the bank. Soon the river was empty. The last of the wood-people were already walking onward towards the glade. Then Linaya turned to me and said, in a low deep resonating voice, like drumming on a hollow log, "Come."

I stared at her. But she only turned and walked away from me through the stream, and after a moment I followed. I was afraid, but somehow instinctively not afraid of her. My feet splashed in the water. Hers didn't. The water where it landed on her skin soaked in.

Time seemed to flow around us strangely. By the time we reached the grove, the wedding was over. The Wood-queen and her king were standing on the green mound with their hands clasped, a chain of braided flowers wrapped over their arms. The wood-people were gathered around them, scattered loosely through the trees, watching and silent. There was a quiet in all of them, a deep inhuman stillness. The handful of men from the tower eyed them warily, and flinched from the rustling murmurs of the heart-trees. The young hard-faced man was standing just to one side of the couple, looking with a twist of distaste at the Wood-queen's strange, long, gnarled fingers where they wrapped around the king's hands.

Linaya moved into the scene to join them. Her eyes were wet, glistening like green leaves after rain. The Wood-queen turned to her, smiling, and held out her hands. "Don't weep," she said, and her voice was laughing as a stream. "I'm not going far. The tower is only at the end of the valley."

The sister didn't answer. She only kissed her cheek, and let her hands go.

The king and the Wood-queen left together, with the men from the tower. The people drifted away quietly through the trees. Linaya sighed, softly, and it was the sighing of wind in the boughs. We were alone again, standing together on the green mound. She turned to me.

"Our people were alone here a long time," she said, and I wondered, what was long to a tree? A thousand years, two thousand, ten? Endless generations, the roots growing deeper every one. "We began to forget how to be people. We dwindled away little by little.

"When the sorcerer-king came with his people, my sister let them come into the valley. She thought they could teach us to remember. She thought we could be renewed, and teach them in turn; we could give each other life. But they were afraid. They wanted to live, they wanted to grow stronger, but they didn't want to change.

They learned the wrong things." Years were slipping past us as she spoke, blurred like rain, grey and soft and piling on one another. And then it was summer again, a different summer a long time later, and the wood-people were coming back through the trees.

Many of them moved slowly, somehow wearily. Some were hurt: they nursed blackened arms, and one man limped on a leg that looked like a log clumsily chopped apart. Two others were helping him. At the end of the stump, I think the leg was growing back. A few parents led children, and a woman carried a baby in her arms. In the distance, far to the west, a thin black pillar of smoke rose into the air.

As the wood-people came, they gathered fruit from the heart-trees and made cups out of fallen bark and leaves, the way Kasia and I had done as children for tea-parties in the forest. They dipped up the bright clear water of the pool and spread out through the grove, wandering apart in ones and twos, sometimes three. I stood watching them, and my eyes were full of tears, without knowing why. Some of them were stopping in open places, where the sun came down. They were eating the fruit, drinking the water. The mother chewed a piece of fruit and put it in her baby's mouth, and gave it a sip from her cup.

They were changing. Their feet were growing, toes stretching long, plunging into the earth. Their bodies were stretching, and they put their arms up towards the sun. Their clothing fell away into blown leaves, dry grass. The children changed quickest; they rose suddenly into great beautiful grey pillars, branches bursting wide and filling with white flowers, silver leaves coming out every-where, as if all the life that might have been in them went rushing out in one furious gasp.

Linaya left the mound and moved out among them. A few of the people, the wounded, the old, were struggling: they were caught half-changed. The baby had changed, a beautiful shining tree crowned with flowers. But the mother knelt crouched and shiver-ing by the trunk, her hands upon it, her cup spilled, her face blind agony. Linaya touched her shoulder gently. She helped the mother stand, stumble a little way from the baby's tree. She stroked the mother's head and gave her the fruit to eat, and a drink from her own cup; she sang to her in that strange deep voice. The mother stood there with her head bent, tears dripping, and then all at once her face lifted to the sun and she was growing, she was gone.

Linaya helped the last few trapped ones, gave them a drink from her own cup, held another piece of fruit to their mouth. She stroked their bark and sang magic into them until they slipped the rest of the way over. Some made small gnarled trees; the oldest ones dwindled down into narrow saplings. The grove was full of heart-trees. She was the only one left.

She came back to the pool. "Why?" I asked her, helplessly. I had to know, but I almost felt I didn't want the answer; I didn't want to know what had driven them to this.

She pointed away, down the river. "They are coming," she said in her deep voice. "Look," and I looked down at the river. Instead of the reflection of the sky I saw men coming in carved boats; they carried lanterns, burning torches, and great axes. A flag streamed at the head of the first boat, and in the prow stood the young man from the wedding-party, older and settled into his hard face; the one who'd bricked up the Wood-queen. He wore a crown of his own now.

"They are coming," Linaya said again. "They betrayed my sister, and imprisoned her where she could not grow. Now they are coming for us."

"Can't you fight them?" I asked. I could feel the magic deep and still in her, not a stream but a well that went down and down. "Can't you run away—"

"No," she said.

I stopped. There were forest depths in her eyes, green and unending. The longer I looked at her, the less like a woman she seemed. The part of her I saw was only half: the crowning trunk, the widespread branches, the leaves and flowers and fruit; below there was a vast network of roots that went long and spreading, deep into the valley floor. I had roots, too, but not like that. I could be carefully dug up, and shaken loose, and transplanted into a king's castle, or a tower built of marble—unhappily, perhaps, but I could survive. There was no way to dig her up.

"They learned the wrong things," Linaya said again. "But if we stay, if we fight, we will remember the wrong things. And then we would become—" She stopped. "We decided that we would rather not remember," she said finally.

She bent down and filled her cup again. "Wait!" I said. I caught her arm before she could drink, before she could leave me. "Can you help me?"

"I can help you change," she said. "You are deep enough to come with me. You can grow with me, and be at peace."

"I can't," I said.

"If you will not come, you will be alone here," she said. "Your sorrow and your fear will poison my roots."

I stood silent, afraid. I was beginning to understand: this was where the Wood's corruption came from. The wood-people had changed willingly. They still lived, they dreamed long deep dreams, but it was closer to the life of trees and not the life of people. They weren't awake and alive and trapped, humans locked behind bark who could never stop wanting to get out.

But if I wouldn't change, if I stayed human, alone and wretched, my misery would sicken her heart-tree, just like the monstrous ones outside the grove, even as my strength kept it alive.

"Can't you let me go?" I said desperately. "She put me into *your* tree—"

Her face drew in with sorrow. I understood then this was the only way she could help me. She was gone. What still lived of her in the tree was deep and strange and slow. The tree had found these memories, these moments, so she could show me a way out—her way out—but that was all that she could do. It was the only way she'd found for herself and all her people.

I swallowed and stepped back. I dropped my hand from her arm. She looked at me a moment longer, and then she drank. Standing there at the edge of the pool she began to take root; the dark roots unfurling and silver branches spreading, rising, going up and up, as high as that depthless lake inside her. She rose and grew and grew, flowers blooming in white ropes; the trunk furrowing lightly beneath ash-silver bark.

I was alone in the grove again. But now the voices of the birds were falling silent. Through the trees I saw a few deer bounding away, frightened, a flash of white tails and gone. Leaves were drifting down from the trees, dry and brown, and underfoot they crackled with their edges bitten by frost. The sun was going down. I put my arms around myself, cold and afraid, my breath coming in white cloudy bursts, my bare feet wincing away from the frozen ground. The Wood was closing in around me. And there was no way out.

But a light dawned behind me, sharp and brilliant and familiar: the *Summoning*-light. I turned in sudden hope, into a grove now drifted with snow: time had moved on again. The silent trees were bare and stark. The *Summoning*-light poured down like a single shaft of moonbeam. The pool shone molten silver, and someone was coming out of it.

It was the Wood-queen. She dragged herself up the bank, leaving a black gash of exposed earth through the snow behind her, and collapsed on the shore still in her sodden white mourning-dress. She lay huddled on her side to catch her breath, and then she opened her eyes. She slowly pushed up on trembling arms and looked around the grove, at all the new heart-trees standing, and her face widened into horror. She struggled to her feet. Her dress was muddy and freezing to her skin. She stood on the mound looking out at the grove, and slowly she turned to look up and up at the great heart-tree above her.

She took a few halting steps up the mound through the snow, and put her hands on the heart-tree's wide silver trunk. She stood there a moment trembling. Then she leaned in and slowly rested her cheek against the bark. She didn't weep. Her eyes were open and empty, seeing nothing.

I didn't know how Sarkan had managed to cast the *Summoning* alone, or what I was seeing, but I stood waiting and tense, hoping for the vision to show me a way out. Snow was coming down around us, brilliant in the crisp light. It didn't touch my skin, but it drifted swiftly over her tracks, covering the ground with white again. The Wood-queen didn't move.

The heart-tree rustled its branches softly, and one low branch dipped gently towards her. A flower was budding on the branch, despite winter. It bloomed, and petals fell away, and a small green fruit swelled and ripened gold. It hung off the bough towards her, a gentle invitation.

The Wood-queen took the fruit. She stood with it cupped in her hands, and in the silence of the grove a hard familiar thunk came down the river: an axe biting into wood.

The Wood-queen halted, the fruit nearly to her lips. We both stood, caught, listening. The thunk came again. Her hands dropped. The fruit fell to the ground, disappearing into the snow. She caught up her tangled skirts away from her feet and ran back down the mound and into the river.

I ran after her, my heart beating in time with the regular axe-thumps. They led us on to the end of the grove. The sapling had grown into a sturdy tall tree now, its branches spreading wide. One of the carved boats was tied up to the shore, and two men were cutting down the other heart-tree. They were working cheerfully together, taking turns with their heavy axes, each one biting deep into the wood. Silver-grey chips flew into the air.

The Wood-queen gave a cry of horror that howled through the trees. The woodcutters halted, shocked, clutching their axes and looking around; then she was on them. She caught them up by the throats with her long-fingered hands and threw them away from her, into the river; they thrashed up coughing. She dropped to her knees beside the sagging tree. She pressed all her fingers over the oozing cut, as if she could close it up. But the tree was too wounded to save. It was already leaning deeply over the water. In an hour, in a day, it would come down.

She stood up. She was still trembling, not with cold but rage, and the ground was trembling with her. In front of her feet, a crack opened suddenly and ran away in both directions along the edge of the grove. She stepped over the widening split, and I followed her just in time. The boat toppled into the opening chasm, vanishing, as the river began to roar wildly down the waterfall, as the grove sank down the new sheltering cliff into the clouds of mist. One of the woodcutters slipped in the water and was dragged over the edge with a scream, the other one crying out, trying to catch his hand too late.

The sapling sank away with the grove; the broken tree rose with us. The second woodcutter struggled up onto the bank, clinging to the shuddering ground. He swung his axe at the Wood-queen as she came towards him; it struck against her flesh and sprang away, ringing, jumping out of his hands. She paid no attention. Her face was blank and lost. She took hold of the woodcutter and carried him over to the wounded heart-tree. He struggled against her, use-lessly, as she pushed him against the trunk, and vines sprouted from the ground to hold him in place.

His body arched, horror in his face. The Wood-queen stepped back. His feet and ankles were bound against the chipped gap where the axes had bitten into the tree, and they were already changing, grafting onto the trunk, boots splitting open and falling away as his toes were stretched out into new roots. His struggling arms were stiffening into branches, the fingers melting into one another. His wide agonized eyes were disappearing beneath a skin of silver bark. I ran to him, in pity and horror. My hands couldn't get hold of the bark, and magic wouldn't answer me in this place. But I couldn't bear to just stand and watch.

Then he managed to lean forward. He whispered, "Agnieszka," in Sarkan's voice, and then he vanished; his face disappeared into a large dark hollow opening up in the trunk. I caught the edges and pulled myself into the hollow after him, into the dark. The tree-roots were close and tight; the damp warm smell of freshly turned earth choked my nose, and also the lingering smell of fire and smoke. I wanted to pull back out; I didn't want to be here. But I knew that going back was wrong. I *was* here, inside the tree. I pushed and shoved and forced my way forward, against every instinct and terror. I forced myself to reach out and feel the blasted, scorched wood around me, splinters piercing my skin, the slick of sap clogging my eyes and my nose, the air I couldn't get.

My nostrils were full of wood and rot and burning. *"Alamak,"* I whispered hoarsely, for walking through walls, and then I pushed my way out through bark and blasted wood, and back into the smoking wreck of the heart-grove.

I came out on the mound, my dress soaked green with sap, the shattered tree behind me. The light of the *Summoning* still blazed across the water, and the last shallow remnants of the pool shone beneath it like a full moon just up over the horizon, so bright it hurt to look at it. Sarkan was on the other side of the pool, on his knees. His mouth was wet, his hand dripping, the only parts of him not blackened with soot and dirt and smoke: he'd cupped water to his mouth. He'd drunk from the Spindle, water and power both, to gather enough strength to cast the *Summoning* alone.

But now the Wood-queen was standing over him with her long fingers wrapped choking around his neck: silver bark was climbing up from the bank over his knees and his legs as he struggled to pry her grip from around his throat. She let him go and whirled with a cry of protest at my escape, too late. With a long groaning above me, the great broken branch of the heart-tree cracked away from the trunk and finally fell, thundering, leaving a gaping hollow wound.

I stepped down from the mound to meet her on the wet stones as she came furious towards me. "Agnieszka!" Sarkan shouted hoarsely, reaching an arm out, struggling half-rooted in the earth. But even as she reached me, the Wood-queen slowed and halted. The *Summoning*-light illuminated her from behind: the terrible corruption in her, the sour black cloud of long despair. But it shone on me also, on me and through me, and I knew that in my face she saw someone else, looking out at her.

I could see in her where she'd gone from the grove: how she'd hunted them down, all the people of the tower, wizards and farmers and woodcutters all alike. How she'd planted one corrupt heart-tree after another in the roots of her own misery, and fed that misery onward. Mingled with my horror, I felt Linaya's pity moving in me, deep and slow: pity and sorrow and regret. The Wood-queen saw it, too, and it held her still before me, trembling.

"I stopped them," she said, her voice the scrape of a branch against the window-pane at night, when you imagine some dark thing is outside the house scratching to get in. "I had to stop them."

She wasn't speaking to me. Her eyes were looking past me, deep towards her sister's face. "They burned the trees," she said, pleading for understanding from someone long gone. "They cut them down. They will always cut them down. They come and go like seasons, the winter that gives no thought to the spring."

Her sister didn't have a voice to speak with anymore, but the sap of the heart-tree clung to my skin, and its roots went deep beneath my feet. "We're meant to go," I said softly, answering for both of us. "We're not meant to stay forever."

The Wood-queen finally looked at me then, instead of through me. "I couldn't go," she said, and I knew she'd tried. She'd killed the tower-lord and his soldiers, she'd planted all the fields with new trees, and she'd come here with her hands bloody, to sleep with her people at last. But she hadn't been able to take root. She'd remembered the wrong things, and forgotten too much. She'd remembered how to kill and how to hate, and she'd forgotten how to grow. All she'd been able to do in the end was lie down beside her sister: not quite dreaming, not quite dead.

I reached out, and from the one low-hanging bough of the broken tree, I took the single waiting fruit, glowing and golden. I held it out to her. "I'll help you," I told her. "If you want to save her, you can."

She looked up at the shattered, dying tree. Mud-tears were leaking from her eyes, thick brown rivulets sliding over her cheeks, dirt and ash and water mingled. She put her hands slowly up to take the fruit from me, her long gnarled twiggy fingers curling carefully around it, gently. They brushed against mine, and we looked at one another. For a moment, through the winding smoke between us, I might have been the daughter she'd hoped for, the child halfway between the tower-people and her own; she might have been my teacher and my guide, like Jaga's book showing me the way. We might never have been enemies at all.

I bent down, and in one curled-up leaf I drew a little water for her, the last clear water left in the pool. We stepped together up onto the mound. She lifted the fruit to her mouth and bit, juices running down her chin in pale golden dripping lines. She shut her eyes and stood there. I put my hand on her, felt hate and agony like a strangler vine tangled deep through her. I put my other hand on the sister-tree, though, and reached for the deep well in her; the stillness and the calm. Being struck by lightning hadn't changed her; the stillness would remain, even when the whole tree had fallen, even while the years crumbled it back into the earth.

The Wood-queen leaned against the tree's gaping wound and put her arms around the blackened trunk. I gave her the last drops of the pool's water, tipped them into her mouth, and then I touched her skin and said softly, very simply, *"Vanalem."*

And she was changing. The last remnants of her white gown blew away, and the charred surface of her scorched skin peeled off in huge black flakes, fresh new bark whirling up from the ground around her like a wide silver skirt, meeting and merging into the old tree's broken trunk. She opened her eyes one last time and looked at me, with sudden relief, and then she was gone, she was growing, her feet plunging new roots over the old.

I backed away, and when her roots had sunk deep into the earth, I turned and ran to Sarkan through the mud of the emptied pool. The bark had stopped climbing up over him. Together we broke him the rest of the way loose, peeling it away from his skin, until his legs came free. I pulled him up from the stump and we sat together, sagged together, on the bank of the stream.

I was too spent to think of anything. He was scowling down at his own hands, almost resentfully. Abruptly he lurched forward and leaned over the streambed and dug into the soft wet earth. I watched him blankly for a while, and then I realized he was trying to restore the course of the stream. I pulled myself up and reached in to help. I could feel it, as soon as I started, the same feeling he hadn't wanted to have: the sure sense that this was the right thing to do. The river wanted to run this way, wanted to feed into the pool.

It only took moving a few handfuls of dirt, and then the stream was running over our fingers, clearing the rest of the bed for itself. The pool began to fill once more. We sat back again, wearily. Next to me he was trying to get the dirt and water off his hands, wiping them on a corner of his ruined shirt, on the grass, on his trousers, mostly just spreading the mud around. Black half-circles were crusted deep under the fingernails. He finally heaved an exasperated noise and let his hands fall into his lap; he was too tired to use magic.

I leaned against his side, his irritation oddly comforting. After a moment he grudgingly put his arm around me. The deep quiet was already settling back upon the grove, as if all the fire and rage we'd brought could make only a brief interruption in its peace. The ash had sunk into the muddy bottom of the pool, and been swallowed up. The trees were letting their scorched leaves fall into the water, and moss crept over the torn bare patches of earth, new blades of grass unfurling. At the head of the pool, the new heart-tree tangled with the old one, bracing it up, sealing over the jagged scar. They were putting out small white flowers, like stars.

THIRTY TWO

I fell asleep in the grove, empty-headed and spent. I didn't notice Sarkan lifting me in his arms, or taking me back to the tower; I roused only long enough to mutter a complaint to him after the unpleasant stomach-twist of his jumping spell, and then I sank down again.

When I woke up, tucked under a blanket in my narrow bed in my narrow room, I kicked the blanket off my legs and got up without thinking about clothes. There was a rip all the way across the valley painting where a jagged chip of rock had torn it: the canvas hung down in flaps, all the magic gone out of it. I went out into the hallway, picking my way over bits of broken stone and cannon-balls littering the floor and rubbing at my gritty eyes. When I came down the stairs, I found Sarkan packing to leave.

"Someone has to clear out the corruption from the capital before it spreads any farther," he said. "Alosha will be a long time recovering, and the court will have to return south by the end of the summer."

He was in riding clothes, and boots of red-dyed leather tooled in silver. I was still a shambling mess of soot and mud, ragged enough to be a ghost but too mucky.

He barely looked me in the face, stuffing flasks and vials into a padded case, another sack full of books already waiting on the laboratory table between us. The floor slanted askew beneath our feet. The walls gaped here and there where cannon-balls had struck or stones had fallen, and the summer-warm wind whistled cheerfully between the cracks and blew papers and powders all over the floor, leaving faint smeared drifts of red and blue on the stone.

"I've propped the tower up for the moment," he added as he laid down a corked, well-sealed flask of violet smoke. "I'll take the fireheart with me. You might start the repairs in the—"

"I won't be here," I said, cutting him off. "I'm going back to the Wood."

"Don't be absurd," he said. "Do you think the death of a witch turns all her works to dust, or that her change of heart can repair them all at once? The Wood is still full of monstrosities and corruption, and will be for a long time to come."

He wasn't wrong, and the Wood-queen wasn't dead anyway; she was only dreaming. But he wasn't going for the sake of corruption or the kingdom. His tower was broken, he'd drunk Spindle-water, and he'd held my hand. So now he was going to run away as quick as he could, and find himself some new stone walls to hide behind. He'd keep himself locked away for ten years this time, until he withered his own roots, and didn't feel the lack of them anymore.

"It won't get any less full of them for my sitting in a heap of stones," I said. I turned and left him with his bottles and his books.

Above my head, the Wood was aflame with red and gold and orange, but a few confused spring flowers in white poked up through the forest floor. A last wave of summer heat had struck this week, just at harvest-time. In the fields, the threshers labored under fierce sun, but it was cooler here in the dim light beneath the heavy canopy, alongside the running gurgle of the Spindle. I walked barefoot on crackling fallen leaves with my basket full of golden fruit, and stopped at a curving in the river. A walker was crouched by the water, putting its stick-head down to drink.

It saw me and held still, wary, but it didn't run away. I held out one of the fruits from my basket. The walker crept towards me little by little on its stiff legs. It stopped just out of arm's reach. I didn't move. Finally it stretched out two forelegs and took the fruit and ate it, turning it around and around in its hands, nibbling until it had cleaned it down to the seed. Afterwards it looked at me, and then tentatively took a few steps into the forest. I nodded.

The walker led me a long way into the forest, into the trees. At last it held aside a heavy mat of vines from what looked like a sheer stone cliff face, and showed me a narrow cut in the rock, a thick sweet rotten stench rolling out. We climbed through the passage into a sheltered narrow vale. At one end stood an old, twisted heart-tree, grey with corruption, the trunk bulging unnaturally. Its boughs hung forward over the grass of the vale, so laden with fruit that the tips brushed the ground.

The walker stood anxiously aside. They'd learned that I would cleanse the sickened heart-trees if I could, and a few of them had even begun to help me. They had a gardener's instinct, it seemed to me, now that they were free of the Wood-queen's driving rage; or maybe they only liked the uncorrupted fruit better.

There were still nightmare things in the Wood, nursing too much rage of their own. They mostly avoided me, but now and then I stumbled over the torn and spoiled body of a rabbit or a squirrel, killed as far as I could see just for cruelty; and sometimes one of the walkers who had helped me would reappear torn and limping, a limb snapped off as by mantis-jaws, or its sides scored deeply by claws. Once in a dim part of the Wood, I fell into a pit trap, cleverly covered over with leaves and moss to blend into the forest floor, and full of broken sticks and a hideous glistening ooze that clung and burned my skin until I went to the grove and washed it off in the pool. I still had a slow-healing scab on my leg where one of the sticks had cut me. It might have been just an ordinary animal's trap, set for prey, but I didn't think so. I thought it had been meant for me.

I hadn't let it stop my work. Now I ducked under the branches and went to the heart-tree's trunk with my jug. I poured a drink of the Spindle-water over its roots, but I knew even as I began that there wasn't much hope for this one. There were too many souls caught inside, twisting the tree in every direction, and they'd been there too long; there wasn't enough left of them to bring out, and it would be almost impossible to calm and ease them all together, to slip them into dreaming.

I stood with my hands on the bark for a long time, trying to reach them, but even the ones I found had been lost so long they had forgotten their names. They lay without walking in shadowed dim places, blank-eyed and exhausted. Their faces had half-lost their shape. I had to let go at last and step away, shivering and chilled through, though the hot sun came down through the leaves. The misery clung to my skin, wanting to climb inside. I ducked back out from beneath the tree's heavy branches and sat down in a patch of open sunlight at the other end of the vale. I took a drink from my jug, resting my forehead against the beaded wet side.

Two more walkers had come creeping through the passageway to join the first: they were sitting in a row, their long heads all bent intently towards my basket. I fed each of them a clean fruit, and when I started working they helped me. Together we heaped dry kindling against the trunk, and dug a broad circle of dirt around the limits of the heart-tree's branches.

I stood up and arched my tired back when we were done, stretching. Then I rubbed my hands with dirt. I went back to the heart-tree and put my hands back on its sides, but this time I didn't try to speak with the trapped souls. "*Kisara,*" I said, and drew the water out. I worked gently, slowly. The water beaded up in fat droplets on the bark and trickled slowly down in thin wet rivulets to sink into the ground. The sun moved onward overhead, coming ever more strongly through the leaves as they curled up and went dry. It was dipping out of sight by the time I finished, my forehead sticky with sweat and my hands covered with sap. The ground beneath my feet was soft and damp, and the tree had gone pale as bone, its branches making a noise like rattling sticks in the wind. The fruit had all withered on the boughs.

I stood clear and kindled it with a word. Then I sat heavily and wiped my hands on the grass as well as I could, and pulled my knees up to my chest. The walkers folded their legs neatly and sat around me. The tree didn't thrash or shriek, already more than half gone; it went up quickly and burned without much smoke. Flakes of ash fell on the damp ground and melted into it like early snowflakes. They landed on my bare arms sometimes, not big enough to burn, just tiny sparks. I didn't back away. We were the only mourners the tree and its dreamers had left.

I fell asleep at some point while the bonfire went on, tired from my work. When I woke in the morning, the tree was burned out, a black stump that crumbled easily into ash. The walkers raked the ash evenly around the clearing with their many-fingered hands, leaving a small mound at the center where the old tree had stood. I planted a fruit from my basket beneath it. I had a vial of growing-potion that I'd brewed up out of river-water and the seeds of heart-trees. I sprinkled a few drops over the mound, and sang encouragement to the fruit until a silver sapling poked its head out and climbed up to three years' height. The new tree didn't have a dream of its own, but it carried on the quiet dream of the grove-tree the fruit had come from, instead of tormented nightmares. The walkers would be able to eat the fruit, when it came.

I left them tending it, busily putting up a shade of tall branches to keep its fresh new leaves from crisping in the hot sun, and went away through the stones, back out into the Wood. The ground was full of ripened nuts and tangles of bramble-berries, but I didn't gather while I walked. It would be a long time yet before it would

be safe to eat any fruit from outside the grove. There was too much
sorrow under the boughs, too many of the tormented heart-trees
still anchoring the forest.

I'd brought out a handful of people from a heart-tree in Zatochek, and another handful from the Rosyan side. But those had
been people taken only very lately. The heart-trees took everything:
flesh and bone and not just dreams. Marek's hope had always been
a false one, I'd discovered. Anyone who'd been caught inside for
more than a week or two was too much a part of the tree to be
brought out again.

I had been able to ease some of those, and help them slide into
the long deep dream. A few of them had even found their way into
dreaming by themselves, once the Wood-queen had slipped away,
her animating rage gone. But that left hundreds of heart-trees still
standing, many of them in dark and secret places of the Wood.
Drawing the water out of them and giving them to the fire was
the gentlest way I'd found to set them free. It still felt like killing
someone, every time, although I knew it was better than leaving
them trapped and lingering. The grey sorrow of it stayed with me
afterwards.

This morning, a clanging bell surprised me out of my weary fog,
and I pushed aside a bush to find a yellow cow staring back at me,
chewing grass meditatively. I was near the border on the Rosyan
side, I realized. "You'd better go back home," I told the cow. "I
know it's hot, but you're too likely to eat the wrong thing in here."
A girl's voice was calling her in the distance, and after a moment
she came through the bushes and stopped when she saw me; nine
years old or so.

"Does she run away into the forest a lot?" I asked her, stumbling
a little over my Rosyan.

"Our meadow is too small," the girl said, looking up at me with
clear blue eyes. "But I always find her."

I looked down at her and knew she was telling the truth; there was a strand of silver bright inside her, magic running close to the surface. "Don't let her go too deep," I said. "And when you get older, come and find me. I live on the other side of the Wood."

"Are you Baba Jaga?" she asked, interestedly.

"No," I said. "But you might call her a friend of mine."

Now I had woken up enough to know where I was, I turned back westward right away. The Rosyans had sent soldiers to patrol the borders of the Wood on their side, and I didn't want to distress them. They were still uneasy about me popping out on their side now and then, even after I'd sent back some of their lost villagers, and I couldn't really blame them. All the songs streaming out of Polnya were wrong about me in different and alarming ways, and I suspected that the bards weren't bringing the most outrageous ones to my side of the valley at all. A man had been booed out of Olshanka tavern a few weeks ago, I'd heard, for trying to sing one where I'd turned into a wolf-beast and eaten up the king.

But my step was lighter anyway: meeting the little girl and her cow had lifted some of the grey weight from my shoulders. I sang Jaga's walking-song and hurried away, back towards home. I was hungry, so I ate a fruit from my basket as I walked. I could taste the forest in it, the running magic of the Spindle caught in roots and branches and fruit, infused with sunlight to become sweet juice on my tongue. There was an invitation in it, too, and maybe one day I would want to accept; one day when I was tired and ready to dream a long dream of my own. But for now it was only a door standing open on a hill in the distance, a friend waving to me from afar, and the grove's deep sense of peace.

Kasia had written me from Gidna: the children were doing as well as could be hoped. Stashek was still very quiet, but he had stood up and spoken to the Magnati, when they had been summoned to vote, well enough to persuade them to crown him with his grandfather as his regent. He'd also agreed to be betrothed to the Archduke of Varsha's daughter, a girl of nine who had evidently impressed him a great deal by being able to spit across a garden plot. I was a little dubious about this as a foundation for marriage, but I suppose it wasn't much worse than marrying her because her father might have stirred up rebellion, otherwise.

There had been a tourney to celebrate Stashek's coronation, and he'd asked Kasia to be his champion, much to his grandmother's dismay. It had turned out halfway for the best, because the Rosyans sent a party of knights, and after Kasia knocked them all down, it made them wary about invading us in revenge for the battle at the Rydva. Enough soldiers had escaped the siege of the tower to carry tales of the invulnerable golden warrior-queen, slaughtering and unstoppable; and people had mixed her up with Kasia. So Rosya had grudgingly accepted Stashek's request for a renewed truce, and our summer had ended in a fragile peace, with time for both sides to mend.

Stashek had also used Kasia's triumph to name her captain of his guard. Now she was learning how to fight with a sword properly, so she didn't knock into the other knights and tumble them over accidentally while they were all drilling together. Two lords and an archduke had asked her to marry them, and so, she wrote to me in outrage, had Solya.

Can you imagine? I told him I thought he was a lunatic, and he said he would live in hope. Alosha laughed for ten minutes without stopping except to cough when I told her, and then she said he'd done it knowing I'd say no, just to demonstrate to the court that he's loyal to Stashek now. I said I wouldn't go bragging of someone asking me to marry them, and she said just watch, he'd spread it around himself. Sure enough, half a dozen people asked me about it the next week. I almost wanted to go and tell him I'd have him after all, just to see him squirm, but I was too afraid he'd decide to go through with it for some reason or another, and he'd find some way not to let me out.

Alosha's better every day, and the children are doing well, too. They go sea-bathing together every morning: I come along and sit on the beach, but I can't swim anymore: I just sink straight to the bottom, and the salt water feels all wrong on my skin, even if I just put my feet into it. Send me another jug of river-water, please! I'm always a little thirsty, here, and it's good for the children, too. They never have the nightmares about the tower if I let them have a sip of it before they sleep.

I'll come for a real visit this winter, if you think it's safe for the children. I thought they'd never want to come back, but Marisha asked if she could come and play at Natalya's house again.

I miss you.

I took one last blurred hop-step to come to the Spindle, and the clearing where my own little tree-cottage stood, coaxed out of the side of an old drowsy oak. On one side of my doorway, the oak's roots made a big hollow that I had lined with grass. I tried to keep it full of grove-fruit for the walkers to take. It was emptier than when I'd left, and on the other side of my doorway, someone had filled my wood-box.

I put the rest of my gathered fruit into the hollow and went inside for a moment. The house didn't need tidying: the floor was soft moss and the grass coverlet turned itself back over the bed without my help after I climbed out in the mornings. I did need tidying, badly, but I'd wasted too much time wandering grey and tired this morning. The sun was climbing past noon, and I didn't want to be late. I only picked up my reply for Kasia and the corked jug of Spindle-water, and put them in my basket, so I could give them to Danka to post for me.

I went back out onto the riverbank and took three more big steps going west to come out of the Wood at last. I crossed the Spindle at Zatochek bridge, in the shade of the tall young heart-tree growing there.

The Wood-queen had made a final furious push at the same time as Sarkan and I were floating down the river to find her, and the trees had half swallowed Zatochek before we stopped her. People fleeing the village met me on the road as I walked away from the tower. I ran the rest of the way and found the handful of desperate defenders about to chop down the newly planted heart-tree.

They'd stayed behind to buy time for their families to escape, but they'd done it expecting to be taken, corrupted; they were wild-eyed and terrified even in their courage. I don't think they would have listened to me if it hadn't been for my ragged flapping clothes, my hair in snarls and blackened with soot, and my feet bare in the road: I couldn't easily have been anything *but* a witch.

Even then, they weren't quite sure whether to believe me when I told them the Wood had been defeated, defeated for good. None of us had imagined such a thing ever happening. But they'd seen the mantises and the walkers go fleeing suddenly back into the Wood, and they were all very tired by then. In the end they stood back and let me work. The tree hadn't been even a day old: the walkers had bound the village headman and his three sons into it, to make it grow. I was able to bring the brothers out, but their father refused: a hot coal of pain had been burning slowly in his belly for a year.

"I can help you," I'd offered, but the old man shook his head, his eyes half-dreaming already, smiling, and the hard knobs of his bones and body trapped beneath the bark melted away suddenly beneath my hands. The crooked heart-tree sighed and straightened up. It dropped all its poisonous blooms at once; new flowers budded on the branches instead.

We all stood together for a moment under the silver branches, breathing in their faint fragrance, nothing like the overwhelming rotten sweetness of the corrupt flowers. Then the defenders noticed what they were doing, shifted nervously and backed away. They were as afraid to accept the heart-tree's peace as Sarkan and I had been, in the grove. None of us knew how to imagine something that came from the Wood and wasn't evil and full of hate. The head-man's sons looked at me helplessly. "Can't you bring him out, too?" the eldest asked.

I had to tell them that there wasn't anything to bring him out *of*, anymore; that the tree was him. I was too tired to explain very well, but anyway it wasn't something people could easily understand, even people from the valley. The sons stood in baffled silence, confused whether to grieve or not. "He missed Mother," the eldest said finally, and they all nodded.

None of the villagers felt easy about having a heart-tree growing on their bridge, but they trusted me enough at least that they'd left it standing. It had grown well since then: its roots were already twining themselves enthusiastically with the logs of the bridge, promising to take it over. It was laden with fruit and birds and squirrels. Not many people were ready to eat a heart-tree's fruit yet, but the animals trusted their noses. I trusted mine, too: I picked a dozen more for my basket and went on, singing my way down the dusty long road to Dvernik.

Little Anton was out with his family's flock, lazing on his back in the grass. He jumped up when I lurched into his field, a little nervously, but mostly everyone had gotten used to my appearing now and then. I might have been shy of going home at first, after everything that had happened, but I'd been so tired after that terrible day, tired and lonely and angry and sad all at once, the Wood-queen's sorrow and my own all tangled up. After I finally finished clearing out Zatochek, almost without thinking my weary feet turned and took me home. My mother took one look at me in the doorway and didn't say anything, just put me to bed. She sat beside me and stroked my hair, singing until I fell asleep.

Everyone was jumpy around me the next day when I came out to the village green to talk to Danka and tell her a little of what had happened, and to look in on Wensa, and on Jerzy and Krystyna. But I was still tired and in no mood to be considerate, so I just ignored the twitching, and after a while of my not setting anything on fire or turning into a beast, it stopped. I learned from the lesson to make people get used to me; now I made a point of stopping into all the villages regularly, a different one each Saturday.

Sarkan hadn't come back. I didn't know if he'd ever come back. I heard fourth- or fifth-hand that he was still in the capital, setting things right, but he hadn't written. Well, we'd never needed a lord to settle quarrels for us, the headmen and -women could do that, and the Wood wasn't the same kind of danger as before, but there were some things a village needed a wizard for, if they could get one. So I went around to all of them, and put a spell on the beacon-fires, and now if they lit them, a matching candle in my cottage lit up to tell me where I was wanted.

But today I wasn't here to work. I waved to Anton and tramped on into the village. The heaped harvest tables were out on the green, dressed in white cloth, with the square in the middle for dancing. My mother was there with Wensa's two oldest daughters, putting out trays full of stewed mushrooms; I ran and kissed her, and she put her hands on my cheeks and smoothed my tangled hair back, smiling with her whole face. "Look at you," she said, picking a long silver twig out of my hair, and some dried brown leaves. "And you might as well be wearing boots. I should tell you to go wash up and sit quietly in the corner." My bare legs were thick with dust to my knees. But she was laughing, joyful, and my father was driving the wagon-cart in with a load for the evening bonfire.

"I'll clean up before it's time to eat," I said, stealing a mushroom, and went to go sit with Wensa in the front room of her house. She was better, but still spent most of her time sitting in a chair by the window, only sewing a little. Kasia had written to her, too, but a stiff, stilted letter: I had read it to her, and softened it a little where I could. Wensa listened to it in silence. I think there was a secret guilt in her to match Kasia's secret resentment: a mother who had resigned herself to an unnecessary fate. That would be a long time healing, too, if it ever did. She did let me persuade her to come to the green with me, and I saw her settled at the tables with her daughters.

There wasn't a pavilion this year: it was only our own small village festival. The big festival was in Olshanka, as it was in every year without a choosing: as it would be every year from now on. We were all too hot eating in the sun, an odd sensation for harvest-time, until it finally sank low. I didn't care. I ate a big bowl of sour zhurek with slices of boiled eggs floating, and a plateful of stewed cabbage and sausage, and then four blini full of sour cherries. Then we all sat around in the sun groaning how good the food had been and how we'd all eaten too much, while the small children ran around wildly in the green until little by little they lay down under the trees and fell asleep. Ludek brought out his suka and put it across his knees and began playing, quietly at first; as more of the children drowsed off, more instruments came out and began joining in, people clapping and singing as the mood took them, and we opened the beer-casks and passed around the cold jug of vodka brought up from Danka's cellar.

I danced with Kasia's brothers and mine, and after that with a handful of other boys I knew a little. I think they were off to one side daring one another to ask me, but I didn't care. They were a little nervous that I might lob fire at their heads, but in the same way I had been nervous to go creeping across old Hanka's yard at twilight to steal the big sweet red apples from her tree, the best ones for eating. We were all happy, all together, and I could recognize the song of the river running through the ground beneath our feet, the song we really danced to.

I sat down in a breathless heap in front of my mother's chair, my hair tumbled loose around my shoulders again, and she gave a sigh and put it in her lap to braid it back up. My basket was at her feet, and I took another of the tree-fruits to eat, golden and bursting with juice. I was licking my fingers and half lost in the bonfire when Danka stood up abruptly from the long bench corner to ours. She put down her cup and said loudly enough to make everyone pay attention, "My lord."

Sarkan was standing at the opening of the circle. One hand perched on the table nearest him, firelight leaping to pick out his silver rings and fine silver buttons and the winding silver embroidery along the edges of his blue coat: a dragon whose head began at his collar and ran all along the borders of the coat until the tail came back up to the collar on the other side. The lace cuffs of his shirt spilled past the sleeves, and his boots were so brightly polished the fire shone in them. He looked grander than the king's ballroom, and perfectly improbable.

All of us were staring at him, me included. His mouth thinned with what I would have called displeasure, once, and now named prickly mortification. I climbed to my feet and went to him, licking my thumb clean. He darted a look at the uncovered basket behind me, saw what I was eating, and glared at me. "That's appalling," he said.

"They're wonderful!" I said. "They're all coming ripe."

"All the better to turn you into a *tree*," he said.

"I don't want to be a tree yet," I said. Happiness was bubbling up through me, a bright stream laughing. He'd come back. "When did you arrive?"

"This afternoon," he said stiffly. "I came to receive the taxes, of course."

"Of course," I said. I was sure he'd even gone to Olshanka for the tribute first, just so he could pretend that was the truth for a little bit longer. But I couldn't really bring myself to pretend with him, not even long enough for him to get used to the idea; my mouth was already turning up at the corners without my willing it to. He flushed and looked away; but that wasn't any better for him, since everyone else was watching us with enormous interest, too drunk on beer and dancing to be polite. He looked back at me instead, and scowled at my smile.

"Come and meet my mother," I said. I reached out and took his hand.

ACKNOWLEDGMENTS

I know this may puzzle many a reader: it's pronounced ag-NYESH-kah. The name comes from a fairy tale that I demanded from my mother endlessly as a child called *Agnieszka Skrawek Neiba* (Agnieszka "Piece of the Sky"), the version by the wonderful Natalia Gałczyńska. The heroine and her wandering yellow cow make a small cameo appearance here, and the roots of the Wood are planted in the wild, overgrown *las* of that story.

This book owes an enormous debt to Francesca Coppa and Sally McGrath, who beta-read and cheered me on throughout the entire writing process on a near-daily basis. Many thanks as well to Seah Levy and Gina Paterson and Lynn Loschin for early reading and advice.

Thank you to my wonderful editor, Anne Groell, and my agent, Cynthia Manson, who encouraged and embraced this book from its very beginnings, and to everyone at Del Rey for their help and enthusiasm.

And most of all so many thanks and so much love to my husband, Charles Ardai, who makes my life and my work better and more true. Not every author is lucky enough to have a fellow writer and brilliant editor in-house for her first reader, and I am so glad that I am!

From my mother, and for my daughter: from root to flower. Evidence, when you are old enough to read this book, I hope it can be a connection for you back to your Babcia and the stories she gave me. I love you so very much.

extracts reading groups

competitions books new

books discounts extracts

competitions extracts

books new reading groups events

events books

extracts reading groups

books new titles reading groups

interviews

reading groups books events extracts

discounts events books

new books events interviews books

events new events new extracts

discounts extracts discounts

www.panmacmillan.com

extracts events reading groups

competitions books extracts new